A Mystery of Venice

FAREWELL to the FLESH

Edward Sklepowich

AVON BOOKS ◆ NEW YORK

To Jeffrey Mason

AVON BOOKS
A division of
The Hearst Corporation
1350 Avenue of the Americas
New York, New York 10019

Copyright © 1991 by Edward Sklepowich
Published by arrangement with William Morrow and Company, Inc.
Library of Congress Catalog Card Number: 91-14112
ISBN: 0-380-71814-6

First Avon Books Printing: April 1993

AVON TRADEMARK REG. U.S. PAT. OFF. AND IN OTHER COUNTRIES, MARCA REGISTRADA, HECHO EN U.S.A.

Printed in the U.S.A.

RA 10 9 8 7 6 5 4 3 2 1

I never tell a lie, but the truth not to everyone.
—PAOLO SARPI, Venetian monk (1552-1623)

Other Avon Books by
Edward Sklepowich

DEATH IN A SERENE CITY

Everything deep loves the mask, said Nietzsche, but the mask has passionate loves of its own. Its favorite time is Carnival—*Carne-Vale* or "flesh, farewell"—and its favorite trysting place is Venice, a city of veils.

DECEIT
AT
FLORIAN'S

U RBINO Macintyre was amused as he sat in the café Florian listening to the Contessa da Capo-Zendrini. Here it was only a few days after the New Year and she was already pining for her summer villa up in Asolo.

"It's the prospect of *Carnevale* that makes me want to wish my life away like this," she said. She leaned back on the maroon banquette in the Chinese salon and slowly shook her head. "You're still a bit too young to realize it but time lost can never be regained, despite what poor Proust in his cork-lined room thought."

A doleful look clouded her attractive face. The Contessa had never told Urbino her precise age but the stretch of her memory and the range of her experience, as well as her frequent references—sometimes playful, sometimes wistful—to what she called his "youth," indicated someone at least two decades older. The wedding photograph in the *salotto blu* of the Ca' da Capo-Zendrini showed a patrician-featured English girl who hadn't so much changed since her days at St. Brigid's-by-the-Sea as gradually aged into the mature look already present in the otherwise fresh face.

She glanced out the window at the Piazza San Marco, relatively empty and quiet now after the recent festivities.

"All those barbarians in masks descending on our serene city! It's intolerable even to think of it!"

She reached out for another tea cake, this one frosted with a deep-rose icing that matched the color of her dress.

"And I can't even go up to London for February. It would be cruel to abandon Josef even if he does insist on staying with the Sisters."

The Contessa was referring to the emigré Pole, Josef Lubonski, who was restoring a fresco at the Church of San Gabriele in the Cannaregio. She had secured him the position after she had seen the work he had done in London in her former parish church and in the townhouse of a friend. Instead of staying at the Ca' da Capo-Zendrini as she had suggested, however, he preferred to lodge at the Casa Crispina, the pensione run by the Sisters of the Charity of Santa Crispina across from San Gabriele.

"But what about abandoning me, Barbara? Doesn't that give you pause?"

"Are you ever anything *but* abandoned during *Carnevale, caro?*" she said with an arch little smile. "And it seems that this year you're determined to be even more shameless than ever."

When Urbino was about to defend himself, she languidly waved a beringed hand temporarily bereft of a petit four.

"Please! I refuse to hear anything more about this masked ball you're thinking of giving at the Palazzo Uccello."

Urbino smiled.

"Oh, I'm not thinking about it anymore, Barbara."

"Thank God for that. The good Sisters at St. Brigid's were right, I see! Even the most inveterate sinner isn't beyond redemption."

"What I mean, Barbara, is that I don't have to think about giving it anymore. I've decided to go ahead."

"To go ahead?" Her gray eyes were round with startle. He might have said that he was going to attempt a translation of *Remembrance of Things Past* into Serbo-Croatian. "But, *caro,* it will be chaos, simply chaos!" She reached out to touch the sleeve of his tweed jacket. "You don't know the first thing about it!"

"I agree."

She nodded with self-satisfaction and reached for another tea cake.

"At least you know the limits of your own presumption."

"Exactly. That's why I've decided to ask Oriana to help me organize things. She'll be my hostess."

The Contessa was holding the tea cake, this one iced in light green. She lost interest in it and put it back on the plate.

"But why Oriana, *caro?* I love her dearly but she isn't the least preoccupied of women."

The Contessa was right. Oriana Borelli and her husband, Filippo, were usually in the thick of extramarital intrigues and domestic disputes that left them little time or energy for much else. Urbino had no idea if Oriana would be able to help him. In fact, he hadn't even brought it up with her yet.

The Contessa took a sip of tea.

"Even if Oriana is a competent woman when she isn't distracted by the *opera buffa* they like to make of their life, what could she hope to do with the Palazzo Uccello? It's a lovely building, but if you're giving a ball, *caro,* you'll need space. The Palazzo Uccello is too *intime*. Oriana can't work a miracle." She looked at him slyly over her teacup. "Because you're an attractive younger man, Oriana might be making promises she can't fulfill. What plans have the two of you made?"

"I wouldn't exactly say we've made any plans yet, Barbara."

"And why not? The storm that's going to disturb this calm"— she nodded out at the Piazza— "isn't so far away. Some people start to think about the next *Carnevale* as soon as the old one is over. Plans should have been made long ago; surely even you can see that." She put her teacup down and paused before adding with quiet firmness, "A great many things."

"Such as?" Urbino prompted.

"A motif, for example! A theme! Do you have that?"

"Not really."

"Not really! You need a theme, Urbino dear, I can't believe that Oriana didn't tell you!"

Poor maligned Oriana, of course, could have told him nothing at all on the topic.

"What would you suggest, Barbara?"

"What would I suggest, *caro*? Whatever in the world have I to do with it? This is Oriana's pet project, and I wish her— and you—the best of luck! You'll both need it!"

"All this is making me feel a bit dispirited," Urbino said, letting his voice drift into a resigned tone. "I hope you realize that I'd prefer you to help me but I know how you feel about *Carnevale*. Quite frankly, I was afraid of asking you."

" 'Afraid!' Am I a person to be afraid of?" she said, shooting him a quick, baleful look. "Don't be a *cretino*! I hate *Carnevale,* yes! But does that mean that I would be happy to see you make a fool of yourself—and of me?"

"Of you? But what would you have to do with it?"

"Even if I have nothing to do with it—absolutely, positively nothing as you have so obviously decided all on your own!— I would be in the thick of it. It would reflect on me! We're associated, we're linked, we're allied! Everyone knows that. Everyone can see it." She gestured around the Chinese salon at the other patrons, who seemed completely oblivious to the two of them enjoying their fabled rapport. "If you make a gaffe—as surely you will if poor, well-intentioned Oriana is seeing to things—they'll laugh at us both. I couldn't bear that for you!" she finished with a commiserative shake of her head and a look that was meant to be devoid of everything else but sympathy for him.

"What would you suggest, then, Barbara?" he asked again.

"I don't see any alternative, do you, Urbino? I feel like sweet, smiling Pope John Paul the First who had things thrust upon him, poor man. What choice did he have but to put his shoulder to the wheel?" she said with more passion than appropriateness in her idiom. "And we all know what happened to him!"

"Does all this mean that you'll help me with my masked ball?" he asked, trying to hide a smile.

"It means nothing of the kind! If I had to provide something at the Palazzo Uccello at this late date, I would be doomed to abject failure! I'd be like Fortuny trying to make do with a pitiful little scrap of material, lovely though the Palazzo Uccello is. Neither of us would survive it." She paused. "Oriana's failure, however, would be even more abject than our own. That's beyond dispute."

For a third time this early January afternoon Urbino asked for her suggestion.

Before answering she caught the attention of the waiter in his formal black and white and ordered a fresh pot of tea.

"I'd suggest, *caro,* that you forget all about having a masked ball at the Palazzo Uccello."

"But—"

"I can see there's no choice," she interrupted. "No choice whatsoever but for me to have one at the Ca' da Capo. You force my hand. Settle things with Oriana. Tell her I've decided to have a *ballo in maschera* and you wouldn't think of having one yourself. She'll understand. She'll probably even be relieved."

"But, Barbara, I wouldn't want you to go through all that trouble."

"You call it trouble, Urbino. I call it a penance willingly embraced before Lent even raises its ashy head. But don't forget what I'm doing it for." She gave him only a moment to consider before informing him, "I'm doing it for you, *caro.*"

She reached across the marble table to pat his hand.

And this was how Urbino, who had never had any intention of giving a masked ball at the Palazzo Uccello, was able to persuade the Contessa to give one herself at the Ca' da Capo-Zendrini. He knew that the Contessa, rather than being offended by his little deception, was just the kind of person to appreciate it. But he also knew that she would no more have admitted to this than admitted to having been aware, all along, of the deceit itself.

The Contessa's appreciation, along with her awareness, shone almost mischievously from her gray eyes as she picked up yet another petit four and waited for her fresh pot of tea.

Part One

DEATH BEFORE LENT

1 JUST the other night, only a few hours after Carnival officially began at midnight, one more aged sister died at the Convent of the Charity of Santa Crispina.

Surrounded by a group of equally ancient nuns, Sister Clara sat up straight in bed and said with a blind, unblinking gaze, "I see her clearly, so clearly, my dear ones. Her face is as young as ours when we took the veil." She smiled and opened her thin arms wide. "Welcome, Sister Death."

Promptly, without any anticlimax, she fell back on the pillows and died.

The sisters started to do what had to be done. Two prepared to wash the body, two prayed, and two argued over whether the smile on Sister Clara's face should be toned down a bit. And no doubt at least one of them was wondering who would be left behind to tend to her own temple of the Holy Ghost when her time came.

Even if you had no other evidence than the smooth, efficient way the sisters went about their business in Sister Clara's cell, as if they were performing the ordinary tasks of housekeeping, you would nonetheless know that death was far from a stranger to this building that housed the convent and its attendant pensione.

Yet death, though familiar, wasn't any more welcome here than elsewhere. It didn't always come so benevolently or wear such a fresh face as it had for Sister Clara, who seemed happy to be delivered into the hands of her Heavenly Bridegroom.

Far from it. Dying sisters at Santa Crispina have been known to scream and even curse when they finally saw the face that death was wearing for them.

Such reluctance on the part of some sisters to leave their building for the bosom of Abraham might lead you to think it was a snug ark whose considerable comforts mocked the order's vow of poverty. You would be wrong, however, as you would immediately have known when you saw the building's leprous stones and chipped statuary, its damp-warped shutters and listing staircases, its buckling floors and crumbling plaster. The furniture was heavy, dark, and minimal, and the paintings scattered throughout the four stories were mainly grim memento mori and martyrdoms. Never did divine motherhood look as consumptive as it did in some of the Madonnas holding their beloved sons in their arms. As for the Last Supper and the Crucifixion that hung in the guests' dining room, you would have been hard pressed to say which of the two was less appetizing.

And yet, despite the dismal quarters, there were several reasons why you might consider staying at the pensione run by the Sisters of the Charity of Santa Crispina.

For one thing, you might be zealously inclined to purify your spirit in the Casa Crispina's austere surroundings, reminiscent of some dark medieval inn where you were frozen in winter and baked in summer. The good sisters saw no need to make you any more comfortable than they were themselves, the charity of their ancient order obliging them not to deny you any of the pleasures to be gained from the mortification of the flesh.

The Casa Crispina provided a clean, sparsely furnished room, three plain meals a day, and the sound of bells from matins all the way through vespers to compline. You were free to ignore these summonses as you wished but the sisters believed that even the mere sound, falling on your ear in sleep or in sloth, had some beneficial effect. To make things as easy as possible, they had placed a prie-dieu and inspirational lithograph in each of the ten rooms so that you could not invoke the excuse of the inconvenience of a long walk to the chapel.

Another, much more obvious reason why you might be attracted to the Casa Crispina was purely a matter of lire since it was one of the cheapest places to stay in all of Venice—unless, that is, you reckoned in the cost of throat and chest medications in winter and all those *aranciate* and ices you were likely to consume in summer.

If these considerations of austerity and cost did not sway you, however, perhaps the retiring nature of the Casa Crispina could, for it was in a remote part of the Cannaregio into which tourists only occasionally strayed from the Ghetto or the Church of the Madonna dell'Orto, the parish church of Tintoretto. Thus you might indulge here the fantasy that almost every tourist has—that he is anything but what he is.

The shopkeeper, the children playing by the covered well-head, the mask maker arranging his display, the two old women in black shaking their heads over the death notice on the bakery-shop window—you could convince yourself that all these residents of the quarter that you saw in only the first few moments of leaving the Casa Crispina couldn't possibly know you for what you really were.

It was much harder to maintain the fiction of your true identity, however, within the somber walls of the Casa Crispina itself where the sisters' domain was clearly separate from that of their guests. You might conceal other things but never that you were anything more than a mere guest, someone initiated into less arcane mysteries than those the good sisters shared.

The pensione, except for its dining area, was confined to the story above the ground level, while the nuns were semicloistered on the next two floors. The two groups mingled only in the chapel and the reception area—both on the ground floor—and on the front staircase that connected all four floors. The sisters, however, usually used their own private entrance and staircase.

The refectory at the rear of the ground floor was divided by a flimsy partition with a door. Large stained-glass windows, which looked out on a narrow canal, were usually shuttered. The guests were served in their own area not by the sisters themselves but by two middle aged women from nearby Mestre who wore perpetually disgruntled expressions.

As Dora Spaak sat down at the empty table in her usual place, she glanced as she always did at the partly opened door into the sisters' refectory. Although the sisters ate earlier, Dora occasionally thought she could see the flutter of dark-gray cloth through the opening. One time when she had come to the dining room earlier than usual, she had heard a voice droning something indistinguishable. A prayer? a homily? the life of a martyred saint? There had been no way for her to tell but it had given her an uneasy feeling.

No, Dora didn't feel at all comfortable staying at the Casa Crispina. She hated it when some of the sisters referred to it by its old-fashioned name, the Hospice, because even though she knew this was supposed to evoke memories of the religious lodgings for the weary in the Holy Land of long ago, all a nurse like her could think of was pain and the end of life.

So much seemed peculiar here. For example, even though it would have been easier for the women from Mestre to bring the food directly from the kitchen to the guests' dining room through the nuns' refectory, they instead made circuitous trips down a corridor even though the nuns had long finished dinner.

As Dora was trying to figure out once again why the door between the two areas was always partly open if no one went through it during meals—was it to tease them all with fleeting glimpses of a better life or to allow the sisters to keep an eye on their guests?—she heard someone approaching. It could be her brother, Nicholas. He had been seeing to their mother in her room, making sure that she really didn't want to come out to dinner, that she didn't want to be coaxed into joining them. Nicholas had more patience with their mother than she did. Dora was already dreading returning to Pittsburgh alone with her.

When she looked away from the door, it wasn't Nicholas standing there but the handsome photographer who had been so nice to her since she arrived.

"Thinking of joining the sisters? They could use some young blood."

He had a soothing, well-modulated voice, one she could have listened to for hours. It was the kind of voice she associated with the best bred of Englishmen.

Dora felt herself blushing. She looked down at her napkin, stained from the meals of previous days.

"You should be careful. The sisters might hear you, Mr. Gibbon."

"Just Val, remember?"

"Val—that's short for . . . ?"

He gave her a dazzling smile. His eyes were as dark as any Italian's but his skin was whiter than hers.

"Guess."

"I couldn't—unless—"

"Yes?"

"Could it be Valentine?"

His quick laugh made her feel foolish. She dared not look up right away but busied herself with her napkin. When she felt strong enough to encounter his dark eyes again, however, she saw that they were no longer alone. Xenia Campi, the Italian woman who lived at the pensione and claimed to be able to see into the future, was standing next to Val, a frown on her heavily made-up face.

"Excuse me, sir." Stout, black-haired, and in her mid-forties, the Italian woman spoke deliberately in heavily accented English. She put her hand on the top of the chair behind which Val Gibbon was standing. "This is *my* seat."

"Excuse *me,* signora! Everything in order here in the convent. What would happen if it wasn't, even during Carnival— or should I say *especially* during Carnival!"

Val Gibbon moved aside so that the woman, wearing a plum-colored, robelike dress with voluminous sleeves, could take her accustomed place next to Dora. Before he went to the other side of the table, the photographer bent down close to Dora's ear and whispered, "Nothing as romantic as that, I'm afraid, but thank you for thinking so. It shows you have a tender imagination."

He went to sit down near the end of the table, his back to the partly open door. As he unfolded his napkin, he looked over at Dora.

"A *very* tender imagination," he added with a smile.

Dora looked away. She had been surprised to see Val Gibbon in the dining room tonight, not because he had come upon her unawares and seemed to enjoy doing it, but because he hadn't eaten at the Casa Crispina for several nights in a row now. She had missed him. No matter what the others might say, she could tell he was in every sense a gentleman. He was like one of those Englishmen who always ended up being especially nice to poor young girls in the books she used to read. They might have seemed strange and even gruff at first, hiding some disturbing secret, but they always made up for it before the end of the story.

On the second evening of Val Gibbon's absence, Xenia Campi had said, "I don't foresee good things for a man who has money to throw away like that."

Whether this was an opinion or the fruit of the woman's supposedly clairvoyant vision, Dora didn't know and didn't want to know. Dora was in almost constant fear that the woman would say something about *her* future. It wasn't that she believed that Xenia Campi—or anyone—could see into the future, but she was superstitious. She was sure that the ill the woman might claim to see would come true, just because she had dared utter it. As for the good she might predict, that was sure to fly away as quickly as the pigeons in St. Mark's Square whenever there was any sudden sound.

Tonight Xenia Campi looked particularly humorless and depressed, and had an unnatural restraint that made Dora feel as if she might strike out at any moment at her or the photographer with some dire prediction or scathing indictment. Dora was relieved when Nicholas, without their mother, took his seat on her other side.

He was soon followed, noisily, by the three teenage boys from Naples. Xenia Campi darted a quick glance at one of the boys, who avoided looking at her and started to talk nervously to his companions. The three boys usually kept very much to themselves, not saying more than a few words of greeting during their meals and never staying longer than was necessary. They were here for Carnival and obviously didn't want to spend any time away from more exciting things in the big square.

"And how are you feeling this evening, Signora Campi?" Nicholas asked.

"Much better, thank you. My cold is almost gone."

"Mr. Lubonski isn't as fortunate, I'm afraid."

The Pole who was restoring the fresco in the nearby church was confined to his room with the flu.

"Signor Lubonski's condition is much more serious than mine, I assure you."

Xenia Campi said this as if, from the privileged position of someone born with a caul, she saw things about the man's lungs that even an X ray couldn't.

Nicholas turned somewhat hesitantly to Val Gibbon. Dora had noticed that her brother was frequently self-conscious with Gibbon and would hardly look him in the face when he spoke to him. She attributed this to his characteristic shyness around very outgoing people. It didn't mean he didn't like them. In fact, she had always thought it was very much the opposite.

As her brother addressed Val Gibbon now, Dora was pleased to note the almost boyish enthusiasm behind his words.

"You must be finding plenty of things to photograph in Venice during Carnival, Mr. Gibbon. It must be difficult to know what not to take a picture of when there's so much to choose from."

Gibbon smiled at him.

"Not at all, Mr. Spaak. That's the difference between an amateur and a professional. Photography is one of the arts, you know. Like all artists, the true photographer is an initiate in mysteries unknown to others."

Xenia Campi, with no attempt to hold her voice down, said to Dora, "There's no more art in taking a picture than there is in making a ragout!"

Dora hoped Val Gibbon didn't think ill of her for being the recipient of the remark. She would have frowned at the woman except for her fear that it might draw even more notice—or that the woman would turn her ill will on her. Her heart went out to the photographer. He might be good at pretending to be strong, but she sensed that he was almost as vulnerable as she was to an unkind word.

"Ah, but Signora Campi," Gibbon said as he turned to the woman, "surely you know that there are cooks and there are chefs, there are holiday picture takers and there are photographers—just as surely as there are Luna Park frauds and whatever might be the opposite in your own profession. You see that I am kind enough to call it a profession."

Xenia Campi's eyes widened but she said nothing. One of the boys at the far end of the table started to laugh loudly and was soon joined by the other two. They began to sing a song in Italian. Dora couldn't understand the song but Xenia Campi frowned in their direction, and the boy she had glanced at earlier stopped singing.

Poor Val Gibbon held his head high but Dora could see his bruised heart. It was just as exposed for her as was the Flaming Heart of Jesus that graced the wall of her room upstairs.

The serving woman came in from the corridor with a tureen of steaming soup. Dora sighed. Another meal at the Casa Crispina was about to begin.

2 URBINO looked down from the window of the Palazzo Uccello straight into the eyes of Death.

Only a few moments earlier, Urbino had put aside the volume of *Remembrance of Things Past* and gone to the window. Someone is in the *calle,* he had said to himself, even though he had heard nothing.

He had been right. The Palazzo Uccello had been visited on this February evening by Death and the Lady of Veils.

Death was tall, dressed almost all in black. Black boots, black leggings and gloves, a black steeple of a hat pulled down over a mad jumble of black crepe Medusa locks. The eyelets of the white oval mask were trimmed in black. Hundreds of featherlike ebony scraps had been sewn together to form a cape that its wearer hugged close.

The Lady of Veils was a vision in white. In fact, with her cascade of short veils framing a delicate mask, her gauze robe, gloves, feathered fan, and slippers—all ghostly white—she seemed to be an emanation of the fog that was curling over the bridge from the canal and drifting into the alley.

Death, conscious of his audience, extended his arms, and suddenly became a burst of color, exposing long tatters of crimson, indigo, yellow, jade, and pink cloth sewn to the torso of the garment beneath. It was like seeing someone eviscerated. The beauty was perversely enhanced for Urbino by the horror of the association.

The Lady of Veils moved closer to Death and let herself be enclosed in the blossom of his embrace.

Was the Lady a woman and Death a man? There was no way of knowing. They carried their secret away with them as they broke their embrace and seemed to glide over the humpbacked bridge. The *calle* was empty once again of everything except the drifting, curling fog.

Serena, the cat he had rescued from the Public Gardens, jumped up on the sill to get Urbino's attention. He turned back into the room and took Schumann's *Carnaval* from the shelf. The Contessa had given him the recording to help him through his recuperation from a bout of the flu that had kept him housebound for almost a week.

"It should more than make up for whatever of *Carnevale* you think you're missing, *caro*." She had sighed and shaken her well-coiffed head. "Why can't our celebration be sane and romantic like Schumann's?"

"But it wouldn't be the Venetian Carnival then, would it?" He did not remind her of the sad suicidal end that Schumann had come to. "I wish it were two months long the way it used to be," he said playfully. "Just imagine if it began the day after Christmas!"

"Even after ten years, you're as much of a perplexity as when I first met you! I thought you cherished your solitude, that you had come here to Venice to be away from it all. Isn't it enough that you're forcing me to give this costume ball?" she said with little regard for how she had actually arrived at this decision a month ago. "Oh, yes, *caro,* you're a perplexity to me—a dear, sweet one but a perplexity nonetheless."

"Am I so different from you? You enjoy your solitude, too, and yet you negotiate drawing rooms like a goldfish in a crystal bowl. You're in your element then."

"Of course I am!" she had said, visibly pleased with his image. "But with you the two are horrible extremes. You could use some order and balance. Listen to *Carnaval*."

That's just what he would do now. He put the record in the player and sat on the sofa. The soothing notes of the "Préambule" filled the room, followed by the movements of Pierrot and Harlequin, those two commedia dell'arte figures of the spirit and the flesh. Naïve Pierrot and coarse Harlequin. Now *there* were two extremes, Urbino thought as he pictured the figures against his closed eyelids. Could the spirit of the one inhabit the flesh of the other? He would have to pose this riddle to the Contessa.

Two screams from the *calle* interrupted the "Valse noble" and Urbino went to the window again. The alley and the bridge seemed deserted. He was about to turn away when a form detached itself from the shadows near the bridge and crept along the *calle* past the Palazzo Uccello. Whether a man or a woman he couldn't tell any more than with Death and the Lady of Veils a little while ago.

The form was swathed in long dark robes, its face covered with an equally dark hood. When it neared the opening of a courtyard, a second form bounded from the shadows and, with another of the screams that had caught his attention, ran down the *calle* and beyond Urbino's sight. The first figure quickened its pace in pursuit as a cry floated back and up to the closed window.

What had he seen? A playful game of hide and seek? One person pursuing another with evil intent? An argument between friends that might end with them kissing each other?

The appearances could cover any of these realities.

Urbino went back to the sofa. The fifth movement had begun. Reaching out to stroke the cat, Urbino smiled to himself.

If Barbara could only see me now, he thought. This was almost as good as a cork-lined room, and he was more than content—at least for the time being.

3 SCHUMANN'S *Carnaval* ended. Urbino poured himself another glass of Corvo and picked up the Proust, opening it to where a postcard reproduction of Man Ray's photograph of Proust's death profile marked his place.

He had read *Remembrance of Things Past* several times before but he was reading it now because of the book on Proust he was adding to his *Venetian Lives* series. *Proust and Venice* would focus on the role the city had played in the writer's life and art. It would have reproductions of paintings by Carpaccio, Titian, Veronese, and Tintoretto and photographs of Venetian scenes and buildings by the city's premier photographer, Porfirio.

Urbino had reached the point where Proust's narrator finally gets to Venice after years of expectation and postponement and after the sudden death of his beloved Albertine. Inevitably, despite Marcel's appreciation of the beauty and secrecy of the city, he finds himself somewhat disillusioned, and by the time he is about to leave, Venice is no longer an enchanted labyrinth out of the *Arabian Nights* but something sinister and deceptive that seems to have little to do with Doges and Turner. It doesn't even seem to be Venice any longer, but a mendacious fiction where the palaces are nothing but lifeless marble and the water that makes the city unique only a combination of hydrogen and oxygen.

Urbino read for a while and then put the book down again, finding it difficult to concentrate tonight on the subjunctive and the imperfect, on the essential melancholia at the lime-blossom heart of Proust's style and story.

Followed by Serena, who had been sleeping on one of the maroon velvet seats of the mahogany confessional on the other side of the room, he went to the study and put *Children of Paradise* in the video machine.

Urbino didn't know how much of the long movie he would be able to watch before dropping off to sleep, but he knew the tragic story of a mime's love for a beautiful actress so well that he could start it at any point without any problem. With its retelling of the story of Pierrot, Harlequin, and Columbine and its great final scene in which the mime Baptiste is separated forever from his beloved Garance by the mad Carnival crowd, it was particularly suited to the season.

He settled himself in his favorite armchair, Serena nestled against him, as the story started to unfold. Garance, the voluptuous yet tenderly maternal woman for whom love was *"terriblement simple,"* was watching a performance in front of the Funambules. In just a few moments Baptiste would fall in love with her forever.

Urbino found himself almost holding his breath. Serena purred. The childlike Baptiste, dressed as a clown all in white, turned in Garance's direction and looked at her with his soulful eyes.

Ah, there, it had happened! The rest—passion, yearning, jealousy, death, and separation—they all were fated now.

4   A small rose-colored object flew through the air at Urbino. He didn't have time to avoid it and it smashed against his black Austrian cape. A colorless liquid splashed out, soaking into the cape and sprinkling his face.

Fortunately the painted egg had been filled with rose water. Urbino brushed the eggshell from his cape and smiled at the boy who had made him his target. Dressed in a multicolored clown costume with a long tail and rabbitlike ears, the boy carried a basket filled with eggs. Another boy, also dressed as a *mattaccino,* stood next to him. They both laughed. Urbino waved. The *mattaccini* continued on their way, throwing an occasional egg but saving most of them for the Piazza.

The Strada Nova was busy with shoppers, tourists on their way to the Piazza, and merchants behind their outdoor stalls. Spirits were high on this clear, brisk afternoon. Urbino had taken a detour on his way to the Church of San Gabriele to get his first, up-close sight of Carnival.

Young children in frilly skirts, tutus, baggy pants, feathers, face paint, and the masks of cartoon characters shouted and raced through the crowd. A mother pushed her daughter along slowly in a stroller. Both had red balloons lifting their ponytails. A group of chess figures—knights, queens, and bishops—strolled along sedately, followed by a pack of devils darting mischievously through the crowd and pretending to steal things from the booths.

Even many of those in street clothes wore masks or had them hanging around their necks or tucked into their pockets. Urbino's own red half mask was hanging around his neck.

In the Campo Santa Fosca, mandolins and guitars played and a high, sweet voice sang Lorenzo Il Magnifico's opening lines from *The Triumph of Bacchus and Ariadne:*

> *"How beautiful is youth*
> *which is fleeing by!*
> *Whoever wishes to be happy,*

let him be so
for tomorrow holds no promises."

The singer was a Gypsy boy about twelve with dark circles under his eyes. The three swarthy musicians continued to play as the boy took off his cap and went around the crowd for money. He brought the money over to one of the men and started another song, his voice just as sweet as before but his face even more weary-looking.

5 HALF an hour later Urbino climbed the paint-splattered ladder in the right nave of the Church of San Gabriele. He stood on the wooden platform, not even six feet square, and looked down at the uneven stone floor more than twenty feet below. The longer he looked at it the farther away it seemed. It had an almost hypnotic effect and only with some effort was he able to turn his attention to the fresco.

It was a sixteenth-century work by one of Titian's followers and depicted Saint Gabriel in three of his heavenly missions: to Daniel, Zachary, and—most prominent of all in the center— to the Blessed Virgin Mary. Giulio Licino had had only a faint glimmer of the robustness and magical color of his master, but the fresco, dimmed now by the years and the pollution that managed to invade even the church itself, deserved to shine with its original beauty, inferior though it might be to Titian's.

Urbino had looked up at the fresco dozens of times since he had moved to Venice. Never had it occurred to him that someday he would be helping to restore it.

He smiled at his exaggeration. He was more in the position of only observing the restoration of the fresco. Lubonski, however, let him do some of the less difficult things that a skilled workman might be trusted with, such as applying the first coat of lime plaster, the *trullisatio,* to the severely damaged areas. Sometimes Urbino felt the way he had one long ago summer fetching and handing tools to his father as he had built a gazebo in their backyard.

Last summer he had studied art restoration on the lagoon island of San Servolo and at the Palazzo Spinelli in Florence to prepare himself for a brief biography of the Minolfis, a renowned Venetian family of restorers. He had taken the commission at the request of the Contessa, who was close to the family.

The courses on San Servolo and at the Palazzo Spinelli would have been more than enough for his purposes, but he had become interested in restoration for its own sake and enjoyed helping, in his small way, to bring things back to the way they once had been.

"I want to do something more," he had said to the Contessa last September as they waited for the Regatta to begin. He had just finished telling her how thrilled he had been the other day on San Servolo when, his face covered with a plastic mask, he had removed some corrosion from the hem of a stone Madonna with the quartz cutter. "I want to do something more than what I've already done here in Venice."

"You've done enough already, _caro_, and you'll continue to," she said. "You've fixed up the Palazzo Uccello and you're writing your biographies. And just think of all the pleasure you give me! My life would be empty without you. What more could you possibly want than all that?"

"Maybe I'd like to be able to see some change—however small—that I've made here. A change for the better that I could reach out and touch. Something that other people could see, too. You're right about restoring the Palazzo Uccello but I live there. It wasn't completely selfless."

The Contessa shook her head and looked down at the Grand Canal.

"Are you speaking from some strange kind of American guilt? You've already turned over the top floor to Natalia and her husband."

"I just want to do something more," he repeated.

"You Americans and your _doing_!" she said with the air of a person whose greater years and British heredity had allowed her to see so much ill-conceived American activity. "Work harder on your biographies! You've got the one on Proust to finish. Find another case to sleuth! Did you know that someone has been stealing the votive candles from the street shrine of the Madonna by the Ca' da Capo? Try your hand at that. Until something better comes along you're going to have to just sit tight and go through the motions of being content. Just don't do anything drastic. Whenever I hear someone talking the way you are and see that same look on their face I think: Beware! You're on the brink of a big mistake. If I didn't know you had a few more years to go, I'd say that you were having a mid-life crisis."

Although the Contessa had continued to chide him about his dissatisfaction, she had ended up providing a solution. A month after the Regatta she decided to finance the restoration of the San Gabriele fresco. She secured the appointment of Josef Lubonski and arranged to have Urbino help him. Everything seemed to be working out well, except that both Urbino and the Pole had come down with the flu. Lubonski's case was much more serious and he was being tended by the sisters at the Casa Crispina across the *campo*.

Actually the San Gabriele fresco wasn't in particularly bad shape compared to other frescoes more exposed to air currents but the pastor wanted to bring the church's patron saint back to a semblance of what the older parishioners could remember as its much greater vividness.

An architect and two contractors had dealt with the problem of the water-soaked plaster on the latticework behind the fresco, and now Lubonski was several weeks into what the Contessa liked to call the "cosmetics."

"If we could only restore ourselves to our original luster!" she had lamented. "Now *that* would be something! Every couple of years we could hang a sign on our doors that says '*In restauro*' and emerge as fresh as we were at forty!"

This afternoon Urbino had climbed the ladder to be alone with the fresco for a few moments. The small areas that Lubonski had worked on glowed with vitality. Several people, including the photographer Porfirio, said that some of the paint was being taken off, that the cølors originally hadn't been so bright. From what he had learned and what he knew about the restoration of the Sistine frescoes, however, Urbino disagreed.

He went down the ladder. He should stop by to see Lubonski before going to Florian's to meet the Contessa.

The English photographer staying at the Casa Crispina was standing near the foot of the ladder looking up at him as he descended the last few rungs. The photographer was burdened with several cameras. Behind him was Paolo, the sexton.

Urbino had met Val Gibbon several times. Because he was lodging in the Casa Crispina and taking some photographs for the sisters, Sister Teresa had pressed the Contessa to have him take the photographs of the fresco for the church records. The Contessa, always easily swayed by Sister Teresa, had agreed, not taking into consideration Porfirio's air of proprietorship about all things Venetian.

Val Gibbon was a handsome man in his late thirties, Urbino's own age, with short, curly dark hair and dark eyes and almost-dead-white skin. The first time Urbino had met him he had been reminded of Caesar's words about Cassius but he was fairly certain that Gibbon's lean and hungry look usually evoked thoughts other than those of danger in the minds of impressionable women.

"Finished dabbling for the day?" Gibbon said with an even, innocent gaze.

"Just having a look. I only 'dabble' when Lubonski is here."

"That might be a while. He was looking like death yesterday. You'd think a Pole would be more hardy. I can't say I mind having him out of the way for a time though. It makes my work easier."

"I thought you were finished with the fresco."

"Not quite. There are still a few things I want to do. I'm also photographing a few of the other frescoes and paintings as a favor to Sister Teresa—although I think I'd do it just to rile that pompous fool Porfirio. He doesn't like the idea of my poaching in his territory—and by that I don't mean only the church but the whole damn city." He looked around the dark Gothic building. His eye rested on a statue of the Virgin to the left of the altar. One of the old women of the parish was arranging a fresh urn of flowers. "I'm also thinking of taking some time-lapse of the Virgin over there. The ridiculous Italian woman staying at the Casa Crispina says she saw a bright halo around the head yesterday. I'd like to give her proof of how foolish she is."

"I doubt if Xenia Campi would accept photographs as proof of anything but what happened *not* to be there at the time they were taken."

Gibbon's immediate laugh had an unpleasant, conspiratorial ring to it. Before Urbino could make it clear that they didn't share a condescending attitude toward Xenia Campi, however, the photographer excused himself and started up the ladder.

6 JOSEF Lubonski, an attractive man in his early forties with short sandy-colored hair and prominent cheekbones, lay in bed beneath several layers of blankets, His face was haggard, and his blue eyes were clouded with dark circles beneath them. He was hardly able to muster a smile of greeting.

"I feel weak like a baby," he told Urbino. "It makes me want to have my mother here, even an old man like me."

Lubonski's mother was in Cracow. He phoned her every week and regularly sent her money. Even in these freer days for Poland, Lubonski preferred not to go back, and his mother, close to eighty, wasn't well enough to visit him.

"Don't worry about anything, Josef. *Carnevale* is still young. As for the fresco, it will wait for you."

A ghost of a smile flickered over Lubonski's face.

"I know the fresco will wait, Urbino. But can you?"

"To be honest, I was just looking at the fresco—but yes, I can wait." Urbino meant it. No more climbing up the ladder and poking around. "Don't worry about me or anyone else. Just get well. Besides, the photographer will be able to finish his work more easily without either of us around."

"I hope he knows he must not flash the bright lights all over!" Lubonski said with vehemence. "He has already given too much light to the three saints. He knows how to take pictures of rich people. He knows how to do it very well, I think. But frescoes and paintings, I am not sure."

A few moments later a sister came in to give Lubonski his medication.

7   URBINO was pushed almost the entire length of the exit ramp at the San Marco boat landing by the crush of passengers behind him. The trip down the Grand Canal had been like a floating party with wine bottles being passed around and couples dancing in the aisle to the music from a transistor radio.

As Urbino reached the end of the ramp, a muzzled cocker spaniel was almost trampled by a huge woman in a Borsalino and a kimono-style robe splashed with vibrant geometrical patterns. The dog's owner, an elderly woman in a fur coat, snatched the dog up and drew as close to the side of the building as she could to let the crowd pass around her.

Urbino joined the flow of people moving exuberantly up the *calle* past Harry's Bar. Although he had never worn a full costume or "cracked the whip" in the Piazza along with a long line of revelers, he seldom tired of the spectacle of this "feast of fools," as it had been called in the Middle Ages. The Contessa assumed that he had been corrupted by all the Mardi Gras back in New Orleans, all the parades and balls, all the business about Mystical Krewes and Comus and Rex.

It was true, but "corruption" wasn't a word he would have used. Some of his happiest memories were of sitting safe and secure on his father's shoulders watching the floats on Canal Street. And even as he had got older he had enjoyed watching the festivities more than taking an active part in them— something that had caused pointless arguments between him and his ex-wife, Evangeline, who had been Queen of Comus before their marriage.

Urbino ducked into the shelter of a shop at the end of the *calle* where it funneled into a main route to the Piazza. Here he had a good view.

An Arab sheikh passed by with the women of his harem dressed in blue veils that revealed considerably more than they concealed. One of them blew Urbino a kiss. Two children, dressed as an angel and a devil, were guided through the crowd by their father wearing a broad, smiling mask. Behind them three figures strolled along with red and purple feathered jackets, sequin-covered leggings, huge gauze fans, and black oval masks. They were followed by five purple-turbaned figures with gold-painted faces who were draped in shiny black material and sported saillike purple wings. They walked haughtily, as if they were royalty, and stopped every few minutes to assume frozen poses. A group of nuns passed by with bawdy laughter and suggestive gestures.

Amid all this clamor five figures in long funereal capes, black capelets with hoods, severe white masks, and black tricorn hats walked in a silent cluster. Dressed in the *bautta* disguise worn by noblemen in the eighteenth century and seen in many Venetian paintings, they seemed to censure the madness around them, to be reminding the other revelers that although *Carnevale* might, by its very name, encourage a wanton farewell to the flesh, that the flesh wasn't forever.

Urbino rejoined the flow of people and soon entered the Piazza through one of the passages across from the mosquelike Basilica. Here the revelers spread out into the square, where pools of water from an *acqua alta* had seeped up through the paving stones. Raised planks provided dry passage over the deeper puddles in front of the Basilica.

A temporary stage, its curtains drawn, faced the Basilica. Outside the café Quadri a covered deck had been set up with tables, chairs, and an area for the house orchestra. The orchestra wasn't playing, but loudspeakers blared "Mack the Knife" so loudly that Urbino could feel it through his whole body. A raised wooden runway dominated the space in front of the stage. People sauntered up and down its ramps, posing, singing, waving, and shouting, while others sat on its edges, fortified against the cold with wine, beer, and their enthusiasm. A group of costumed men and women was dancing wildly to the music around two boys on stilts, dressed as crows. Above all this activity, a huge chandelier hung in the middle of the Piazza, waiting to be lighted the last evening of *Carnevale,* when the square would become an open ballroom.

Photographers were everywhere in their high boots, posing the masqueraders who were only too eager to please someone other than themselves after hours in front of their mirrors. Sometimes one of them would seduce a photographer away from someone he was about to shoot. Fights erupted between the abandoned masquerader and the photographer's new subject but they were usually short-lived. The maskers returned to their strolling and posing, seeking another opportunity to be the center of attention.

Surely it would soon come their way. Wasn't something new, something different and unexpected supposed to happen at *Carnevale*? Wasn't it when anything could happen? When you could do anything you wanted?

As Urbino sidestepped the fake Gucci purses, belts, and wallets spread out on a blanket at the feet of a glum-looking Senegalese, shouts farther down the arcade caught his attention. A group was gathered around a brightly costumed figure and a woman in a long dark cloak with a knit cap pulled low over her ears and forehead. A red-bearded man in a bridal dress stood next to the woman and mimicked her movements. She seemed unaware of what he was doing and of the amusement of the group around them. She was shouting shrilly in a rapid Italian at the blue-and-green-robed figure in a high headdress with silver baubles. This figure—whether a man or a woman Urbino couldn't tell because of the turquoise and silver mask with Oriental features—held a large black feathered fan inset with tiny mirrors.

"You should be ashamed of yourself! You're just as bad as everyone else. Even worse! If the Venetians don't care about what's happening, then what hope is there? Everything is going to return to the hungry sea, every last building, bridge, and painting!" She looked the figure up and down with disdain. "Here"—she thrust at the masquerader a sheet of paper that fluttered down to the pavement—"spend your time reading this. Think of the future—yours and Venice's! Either save yourself or prepare yourself!"

This thrusting of the sheet of paper at the masquerader and her comments identified the woman for Urbino. Beneath that cap was Xenia Campi, whom Val Gibbon had mentioned earlier. She lived at the Casa Crispina, partly on the eponymous charity of the sisters and partly on what she got from her ex-husband Ignazio Rigoletti. Her ranting and raving against commercialism and her predictions of the "final destruction of the Serene Republic" had made her a source of both amusement and irritation to the Venetians. Her proselytizing and claims to clairvoyance had begun more than ten years ago, shortly after the death of her teenage son in a car crash.

The masquerader responded to Xenia Campi's diatribe not by picking up the flyer but by standing up straighter and, with one quick motion, taking off the Oriental mask. When it was completely removed, Xenia Campi gasped, for the unmasked face beneath the headdress was clearly hers: the same small eyes, square face, thin mouth, and cleft chin.

It was a portrait mask, the kind gallants wore beneath another mask in the seventeenth century to deceive women with the face of their lovers or husbands—or, in some cases, to give the women a good excuse to claim they had been deceived. The man would briefly lift the first mask, revealing the familiar features beneath, and then proceed to take advantage of the apparently deceived woman.

Xenia Campi grabbed the mask. The high-pitched laugh of her mocker gave no clue to its owner's sex. Not until Xenia Campi held her papier-mâché image of herself triumphantly in her hand did Urbino recognize one of the most familiar figures of *Carnevale* beneath the headdress.

It was Giovanni Firpo, a pharmacist at the Municipal Hospital. Ever since Venice's Department for Tourism and Cultural Activities had resurrected *Carnevale* ten years ago, Firpo had been one of its most enthusiastic participants, sporting a different costume every year. Like many other masqueraders who came to *Carnevale* decked out in elaborate costumes, he hoped to get on a postcard, a poster, or a calendar, to have not only these brief days of fun and attention but something more substantial, something that distinguished him above all the others.

Firpo didn't seem to mind that his mask had been confiscated. It had already had the best effect possible. Putting on the Oriental mask again, he laughed and walked into the Piazza toward the ramp.

Xenia Campi stuffed the portrait mask into her carpetbag. The little group around her and Firpo dispersed, off to seek fresh amusement. As Urbino approached the woman, he smiled. He knew she was eccentric, even somewhat offensive at times, but he couldn't help admiring her enthusiasm and her love for Venice. It still rankled that Val Gibbon had been left with the impression earlier that Urbino considered the woman a fool.

Xenia Campi's response to Urbino's smile was a frown.

"Read it, Signor Macintyre, read it and do something!" She thrust one of the sheets into his hand, then took another from the pile cradled in the crook of her arm. "And one for your friend the Contessa. I notice she's enjoying herself in Florian's as usual. Maybe the two of you can do something more than pay a fortune for tea and little cakes while everything is falling down around your ears."

She set off down the arcade, handing out more sheets as she went.

Urbino looked at the flyer. There were several short paragraphs in Italian, French, Spanish, German, and English. They all said the same thing, in better or poorer style, with more or fewer errors, depending on the translation:

THIS IS NOT VENICE! THIS IS MADNESS!

Carnevale brings this city closer to destruction every year. I mean moral *and* physical destruction.

What you see destroying this beautiful city is the Venice of speculators, money-crazed merchants, and a corrupt civil government. Everyone who encourages this madness—foreigners, Italians, and (most shameful of all!) Venetians themselves—gives death blows to the serene city.

Venice is a peaceful and peace-loving city, a city of art and culture. Do you want to see all this destroyed during *Carnevale*? Do you want to see our dream city become a nightmare? Do you want to murder Venice? Where will it all end?

VENICE IS NOT DISNEYLAND!

Urbino smiled to himself. The irrepressible Xenia Campi! Not a stylist perhaps, but—as always—there was more than a little sense in what she said.

8 "THE pathetic and the deluded," the Contessa said when Urbino told her about Giovanni Firpo and Xenia Campi Who was pathetic and who deluded she left for him to sort out as she glanced disdainfully at the flyer.

The Contessa's choice today of her multicolored Fortuny dress that had belonged to the actress Eleonora Duse indicated that she was either weary or depressed, perhaps both. Urbino had never known her to wear it in any other circumstances. She seemed to believe there was something talismanic in the garment that would lift her spirits. It didn't seem to be working this afternoon, however.

"Is that poor soul still talking about Disneyland? She said the same thing last summer."

She sighed and absently fingered her strand of matched pearls.

"And she probably will again this summer. She does have a point though."

"Of course she does! There's nothing worse than an idealist gone wrong. You should be able to appreciate that."

"I would think that you'd be more sympathetic, Barbara. You don't care for *Carnevale* any more than she does."

The Contessa looked out the window into the crowded Piazza.

"I endure it like so much else in life. Just a week until it's all over."

The waiter brought over a Campari soda for Urbino and a fresh pot of tea for the Contessa, made with the first flush jasmine tea her majordomo Mauro brought over every month. The needs of the Contessa and Urbino were anticipated here at Florian's, where the Contessa was almost a daily figure, usually in the company of her American friend or some social, political, or artistic luminary of the city.

She favored the Chinese salon, one of the smaller rooms, with its floral patterns, vaguely Oriental portraits, and wooden parquet floor. It had an intricate ceiling of lace and flower designs sheeted in clear Murano glass and framed by dark, shining strips of wood in geometrical configurations. The walls had the same Murano glass but many of the strips of dark wood on the walls were gilded. Here in the Chinese salon, surrounded by its painted panels and carved wood, its velvet and marble, its stucco and its gilding, and its heavy mirror and bronze *amorini* holding delicately fluted lamps, the Contessa had one of her best settings. From the plush maroon banquette by the windows, she was mistress of all she could survey in the Piazza outside or in the small room itself. But right now she was staring at Urbino.

"Whatever is that *thing* around your neck?"

"I'm going to Porfirio's party before the Fenice tonight." He quickly added, "Don't worry. I won't be late."

He felt uncomfortable mentioning Porfirio's party, knowing that there was bad blood between her and the Venetian photographer. Had she been invited? Perhaps she was brooding about it.

"I'm *not* worried but do put that thing away. It's distracting. There's something I want to talk about."

Urbino slipped the mask into the pocket of his blazer.

"I thought it gave a rather nice touch of color."

"I'm beginning to wonder about you, Urbino. Are you sure you aren't a closet masquerader or whatever one would call it? Trying to relive your adolescent days of those 'mystical crows' or whatever they're called? Do you have a wardrobe of bizarre costumes at the Palazzo Uccello like Giovanni Firpo? It's the kind of thing one would expect of an admirer of that decadent duke Des Esseintes! I've probably passed by you during *Carnevale* on any number of occasions and not even known it was you. Of course, one has absolutely no way of knowing who most of these mad men and women out there are, either. And I probably wouldn't want to know. Shocks like that add lines to the face and gray to the hair!"

A figure was standing at the window looking at them. It was wearing a large mask designed after one of the weird portraits of the sixteenth-century painter Arcimboldo, composed of vegetables, fruits, and flowers. This comestible mask had a thicket of roots for hair, mushrooms for ears, a tuber for a nose, and a sprouting potato for a chin. The Contessa sighed and shook her head.

"You said you had something to talk about," Urbino reminded her.

"So I do, *caro*. Three days ago I was rung up by someone I haven't seen for longer than I care to remember. We were only about fifteen the last time we saw each other. Can you believe such an atrocious thing? Her name is Berenice Reilly—or rather it *was*. It's Berenice Pillow now."

"Pillow! You British have some of the strangest names."

"Actually, *caro*, the name is American—or at least her husband was American. The family was probably British originally. She read about the Ca' da Capo in the article in *Casa Vogue*. She couldn't believe it was me—a Contessa, she said, little Barbara Spencer—and to think we had been girls together at St. Brigid's-by-the-Sea." She looked at Urbino with a little smile. "She recognized me, I believe. That picture taken in the library *was* a good one."

"Recognized you after all these years? The article *did* give your maiden name and some other information."

"In any case, *caro*," the Contessa went on, "she said she remembered me quite well. She was a rather plain girl with a fiery temper to match her red hair. I never heard from her, or even *of* her, again until three days ago. Can you believe a person from your past just popping up like this?"

She took a sip of tea.

"She wanted to see me for old times' sake and to find out about my life since St. Brigid's. She said I was just the person she needed to talk to, to confide in the way we used to on those winter nights at St. Brigid's. It's rather flattering, don't you think, after you get over the initial shock? It should be fun showing her around to Oriana and some of my other friends—and, of course, you, *caro*—as long as she promises to be discreet!"

A figure in a domino with its ample hood pulled up over a paint-whitened face paused before their window. He was about to move along when he saw the Contessa looking out. He raised his hand, bowed his hooded head, and called out "Benedicite!" to her. The Contessa turned away, not waiting to see what he might say or do next. The man blessed himself and continued along the arcade.

"Berenice and I decided to meet here at four-thirty yesterday. Well, I must tell you that I waited almost a full and complete hour! I had some diversion while I was waiting, but not completely pleasant. Gibbon came in with a plain young woman who's also staying at the Casa Crispina. I talked with them for a while although she hardly said a word. I wish the same could be said for Gibbon. Every time I meet him he makes me regret ever listening to Sister Teresa. Somehow, within only a few minutes, he managed to disparage both Josef and Porfirio. There was a malicious edge to everything he said. The girl was quite amused but I definitely wasn't. One of Porfirio's friends was sitting at the table over there and heard everything. I have no doubt he repeated every single word back to him. When our local dragon Xenia Campi descended on us with her flyers, Gibbon and the girl left. The girl didn't seem comfortable with Xenia Campi in the room although if she had waited only a few moments she would have had the pleasure of seeing her escorted out."

Her eye ran over the flyer again before going on.

"Berenice finally came. She looked a wreck! You would never think we had been in the same form together although she was a year older, I think. I would never have recognized her but she came right over to my table without any hesitation. She was loaded down with enough things to outfit an army! She had her purse, a guide book, a Missoni shopping bag, and one of those folding lap desks. It wasn't the most dignified entrance Florian's has ever seen. She ordered a martini—a martini, mind you!—and drank it faster than I drank the rest of the tea in my cup. She asked me all about myself but we didn't come close to sharing any confidences. Maybe once she saw me she decided she didn't want to confide in me after all, and I admit I held myself back. I think we have to get reacquainted first. Just about the only things I learned were that she has been married twice, once to an Italian—and twice widowed, poor thing—and that she has a son. That is, I think she has a son. She was so confusing that I wasn't able to figure out if he was a stepson or a son by one of her two marriages."

She shook her head slowly.

"She'll be stopping by the Ca' da Capo tomorrow with her son—or her stepson. Why don't you stop by, too? It might be fun, meeting an old school chum of mine—as long as you don't ask any personal questions."

"I'll come just to see what a woman with a name like that is like!"

"As I said, she doesn't look anything like my age. Or I should say," she emended, realizing that this might be misinterpreted, "that she looks as if she had been at St. Brigid's years before me! But you'll see for yourself!"

She said this with a bright smile of confidence.

9 URBINO, wearing his scarlet mask, looked around Porfirio's living room. The swaggering, violent music of Stravinsky's Blackamoor was playing a little too loudly.

This might only be Urbino's second visit to Porfirio's but even a hundred wouldn't reconcile him to all the laminated plastic, glass, and chrome. The living room, mercilessly illuminated and filled with hyperpatterned, bright-colored furniture and rugs, was straight out of the contemporary design collaborative of Memphis/Milano.

Porfirio—because his last name was the comically inappropriate "Buffone," he used only his first one—lived in the Cannaregio between the Ghetto and one of the long canals. He wasn't a particularly popular man in the quarter precisely because of his apartment. Not that the residents had little fondness for modern architecture and up-to-date improvements. On the contrary, most of them liked them very much. It was why so many, like Venetians from the other quarters, were moving in large numbers to the mainland for something "high, dry, and modern."

No, it wasn't the apartment's modern design—all of it behind the building's nineteenth-century facade—that disturbed the residents of the Cannaregio, but that, after greasing enough palms and pressuring the right people as far as Rome, Porfirio had managed to evict two Venetian families so that he could begin his renovations. One of them had been Xenia Campi and her husband, Ignazio Rigoletti. It was as if the *equo canone*—the fair rent law—protecting apartment dwellers didn't exist for him. Although Porfirio wasn't the first person to be involved in what an editorial in *Il Gazzettino* had called "a violent gentrification that strikes at the pocketbook, the stability, and the very heart of long-resident families," he was one of the most disliked. As the last member of a Venetian family with a long, distinguished history of philanthropy, Porfirio had been expected to act differently, to be a protector, not a spoiler.

Also fanning the flames was Porfirio's much-acclaimed photography that celebrated Venice. Wasn't there something vampiristic—certainly hypocritical—about a man whose art and reputation fed off a city whose residents he obviously had little regard for?

Urbino, whose own Palazzo Uccello had been almost uninhabitable when he had inherited it, didn't approve of the way Porfirio had gone about emptying and renovating his own building, but he did approve of his photography. He was pleased to have him providing the photographs for his book on Proust. All Porfirio's collections were of Venice—its palaces, gardens, bridges, squares, and festivals, including a particularly popular one several seasons ago on *Carnevale*. He had taken photographs of the Palazzo Uccello for Urbino to send back to his two great-aunts in New Orleans, who were understandably curious about his living in a palace but whose advanced age didn't permit a trip. The photographs had been a great success with the women.

Porfirio had therefore been the logical choice to take the photographs at San Gabriele, not the English photographer Gibbon. Porfirio didn't need the Contessa's commission or whatever limited recognition he might get from taking photographs of the paintings and frescoes at the church. They would only end up in the parish files anyway. What upset him, the Contessa had assured Urbino, was that a man of his reputation had been rejected before he could refuse the project himself.

The fifty-five-year-old Porfirio, who had an arrogant face and carried his more than six feet with a commanding air of self-confidence, was dressed as Pantalone, the Venetian merchant. He wore knee-length red trousers and a red waistcoat, a long black cape, a floppy red hat, and a mask with a hooked nose. In keeping with the character, Porfirio would occasionally use expressions from the Venetian dialect.

Not everyone was in costume but those who were conformed to the commedia dell'arte theme of Porfirio's little gathering. There were Harlequins, Columbines, Pierrots, Brighellas, Pulcinellas, Dottores, and Capitanos. Porfirio, however, by either design or circumstance, was the only Pantalone.

As Urbino and Porfirio stood in front of the large windows that looked out on a back canal, now obscured by night, Urbino decided to mention Val Gibbon. Knowing how upset Porfirio was about having been passed over by the Contessa made Urbino feel, perhaps wrongly, that not bringing up the topic might only make things fester the more.

"What do you think of Val Gibbon's work, Porfirio?"

"Gibbon, Gibbon."

Porfirio repeated the name slowly in a musing way as if he didn't recognize it. He looked across the room at a massive expressionist canvas in reds and yellows that would have been just as much at home on the other side of the Grand Canal at Peggy Guggenheim's.

"He's taking photographs of the San Gabriele fresco that Lubonski is restoring."

"And he's one of the hundreds of other photographers who have descended on our Piazza these days in their high boots!" Porfirio said contemptuously, turning his gaze back to Urbino.

Urbino, who had seen his host in high boots in the Piazza on numerous occasions several *Carnevali* ago—albeit stylish models and not the cheap plastic ones hanging by huge clothespins in the Rialto shops—restrained a smile. After sipping his whiskey, Porfirio continued.

"They have no dedication, this kind of photographer, no commitment to one thing more than any other. Every time I see someone with a camera here in Venice, it makes me angry, even a little ashamed—yes, ashamed for them and for myself. Why does almost every person with a camera think he is an artist? Tell me that! They think it is so easy, but photography is one of the arts. You must be *consacrato*! to the art and to a special subject. I will be known as *the* photographer of Venezia! You see, my dear Urbino, you have chosen well for your Proust!" he finished with a little smile that he probably wanted Urbino to think was meant as an ironic qualification of his self-praise.

He excused himself and went over to the bar on the other side of the room where Pietro Basso, the architect who had designed Porfirio's apartments, was standing with a young woman Urbino didn't recognize. She had tawny hair cut in a short blunt style and was wearing a long dark-green dress with a lacy white apron attached in the manner of the character Columbine. She wore no mask, however, and her eyes flicked briefly in his direction before she responded to something Porfirio had said. After a few minutes Porfirio drifted off to join another group.

Urbino went over to the bar to get some more wine. Basso was looking pleased with himself as he finished his favorite lecture on the virtues of all modern architecture. The young woman looked relieved when Urbino joined them and introduced himself.

"Hazel Reeve," she said, smiling and extending her hand.

She looked directly into his eyes. She was about twenty-five with an assured and intelligent manner. Her face was oval with a generous mouth and widely spaced sea-green eyes.

"Signorina Reeve is English. She is staying here with Porfirio," Basso said. The architect was a man whose shortness and rotundity were amusingly at odds with the angularity of his architecture. "She is doing some translating for him, isn't that right, Signorina Reeve?"

"That's right, although I think he feels somewhat compromised that his photographs need a text at all, whether in Italian *or* English," she explained, looking over at the photographer, who was now talking with a journalist from *Il Gazzettino*. After having looked at Urbino so directly a few moments ago she now seemed to be avoiding his eyes.

"When he came up to London before we published his first book on bridges," she went on, "he defended the purity of his art quite impressively. 'A photograph should stand alone, isolated,' he said, 'a clear statement in itself and by itself'— something very much like that. It was decided nonetheless that if the Italians needed a text, then surely the benighted Brits did as well."

She laughed lightly, showing even white teeth.

"Ah," Basso said after taking a sip of his drink, "a bridge is a bridge is a bridge is a bridge."

"Do you speak from your knowledge of architecture, Signor Basso, or your familiarity with Gertrude Stein?" Hazel Reeve asked playfully. "Porfirio's photographs of bridges could have stood on their own, perhaps, but not the ones on relics that we're publishing in the autumn. However could the photographs be enough, even for the Italian reader?"

"But most of the chests, reliquaries, and altarpieces are beautiful in themselves," Urbino said.

"That's certainly true, but it's the story behind the relics—
the story *of* the relics—that's of interest for most people,
wouldn't you say? It's a whole fascinating history of thefts
and concealments, pillagings and supposed miracles." The
quick, brief glance her green eyes now gave Urbino was all
the more forceful for having been withheld for what seemed
much longer than it actually was. "At any rate, it's not up to
me. I get my assignments, I do my work. Not that I'm not
thrilled to be working on another of Porfirio's collections.
They're quite magnificent."

"They certainly are!" Basso agreed heartily. "And don't
forget that you get to come to our beautiful city."

"Believe me, Signor Basso, such extravagances are beyond
our budget. I know my Italian and, as far as my editor is
concerned, that's supposed to be sufficient. But it's *Carnevale*
and I thought I'd take a look for myself at the relics—although
I'm not exactly sure what the advantage might be for a mere
translation."

"I wouldn't denigrate your work like that, Miss Reeve,"
Urbino said.

"*Traditore, traduttore,*" Basso said loudly with his small,
round head thrown back, reciting a popular Italian saying
that played on the similarity between the words "betrayer"
and "translator."

"I hope that *my* translations aren't in any way a betrayal,
Signor Basso. What you say is more appropriate for a translator
of Dante or Petrarch." Then, without any preliminary except
for a slight intake of breath and as if she were doing the most
natural thing in the world, Hazel Reeve recited the opening
canto of Dante's *Inferno:*

> "*Nel mezzo del cammin di nostra vita*
> *Mi ritrovai per una selva oscura*
> *Che la diritta via era smarrita.*"

After finishing she said quickly, as if to discourage any
possible praise or criticism of her Italian, "I've read at least
a dozen English translations of those lines and not one even
comes close to the original. How would it be possible! When
it comes to Dante," she said, directing herself to the architect,
"the translator *is* a betrayer, even if he does have the purest
of hearts and the best of intentions."

Urbino paid little attention to Basso's response. Hazel Reeve's recitation was still sounding in his ears. He, too, like Dante, was midway in his own life's journey—if he were, in fact, to be blessed with the three score and ten the Bible allotted. In no way had he, like Dante, gone astray in a dark wood—or even among all the beauties of Venice that could be so disorienting. Yet Dante's words, spoken so well by this young Englishwoman, had seemed to be speaking directly to him, reminding him somehow of the warning the Contessa had given him on the day of the Regatta.

"You seem lost in thought, Mr. Macintyre," Hazel Reeve said. "I didn't mean to be superior, rattling off Dante like that. You'll have to forgive me. I love Italian so much that I forget it's not a language most people are inclined to study, certainly not the way they do French and Spanish."

"I know Italian well enough," Urbino said with what he hoped would be taken as neither pride nor injured feelings. "It was just that the Dante—" He stopped. How could he explain something that he didn't understand himself?

"It's just that you spoke so well," he finished.

"*D'accordo!*" Basso said with a lift of his glass. "But your Italian is equal to hers, Signor Macintyre. There's no cause for envy."

Feeling completely misunderstood and yet not up to explaining himself, Urbino said nothing. He drew comfort, however, from the look that Hazel Reeve gave him as she took a sip of her wine, another look from her brilliant green eyes.

She seemed to know exactly how he felt. He had no need to make explanations.

"Signor Macintyre is a writer," Basso said.

Interest flickered in Hazel Reeve's eyes.

"Do you write novels?"

"Not novels, although on occasion I've been accused of writing fiction. I write biographies—biographies about Venice."

"Biographies about Venice?"

"Not about Venice itself but about some of the people who have had an association with it. Mainly writers and artists—and not only Italians."

"But you have so many to choose from! Browning, Ruskin, Mann, Turner, Vivaldi, Tintoretto, James—there must be dozens!"

"Exactly, although so far I've done books only on Ruskin, Casanova, Canaletto, and Browning and monographs on Pound and a Venetian family of restorers. I'm doing one on Proust now. Porfirio is providing the photographs."

"How interesting. I absolutely adore Proust."

"Proust!" Basso said with a frown after taking a sip of his whiskey. "I tried to read the book years ago but never got any farther than the first pages. The man was using so many words but he wasn't saying anything that I could see. Something about kissing his mother."

"Perhaps you should try again, Signor Basso," Hazel Reeve suggested. "The book is like a cathedral—but to begin to see that you would have to read more than just a few pages."

The comment seemed directed less at Basso than Urbino. She smiled, her green eyes looking directly into his.

10 THE Teatro La Fenice was ablaze with lights as Urbino slipped into the Contessa's box in the second tier. The Contessa's restrained black and ecru Pirovano gown and Bulgari ruby necklace complemented La Fenice's dominant beiges, golds, and reds. She was talking with her friend Oriana Borelli, who was alone in the next box. They gave him a quick greeting and returned to their low conversation, which was probably about the most recent marital explosion at the Ca' Borelli on the Giudecca.

Urbino looked around the crowded theater. The crystal, gilt, and velvet enhanced the well-dressed audience, some of whom were in elegant masks and costumes. Urbino was curious about this new production of Rossini's *Otello*. For him as well as the Contessa it would be the first production he had seen of the opera that had been eclipsed by Verdi's version. He was familiar with the music but not the libretto. The librettist, the Marchese Berio di Salsa, was related by marriage to the da Capo-Zendrini family, and the Contessa hoped that her friend would disagree with the almost universal low opinion of his work. Her own opinion, it would seem, was a foregone conclusion. Ever since her marriage to Alvise da Capo-Zendrini—but especially since his death twelve years ago—she had become the champion of the family, drawing attention to their considerable contributions and deemphasizing, when not simply ignoring, their almost equally numerous peccadilloes.

The Contessa finished her conversation with Oriana and turned to Urbino. He was glad Barbara wanted to do most of the talking as they waited for the performance to begin. He was thinking about Hazel Reeve. She had managed to insinuate herself into his thoughts not only by what she had said but also by what she had left unsaid and implied. Urbino wasn't flattered easily—or at least he didn't think he was. Yet he had felt sought out, even favored in a subtle way by this young Englishwoman with the widely spaced green eyes and had stayed longer at Porfirio's than he had intended. After Basso had gone off, they had discussed Browning and Proust.

When the performance began, it didn't take Urbino long to realize that the libretto travestied Shakespeare's tale of passion, pride, and jealousy.

During the intervals the Contessa, however, praised the opera, looking at him with an amused expression as she singled out the libretto for special comment, calling it "unique." He didn't dispute her for indeed the libretto was unique in the worst sense. He mumbled something innocuous about the recitatives and the similarity between one passage and a Verdi aria, surprised that aspects of the opera had managed to penetrate his abstraction.

"What did you think, Urbino?" the Contessa asked when the performance was over and they stepped out into the night air with Oriana Borelli.

"Any version that substitutes a love letter for the hand-kerchief can't be anything but all wrong, but thank God he smothered her instead of forgiving her."

Oriana, who knew that the Marchese Bario di Salsa was related to the da Capo-Zendrinis, reached out to touch the sleeve of the Contessa's sable coat in consolation and turned surprised eyes, magnified behind her outsize black frames, in Urbino's direction. Her gaze was transferred to the Contessa the next moment when the Contessa laughed and said,

"I couldn't agree with you more, *caro*. Abominable, wasn't it!" Then, with a tug at his arm as they went down the steps into the square after saying good night to Oriana, she added, "Alvise always said he wasn't absolutely convinced that the da Capo-Zendrinis were related to the di Salsas."

In the darkened cabin of the Contessa's motorboat, the Contessa asked him about Porfirio's party. Urbino didn't go into much detail, not mentioning the photographer's houseguest, but the little he said seemed to satisfy her. For most of the trip up the Grand Canal, she mused about the unexpected visit from her schoolgirl friend and said she was looking forward to getting Urbino's opinion of her.

"I hope," she said, "that you'll be over whatever is troubling you. I also hope that you've noticed, with a keen appreciation for the reticence of true friendship, that I haven't asked you one single, solitary question about the cause of that scrunched-up look on your face. At least I haven't asked you yet. Go home and go to sleep. Good night and God keep you from any nightmares."

11 WHEN Urbino got back to the Palazzo Uccello, the phone was ringing. It was Lubonski.

"Remember that you promised not to go near the fresco until I am well," he said in a barely coherent voice. "I want to be the only one responsible for any damage done."

Not waiting for a response, the Pole hung up. Feeling somewhat put out by Lubonski's reference to "damage"—even if he had included himself in it—Urbino went to the study and sat down to read Proust.

He seldom had premonitions, if that was the name he might give to the uneasy feeling he now had as he opened the book. He had felt this way on the day of his parents' accidental death and on a Mardi Gras evening almost fifteen years ago as he had paused in front of a closed door his wife had gone through half an hour before with her cousin, Reid.

As he sat stroking Serena absently, he couldn't shake the feeling that something bad was going to happen—unless it had already.

12 IGNAZIO Rigoletti, returning to the Corte Santa Scolastica after buying cigarettes, was glad he didn't encounter anyone in costume. He wasn't in a good mood and he didn't know what he might say or do.

The only *festa* he enjoyed was the Regatta. As a teenager he had rowed in the two-oar *puparino* and had eventually been among the *gondolini* champions and a district representative for the six-oar *caorlina*. Hadn't he even helped row the Bucintoro thirty years ago when the golden barge had carried Pope Pius X's body in a crystal coffin down the Grand Canal? Now he only occasionally rowed for the Querini club, at the age of forty-nine leaving most of the rowing to his nephews.

Rigoletti had hoped that his son, Marco, killed in a car crash on the autostrada, would become a rowing champion. He had been a fine specimen of a young man and the Regatta was a *festa* for real men. Even though they now allowed women to row in the two-oar *mascareta*, it was nothing more than just something to appease the crazy women liberationists. All eyes—at least the ones that counted—were always on the men.

But *Carnevale*! Men and women indistinguishable from each other, behaving like inmates of an asylum, every one mocking the values he—and other upright Venetians—believed in. It was for the tourists, the merchants, and a small group of poor, confused Venetians for whom it was the pinnacle of the year. Even Marco's old girlfriend made a living off it now.

Unfortunately, Rigoletti could hardly avoid the most boisterous aspects of *Carnevale,* for his apartment was off the Calle Santa Scolastica only a few minutes from the Piazza and practically within touching distance of the Bridge of Sighs. In addition to being so close to the crowds, the Calle Santa Scolastica, although it dead-ended on a canal, got quite a few tourists who had lost their way or wanted to take a photograph of the Bridge of Sighs from an unusual angle.

It wasn't these people who bothered him, however. Although he hated *Carnevale*, he certainly didn't want to see the city empty of tourists. Where would he be—a man who delivered supplies to the big hotels—without them? One of the many things he didn't agree with his ex-wife, Xenia, about was keeping as many people as possible away from Venice.

No, he wasn't bothered by the tourists but by the men who used the end of the *calle* by the water steps for furtive meetings, the kind of men who probably never rowed in the Regatta. He often came home late in the evening like this to find two or even three and four men merging in the dark under the portico, silhouetted against the Ducal Palace.

The *calle*'s attraction resulted from a topographical peculiarity that could be found throughout the city. All you could see from its entrance and for ten or fifteen feet of its length was the wall of the courtyard building beyond. Not until you reached the courtyard itself could you see that it extended farther to the canal. Men seeking privacy together took advantage of this typically Venetian formation. There was absolutely no chance that they might be observed by anyone passing along the main alley—the Calle degli Albanesi down which he was walking now—or by anyone who had ventured into the first part of the Calle Santa Scolastica.

Whenever he came upon these men, they would pretend an interest in the view or retrace their steps back to the Calle degli Albanesi. Fifteen minutes ago when he had stepped down from his apartment he had seen a man lounging against the wall. Sometimes Rigoletti lost his temper with these men, and he certainly had lost it tonight, hadn't he? He still remembered the frightened, almost desperate look in the good-looking young man's face. He laughed at the memory.

Tonight a wind was blowing up the Calle degli Albanesi from the lagoon. The narrow opening by the water channeled the wind into the alley with unusual force, creating an eerie noise that sounded like souls in infernal pain. Tonight, however, the wind wasn't as strong as it could be on these February nights but carried a warmth and dampness that weren't completely comfortable. A fog was already rolling in.

As he was turning into the Calle Santa Scolastica, he almost collided with a dark, attractive young man who was rushing from the *calle* with an impassive look on his face. He seemed in a desperate hurry but showed no emotion. Rigoletti watched him walking briskly toward the Riva degli Schiavoni.

The *calle* itself was empty. When Rigoletti reached the courtyard, he looked down the remaining length of the *calle* to where it ended at the water.

There under the portico he saw the dark form looking like a pile of trash.

He went over to the prone man sprawled on the wet stones, whose hands were reaching out toward the water steps. He nudged his foot with his shoe tip but the man just lay there motionless in his rubber boots and flannel shirt jacket.

Rigoletti kneeled down. Thick dark hair curled over the man's jacket collar. He turned the face toward him. The bulb encaged in metal in the portico gave Rigoletti just enough light to peer into the open eye of the man.

The eye, frozen in focus elsewhere and on a former time, didn't peer back. Rigoletti's hand touched the man's flannel shirt and came away damp and sticky.

He stood up. He had to call the Questura.

Rigoletti left the dead body and went into the courtyard, only to stop suddenly, undecided if he should go back. Could he have left fingerprints on the body? But surely the police would accept his explanation, wouldn't they? He had had to turn the man around to see if he was all right. It would be more suspicious if his fingerprints weren't found.

Not exactly sure if he had made a mistake or not, Rigoletti crossed the courtyard. He would call the Questura from the restaurant where he had just bought his cigarettes. He went into the other part of the Calle Santa Scolastica that led to the Calle degli Albanesi.

A young blond man was coming down the Calle Santa Scolastica tentatively, looking warily ahead of him. When he saw Rigoletti, he started, and a frightened look came over his face. He turned quickly back into the Calle degli Albanesi. Rigoletti was right behind him. The young man was hurrying toward the Riva degli Schiavoni and the lagoon.

Rigoletti went to the restaurant to call the Questura.

Part Two

VEILS

1 THE first thing that occurred to Urbino when he went into the Contessa's *salotto blu* at five the next afternoon was that the woman looking up at the Veronese over the fireplace, crackling in homey fashion with wood brought down from near the Contessa's villa in Asolo, could not possibly be named Pillow even if by marriage.

She was at least five ten and all sharp angles, from her gaunt face with prominent cheekbones and aquiline nose to her narrow feet shod in stylish black flats. Her dress in thin violet and black vertical stripes accentuated her long spare lines as did the gold chains and pendant that fell from her neck. With her reddish hair, fading into yellow-gray and pulled back in a bun, she did look about ten years older than the Contessa. Urbino wondered if the look of weariness in her face was something that several nights' good sleep would banish or if it was the look she usually wore.

A young man about twenty-five in a dark-gray, generously cut suit and a crisp black T-shirt sat in the rococo chair next to the Contessa. He had one of those handsome narrow faces with Florentine lips that stares out from so many Italian portraits. His hair was matte black and medium long. Parted in the center, it swept down to either side of his forehead in two bold waves that drew attention to his large dark eyes.

"Urbino, you have the most marvelous capacity of turning up just when I need you. My friend Berenice was just asking me about the Veronese and I give you the question to answer."

Before explaining further, she made the introductions. The young man, Antonio Vico, gave Urbino a firm handshake.

"He's Berenice's son—her stepson, excuse me."

"We make no distinctions either way, Barbara dear," Berenice Pillow said with a fond look at Vico. "Tony is my first husband's son, yes, but he's my own son as well."

"You can see, Urbino, that she's made his name into her own as well! I prefer Tonio!"

"So does he, but if mothers aren't entitled to their own pet names for their children, then who is?"

"But, Berenice dear, it puts me in a difficult situation to choose between an old friend and a handsome young man."

"Remembering what you were like at St. Brigid's, Barbara, I think I know what the decision will be."

"I have no idea what you are talking about, Berenice!" But the Contessa seemed pleased. "As a matter of fact, I was rather backward in those areas but I remember how—how impassioned you got over that rude stable boy. I always thought it was your red hair that drove you to it."

"The Contessa makes you sound like Lady Chatterley, Mother," Tonio Vico said in perfectly modulated English without the faintest trace of an accent.

Berenice Pillow blushed.

"Such a thing for a son to say to a mother, Tony! I was only a child at the time!"

"The heart never changes, my dear Berenice—and yours was always ardent."

Mrs. Pillow turned back to the Veronese.

"Ah yes, my Veronese," the Contessa said with less an air of possession than of the Pre-Raphaelite languidness she frequently liked to affect. "I'm thinking of importing a niece from London to do some of the social for me—at least to convey information about *mes choses*. It gets a bit tiresome, I must say, and when it isn't it seems rather self-absorbed to run on and on about one's own things."

"But, Barbara, you don't *show* your place like that old woman at the house we visited with the other girls!"

She had a shocked look on her long thin face. The Contessa's face mirrored her friend's.

" 'Show my place,' Berenice dear! God forbid! I have never shown—except occasionally for magazines like *Casa Vogue*. What I meant was showing someone like yourself—a *friend*"— she emphasized the word. "Of course, that's not the same thing, but even in such circumstances—and don't hold it against me, Berenice dear—it can be tedious. That's why I'm pleased to have Urbino here now."

Urbino felt uncomfortable. When the Contessa asked Mrs. Pillow to tell him what she had been saying before he came in, he felt no better. It was as if the Contessa were forcing Mrs. Pillow to confide something in him.

She looked away from the painting at Urbino, at the Contessa, and then back at the Veronese. She seemed reluctant to repeat what she had said.

Before Urbino had any time to wonder what embarrassing question might have been posed, the Contessa said, with a quaver in her voice, "She was wondering why it was so small."

"Small?" Urbino involuntarily echoed.

The Veronese, an allegory of love with a stout golden-haired barebacked Venus dividing her attention between two handsome bearded swains beneath a lush tree, was at least six feet square. It dominated the Contessa's intimate *salotto* where she kept most of her favorite bibelots and books and where she entertained only her closest friends.

"Small for a Veronese, she meant," Vico said. His tone was ameliorative as he moved closer to his stepmother. "She was comparing him with himself, not with anything American."

He smiled at Urbino.

"Of course," Urbino agreed, "compared to the ceiling paintings at the Ducal Palace or *The Last Supper*."

"Whether they're large or small, I don't very much like his paintings. No offense to you, Barbara. It's a perfectly lovely painting and looks very nice here in your little parlor. It's just that I prefer Tintoretto."

The Contessa laughed.

"And so does Urbino. Sometimes he attacks me mercilessly, but so far I've stood my ground."

"You have to admit, Barbara, that I've always granted that a Tintoretto would be a bit out of place here."

"True, but that's not so much praise of my Veronese as, perhaps, criticism of the secular spirit of my little nest."

Urbino began to describe the Veronese—not only the meaning of its somewhat obscure allegory but also its provenance. How it had hung in the Imperial Palace in Prague, in Rome in Queen Christina's collection after her abdication, and then in the palazzo of a Roman duke from whose family Alvise da Capo-Zendrini had bought it for his wife on their marriage. When he reached this point, Berenice Pillow seemed about to say something. Urbino suspected it might be about the dubious appropriateness of such an allegory—a woman positioned seductively between two handsome men—as a wedding gift from husband to wife.

Urbino was prepared to give a few more details about the painting when Berenice Pillow said, "I don't remember seeing it in that article in *Casa Vogue,* Barbara."

"Oh, but it definitely was, Berenice dear. I would have insisted on it even if they hadn't wanted it."

"I'm sure you know what you're talking about, but I just don't remember." She narrowed her eyes for a few seconds. "But of course! I don't believe I saw the whole article."

"The Veronese was on the very first page."

"That's it! I'm afraid the copy I had—it was at my lawyer's in New York—was a bit mutilated. Now that I think of it, the first part *was* missing. That's why I didn't recognize the Veronese." She looked at the painting again for a few moments and then sat down on the sofa beside the Contessa. "You wouldn't have a copy of the magazine, would you, Barbara? I would so love to see the whole thing."

"I have hundreds! Urbino, would you be so kind as to go to the library? You know where they are."

Tonio Vico got up.

"You'll have to excuse me. I'm meeting someone at Harry's Bar. I'm sure I'm leaving Mother in good hands. She's been so anxious to see you again, Contessa. We couldn't keep her down in Napoli when she knew you were up here. I hope you'll be kind enough to share your memories of St. Brigid's with me on another occasion, without Mother around to try to deny everything, however."

After he left, Urbino went down the wide central hall to the library, a large room that overlooked the walled garden. The da Capo-Zendrini book collection, most of which dated back to the sixteenth and seventeenth centuries, had some of the most important works about the Venetian Republic.

Urbino went to the glass-doored cabinet, noting that a copy of Lorenzetti's *Feste e Maschere Veneziane* lay open on the table. Could his friend be more interested in *Carnevale* than she pretended to be? She was probably looking forward to her costume ball much more than she was willing to let on.

He searched through the magazines until he found a copy of *Casa Vogue.* Despite what the Contessa had said, there were only three copies.

When he returned to the *salotto,* the women had been joined by Sister Teresa. The sister, a tall, dark woman in her early fifties, was standing nervously in her gray coat. She turned to him with a worried expression.

"Signor Macintyre, you must help us!"

Sister Teresa, who had recently become tour guide at the Casa Crispina, had good English, but Urbino could tell that she was in danger of losing it. Usually calm and in control, she was now very nervous. Her bony hands were tightly clenched. Putting the magazine down on the table next to the tea service, he went over to her.

"What is it, Sister?" he asked in Italian.

"Santa Crispina is accused of murder, that's what it is!"

2 A few minutes of gentle interrogation in her native Italian clarified the situation, but only slightly. Sister Teresa didn't mean that the patron saint of her order was under suspicion—a rather difficult turn of events since Santa Crispina, though not her charity, had been dead since the fifteenth century—but that the convent and its pensione were.

"It's the murder in the Calle Santa Scolastica. Don't you know? It's one of our guests! The English photographer! He was stabbed in the heart!"

The Contessa went over and took her hand.

"Signor Gibbon!" the Contessa said. "But it can't be true! Murdered!"

"It *is* true, Contessa, God rest his soul. And now all of us at Santa Crispina are suffering as well."

"A murder here?" Berenice Pillow said, putting down one of the miniature icons she had been examining. "How dreadful! But isn't that a bit unusual for Venice?"

"And why *not* here in Venice?" the Contessa asked as if her friend's comment had been meant as a criticism of the city. "Tell us what happened, Sister. You can speak Italian. My friend understands it."

Sister Teresa gave Mrs. Pillow a thin smile of acknowledgment as the American woman drew closer so that she could hear better.

"He was found stabbed in the heart in the Calle Santa Scolastica last night or early this morning. The police are asking questions at the Casa Crispina. You can be sure they are thinking the worst thoughts about us all! That's why I've come for you, Signor Macintyre. You must do something! You know Commissario Gemelli. You have experience with murder!"

Berenice Pillow looked at Urbino in surprise.

"Experience with murder!" the Contessa said, allowing herself a little smile. "You make it sound as if he had been the perpetrator. He was involved in an investigation." She directed this reassuring clarification to her school friend.

"A murder investigation, yes," Sister Teresa said. "That's why he can help us."

"I still don't understand what it is I can do, Sister."

"A great deal, Signor Macintyre. And you can start right now. Come back to Santa Crispina with me."

"A murder!" Mrs. Pillow said as if the reality was only now sinking in. "How terrible! And during Carnival."

Sister Veronica nodded her head and said, "That's right, signora. It could not be worse for us all. This would have to happen during Carnival."

"Milo will take you in the boat," the Contessa said. She hurried from the *salotto*.

3   TEN minutes later, when Urbino and Sister Teresa stepped into the reception area of the Casa Crispina, Urbino was surprised to see Hazel Reeve, the woman he had met at Porfirio's last night. She gave him a blank look.

The reason for her presence became evident when Commissario Francesco Gemelli of the Venice Questura came down the staircase and went up to her.

"Would you mind coming this way, Miss Reeve?" he said in his heavily accented English, indicating a room behind the reception desk. "I have a few more questions."

As the Commissario turned, he saw Urbino. Annoyance

crossed his ruggedly good-looking face and he was about to say something but decided against it. He went into the room and closed the door firmly behind himself and Hazel Reeve.

Urbino took off his cape and followed Sister Teresa up the main staircase and along one of the corridors to a small room where Mother Mariangela was sitting behind a mahogany desk. She was a heavy woman in her early seventies who had little angelic about her but her name and her round face. Her dominant feature was her eyes—sharp and piercing—which Urbino was sure saw everything that should be seen among her charges and quite a few that they might try to conceal.

"Let me tell you why we've asked you to come, Signor Macintyre." As did Sister Teresa, she spoke good English. "Commissario Gemelli has been creating a lot of confusion here today." With a little smile, she added, "Of course, the murder of Signor Gibbon is the real cause of the confusion. It's the consequences of that terrible event that we now have to deal with, however. Such things always bring consequences."

Urbino nodded, taking the chair to the left of the desk.

"Yes, consequences," she repeated. "You see, Signor Macintyre, it is not only that Signor Gibbon was associated with the Casa Crispina. That would be bad enough. But you must not forget that we have other guests, and *these* guests knew Signor Gibbon."

Urbino, not exactly sure of what she meant, remained silent.

"The problem, you see," she said a bit impatiently, "is Commissario Gemelli."

"How is he a problem?"

He asked the question even though his own previous experiences with the Commissario had shown just how much of a problem the Sicilian could be.

"He's been asking questions of the guests all day—and he isn't finished yet! He's disturbing them."

"But it's the police's job to ask questions."

Mother Mariangela looked at Sister Teresa, who was sitting in a high-backed chair beneath a lithograph of Saint Catherine of Siena. Sister Teresa must have understood the import of the look, for she said, "Yes, of course, it is their job to ask questions, Signor Macintyre, but Commissario Gemelli is not the most delicate of men. He treats everyone like a criminal."

Ah, yes, Urbino thought, he had noted this in Gemelli

before: guilty until proven innocent.

"Pardon me, Sisters, but the Commissario has to begin somewhere. What better place to begin—what *only* place to begin—but with the people Gibbon was lodging with?"

"He's stirring them up!" Mother Mariangela said impatiently. "Can you imagine what can happen? The reputation of our lovely Casa Crispina would suffer! We need the money we get from it. If the shadow of a murder hangs over the Casa Crispina, we will be ruined! Not one guest must leave with a question in his mind. It will be like feathers in the wind. Do you think they will find out what really happened when they go home? No! They will have doubts, suspicions! Maybe one of the sisters was the murderer, maybe one of the other guests! No, Signor Macintyre, we cannot permit such speculation."

She pointed to a large, worn black book open on the desk.

"This is our ledger. Our guests will not stay forever. Signora Campi and Signor Lubonski—who, by the way, was rushed to the hospital last night—will remain, of course. The first of our guests will start to leave on Ash Wednesday, and soon all of them will be replaced by new guests. You see what the problem is."

"I understand, Mother Mariangela, but it doesn't explain why you're upset about Commissario Gemelli. It's his job to find out the truth. And one of the things he must do is to meet with each of the Casa Crispina's guests and—"

"I have no faith in Commissario Gemelli."

"What Mother Mariangela is saying, if she will excuse me for interrupting, is that she has more faith in you, Signor Macintyre."

"In me? To do what?"

"To do what the Commissario must do but to do it better."

"You are gentler than the Commissario," Mother Mariangela said. "He stirs people up, as I said before. You do the opposite. You can calm everyone down while finding out the truth before Ash Wednesday. I want this settled by then."

When he pointed out that he had none of the authority or any of the resources of the police, she reminded him that being a policeman here in Italy could also be a limitation.

"A private person like yourself, with your excellent Italian and your commitment to Venice, is the best one to get at the truth. We believe that you have the best chance of doing just that by Ash Wednesday."

"And if the truth is that one of the guests himself is the murderer?"

Mother Mariangela shrugged her shoulders.

"The truth, Signor Macintyre, we need the truth by Ash Wednesday—yes, even if one of our guests remains behind in the custody of the police. But I have no doubt that the murderer has absolutely nothing to do with Santa Crispina. I will prepare the guests for your visit. Here is a list of their names." She handed Urbino a sheet of paper. "You can return later in the evening after Commissario Gemelli has left."

Before going out into the Campo San Gabriele, Urbino stopped by the reception desk, hoping he would see Hazel Reeve. Had Gemelli finished his business with her or were they still behind the closed door? He was staring at the door when he heard footsteps behind him.

"If you're waiting for the attractive young lady, I'm afraid that she has already left."

Urbino turned around to confront Gemelli's characteristically supercilious smile.

"I suppose you'd like to begin your little investigation with her. Oh, don't look so surprised. I know why you're here, and I know it without Mother Mariangela telling me. I'm sure she's prepared to give some elaborate excuse that goes back to the Dark Ages and involves her order's rules. No, I don't need her to tell me, I knew it the minute I saw you come in with Sister Teresa."

"With such uncanny detecting skills, Commissario, you should be able to have this case wrapped up in record time."

"Or else you will do it for me? Oh, you don't have to commit yourself in any way. Just remember that there's a thin line between well-intentioned help and reckless interference. Good evening, Macintyre."

4   URBINO struck out across the Campo San Gabriele. He
    would try to be back at the Casa Crispina by eight-
thirty.

It was a clear cold night. Tourists seldom ventured into the
San Gabriele parish. Only during the recent notoriety over
what came to be known as the Relic Murders had there been
anything like tourist traffic in this relatively remote area.

What activity there was in the square—mainly residents
hurrying home from shopping, work, or their *passeggiate*—
was undisturbed by the frenzy of *Carnevale*.

When Urbino reached the other side of the square, he heard
someone behind him calling his name. The voice—a woman's—was vaguely familiar. He turned. It was Hazel Reeve
muffled in a dark hooded coat. She was shivering.

"Miss Reeve. You look cold."

"I am. I've been waiting for you to come out. I didn't want
to wait inside. I've had enough of that policeman." She looked
dispirited and her mouth was slack.

"I was on my way home. Why don't you come with me and
have a drink to warm you up. It isn't far."

Hazel Reeve didn't object and he took her arm. As they
walked, Urbino described some of the buildings and canals, all
the while wondering what her relationship was to Val Gibbon's
murder and why she had waited for him in the Campo San
Gabriele. Did she think Commissario Gemelli had told Urbino
all about her?

When they were approaching the Palazzo Uccello, Urbino
pointed to a bridge in the distance and, without thinking,
said, "That's where the monk Paolo Sarpi was stabbed in
the seventeenth century."

Hazel Reeve stiffened but there was no break in her stride.
Urbino quickly explained that Sarpi's wounds weren't fatal,
and they went the rest of the way in silence.

When they reached the Palazzo Uccello, at first Hazel Reeve
acted as if she were paying a simple social visit. Underneath

her casual manner, however, was an urgency kept in check by what Urbino suspected must be a powerful self-mastery.

When they were settled with brandies in the cramped parlor next to the library, she said, "You used to live in the attic story, too, didn't you? Porfirio told me last night. The maid and her husband live there now."

"Actually I lived on just two floors, but mainly on this one. The attic had guest rooms and I would go up there only to get to the *altana,* the wooden terrace on the roof. The ground floor is still empty. I might turn it over to the city for municipal offices."

"Porfirio is surprised that you don't care to live in the whole building. He made your palazzo sound much smaller than it actually is."

"But it *is* small, Miss Reeve, more like a little house than anything else. That's why I like it."

"You inherited it through your mother's side of the family, right?"

Urbino nodded but he didn't go into more detail. Despite his interest in other people's lives, he wasn't comfortable giving out personal information about himself.

Hazel Reeve took a sip of her brandy and closed her eyes as she waited for it to warm her. For a moment her face lost much of its tenseness. Then she looked around the room, crowded with some of Urbino's favorite pieces with little regard for what might go well together. On the wall behind the sofa was a Bronzino of a pearled-and-brocaded Florentine lady that the Contessa had given him. When Hazel Reeve turned around to look at it, Urbino wondered if she could see beyond the angularity that she and the Florentine lady didn't share to the tenseness that they did.

"I envy you," she said, turning back to Urbino. Then as if to consolidate the implied compliment, "Please call me Hazel."

"Only if you call me Urbino."

"It's an unusual name."

"Not to me, of course. My great-grandmother was born not far from the city and my mother loved Raphael."

"Why didn't she name you after him instead of his city?"

"She did. Raphael is my baptismal name but I've never used it. My mother and father called me by my middle name since I was born."

"Maybe it's just the power of association but you look a little like a Raphael."

"Not even my mother went that far," he said, thinking of how ironic her comment was in light of what he had just been thinking of the Bronzino. From the puzzled look on Hazel's face he could tell that she wasn't quite sure of what to make of his response. "I meant that a mother is inclined to see her child in an ideal light. I hope you didn't think I took what you said as anything but a compliment."

"A compliment?" Hazel frowned. "I suppose it is, but I was merely being descriptive. I was thinking of a specific Raphael—the portrait of a young cardinal at the Prado. Do you know it?"

Urbino nodded, having studied the painting in college and seen it three summers ago in Madrid. But he could see little resemblance between himself and the confident-looking cardinal in his watered-silk, scarlet *mozzetta* and matching hat.

"There *is* a resemblance," Hazel insisted, as if she knew what he was thinking. "Your face is sharper and more attractive, but you both have the same controlled look and," she added with a little smile, "very intelligent eyes."

She took another sip of her brandy. Urbino was prepared for further embarrassment when Hazel went on, but what she said had nothing to do with the Raphael.

"They're dead, your parents."

"A car accident almost fifteen years ago."

"Such a violent death must surely—" She stopped and shook her head slowly. "You must find me frightfully rude—rude and rather unfeeling. What I mean is that I'm here jabbering away when poor Val is lying dead—murdered."

Not knowing as much about her as she obviously did about him, Urbino didn't know exactly how to respond.

Hazel looked up at him with wet eyes.

"You're being very patient, Urbino. There I was in the square waiting to pounce on you when you probably wanted nothing better than a nice quiet walk back here. The least I can do is to tell you about Val and me." She said this as if it hadn't been her intention all along. "Did you know him?"

"I met him only a few times."

"I suppose I need tell you only that Val and I were in love," Hazel began with a deep breath and nervous smile. "That should be enough explanation and perhaps all that you even want to know—but there was more to it than that. Love affairs are never simple, are they?—and I'm not thinking only of Proust, believe me."

She reached down and picked up the volume of *Remembrance of Things Past*. When she opened it to the bookmark and saw that it was Man Ray's photograph of the dead Proust, she turned white and quickly closed the book and put it down.

"In any case, Proust is a rather poor example when talking about love, don't you think?" Urbino said. "For him love was more an illness than anything else. *Maladie d'amour*."

Hazel nodded abstractedly.

"Here we've known each other only a few hours, counting last evening, and I'm talking about something personal. Not your usual English reticence, is it? It's just that I'm at wits' end. I need to talk, and quite frankly I feel I can say things to you without your thinking ill of me. I need that tonight. Believe it or not, you're the person I feel I know best in Venice, now that Val is—is gone."

"What about Porfirio?"

After he said this he realized she might take it as a rebuff, as a not-too-subtle suggestion that she burden the Venetian photographer with her story instead of him.

"Oh, Porfirio! He would be the last person I would confide in about Val."

"Don't you find him sympathetic?"

"I'm afraid he would be too sympathetic."

"Do you mean he's interested in you?"

She laughed but it was a laugh almost empty of humor.

"Interested in me? I've never thought of that. What I meant was that he didn't like Val, not personally or professionally. Whatever sympathy he might have to give would have more to do with that than any possible interest in me—which I doubt."

The implication behind what she was saying was that Gibbon's behavior to her might be open to an unfavorable interpretation. Otherwise there would be no reason for her to be sure of Porfirio's sympathy precisely because he hadn't liked Gibbon. Urbino sensed that she was trying to prepare him for something negative about the photographer.

She took a handkerchief from her skirt pocket.

"I feel so empty and violated after having spoken with the Commissario. And to think I have to go through it all over again tomorrow at the Questura."

She took a sip of the brandy.

"I cared a lot for Val and he did for me—at least I thought he did," she went on. "We had planned to marry but we had a few problems we had to work out. I *do* think I might have made him see things differently." She looked at Urbino with a little smile. "You know, you have the same expression on your face that the Commissario had. Almost as if you're thinking bad thoughts of me. I'm sure *he* was. But I can't be afraid of what people will think, can I? I have to tell the truth. Val is dead and I have to tell as much as I know, even if it's private and doesn't put me—or Val—in a good light. The dead have no privacy and neither do the people they knew, not when it's a question of murder."

She let Urbino consider this for a few moments as she returned her handkerchief, unused, to her pocket. Then she stood up abruptly, surprising him by saying that she had to be going. Urbino had thought she had been about to plunge into a detailed account of her relationship with Gibbon but now, for some reason, she seemed eager to leave.

As he was helping her on with her coat, she said, "Could you tell me how to get back to Porfirio's? I wasn't paying much attention as we came here from San Gabriele."

"I'll go with you back to San Gabriele and give you directions from there. I have to go back to the Casa Crispina."

Hazel was quiet as they retraced their earlier walk. When they reached the Campo San Gabriele, Urbino gave her directions to Porfirio's, but something more seemed to be called for and he found himself asking her to dinner tomorrow. He would come by Porfirio's at eight the next evening.

As Urbino stood in front of the Casa Crispina and watched Hazel walking to the other side of the *campo,* he hoped he would learn more tomorrow about her relationship with Gibbon. She actually hadn't told him much at all tonight, even though she seemed to have sought him out to do just that. Or was this the impression she had wanted him to have? Their conversation tomorrow during dinner might make things clearer.

5 "IT would be a better use of your precious time, Signor Macintyre, if you were to do something about the people who are trying to kill Venice," Xenia Campi said, her voice heavy with sarcasm, looking not at Urbino but at her lapis lazuli ring. "As for Gibbon, I didn't like him and I wasn't surprised when something happened to him."

She wore a large, loose dark-blue dress with green brocade, and an embroidered shawl was draped over her shoulders. A blue snood caught her black hair from behind. She was sitting in the high-backed chair under the Catherine of Siena lithograph in Mother Mariangela's reception room.

"And I said the same thing to Commissario Gemelli," the heavyset woman added firmly, finally looking up at Urbino and pulling her shawl more tightly around her shoulders.

"Why did you think something was going to happen to Gibbon?"

"An aura," she said. "He was always surrounded by an aura, a violent red one. And I saw flames, bright orange-red flames tipped with yellow."

Her eyes lit up as if from a reflection of the flames she was describing. There was a faraway, almost sad look on her heavy face. Could she be thinking about her dead son? Her clairvoyance—or whatever gift she claimed to have—had been bestowed only after his death. How many times might she have thought that if she had only had the gift before his death, she might have seen an aura around him and warned him?

"The aura told me that he was either going to be consumed or be the instrument of someone else's fiery destruction. Fire burns the good but punishes the wicked."

"As you know, Signor Gibbon didn't die in a fire."

She shook her head slowly and gave him a wry smile. Her heavy makeup barely showed a crease or fold.

"Sometimes the flames are real, Signor Macintyre—they burn the flesh—and sometimes they are symbolic. But it isn't finished yet, is it? Mother Mariangela is worried about the reputation of her Casa Crispina. She said I should be grateful for staying here and I am, but I told her she should be thankful things weren't worse than they are. He could have been killed right here—hit over the head with a pitcher of wine during a meal, don't think any different!"

"Why was that?"

"I'll tell you why just as I told Commissario Gemelli. Because Signor Gibbon was insolent! He was the kind of person you wanted to slap or hit over the head. Believe me, you would have felt the same way."

"I knew him slightly. He did have a certain way about him but—"

" 'But,' nothing! Unless you were with him when there was a lady present, you couldn't possibly know what I mean. He went after women, he did—the younger ones."

She rearranged her shawl.

"Went after them?"

"I saw what he was up to. I didn't need my special powers to make it any clearer than it was to anyone else. Yes, he went after them! He played with their feelings, toyed with them. I saw it all. He flattered them to flatter himself. I warned the girls I saw him with and I warned him, too, but it didn't seem to do much good."

"What young women did you see him with, Signora Campi?"

Xenia Campi stood up. She wasn't a tall woman. She was, in fact, on the short side, and her heaviness made her seem even shorter. But now, as she answered Urbino's question, she seemed inches taller.

"Signorina Spaak!"

Amusement lightened her blunt features. She seemed pleased to be able to give him the American girl's name.

"You mentioned other young women. Who were they?"

"Oh, just girls in the Piazza," she said vaguely. She moved to the door. "I know you have other questions to ask me, but not this evening, if you don't mind. I'm not feeling well and I have to save my energies for the Piazza." She leaned her head back and gazed up at Urbino. "Speaking of Signorina Spaak, look deep into her eyes when you see her, Signor Macintyre. Deep, deep into her eyes." Xenia Campi's own eyes seemed suddenly veiled. "You'll see the ghost of death—of murder. It entered her through her eyes. But will it ever come out?"

Urbino thought she was finished, but just before she opened the door she answered a question that he hadn't had a chance to ask yet.

"And if you want to know where I was yesterday evening, I was right here in the Casa Crispina. I was in the lounge reading Madame Blavatsky and had a chat with Sister Agata before she dropped off to sleep at the desk. Then I went to bed. As I'm going to do now. Good evening, Signor Macintyre."

6 DORA Spaak, dressed in tweed slacks and a heavy sweater, was dwarfed by the high-backed chair. She couldn't have been more of a contrast to Saint Catherine, pale and thin on the wall behind her. Dora Spaak was rosy and rounded, from her short haircut with bangs above surprised-looking brown eyes to her feet in pink angora slippers that barely touched the floor. Even her voice was full of rounded tones that would have been even more rounded if she had spoken with less breathlessness.

She held a crumpled tissue in her hand.

"Poor Mr. Gibbon. Whatever could have happened? He was such a nice man. It must have been an accident."

An accident? Urbino repeated to himself. Could she possibly mean that being stabbed in the heart qualified as an accident? The next moment, the tissue at her snub nose, she added, "It was dark. Maybe they thought he was someone else. Mistaken identity, you know."

"I'm sure the police are considering that possibility."

"Except you don't think it was an accident, do you?" She looked at him accusingly with her round eyes. "You think someone hated him and killed him, but it's not true! Everyone here liked him, except for that crackpot Signora Campi. Even my brother, Nicholas—"

She stopped.

"What about your brother, Miss Spaak?"

She blew her nose before answering. When she did answer, there was a more cautious note in her voice.

"Nothing. Just that Nicholas liked Val, too, even if he didn't always show it. Signora Campi probably wants to put us all in the same group with her! She was always so unkind in the things she said. She almost always said them to me and it made me feel awful. Most of the time Val was there and he heard. I hope he didn't think I believed what she was saying. He couldn't do anything right as far as she was concerned! She said being a photographer was nothing at all. It wasn't work and it wasn't art. She said he fed off other people. She criticized him for not having all his meals with us here even though he had to pay for them. I think she resented that he had the money to do that. She didn't have two nickels to rub together—or whatever they call them here. And another thing," Dora added almost eagerly, the sodden tissue clutched in her chubby hand. "She was always saying he had a fire around his head that wouldn't bring him or anyone else any good. She sends chills down my spine when she talks like that! No wonder she frightens the boys from Naples if she can frighten a grown woman like me. I wouldn't be surprised if—"

Once again she broke off.

"If what, Miss Spaak?"

"Nothing. It's just that she frightens me so much."

"When was the last time you saw Mr. Gibbon?"

She wiped her nose.

"Last night after dinner," she said softly. "You see, I wasn't feeling too well. I caught a chill early in the day and my shoes and stockings got soaked in all the high water when I was looking for a post office. By the time I got back here I was sneezing. Later, sometime after nine, I was in the dining room having a cup of tea that the woman made for me before she left for the night. Val came down the backstairs. He was on his way out with his camera case. I figured he was going to join the fun in the big square. But he had on only a scarf and a light flannel shirt and I told him it didn't took as if he was going to be warm enough. He sat down and we had a chat." She applied a fresh tissue to her eyes. "He was so kind. He said he would go to the kitchen and get me some biscuits. It would be an adventure, he said, there would probably be a sign over the pantry door, something about abandoning hope or whatever if you went in, but he said he would do it anyway."

Hearing these garbled words from Dante had Urbino wondering if Val Gibbon had picked up Hazel Reeve's habit of quoting the Italian poet.

"He said that if I happened to know where it was, I could be his Be—Be—I forget what he said, some strange name."

"Beatrice," Urbino offered, pronouncing it in the Italian way with four syllables.

"That was it." Dora Spaak looked at him suspiciously. "I said I had no idea. I told him not to bother, that I was fine. All I needed was my tea. He said he would join me and started to take off his scarf. He would stay in and devote himself to making me feel a little better. Of course I insisted that he continue with his original plans. It was very kind and sweet of him, I said, but I was just fine. Yes, I—I told him to go. If I hadn't sent him away, he would be alive—and—and no one would have had to kill him!"

It was now that Urbino remembered what Xenia Campi had said about looking deep into Dora Spaak's eyes. What he saw when he did, however, wasn't the "ghost of death," as Xenia Campi had called it, but fear.

"He stayed a few minutes longer and left," Dora Spaak said, averting her eyes. "He said he liked my slippers."

She looked down at the slippers and started to cry as she considered the poignancy of his last words to her.

7 A slim blond man in his late twenties, with dark blue eyes and less than firm features, was standing outside the door when Urbino opened it to let Dora Spaak out after their interview.

"I'm Nicholas Spaak," the blond man said, frowning at Dora who said a quick good-bye and shuffled down the hall, the tissue pressed against her nose. "My mother needs to be asleep by nine. Dora insisted on seeing you first. If you wouldn't mind talking with my mother in her own room, we would appreciate it. She's more comfortable when she has all her things around her."

What Spaak meant by all his mother's things became apparent as soon as Urbino entered the room on the floor below. In addition to the bed, night table, prie-dieu, religious lithograph, and washbasin found in all the rooms, there was also a large electric heater making the room almost unbearable. It was about five feet from the bed in which Spaak's mother was lying, not beneath the regulation dark-brown blanket but beneath a brightly colored quilt. On the night table squatted a plastic object about the size of a small portable television. A cord ran from it to a socket in the wall and there was a hoselike apparatus from the other end that terminated in a plastic covering for the nose and mouth. Various American magazines—*Time, Redbook, Reader's Digest,* and *Health*— were scattered on the floor, and on the bed was a messy pile of clippings held in place by a pair of scissors. Several boxes of cookies were next to the machine on the bedside table, all of them opened, and a full yellow plastic mask was hanging from the knob of the table drawer.

"Mr. Macintyre, my mother, Stella Maris Spaak."

Stella Maris Spaak was a small woman in her early sixties who resembled her daughter much more than her son. Her form under the bedclothes hardly extended half the length of the bed. She was propped up with several pillows and showed a sweet, open face framed by short light-brown hair in need of a touch-up. Around her neck was a gold chain holding a little pendant embossed with what seemed to be the crossed keys of the Vatican coat of arms.

"I'm sorry to inconvenience you so late, Mrs. Spaak, but it won't be for long."

"It's all right, Mr. Macintyre. I'm sure my Nicky has been warning you not to trouble me but I'm not as bad as he thinks. I've held up very well during our three weeks in Italy, haven't I, Nicky?"

She smiled at her son, who was sitting on the bed. Urbino was in the room's only chair.

"We've already talked with the police, Mr. Macintyre," Nicholas Spaak said.

"Don't be upset, Nicky dear. He's really upset for me, Mr. Macintyre, but I'm fine. As you know, Nicky, Mother Mariangela said we should be nice to Mr. Macintyre. And you do seem like a very nice man, just as she said you were."

"Can't we get on with this, Mr. Macintyre?" Nicholas Spaak said in an irritated tone that drew a disapproving glance from his mother.

"Of course. All I wanted to know was if you noticed anything unusual here last night."

"Nothing whatsoever," Spaak answered, "and I think that at a place like this—a convent, I mean—where everything is so usual, you would be bound to notice anything that was otherwise, wouldn't you say?"

Urbino had to agree, although the Convent of the Charity of Santa Crispina did tend to have its unconventional aspects, one of which was the somewhat loose way it ran its pensione. Most establishments attached to convents and monasteries had much stricter rules about coming and going and the mixing of the sexes.

"Nicky is right. I'm afraid we can't be of much help to you or to poor Mr. Gibbon, God rest his soul. Every evening here is the same. We have dinner with the others at seven. Last night we finished about eight as we always do. Mr. Gibbon was looking very healthy and happy. I went to the chapel for half an hour. When I got back here, Nicky got me all set up for the night. I was in bed by nine."

"That's right, Mr. Macintyre. We keep to a schedule, my mother and I. It's best for her."

"Now, Nicky, don't give him the wrong impression. You like it, too. Ever since he was a baby, Mr. Macintyre, my Nicky has been like a clock."

Nicholas Spaak blushed.

"You see how sensitive he is, Mr. Macintyre? Ever since he started to go to school, he wouldn't let me praise him one bit, and what greater pleasure is there for a mother than to talk about her children? He's one of the best young English teachers at the community college in Pittsburgh."

Spaak's blush had deepened.

"What did you do after getting your mother ready for bed?"

"I went to my room next door. I read for a while, then fell asleep and slept until about seven this morning."

"I didn't hear anything unusual either, Mr. Macintyre. Nicky looked in on me after nine, and Dora came in about half an hour after he did and once again later. I'm not a good sleeper, but I don't like my children to worry, so I sometimes pretend to be asleep." She gave her son a nervous little glance. "It wasn't until the next morning at breakfast that we knew something was wrong."

"And now you'll want to know what we thought about Gibbon," Spaak said, "and whether we liked him or not."

"Liked him or not! What a thing to say! Of course we liked him. You never should speak ill of the dead."

"I'm sorry, Mother, but you know I didn't care for him. My mother has never been a person to say anything hurtful about anyone else."

"Why didn't you like him, Mr. Spaak?" Urbino asked, thinking of how Dora had said that her brother had actually liked Gibbon but didn't show it.

"I found him insufferably snide. Sometimes I thought he needed a smack in the face."

Xenia Campi had said very much the same thing.

"Nicky, that's not like you!"

Spaak got up and thrust his hands into the pockets of his corduroy trousers. His mother's eyes followed him with concern as he went to the door and turned around.

"You should understand, Mr. Macintyre, that I'm not the kind of person to dislike without good reason." He shrugged, as if to say that this was the form his own charitableness took—to have at least a reason for speaking ill of the dead. "Gibbon had an insidious way about him. I didn't like the way he talked to Dora, being sweet and encouraging but really making a fool of her. And he would always try to take you unawares with one of his insinuating comments."

"Nicky, you're still not letting what he said at dinner bother you, are you? If Dora thought there was anything bad in it, she never would have told me, you can be sure of that. You know how devoted she is to you. According to Dora, Mr. Macintyre, the other night at dinner when I wasn't there Mr. Gibbon was joking around. Nicky asked him how he decided what to take pictures of. Mr. Gibbon said something about wanting his pictures to show what people couldn't see on their own. But Nicky was upset because Mr. Gibbon said he wouldn't want to take *his* picture, that everyone could see what my Nicky was like, and that if I were in the picture with him it would be even more clear. I think that was a very nice thing to say, Mr. Macintyre, don't you? Dora thought so too. He was paying Nicky and me a compliment."

Mrs. Spaak paused for a telling moment as she looked at her son, who was standing very still, avoiding her eyes.

"Of course, Nicky understands things Dora and I don't," she went on. "It hurts me to see him upset. But Mr. Gibbon is dead now. If what he said wasn't nice in some way, it's not for us to judge him now. He's met his justice."

She closed her thin lips firmly after the last word, a hard look coming into her eyes and taking away almost all the sweetness in her face.

8 OUT in the hall Spaak asked Urbino to come into his room. Unlike his mother's room, Spaak's held only the regulation items, a carry-on valise, an Italian dictionary, and a paperback copy of D. H. Lawrence's *Twilight in Italy*.

"There's one thing I'd like to clarify, Mr. Macintyre. Just now with my mother I may have misled you."

He made a long pause.

"Mr. Lubonski," Spaak said slowly as if offering Urbino a generous hint. "I didn't stay in my room after I saw my mother last night. I went out about nine-thirty. Mr. Lubonski saw me as he was coming in. He looked as if he was in a daze. Didn't he tell you he saw me?"

"I haven't been to the hospital yet."

"I wonder if the Commissario has. I didn't tell him I had been out last night. I didn't want to disturb Mother. I do it every once in a while, you see, after she goes to bed, but I don't like her to know. If I had told the Commissario, he might have asked her all sorts of questions and then she would have known. I'm sure you understand that sometimes I need to get away. And Dora was here. She's a nurse and is much more qualified to care for Mother. Each of us looks in on her once a night, both here and back home. Dora covers for me. She's devoted to me, as Mother said—a typical kid sister, I guess."

"What did you do last night after you left?"

"I did what I usually do. I went for a walk for about an hour. I ended up in a bar where I had a few drinks." He gave a nervous laugh and added, "But if you're going to ask me where I walked and where the bar was I can't tell you. It could have been around the corner—or miles away. All I know is that I didn't go over one of the big bridges."

So he didn't walk over to the other side of the Grand Canal. The Calle Santa Scolastica, however, was on the same side as the Cannaregio and could be reached through the network of alleys, squares, and small bridges.

"I came back about midnight. No one saw me come in. I used my key."

Urbino didn't know when Gibbon's body had been discovered or the probable time of his death. He knew only that it had to be after Nicholas Spaak's sister had seen Gibbon in the dining room—if Dora was telling the truth about the encounter. But if Urbino couldn't be sure of exactly what had passed between Gibbon and Dora in the dining room, it should be easier to verify when Gibbon had left the Casa Crispina last night. He must talk with Xenia Campi again. And then there was Sister Agata who had been at the reception desk. Urbino was going to have to try to get information from Commissario Gemelli, too, a prospect that didn't please him.

"I'd rather Mother didn't know about all this, Mr. Macintyre. She's an asthmatic and her attacks can be brought on by emotion." Spaak had an imploring look on his face. Urbino could see the little boy who wanted to please his mother, who never wanted to be in her disfavor. Was Spaak in the habit of using her as a convenient excuse for things he himself didn't want to do anyway? There seemed to be a core of strength in the woman that Spaak either didn't see or didn't want to acknowledge.

"You should tell the Commissario. Perhaps you could speak with your mother first."

Spaak shrugged. Fear flickered in his eyes, but whether because of his mother's possible response or the Commissario's there was no way for Urbino to know.

The only other guests Urbino needed to see were the three boys from Naples, but they were out for the evening. As for Sister Agata, she was fast asleep at the reception desk.

9 WHEN Urbino returned to the Palazzo Uccello he fed Serena and fixed himself a *frittata*. He had almost finished eating it when the phone rang.

"My God, Urbino, I've known you for ten years and I never knew you had a sadistic streak," the Contessa said as soon as he picked up the receiver. "Why have you kept me waiting? I've been ringing and ringing."

"I just got in."

He told her about his visit to the Casa Crispina and his conversations with Xenia Campi and the Spaaks.

"Dora Spaak must have been the girl you saw Gibbon with at Florian's the other afternoon. She was obviously infatuated with him."

"I could see that. But what about the other girls Xenia Campi mentioned that Gibbon flirted with?"

"She seemed reluctant to give more details. I think she regretted having mentioned it."

"From what you've learned already, I'd say that the brother is the most likely suspect. He obviously didn't like Gibbon."

"Neither did Xenia Campi."

"*Caro,* you know that's neither a recommendation nor a condemnation when it comes to Xenia Campi! No, I'd say it was the brother. He didn't return to the Casa Crispina until midnight. Even if we learn that Gibbon was killed after then, the brother really isn't off the hook, is he? We only have his word for when he got back. Gibbon not only insulted him— and his mother—by his snide comment but was also making a fool of his sister. But perhaps those aren't strong enough reasons to kill someone, are they?"

"People have been murdered for less. I can't shake the feeling that the Spaaks are hiding something, but whether in concert or individually I can't tell."

"Surely you don't think that Mrs. Spaak could have done it! I can't imagine a woman like her—a semi-convalescent from what you say—dragging herself to the Calle Santa Scolastica and back again in the middle of the night. It was impossible for her to have killed Gibbon!"

"I haven't told you yet, Barbara, but Nicholas Spaak saw Josef coming in about nine-thirty."

The Contessa didn't say anything for a few moments.

"But, Urbino, he was coming *in,* not going out. He couldn't have killed Gibbon, who had left only a short time before Josef returned."

"You miss the point, Barbara. If Josef was well enough to go out one time that night, perhaps he went out again later. He wasn't rushed to the hospital until the early hours of the morning. He called me when I got back from the Fenice at at eleven to tell me not to work on the fresco until he got well."

"I don't believe Josef could harm a fly. Besides, what motive could he have?" She sighed. "All I would need is to have Josef turn out to be a murderer. *I* recommended him for the job. No one would ever let me forget it."

"Are you concerned about Josef or yourself, Barbara?"

"Urbino! How can you say such a thing! But if Josef turns out to be the murderer, I'll never forgive you—for *both* our sakes!"

Having run through the lodgers at the Casa Crispina—except for the three Neapolitan boys—Urbino realized that he could no longer avoid telling the Contessa about Hazel Reeve.

"Cherchez la femme," the Contessa said without much enthusiasm and even less originality. "But it would seem, *caro,* that *la femme* has found you instead! It's strange, don't you think? A complete stranger—a bereaved woman with an emotional involvement with the murdered man—seeks out another man. It's not what one would expect."

"Emotionally speaking, it's probably not unusual at all if you think about it. Besides, Barbara, she's not a complete stranger."

"Then, my dear, you are a complete liar. I never heard of this Reeve woman before."

"I met her last night at Porfirio's."

There was a charged silence.

"Didn't we talk about Porfirio's party on the way back from the Fenice? I don't remember any mention of this woman then.

I do seem to remember, however, that you were preoccupied. I refrained from probing then and now it seems unnecessary. It was this Reeve woman, wasn't it?"

Urbino felt uncomfortable. He and the Contessa were very good friends, and there had even been unfounded rumors about them because they were so often out together that they appeared more inseparable than many married couples. "The Anglo-American alliance" they were sometimes called. His personal life was seldom something he discussed even with her, yet she had a somewhat proprietary attitude toward it. It had often occurred to him that this was probably because of his own reticence, for, with good reason, she couldn't help believing that she—and only she—was always sitting squarely in the center of his personal life. With a bit of a shock Urbino realized that he felt a little guilty, almost as if he were displaying a peculiar kind of infidelity by his interest, vague and unformed though it was, in Hazel Reeve.

"I don't assume this conversation with Miss Reeve took place in the middle of the Campo San Gabriele."

It didn't make him any more comfortable when he detected something in the Contessa's voice. It wasn't quite a quaver, it wasn't quite a breathiness, but he knew her well enough to know what it meant. She was hurt, disappointed. She made an attempt to control it as she said with certainty, "You went back to the Palazzo Uccello."

"Don't make it sound like an assignation! It seemed the most convenient thing to do. I couldn't go back to the Casa Crispina until I was sure Gemelli had left, and a bar—"

"Spare me a long explanation, Urbino dear. It will only make me more suspicious. I suppose you're entitled to have your secrets from a poor old woman like me. I'd prefer not to talk about your Miss Reeve right now or about all this sad business at the Casa Crispina. Call it selfishness on my part, *caro*, but at the end of my day I'd prefer tranquil thoughts. How did you find my old school friend?"

"I rather liked her. It must be a good feeling to have someone look you up like that—once you get over the initial surprise. And her stepson is pleasant enough. The two of them seem to have a rapport."

"Yes, they do, don't they?"

The Contessa's voice sounded suddenly tired. She and Alvise had been childless and Urbino knew that she felt the lack the older she got. Seeing her old school friend with her stepson might be difficult for her.

"Berenice didn't stay much longer. Take it as a recommendation of your own social charms that were so abruptly snatched from us. We avoided the murder and talked about the *Casa Vogue* piece. Then she told me a few more things about her life. She has an antiques business and spends a lot of time in Florence around the Via Maggio and the Borgognissanti quarter. She met Vico's father in the mid-sixties when she was in Naples scouting around for things. He was a widower with the one son. She was in her thirties by then—I *think*," the Contessa emended, realizing any specific references to her friend's age would be more than a clue to her own—"anyway, she hadn't married yet. She raised the two-year-old Tonio as her own."

"And her second husband?"

"Malcolm Pillow. *He* had money too. He owned several factories in America and died about eight years ago in London. Collapsed during a business trip and was hospitalized for several months. It took a lot out of Berenice. When she's in Italy, she's usually at the Villa Vico in Naples. It belongs to Tonio now. He's an architect with a degree from London University."

"It's unfortunate I had to rush off. I was hoping I might learn a few secrets about you."

"I'm sure you were, but after you left we made a pact that we would reminisce mainly with each other, especially since she'll be meeting many of my friends. We agreed that I would say nothing to Tonio—nothing possibly embarrassing, that is—and she would do the same for me. All memories will be in a golden bath. You can see how well we keep to our pact tomorrow evening at dinner."

"Tomorrow?"

"Yes, *caro*, tomorrow. Is there a problem with that?"

"I already have a dinner engagement for tomorrow, Barbara."

In the brief silence he knew that she knew.

"With the Reeve woman. She sounds like someone out of Thomas Hardy. You surprise me, Urbino. You work faster than I thought. Unless it was her suggestion."

"No, mine." Then, as if it would make a difference to be more specific, he added, "The Montin."

"The Montin! That's where we're going! Please don't think we'll squeeze your Miss Reeve in at our table. A forward girl like she seems to be is certain to dominate the entire conversation."

Before Urbino had time to respond, the Contessa had said good night and hung up.

10 "YOU are about forty-five minutes later than I thought you would be, Macintyre," Gemelli said the next morning when Urbino called the Questura. "I was sure you would be the first call that came through today."

Urbino had rehearsed what he would say to Gemelli but now it all slipped away from him. If he was going to make any sense of things, he needed some specific information. Being only an alien resident of Italy and considered somewhat of a meddler made whatever information he could get from Gemelli a function of the man's whim, craft, or weariness.

"I'd like to know roughly when Gibbon was murdered," Urbino said, deciding to be as direct as possible.

" 'Roughly,' you say. Privileged information nonetheless, as you well know."

"Yes, I know, but—"

"Consider looking in today's *Il Gazzettino,* Macintyre. We released the time Gibbon's body was found. I'm sure you have a good idea when he was last seen at the Casa Crispina. Put the two together and you get the rough idea you've asked for." Gemelli paused. Urbino could hear him exhaling smoke from a cigarette. "But that's not all you want to know, is it, Macintyre? You have a few more questions. I don't know why you like getting involved in these things. All this is a job, a profession, some say it is even a kind of art—but one thing it isn't is a hobby."

"I didn't go looking for this, Commissario."

"No, Mother Mariangela came looking for you with a string of rosary beads in one hand and her precious guests' ledger in the other. I know. But I don't see you moving in the other direction."

"Should I?"

"It might be a good idea."

"From the point of view of danger?"

"I wasn't thinking of that—but yes, that's something always to be taken into consideration. I was thinking more of myself, though—or, to be more exact, more about the Questura and the success of this case. Having you involved, in whatever capacity, could throw everything out of balance."

"I've been of help before."

"It might have worked out differently. We might have lived to regret it—or maybe even worse."

"What harm could there be in telling me something more? If you're afraid I might 'throw everything out of balance,' as you just said, wouldn't I be more likely to do it because of what I didn't know than what I did?"

Gemelli laughed.

"If I tell you anything more, Macintyre, don't think it has anything to do with your powers of persuasion. I'll satisfy your curiosity up to a certain point because otherwise I'll probably get calls from both Mother Mariangela and the Contessa da Capo-Zendrini. And if those calls don't get you an answer, we both know what will happen next. Corruption of a public official—or something close to it. One of you—most likely the Contessa with all her wonderful connections—would manage to get to Brilli"—Franco Brilli was the medical examiner—"and get information out of him. And just think how guilty that will make poor old Brilli feel after being so circumspect all these years and so close to retirement! So to avoid the waste of any more of my time, the corruption of a public official, and the disturbance of poor old Brilli, I'll tell you that Gibbon died sometime between ten o'clock and eleven-thirty, when Ignazio Rigoletti discovered his body. He was stabbed once in the chest and seems to have died instantly. The attack and death occurred where the body was found—near the water steps in the Calle Santa Scolastica. We assume the perpetrator escaped on foot back along the Calle Santa Scolastica and then went either down to the Riva degli Schiavoni or up to the Campo Filippo e Giacomo. There's also the possibility, of course, that the perpetrator used a boat of some kind—a motorboat, a *sandolo*, maybe even a gondola. We *haven't* found anything yet that might have been the murder weapon."

Before Urbino could ask what kind of weapon they were looking for, Gemelli said he had to hang up. Another call was waiting.

Urbino was left not only feeling pleased that he had got as much information as he had from Gemelli but also wondering why Gemelli had passed it on. Something else must be behind it other than the reasons he had given.

11 URBINO went out to the nearest news kiosk and got a copy of *Il Gazzettino*. He stopped in a café and ordered an espresso at the bar. Urbino hadn't read yesterday's paper so he didn't know how much of today's article about Gibbon's murder was a repetition, if any. Gibbon's murder might not have made the morning paper except for a brief piece.

Urbino noticed that most of the other people in the café, including a man dressed as a matador, were engrossed in the account. After changing his order of a simple espresso to one "corrected" by a dollop of anisette, he read the article.

ENGLISH PHOTOGRAPHER MURDERED NEAR BRIDGE OF SIGHS

Signor Val Gibbon, 38, of London was found stabbed in the Calle Santa Scolastica on Wednesday evening. Ignazio Rigoletti, a resident of the area, discovered the body at approximately 11:30 P.M. when returning to his apartment in the Corte Santa Scolastica. Mr. Gibbon was pronounced dead on the scene at 11:57 by Dr. Franco Brilli, the medical examiner.

Mr. Gibbon had been in the city for two weeks and was staying at the Casa Crispina of the Charity of Santa Crispina in the Cannaregio. He was in Venice to photograph Carnival for a forthcoming book.

Commissario Gemelli of the Venice Questura did not wish to comment on the investigation except to say that the Questura is following various leads it expects will soon prove successful.

Urbino sensed that although the story was on the first page of the Venice news, there was an attempt to deemphasize it. He had seen other examples of this in the city, several of them around *Carnevale* or another of the crowd and revenue-gathering festivals like the Regatta in September or the Feast of the Redeemer in July.

More than the other festivals, however, *Carnevale* brought Venice considerable national and international publicity, precious during a time when the media often emphasized the ecological plight of the city. Opinions—pro and con—ran high about this holiday that had been revived in 1980. Urbino thought of Xenia Campi and how she had been handing out the flyers in the Piazza on the afternoon before Gibbon's murder. Many Venetians felt the way she did, even if they might find her methods strange. Yet there was a sizable group of Venetians in the municipal government and the tourist business, not to mention people like Giovanni Firpo, the man who had mocked Xenia Campi in the Piazza, who were strongly opposed to anything and anyone that might undermine the success of *Carnevale*.

Urbino read the article again. There was nothing in it he didn't already know. He finished his coffee and headed for the Piazza San Marco. Wanting to think and not to be distracted, he chose his route carefully. He saw relatively few people and only one in costume, a young woman dressed as a butterfly hurrying off to join her friends.

As he walked down the chill back alleys, he reviewed the little he knew but it yielded nothing more than questions. If it was true that anyone could be driven to murder, what might have driven the Cassandra-like Xenia Campi, obsessed with the fate of Venice and still not recovered, as no parent could ever be, from the death of her child? Was Dora telling the truth about her last encounter with Gibbon in the dining room of the Casa Crispina? She had insisted that her brother liked Gibbon, whereas Nicholas himself had made it more than clear that he hadn't. Could Nicholas not be completely aware of how he had felt about the photographer? And what role might have been played by Mrs. Spaak or Lubonski, both of whom were supposed to have been restricted in their movements the night of the murder because of illness?

Then there were the questions about Hazel Reeve, perhaps the most disturbing of all. Why had she waited for him outside the Casa Crispina last night? Why had she chosen him to be the recipient of her confidences? He was afraid of being misled by either his vanity or his suspicion.

One of his weaknesses was being attracted to people in distress and encouraging their confidences. He considered it a weakness because it had led in the past to relationships doomed from the start. The burden of responsibility for the other's problems had often proved too heavy and he himself had eventually started to suffer under their weight. He sometimes thought of it as a kind of emotional vampirism in which he willingly offered himself up to be fed upon, only to be weakened and resentful in the end. What amazed but never amused him was the way that he hardly ever had to seek these people out. They somehow managed to find him and, once found, he was often, at least for a time, lost.

The most disastrous of these relationships had been his short marriage back in New Orleans to Evangeline Hennepin, the daughter of wealthy, manipulative parents. Who had ended up failing whom in the marriage was still difficult for Urbino to sort out but he took a lot of the blame himself. Even after all this time, however, he was still wary when he found himself attracted to someone in distress.

Urbino put aside these troubling thoughts when he eventually was forced to join the stream of people moving toward the Piazza.

As soon as he entered the crowded Piazza, he was surrounded by a group of *gnaghe,* young men in plain dresses and the black oval *moretta* masks customarily worn by women. It was a traditional costume that went back to the early days of *Carnevale* when it had created a lot of controversy because of its association with sodomy. These boys around Urbino mimicked the voices of women and made the catlike sounds that gave them their name. They plucked at his cape and made kissing noises before running off in a flock to another man.

Urbino crossed over to Florian's. On the steps going up to the arcade a young woman was painting the face of a teenage boy while a group watched and waited for their turn. Her own face was painted a bright red.

"Your name is Macintyre, isn't it?"

Urbino looked up at a tall thin boy of sixteen or seventeen standing at the edge of the group. He was wearing a checkered Arab headdress. Next to him was a boy with his face painted as a clown. They wore jeans, sneakers, and short woolen jackets.

"My name's Leo, this is Fabio. We're staying at the convent, the one where the murdered Englishman was staying."

Leo spoke with a rough Neapolitan accent.

"You want to talk to us," Fabio said in smoother Italian.

"I'd like to ask you a few questions. It wouldn't take long. I thought there were three of you."

"There are. Giuseppe!" Leo shouted and whistled over to a chubby boy leaning against a column. Giuseppe came over with a scowl on his round face. He wore a cowboy hat and a holster with a beat-up flask in it. "The girl painting faces told us who you were."

Urbino looked at her again. He didn't recognize her although he might have if she hadn't been wearing makeup and had shown him her face more fully.

"We can't talk here, can we?" said Leo, who seemed to be the leader of the group. "Why don't we go inside?" He nodded toward Florian's. "You buy us some coffee and sandwiches and we'll tell you what we know. Fair exchange? The only way we're going to get into a place like that is with someone like you. How about it?"

"Fine," Urbino said.

Florian's was filled with merrymakers but they found a table in the back away from the windows. The room was thick with smoke. The boys stared at the furnishings—at the marble tables and velvet banquettes, the little round mahogany serving tables, the putti lamps, the mirrors, the frescoes under glass, the ornate ceiling. After joking over the menu cards, they ordered their coffees and the small crustless sandwiches called *tramezzini* but surprised Urbino by eating and drinking carefully and slowly. He smiled to himself. What had he expected? A ravenous pack of dogs?

"Nice place," Leo said, "nothing like old Crispina!"

"Why are you boys staying there?"

"Our folks thought we'd be safer there than a youth hostel. Can you believe it? Look what happened to the photographer!"

Leo and Fabio laughed but Giuseppe kept a grim face, looking at Urbino sullenly.

"Were you boys at the Casa Crispina the night of the murder?"

"Just for dinner. We try to stay there as little as possible," Fabio said. "Just to eat and sleep. Our folks already paid for the rooms and the meals. Otherwise we'd use the money in a better way."

"Did you notice anything unusual that night—or any other night? Something that you think might be important now that you know that the English photographer was murdered?"

"We keep to ourselves," Fabio said. "The other guests are old and weird. The photographer—he wasn't a bad sort. Took our picture here in the Piazza. Said he would mail us a copy. Giuseppe gave him his address. Giuseppe is Leo's cousin. We all come from Naples."

"Most of the people are strange there, starting with the nuns!" Leo said. "They give me the creeps. I never saw so many old women in one place at one time. I bet one of them killed him. Probably found out he was taking dirty pictures or something."

"The crazy woman," Giuseppe said in a low voice. "She's the one."

"Xenia Campi?" Urbino asked. "The woman who makes predictions?"

"That's the one," Leo said. "Beppe hates her. She's always coming after him. She's always coming after *all* of us but she has it in for Beppe. I think she likes him!"

Leo and Fabio laughed.

"Why do you say she might like him?"

Leo looked over at Giuseppe and was given a warning glance.

"Oh, I don't know. She says he's such a nice boy, that he's going in the wrong direction. I think she's even trying to fix him up with a girl! She doesn't seem to care about us so much. All she does is curse at us."

"She says I remind her of a dead boy," Giuseppe said, looking down into his coffee cup.

"I thought you didn't want anyone to know!" Leo shouted.

Giuseppe shrugged.

"Maybe he should know. Maybe he doesn't know how crazy she is, always talking about nice-looking dead boys. Maybe she thought the photographer was nice and killed him, too. She said I was nice but that she saw something bad around me, something around my head that meant death if I wasn't good."

"Don't be afraid of *her* if she says you're nice," Leo said. "Be afraid if a man says it!" He looked at Fabio who burst out laughing again. "We know what kind of place the photographer was found in. It's where the *finocchi* go."

"Did the photographer ever bother you in that way?"

"What do you think we are?" Fabio said angrily, no longer amused. "Nobody ever bothers us anywhere—not at old Crispina's or anywhere else. We keep to ourselves."

"That's right," Leo said. "Whatever might have been going on at old Crispina's had nothing to do with us. Thanks for the coffee and sandwiches. Let's go, *ragazzi*."

Grabbing some of the little sandwiches, the three boys hurried out into the Piazza.

Urbino stayed a while longer, finishing his *caffelatte* and trying to give his attention to the other news in *Il Gazzettino*, but when he found himself rereading a piece on a ten-car pileup in the fog between Venice and Florence, he put the paper aside and asked for his check.

He left Florian's and walked around the arcade past the Campanile to the Molo where there were fewer people. Between the two columns a white-faced mime dressed in a black skullcap and a baggy white suit with large, white buttons was dramatizing the defeat of all his amorous hopes in front of a small but enthusiastic audience. Closer to the water three acrobats dressed as jesters in particolored suits were doing handstands and tumbles. One of them threw a dagger in the air as he cavorted beneath it. Another caught it by the handle and, with exaggerated stealth, stalked and stabbed their oblivious companion, whose death throes were marvelous feats of balance and contortion

The sky above the lagoon was a pale blue and the air, blown south from the Dolomites, was clear and crisp. The last time it had rained was the day before Val Gibbon had been murdered. Beyond the moored gondolas and motorboats and aloof from all the revelry floated the monastery island of San Giorgio Maggiore. Vaporetti, motorcraft, and barges negotiated the broad stretch of lagoon, slipped in and out of the Grand Canal, and made their way through the Giudecca Canal. A car ferry overtook a freighter slowly moving toward its berth at the Maritime Station.

Urbino went past the cream-colored filigree pillars of the Ducal Palace and up the steps of the bridge. Gondolas filled with merrymakers were floating up and down the canal. One of them had stopped so that the gondolier could take a picture of a young couple with the Bridge of Sighs in the background. The couple smiled, then kissed for the camera.

Urbino quickened his steps as he went down the bridge and under the arcades of the old prison building into the narrow opening of the Calle degli Albanesi. A wing of the Danieli Hotel was on his right. He could have touched both sides of the *calle* by extending his arms. After passing under a little arch, he turned left into the Calle Santa Scolastica.

It was empty. He went along it, crossed the intervening courtyard, and continued to where the *calle* ended abruptly at water steps.

This was where Val Gibbon had been murdered and his body had been found by Xenia Campi's ex-husband. When darkness fell, the Calle Santa Scolastica provided a convenient rendezvous point for men who might have met by the lagoon or in the Piazza. The city had many places like this, ideal for privacy and concealment, but the Calle Santa Scolastica was one of the most popular because of its proximity to the Piazza and the Bridge of Sighs, which you could see if you carefully looked up the canal while grasping the wall.

Urbino didn't know what he expected to find in the Calle Santa Scolastica but he wanted to take a look. Gemelli's scene-of-crime people would have been through it very thoroughly. Despite the odor of urine, the area was fairly clean, without even any boxes or plastic garbage bags set out for pickup. On the top water step was a used condom that must have been deposited or been washed up by the tide after the scene-of-crime crew had been there. They certainly wouldn't have missed something as important as that.

Urbino didn't venture down onto the moss-covered water steps but, from a more secure footing, looked down the canal toward the lagoon. He could see the Bridge of Sighs. A gondola was passing under it in his direction, crowded with a group of costumed men and women. When they saw him, they waved and shouted and one of them, dressed as a sorcerer, threw him a handful of golden-colored coinlike disks. It reminded him of the trinkets thrown from the Mardi Gras floats as they made their way along Canal Street. The people would scramble for them as if they were the most precious of objects. Urbino did no differently now. He picked up several of the disks and put them in his pocket, waving a thank-you to the gondola as it went up the canal.

12 AFTER leaving the Calle Santa Scolastica, Urbino wandered for a while through the nearby working-class quarter of the Castello. Very few of the people in this area wore costumes and those who did had simple affairs that bore the look of altered bridal gowns and military uniforms, of hastily sewn sheeting material and remnants.

One figure stood out from the rest, however. Urbino saw it on the other side of one of the squares. It was vaguely familiar, with its green and blue embroidered robe and high headdress with silver baubles, Oriental mask, and feathered fan. It was surrounded by a group of young children who were tugging at the skirt and making gesticulations. Urbino couldn't hear what they were saying. A woman shouted something down from a window and the children ran off, but not before one of them had scurried back to try to pull a feather from the fan.

As the figure continued across the square in the general direction of San Marco, Urbino recognized it. It was Giovanni Firpo, whom he had last seen in the Piazza taunting Xenia Campi as she handed out her pamphlets decrying Carnival. Firpo, who lived in the Castello, probably had spent close to a month's wages from his job at the hospital on this year's costume. It was the same every year.

When Urbino reached the Public Gardens where the Biennale art festival was held every other summer, he sat down on one of the benches by the water. The odor of cat urine engulfed him. In a large fenced-in area behind him, hundreds of cats made their home in the dead leaves and under the bushes and trees. It was the fate he had rescued his own Serena from when he had found her shivering under a bush by the statue of Wagner on a wet day in November.

A girls' gymnastics class was jogging along the path that bordered the lagoon. Several of the girls jumped up on the stone wall and walked along it fearlessly.

Urbino sat thinking of what he had learned from the guests so far. No one seemed to have noticed anything unusual the night of Gibbon's death. Perhaps the most unusual fact had been that Lubonski had got up from his sickbed to leave the Casa Crispina and then had called Urbino. The only other person who Urbino knew for sure had been out that night was Nicholas Spaak, who had gone for a walk and had a drink at a bar. This didn't mean, of course, that no one else had gone out. It was ironic, but it might have been easier tracking the comings and goings of guests at one of the big hotels than at the Casa Crispina, where the guests had individual keys that they kept with them at all times. He would have to ask Xenia Campi a few more questions, since she had been sitting in the lounge that evening and would have been able to see whoever might have gone in or out. And he supposed there was a possibility that Sister Agata had seen or heard something even after nine-thirty although, from what he had heard, she was usually fast asleep by then.

Urbino was less clear now about what kind of person Gibbon had been than before he talked with the guests. Was there any consistency in their different views of Gibbon? The men—Lubonski and Nicholas Spaak—hadn't cared for him, whereas Dora Spaak and her mother seemed to have more benevolent opinions. But Xenia Campi hadn't liked him and the boys from Naples hadn't had anything bad to say about him. No, there wasn't much consistency in this direction, he said to himself as he got up and started back toward the Piazza.

13 "WHEREVER are you taking me, Urbino?" Hazel asked after they left the busy *calle*. "Is there really a restaurant around here?"

She looked down the length of the quay that bordered the still canal with its moored boats, many in need of paint and repair. Although the canal was only a few minutes' walk from the Grand Canal and the Zattere, it always had a quiet, secretive air. It was at its most charming in the spring and summer when flowers cascaded from the balconies and when the boats were freshly painted. Most of the windows of the buildings were tightly shuttered now, however, emitting only the faintest light between their chinks. The loudest sounds were their own footsteps and the gentle lapping of water against the water steps and boats.

On the other side of the canal a door opened and two clowns emerged, the white ruffles around their necks blowing in the slight wind. They hurried toward the nearby Campo San Barnaba.

"It's not only a restaurant but a simple one-star hotel with only seven rooms," Urbino said. "The restaurant is on the ground floor. It has one of the best reputations in town. We were lucky to get a table tonight." He pointed ahead. "Can you see the lantern?"

"Barely." When they reached the unassuming front of the Montin with its two small iron-grille windows flanking the wooden door and its four-sided lantern with the establishment's name painted on it, Hazel said, "I like it already."

The *padrona* greeted them with a big smile from the bar-reception area next to the door. A freshly lit cigarette was between her fingers. She was an attractive, slightly overweight woman in her fifties with blond hair and large, fashionable glasses. She led them between the double rows of long tables to a less than choice table near the kitchen and the doors leading out to the rest rooms and the garden restaurant, closed until spring. Urbino had Hazel sit so that she could have a view of the length of the long, narrow room.

"*Buon appetito*," the woman said in her smoke-hoarse voice. "Lino will be with you in a few minutes."

Urbino didn't see the Contessa, Mrs. Pillow, and Tonio Vico anywhere. Either they hadn't yet arrived or were in the intimate room with the fireplace to the left of the entrance.

The walls were crowded with paintings—watercolors, charcoals, and oils of Venetian scenes along with portraits and modernist paintings suggestive of Picasso, Matisse, and Chagall.

"Some people say the paintings were left by artists as payment for their room and board but most of them are by Venetian artists of the fifties and sixties who patronized the place. I don't think they have room for many more, if any."

Lino, a distinguished-looking man in his sixties, came to take their order. Hazel closed her menu and told Urbino to order for her.

"I'm sure everything is delicious here. Just order some of your favorite things."

After Urbino ordered, he thought that some small talk was in order and told her how the director Salerno had used the garden of the Montin in one of his films. Although she looked at him attentively and asked an occasional question, Urbino could tell that her mind was elsewhere. After Lino brought a bottle of Bardolino and some mineral water, Urbino expected her to mention Gibbon but now she seemed to want to talk about the paintings near their table.

Urbino tried to be patient and reminded himself that he had been the one to ask her to dinner. On the walk to Porfirio's to pick her up, he had run through their conversation of the evening before and realized that she had ended by telling him very little about herself and Gibbon. Not much more than that they had planned to marry and then decided not to—although her implication had been that the breaking off of the engagement had been his idea.

After Lino brought the antipasto, Urbino surprised himself by asking, without any preliminary, how she had met Val Gibbon.

Rather than being ruffled by the abruptness of his question, Hazel seemed relieved. She took a sip of her Bardolino before answering, beginning in a neutral way, without much inflection.

"He appeared in my life as if out of nowhere. I was looking for someone to take photographs of Mother and Father's art collection after Father died, and I had hardly made an attempt to find someone, when there he was. He never told me how he knew. He said it would be one of our romantic little mysteries. All I cared about was that he had shown up in my life." She had a faraway look in her eyes, then focused them on Urbino as she added, gradually becoming more animated, "Val was the first person I ever fell in love with. Before I met him, I thought I was in love with someone else, but after being around Val I knew I wasn't. I haven't mentioned this other man to the Commissario. He would just want to know who he was and then make his life miserable. He's an innocent in all of this, believe me—the quintessential innocent!—and he's nowhere near Venice. There's no point in dragging him into everything. I broke things off with him as soon as I realized how I felt about Val. Val was seeing someone at the time, too, but it was nothing serious. Not like us, he said. Oh, Urbino, I want Val's murderer found as soon as possible—found and punished! And I want to help in whatever way I can! He has no living relatives. None! At least I have an aunt and an uncle and cousins, but poor Val has been all on his own for the last twenty years, even before he went into university. There's no one to care about his being dead—murdered—except me!"

Without any warning Hazel burst into tears and took a handkerchief from her purse. She composed herself before going on with what was meant to be a brave little smile.

"The Mother Superior and Porfirio told me about your reputation for getting answers and knowing if they're the right ones. I can tell you go about it in a much more gentle way than Commissario Gemelli."

"How did your visit to the Questura go?"

"It was like cat and mouse. I had to account for every minute between Porfirio's party and when they found Val. I told him that just because I didn't have a verifiable alibi didn't make me guilty. From what I understand it's frequently the people with the alibis who are the criminals."

"You weren't at Porfirio's for the whole evening?"

"I wish I could say I was, but I went out about nine, after everyone had left, and walked around for a few hours. I got lost a few times but that only made my walk more enjoyable. To think that at the same time Val was being stabbed to death!"

Lino brought over two plates of yellow and green angel-hair pasta with a cream sauce and mushrooms.

"Commissario Gemelli seemed disturbed that I didn't have anything bad to say about Val," she went on after Lino had left. "He said that usually a woman disappointed in marriage didn't have good things to say about her former fiancé. I pointed out that we had been having our disagreements but that it wasn't definite that we wouldn't be married."

About to gather her pasta with her fork and spoon, she gave Urbino a quick glance, as if gauging his reaction to what she had been saying. She seemed to be waiting for him to ask her another question. When he didn't, she abandoned Val Gibbon as a topic and started to ask Urbino about himself—how he liked living in Venice, what his life had been like back in New Orleans, whether he had any brothers or sisters.

When he told her he was an only child, she said, "So am I! People usually feel sorry for me but it's never been a problem—that is, not until Mother and Father died and I was all alone. Father had a heart attack and—and Mother took her own life a year later."

"I'm sorry."

She put down her fork and spoon.

"Have you ever been married?"

"I'm divorced and"—he anticipated her—"I don't have any children."

"Is your ex-wife Italian?"

"No, American, from New Orleans."

There had obviously been a limit to what Porfirio had been able to tell Hazel about him. Hazel stared at him for a few moments as Lino took away their dishes. When he had gone, she asked, "Do you ever see her?"

"The last time was more than ten years ago, before I moved here."

She waited for him to go on but, taking a sip of wine, he said no more. Hazel rested her chin on her hand and looked at him with a bemused smile.

"You're not comfortable talking about yourself, are you? That's all right. I'm sorry for being so inquisitive."

"It's only natural that you would want to know something about me when you've been telling me such personal things about yourself."

"To even things up? But there's one big difference between us, isn't there? I'm the one with the dead fiancé to account for, aren't I?" She said this in a light way, but her eyes were full of pain. "I promise I won't ask any more personal questions. It's Val I should be talking about anyway, isn't it?"

They finished their pasta in an awkward silence. Lino brought over the fish dish.

"Absolutely delicious," Hazel said but despite her enthusiasm she put down her fork. "I was telling Commissario Gemelli the truth, you know, when I said that it wasn't definite Val and I wouldn't be married. I came down to Venice last week to see if we could work things out. It was nothing like infidelity or his being in love with someone else. It was something quite different, yet it was very important to us both. My parents were well off. My mother was a Baskew of Baskew and Baskew Milliners and my father owned several factories."

Was Hazel going to tell him that Val Gibbon had been so good as to have qualms about marrying into wealth? Somehow he doubted it.

"We have to be very careful of the promises we make to the people we love. They can take on an unbelievable force once the people are gone. I promised my father that when I married I would have my fiancé sign a prenuptial agreement. He was worried that I might attract fortune hunters. I saw no reason not to promise. Money has always been the last thing I've thought about."

What she was saying was leading into such a delicate area that Urbino thought it best not to say anything, but to wait for her to tell him what she wanted to tell him in exactly her own way. Now that she had reached this point she seemed to want to get through it as quickly as possible.

"Val and I planned to be married this summer. I told him about the promise I had made my father, told him that I felt I couldn't break it. We had a fight. He said that he had no interest in my money, but that asking him to sign meant that I didn't trust him, that I didn't believe he loved me. I was so confused. Val in no way acted like someone who was after my money. I've developed a sixth sense about it. His pride was hurt, you see. He even had tears in his eyes." She blinked back tears of her own as she stared at Urbino. "It wasn't the same between us after that. Nothing I said seemed to change anything. Sometimes I thought all he wanted me to say was that I wouldn't ask him to sign and then he would tell me that he would, that he just wanted me to trust him. But I just couldn't, even if there was a good chance he would end up signing the agreement on his own. It would have been the same as not honoring my promise at all, don't you see?"

Urbino did see but he was surprised. This kind of fidelity to a promise was from a more scrupulous generation, one that had believed in the value of renunciatory gestures, that hadn't been so concerned with personal gratification. It didn't seem to suit Hazel Reeve.

"I know what you're thinking," she said, and then went on to show how little she did. "You're thinking that Val was a cad, that he had been after my money all along, but you're wrong. He always had plenty of money of his own. He didn't need mine. He wouldn't let me pay for anything. Things would have worked out for us. He was a good man but he was hurt. I could have made him see things differently."

What powers of persuasion did she think she had? She seemed confident of them. Or was she being too optimistic, misjudging both her own powers and Val Gibbon's good nature?

For the next few minutes she gave her attention to the fish but seemed even less interested in it than before. Urbino thought it might be a good idea to leave her alone and excused himself to go to the rest room. It was occupied so he slipped into the garden for a few minutes, turning his jacket collar up against the chill.

Taking a turn under the grape arbor, bare of leaves at this time of year, Urbino mulled over what Hazel had told him so far this evening. It certainly added a great deal to the little she had told him last night at the Palazzo Uccello. He wondered if she would have kept her promise to her father. Would she have had a greater fidelity to him or to the man she loved? Either way, a betrayal was involved. He didn't envy Hazel her dilemma, but it was a dilemma she had been delivered from by Gibbon's death. Had she faced the same problem with the man before Gibbon—the "quintessential innocent," as she had called him? She seemed to be particularly concerned to protect him.

Hazel appeared to be in the grip of a great emotion but it might just as plausibly be fear as grief. But was it fear for herself or someone else?

When Urbino got back to the table, Hazel wasn't there. He thought she had gone to the rest room herself until the *padrona* told him that the young lady had gone outside, that she had said she was feeling overheated. Urbino paid his check, got his cape, and was opening the door out to the quay when he heard his name called. It was the Contessa. She was in the little room with the fireplace, sitting, as she always liked to, with a view of the door.

He went over to her table and said good evening to a tired-looking Mrs. Pillow and her stepson, who seemed to be in high spirits. The Contessa gave him one of her radiant smiles.

"I see you're on your way out already. We're barely settled in our seats." She looked pointedly behind him. "Were you dining alone? You should have joined us."

"Not alone, no, but my companion isn't feeling well. She's getting some air outside. You'll have to excuse me."

"But of course, *caro*. Perhaps we can meet her when she's feeling better."

Urbino went out to join Hazel.

14 HAZEL assured him that she was fine, that she had suddenly felt hot and needed some air, just as she had told the *padrona*. It was too dark to see how well—or ill—she looked but it was obvious from the slight crack in her voice and the way she kept touching the hair at her forehead that she didn't feel well. He gave her his arm and they walked toward the Ca' Rezzonico boat landing, retracing their earlier steps. Within a few moments they had left the isolation of the quay and were among groups of laughing revelers.

Hazel seemed disinclined to talk. He mentioned the Montin but she only nodded absently. At one point she shivered and he was tempted to put his arm around her but there was something about her manner—something, it seemed, apart from her not feeling well—that put him off. He felt that she was behaving coolly and he assumed it was because of what she had told him. She was probably already regretting it. Maybe she had discovered that it was much easier to tell these things to Commissario Gemelli.

For his part, Urbino felt a little upset with her. He hadn't sought her out last night and she *had* said that she wanted to be of as much help as she could. She should have known that this would entail revealing some things that might be painful and embarrassing to her.

By the time they reached the Campo San Barnaba, however, Urbino had softened. The poor woman had suffered through a great deal during the past two days. He was little more than a stranger. It was only understandable that she might be regretting having told him what she had. With Gemelli she had had no choice. Urbino might be striking her as a Nosey Parker.

And she had seemed to be a little upset with him when he had been reserved about the details of his own personal life.

The silence between them was becoming more uncomfortable. Most of the people around them were in high spirits. One of them, wearing a black half mask and floppy jester's hat with a bell, threw confetti over them. Hazel brushed the confetti from the top of her head.

"That's where Katharine Hepburn fell into the canal in *Summertime*." He pointed to the other side of the busy *campo*. "And that shuttered shop to the right is where she met Rossano Brazzi."

"I never saw the movie."

She stopped. As she looked across the *campo*, he thought she wanted him to explain the movie.

"It's about this middle-aged American schoolteacher who comes to Venice one summer and—"

"I know the story. I just never saw the movie." Her face caught the light from the lamp overhead, giving it a washed-out appearance. Its impassive cast contributed to the masklike effect. She touched his sleeve. "This is all very nice, Urbino, but I'd like to go back to Porfirio's by myself. I have a lot of things on my mind. A long walk might help. No, don't insist and don't be upset. I wouldn't be a good companion for what would remain of our evening."

She made an attempt at a smile but it only succeeded in giving a grotesque expression to her face. "I'd either retreat completely into silence or snap out at you. Thank you, Urbino. It was enjoyable."

She turned around to go back under the *sottoportego*.

"It would be better if you went the other way."

If she heard him, she didn't respond. He watched her until she went up the steps of the bridge beyond the *sottoportego*, the lights striking golden highlights from her bent head. Along with most of the shouting, singing people around her, she was headed away from the Cannaregio toward the chaos of the Piazza San Marco.

15 "I accept your apologies," the Contessa said without any preliminary the next morning when he called her. "Not yours exactly, *caro*—but your dinner companion's last night. Don't try to spare me. I'm beyond the age of illusion. How could she want to meet me, especially after what you've told her about me—or *failed* to tell her! I noticed this little thing hurrying out as fast as she could. I thought to myself that a nervous wren like her—whoever she was—seemed to be impatient to fly to her fate in the Piazza."

"I'm not exactly sure where she went after dinner."

"You're not? I guess she did fly away then. I hope you had a pleasant evening."

"What about you and Mrs. Pillow and her stepson? She looked a bit haggard. Was anything the matter?"

"A poor night's sleep, *caro*. After a certain age it adds a decade to your looks. It's unfortunate they're staying at the Splendide-Suisse. It's in the middle of everything. Berenice heard people shouting all night in the *calle*. While I was waiting for her in the foyer, I thought I would go mad. Such confusion! I know it's *Carnevale*, but the desk should have more control. I've been thinking of asking them to stay here but I'm not sure how she'll take it. She's always been independent," she said as if she had stayed in contact over the decades with the Berenice Reilly of her adolescence. "We enjoyed ourselves last night. I'm afraid I did all the talking. Tonio kept asking me questions about Berenice."

"I thought you and Berenice had a pact not to say anything about the past."

"Not to say anything *embarrassing*. My memories were all flattering. She wasn't upset at all, and Tonio enjoyed hearing about those days. I'm meeting her today at Florian's at four-thirty. Why don't you join us? It will probably be the last time I'll go near the Piazza until after Ash Wednesday."

"I'll come a little earlier and tell you what I've learned since we discussed the Casa Crispina guests the other night on the phone."

16 URBINO got to the Casa Crispina just as Xenia Campi was about to leave for the Piazza. She was standing by the reception desk in her long dark coat and knit cap. Her face seemed larger and rounder than usual, almost swollen, but her eyes, without their usual heavy makeup this morning, were disconcertingly smaller.

"It's about the aura I saw around Signor Gibbon, isn't it?" she said with a self-satisfied smile. She loosened her heavy woolen scarf, preparing herself to go into more detail. When Urbino didn't immediately respond, she quickly added, "It's about my alibi." She was clearly determined to display her prescience one way or another.

"I do want to ask you about the evening of Gibbon's death, Signora Campi."

"Aha!" Her sound of triumph rang with all the conviction of her belief in her powers.

"You said you sat in the lounge that evening."

"Yes, reading my Madame Blavatsky in the chair over in the corner—the one with the ottoman." The chair was to the left of the reception desk and would have given her a good view of the front door and the staircase going up to the second-floor guest rooms. "I was tired and went to bed about a quarter to ten. I was in the Piazza all day. Gibbon was running around there, taking photographs. He even took some of me until I stopped him."

"When did you get here?"

"About eight-fifteen, right after dinner. I stopped in my room first for my shawl."

"Was anyone else here while you were?"

"Only Sister Agata, but she was asleep most of the time. The Polish man staggered out fifteen minutes after I got here. Maybe, being a Pole, he wanted some cold air but he obviously should have been in his bed under blankets. I wasn't surprised when the boat came for him later. It was about nine-fifteen when Gibbon left. I've worked it out in my mind because I

know it's important. The American staying with his mother
and sister left ten minutes later. He practically bumped into
the Polish man, who was coming back in. I don't think either
one of them noticed me."

"Was there anything about Gibbon that was unusual?"

"Not that I could see, except that he wasn't dressed warmly.
He had his camera with him. I guess he was going back to the
Piazza."

"Did you leave the lounge at any point?"

"Only for five minutes right after the American man left. I
went to my room for a glass of anisette to take the chill off. I
saw the American girl coming out of her mother's room and
asked her if she wanted some anisette, too. She wasn't very
friendly and seemed to be in a hurry. I might as well have just
stayed in my room after I had the anisette. It made me sleepy
and I didn't last much longer out here after I got back. When
I went to bed, Sister Agata was snoring away as she always
does. I don't know why they put the poor woman on the night
shift. We could all be robbed blind—or worse."

"After you went to your room, did you hear anything out
of the ordinary?"

"Not a thing." She rearranged her scarf more tightly around
her throat and started to pull on her gloves. "My room is away
from most of the noise. Thank God those young people are at
the far end of the hall."

Once again Urbino asked her if she knew any young women
other than Dora Spaak whom Gibbon had been attentive to, but
she shook her head vigorously, then gave a knowing smile.

"Did you remember to look deep into the American girl's
eyes for the ghost of death, Signor Macintyre?" Xenia Campi
looked deep into Urbino's own eyes with her small ones. When
he didn't answer, she laughed. "I can tell that you did! I hope
she didn't think you were interested in her. She's starving for
attention. Visits to her mother's room aren't enough for her
when she wants to be in the Piazza like the other fools."

This seemed to awaken an unpleasant train of thoughts. A
sad expression crossed her large face.

"A child is always enough for a good mother though," she
said, her voice seeming to come from far away. "More than
enough."

Xenia Campi then said a hurried good-bye and went out into
the *campo* with her flyers.

A few minutes later Mother Mariangela discouraged Urbino from speaking with any of the sisters, assuring him that they had been in their rooms since seven on the night of the murder and had heard nothing strange, but she agreed to summon Sister Agata to her study.

With embarrassment the old nun admitted that she had dozed on the evening of Signor Gibbon's murder and hadn't noticed anyone coming and going. All she remembered was that Signora Campi came to the lounge after the guests' dinner. Mother Mariangela said a few soothing words to Sister Agata and dismissed her.

Urbino left the Casa Crispina and walked briskly toward the other side of the Grand Canal to clear his mind.

Other than the sisters, the only ones in the Casa Crispina after nine-fifteen when Gibbon had left were Xenia Campi, Lubonski, Stella Maris Spaak, and her daughter, Dora. But someone might have slipped out during the time Xenia Campi had gone to her room for some anisette, and even though Xenia Campi said that she had gone to bed, she herself could have left the Casa Crispina. Sister Agata wouldn't have noticed a thing.

17 AFTER Urbino left the Casa Crispina, he went on a long, meandering walk that eventually took him to the other side of the Grand Canal to the broad embankment of the Zattere. He watched the busy water traffic in the Giudecca Canal, dominated by a sleek French liner and a Yugoslavian tanker, as he had some *tramezzini* and wine in a café and went over what Xenia Campi had just told him. The times she gave for Nicholas Spaak's and Gibbon's departures from the Casa Crispina the evening of the murder coincided with what Spaak and his sister had told him. Spaak hadn't returned, he said, until midnight, and Gibbon, of course, had never returned. As for Josef, he had been away for an hour from eight-thirty to nine-thirty. Where had he gone? Could it possibly have had anything to do with Gibbon's death later in the Calle Santa

Scolastica? And could Josef have left the Casa Crispina for a second time that night? Urbino had assumed, perhaps wrongly, that Josef had phoned him from the pensione.

After leaving the Zattere, Urbino walked for a while longer but could formulate nothing but more questions, many of which were in direct conflict with each other.

More confused than anything else, he approached the *traghetto* stop at the end of the Calle Corner. Because only three bridges crossed the Grand Canal, *traghetti,* or ferries, had been established at various strategic points. They provided not only a convenient way to make the crossing but a cheap, if short, gondola ride, although it was mainly Venetians who used them, almost always standing up in no-nonsense fashion for the trip.

The gondola would take him from the San Polo quarter across to the Cannaregio. From there it would be a quick walk to Porfirio's. He wanted to see Hazel. Perhaps they could have a drink at a bar somewhere.

Three women were waiting. One of them was Berenice Pillow, burdened, as the Contessa had said she had been at Florian's a few days ago, with her purse, a shopping bag, and a delicate wooden lap desk in an Oriental design. She was looking more rested this morning than she had last night.

"Mr. Macintyre, what a pleasant surprise. You've come at exactly the right time, as Barbara says you do! I was just at the Ca' Pesaro and want to get to the other side. The young woman selling postcards said this would be the quickest way but now I'm not so sure. I was just thinking I should take the vaporetto instead."

"Not at all, Mrs. Pillow. This is the way the *veneziani* do it."

He indicated the two women with their mesh shopping bags waiting along with them.

"I was just wishing that Tony was with me but he went to Vicenza for the Palladian architecture."

She became distracted as the gondola came up to the landing and the four passengers got off. She seemed nervous and held her objects close to her. Urbino offered to take something but she shook her head. He stepped into the gondola and helped her after him, paying both their fares.

"Don't worry, Mrs. Pillow. Just stand as still as possible. Maybe it would be better to look straight ahead."

As the gondola moved into the Grand Canal, allowing a vaporetto to pass on its way to the San Stae landing, Berenice Pillow gave him a nervous smile. The two other women were busy chatting about food prices. Suddenly the gondolier burst into "La biondina in gondoleta," a favorite song among the men of his profession.

"I thought all they sang was 'Santa Lucia' and 'O Sole Mio,' " Mrs. Pillow said with a little laugh. She looked up at Urbino for his reaction, and this proved her undoing. A startled look came into her eyes as she started to move, then flail her arms. Urbino reached out to grab her arm. The two women stopped their conversation and looked with a measure of scorn at the *forestiera* who was threatening to capsize them all. The gondolier compensated with his oar for the unexpected movements but this didn't help Berenice Pillow. Her purse and lap desk fell into the water. The shopping bag landed at her feet.

"Sit down," Urbino told her as he took her elbow and helped her onto one of the flat wooden seats.

"My purse!" Mrs. Pillow shouted. "It has everything."

The gondolier stopped the movement of the boat. The purse and the lap desk were floating about five feet away, but they wouldn't be for long. Urbino asked the gondolier to try to move closer to them. The two Venetian women were clicking their tongues and shaking their heads. With the gondolier's skillful maneuvering, Urbino was able to reach the strap of the purse but at first it slipped through his fingers. He could finally grab it and pull it back into the gondola. The gondolier used his oar to bring the lap desk closer. Urbino tried the best he could to reach it but it was moving beyond rescue, pushed farther by the wake of a motorboat.

A vaporetto was coming down the Grand Canal and approaching the Ca' d'Oro landing. The little lap desk disappeared in the froth of its prow.

Mrs. Pillow hugged the purse against her.

"Don't worry about it, Mr. Macintyre. Thank God you got the purse. I don't want you falling in yourself. Everything must be ruined anyway," she said philosophically. "I've got what I want. Thank you."

She looked pale. When they were approaching the landing, she had recovered somewhat and was talking with the two women in perfect Italian, telling them that she was an American but had been married to an Italian, a Neapolitan.

"*Un napolitano*," one of the women said, rolling her eyes.

Hearing this, the gondolier started in with "Santa Lucia." They arrived at the landing without further incident. Urbino walked with Berenice Pillow as far as the Strada Nova where she turned toward the Ca' d'Oro. She thanked him again. He told her he would be joining her later at Florian's.

18 "I must admit I feel in a peculiar position," Porfirio said half an hour later in his clipped British English. He was wearing a Missoni cardigan in beige, rust, and silver. "You come to my house calling for a young lady. Yes, a most peculiar position. I don't think I have the temperament for either a benign father figure handing over his fresh young daughter to an importunate suitor or—God forbid!—a Pandarus. Unfortunately, the charming Miss Reeve is not in. She's been out since early morning, it seems. Why don't you join me for a drink. She might come in at any minute. I'm sure she would be distressed if she just missed seeing you."

As Urbino followed the photographer from the foyer into the living room, he was assaulted by all the chrome and glass and tubing. The effect was much sharper and stronger this early afternoon with the bright Venetian light pouring in than it had been three nights ago.

Urbino couldn't help feeling that someone who lived with so much brightness and open space and lines was trying to give the impression he had nothing to hide.

As if to show how little he did have to hide, the photographer said, "I hear that you're trying to get to the bottom of this murder."

He poured Urbino a glass of red wine. On the long shining coffee table was a folio-sized volume with a photograph of the throne in San Pietro di Castello, said to have been used by Saint Peter at Antioch. In tasteful letters was spelled out LE RELIQUIE DI VENEZIA DI PORFIRIO.

"Mother Mariangela asked if I might try to smooth things over at the convent."

"It certainly provides you with a convenient excuse, this request of Mother Mariangela. Oh, don't be offended. I only meant that a man in your profession—that of a biographer, I mean—doesn't need too much encouragement to satisfy his curiosity about people. Violent death certainly gives an extra interest."

"Couldn't the same be said of people in your own profession?"

"You forget I'm not a photojournalist, or even a portrait photographer. As you know, I try to have as few people in my photographs as possible."

"What kind of photographer was Val Gibbon?"

Porfirio stirred uneasily in his tubular chair.

"I haven't seen that much of his work, but what I have seen confirms my feeling about most photographers, especially the ones who swarm over Venice at this time of the year—or at any time, for that matter. They have no real love for anything. They're exploiters."

Urbino involuntarily looked down at the book on the relics of Venice. Porfirio caught his glance.

"And what they also lack is concentration. You can't be anything but a passable photographer without it. Choose one subject and stay with it. That's what most of the great photographers have done."

"Did you have a personal opinion of him?"

"I barely knew the man, although what I knew of his work told me as much about him as a day of intense conversation. There's something to be said for types, and maybe even the Renaissance humors. I would say that Gibbon was of the sanguine temperament, ever hopeful, ever optimistic about a relatively small talent."

Had he explained it in this way to Hazel? Was this what she had meant when she had told Urbino that Porfirio hadn't liked Gibbon professionally or personally?

"It's a bit ironic that Hazel Reeve is a link between the two of you," said Urbino.

"To be honest with you, I didn't have the slightest idea that she knew Gibbon any better than I did. I'm not upset, but it does seem as if it might have come up at some point."

"Maybe she assumed you knew."

"In that case she assumed wrong. No, I don't think that's it at all. She told me about him only after he was murdered. How could she keep it a secret after that?"

Urbino didn't know how much Hazel had told Porfirio or how much she wanted him to know about her relationship with Gibbon. Hadn't she said Porfirio would be the last person she would confide in about him?

Porfirio had an insinuating smile on his face. He seemed happy to be putting his houseguest in a somewhat bad light. It might be simply jealousy—but jealousy about what? About Hazel's interest in someone he considered artistically inferior to himself? About Gibbon's work itself? Urbino suspected that Porfirio didn't have quite as low an opinion of the English photographer's work as he said he did.

Urbino stayed only a few minutes longer. Porfirio said that he would tell Hazel he had stopped by to see her. He was sure she would be disappointed to have missed him.

19 THE Piazza had a fey, elfin spirit this afternoon, the kind that came in fairy tales from the passing of a wand. Revelers walked under the arcades, sat on the steps, leaned against the pillars, and thronged the square. Laughter and shouts were a counterpoint to the Vivaldi playing over the speakers. Brightly costumed men and women danced the *moresca* on the large stage while on a miniature one a Punch and Judy show was entertaining a group of children. A Queen of Hearts and an Ace of Spades were doing a *pas de deux* of love and death near one of the souvenir wagons.

In front of the Basilica a family of tumblers in white suits with large white buttons and ruffled collars were performing their act and a man in a tall turban was cavorting agilely on stilts. Three young women walked slowly on huge wooden platform heels—the *zoccoli* of Renaissance Venice. They wore long, richly embroidered gowns of green and gold. On their heads were straw hats with the crowns removed so that they could pull their long, blond hair out to be bleached by the sun as Venetian women used to do in former days.

Involuntarily, Urbino's eyes looked up at the space between the Campanile and the Basilica, half expecting to see a wire on which an acrobat was balancing. It would have fit perfectly into the dreamlike scene. Urbino felt as if he had stepped into the pages of a children's book.

Amid all this carefree activity, solitary figures in fanciful and grotesque costumes stood immobile as if part of the city's architecture. They leaned against the columns, perched on the base of the Campanile, and secluded themselves in niches and narrow openings where they could easily be mistaken for pieces of colorful sculpture.

As Urbino walked past one of these silent figures dressed in orange robes, a shaggy silver wig, and a huge five-pointed star glistening with silver sequins, Giovanni Firpo emerged from a lively cluster of people, carrying his mask in one hand, his mirrored fan in the other. He moved almost majestically in his blue and green robe and baubled headdress, his fan fluttering in the chill wind that blew across the domes of the Basilica. In order to take part in *Carnevale* the way he wanted to, Firpo had a reduced schedule at the hospital. He made up for it by working extra shifts during August when everyone else was running off to the seashore and countryside.

Firpo came over, revealing pointed azure boots beneath the embroidered hem of his gown. His costume gave his paunchy body svelter lines. So far his ambition to get on a calendar or a postcard hadn't been realized but neither had his enthusiasm been dampened. Each year he tried to outdo himself, expecting each year to be the one when he would finally achieve his goal. Urbino hoped that he would eventually get what he wanted. There was something to be said for such a simple dream.

"Have you been having any success?" Urbino asked him.

"Marvelous! Everybody's been taking my picture today."

"Did you know the English photographer who was murdered in the Calle Santa Scolastica Wednesday night?"

"I didn't know him, no, but I knew who he was."

"Did he take any pictures of you?"

The baubles on Firpo's headdress tinkled as he shook his head.

"No, unfortunately."

Firpo seemed about to add something but his attention was caught by a man in a heavy black turtleneck aiming his camera at two women in pink gowns, white stoles, pearls, and large sunglasses with pink feathers sprouting from them.

"Were you anywhere near the Calle Santa Scolastica on Wednesday night?"

"Why would I go there? This is where most of the action is." He looked over at the photographer, who was finishing with the two women in pink. "I didn't see the English photographer that night, if that's what you want to know."

"What about Xenia Campi?"

"I'm sure I would have known if *she* was around!"

Urbino had to agree. If Xenia Campi had been there in her usual capacity that night, she certainly would have made her presence known, but suppose she hadn't wanted to be seen? He had only her word that she hadn't left the Casa Crispina after Gibbon and Nicholas Spaak had left and Josef had come in.

"Did you ever see the English photographer paying attention to any young women in particular?"

"In particular? No." Firpo was getting impatient to be off. The photographer in the turtleneck was now exchanging names and addresses with the two women. "He talked to a lot of the girls."

Firpo excused himself and hurried away, holding his head-dress as it swayed perilously in his effort to get the photographer's attention before it was caught by someone else. But the photographer passed Firpo by and started taking pictures of a figure dressed as an *Inamorata* from the commedia dell'arte, voluptuously robed in gold, scarlet, and silver. Firpo stood watching the figure pose at the foot of the ramp, then started to walk up the ramp sedately, off again in search of the photographer who might make him an icon on next year's calendars or collection of *Carnevale* postcards.

20 ON the edge of the crowd, looking as sullen as he had yesterday, was Giuseppe, wearing his cowboy hat and holster. He recognized Urbino, too, and seemed to want to slip away but Urbino went over to him before he could.

"Giuseppe, how are you? Where are your cousin and Fabio?"

"Somewhere."

His eyes shifted over the crowd in the Piazza, not meeting Urbino's gaze.

"I was wondering if you saw Xenia Campi anywhere around here on Wednesday night." He paused. "It was the night the English photographer was murdered."

"She could have been."

"But did you see her?"

Giuseppe took a few moments to think. He still didn't look at Urbino.

"People wear masks and costumes. Maybe she did. She could have been here but I might not have known it was her." He finally looked at Urbino. "Are you trying to get me in trouble? If she thinks I told you she was here, she'll have it in for me. No!" he said. "I didn't see that *strega*, that witch! None of us did."

"Leo said something about a girl she was trying to get you interested in. Who is she?"

"I don't remember her name. She was the girlfriend of a dead boy. She's the girl who paints faces sometimes, the one who told Leo who you were. She's too old for me, and even if she wasn't I don't want anything to do with someone that crazy woman likes. Good-bye!"

He disappeared into the crowd.

21 THE waiter brought over Urbino's Campari soda. A teapot and a plate of little cakes were already on the table. Despite the press of people waiting in the foyer, Urbino had found the Contessa comfortably ensconced at her usual table by the window in the Chinese salon.

"Tell me everything," she said. "And when you're finished I might have something of interest for you, too."

As he filled the Contessa in on what he had learned since yesterday morning from the Neapolitan boys, Hazel Reeve, and Xenia Campi, he was grateful for the opportunity to review it all himself.

"So what do we know about Gibbon?" the Contessa said when he had finished. "He was a good-looking man, he was talented, he flirted with women, he wanted to marry Hazel Reeve but didn't want to sign a prenuptial agreement, and he was found stabbed to death in a rather *louche* area. He also rubbed people the wrong way. Josef, Porfirio, Xenia Campi, and Nicholas Spaak didn't like him. Hazel says she loved him but can we be so sure of that? She might have loved him at one time but love can turn to hate. So what do you think, Urbino? Did the girl love him or hate him?"

The Contessa smiled at him in a playful way that he found somewhat inappropriate. When he didn't answer, she said, "Or is that too much like the Lady or the Tiger?—or rather, the Devil and the Deep Blue Sea?" She paused and nodded knowingly. "She's having her little success, isn't she, Hazel Reeve? Or perhaps I should call it a big success."

"What do you mean?"

"She's succeeded in confusing you."

"It's you who are trying to confuse me, Barbara!"

"I'm trying to help clarify things, *caro*. Hasn't it occurred to you why she cares what you think, what you know?"

"Of course it has."

"Well, then, I hope that you're just a little bit suspicious that she's giving you all these confidences. Look at the way she said that she hadn't told the Commissario about her old boyfriend but was telling you. That itself should make you suspicious. You're proving yourself to be just like a man, and I had such great hopes for you! Don't be too eager to assume that what Xenia Campi or Nicholas Spaak has to tell you about Gibbon is more to the point than the positive things you've heard from the others."

"I wasn't aware that you had liked Gibbon so much."

"I didn't particularly care for him or didn't care for the little I knew about him. That's just what I mean. I knew so little."

"Someone else might say that to dislike someone after only limited contact means that there's a good, visceral reason."

"The viscera can lead you astray, as anyone who's been blindly in love can testify. No, Urbino, you have to put your faith in a different part of the anatomy"—she tapped a well-manicured finger against her temple—"and you have to separate the facts from the opinions. You're in search of truth, after all! That's what your wonderful little lives are all about, aren't they? But I certainly don't mean to lecture you, *caro*—all the more so because I know you've saturated yourself in Proust of late, and if I remember correctly, he has almost as much to say about the elusiveness of *la vérité* as he does about *l'amour* itself."

Urbino nodded absently, feeling a little dispirited. He looked around the crowded Chinese salon, filled with the aromas of coffee and of the mint, cocoa, and cherry in the small Rosolio glasses.

Most of the other patrons were wearing costumes. Two tables were occupied by men and women in black capes, high-heeled shoes, white stockings, beribboned black-velvet pants and lace-frothed white shirts. The women carried black masks on long sticks and the men had black *bautta* demi-masks. In the eighteenth-century surroundings of Florian's, Urbino felt as if he were in a Pietro Longhi painting. Casanova or Goldoni would have felt right at home.

The Contessa was peering with particular attention into the crowd beyond the windows, apparently in search of her friend. An elderly man started to strum his mandolin in front of the window, as if he were serenading her. When he finished the Contessa smiled at him and he took off his tricorn hat and bowed.

Urbino hadn't yet told her about the incident on the *traghetto*. Before he did, he wanted to pursue something she had said a few minutes ago.

"You said you had something interesting to tell me."

"A piece of factual information. Gibbon was found with money on him, all in hundred-pound notes. Thirty of them."

Urbino was too surprised to do anything at first but stare at her. Then he asked her how she knew.

"Corrado Scarpa." She named a friend of her husband attached to the Questura. "You know what he thinks of Gemelli. They haven't got along since they were both in Verona. I hardly had to ask him for any information. I met him at the hospital when I went to see Josef—who isn't much better, by the way. Corrado was checking some medical records."

"Gemelli would be furious if he knew," said Urbino. "It wasn't in *Il Gazzettino* and it wasn't one of the things he condescended to tell me about. The Questura obviously doesn't want the public to know."

"I have never thought of myself as the 'public,' *caro*."

"It certainly seems to rule out random violence or a mugging gone wrong. But what was Gibbon doing with all that money? Three thousand pounds!"

"Maybe it was the price of his death. People are killed for less than that."

"But the money was still on him. It doesn't make sense. Why murder a man and not take the spoils?"

"The murder might have been interrupted," speculated the Contessa. "It's *Carnevale*. Any number of people might have wandered into the Calle Santa Scolastica—other than the ones who usually do, I mean. Do you think he was going to give the money to someone?"

"Someone might have given it to him that night."

"Or he could have taken it from someone."

"It seems more logical that he was given the money, that he rendezvoused either in the Calle Santa Scolastica or somewhere nearby and then went there. He was a photographer, don't forget, which means he was in a classic position to blackmail someone."

"True, but blackmail isn't the only motive for murdering a photographer—or even the best." A mischievous gleam came into her eye. "Anyone who has ever had a bad photograph taken would understand wanting to do it."

If the Contessa was trying to lighten his mood with her little jokes this afternoon, she wasn't having much success.

"You said a little while ago, Barbara, that I should use something other than my viscera. When you find a murdered photographer with so much money on him, blackmail is probably the first and most logical thing to come to mind. Hazel said he always had plenty of money. Maybe that's why."

"Except why give Gibbon the money and then kill him? Why not kill him before, or take the money back after you've killed him?"

They were contemplating this when the waiter came over and told the Contessa there was a call for her.

While she was gone, Urbino considered various possibilities. Although it made more sense to kill a blackmailer before you turned over any more money, there were other scenarios as well. The money could have been given as a distraction, to put

Gibbon off his guard, to gain some vital time, and then been forgotten in the confusion or because of an interruption. It was even possible to imagine someone who didn't care about the money, but only cared that Gibbon was now dead. Or Gibbon could have been given the money by one person and murdered afterward by someone else.

If Hazel knew about the money found on Gibbon, she would most likely see it as further proof of how little he had been interested in her own. Unless, of course, she had given it to him herself and already knew about it.

"It was Berenice," the Contessa said as she slipped back onto the banquette. "She's not feeling well, poor thing. Probably another bad night at the hotel."

Urbino quickly told her about the incident on the *traghetto*. The waiter brought over a fresh pot of tea and another Campari soda.

"All along you obviously knew she wasn't coming!"

"I had no idea! She was upset at first but she seemed fine by the time I left her."

"Poor Berenice." She laughed. "I know I shouldn't be laughing but her experience on the *traghetto* reminds me of when she fell into the Cam. Were there any good-looking young men around who might have caught her eye? Other than you, I mean? That's what happened on the Cam. All this good-looking boy had to do was take his straw hat off to her and she was lost. She waved, she stood up and called something to him—and she was lost."

"Lost?"

"What do you call it when a person falls into a river from the exuberance of her own emotions? She was passionate about so many things. We used to think it was because she was American. We had a lot of laughs about it." Her face suddenly clouded. "Berenice's appearing out of the blue like this after all these years wasn't the best thing that could have happened to me—not with another birthday coming up. I've been resenting her a little—resenting her for remembering so much, even more for reminding me of so much. I know it's wonderful to have old friends, people you've shared so many things with, who remember how you once were, but it's also unsettling. Sometimes I feel as if I want to forget most of it—or remember it only when I'm all alone. I'm not in search of lost time, not like your Monsieur Proust, by any means! I treasure my past but I like to keep it in a chest I can open from time to time when no one else is there. Quite frankly, if someone else brings up the past I feel so abominably old!''

Urbino was touched by his friend's admission but thought he would use a little humor to distract her as she had tried to do earlier with him.

"I'll have to remember all this and be sure never to mention anything much before last week.''

"There's no need of that, *caro*. The main reason I like you so much is not because of your indisputable charm and delightfully un-American ways, your refined sensibility and intelligence, your love for our serene city—need I go on and on?—but because, quite simply, you are a relatively recent friend. You didn't know me in my first prime—and that's comforting, believe it or not!''

Her smile seemed a pledge to her feelings about him—as long as the two of them, he assumed, didn't reach a point when his memory would be able to go upstream for decades and decades.

"Berenice was probably thinking of the Cam when her things fell into the Canalazzo,'' the Contessa went on. "After it happened, she was always afraid it might happen again. We don't change all that much down through the years although she *has* changed considerably in appearance. She wasn't blessed, poor thing, with good genes and bone structure.''

The Contessa tilted her face toward Urbino on the pretext of looking over his shoulder at the group of eighteenth-century men and women on the other side of the Chinese salon, managing to display her flat planes and sharp angles as a silent commentary on her evaluation of her friend.

"She wants to see us both later,'' she said, turning her attention back to him. "Tonio is coming too. I suggested the Ca' da Capo. Shall we say about eight-thirty, *caro*?''

22 URBINO declined the Contessa's invitation to go back to the Ca' da Capo-Zendrini directly with her, have a light dinner, and wait there for Berenice Pillow and Tonio Vico. After she left, he called the hospital from the upstairs phone and learned that Lubonski was still unable to have visitors but that his condition had improved slightly.

He struck out for the Fondamenta Nuove, each step taking him farther from the turmoil of the Piazza. It was cold but clear. So far there had been relatively good weather for *Carnevale* except for several rainstorms, but an icy *bora* could blow down from the north with little warning.

When he reached the Fondamenta Nuove, he looked out into the lagoon, searching the sky over Murano for some sign of a change for the worse, but it was cloudless, the waters calm. On an impulse he hurried to catch the boat about to leave for San Michele, the island of the dead and the site of the mortuary where Gibbon's body would have been brought and where it probably still was. He frequently went to San Michele to think, far away from any distractions except the grim silent ones of the island.

Ten minutes later as he walked through one of the *campi* of the cemetery, crowded with its tombstones and mausoleums but empty of everyone except himself, an attendant or two, and a few women in black coats visiting the graves, he wondered why Berenice Pillow wanted to see him along with the Contessa. Was she including him because of his rescue of her pocketbook on the *traghetto*?

He left the main part of the cemetery for the walled Orthodox section where Diaghilev, Stravinsky, and many other Russians and Greeks were buried. Diaghilev's grave had one of its mysterious, lone ballet slippers as it always did. Were these slippers left by the same person or by different pilgrims to the famous ballet producer's grave? He had never seen anyone leaving a slipper. It was one of Venice's little mysteries—and one that he really preferred not to solve. It was more romantic without a solution.

After leaving Diaghilev's grave he went to another of his favorites, this one of a Russian woman named Sonia—there was no last name—who had died at twenty-seven. Her grave was dominated by a life-size, lifelike reclining white marble statue of the young woman. Fresh red roses had been placed in the curve of her arm.

Urbino knew he was sentimental when it came to death. The Contessa, who avoided the topic and the cemetery island whenever and however she could, thought she had a better name for it. She called it morbid. But Urbino was comforted by the sight of well-tended graves, of the bereaved making their visits, leaving their flowers and tokens, and avoided thinking of how few of these people there were compared to the thousands of forgotten dead. He had often tried to decide whether he would prefer being one of those who were remembered or one of those who did the remembering, as if the choice were up to him. It was like trying to decide between being the beloved or the lover, except in this instance death hadn't yet made its great separation.

On the boat back to the Fondamenta Nuove, Urbino wondered if Gibbon had returned Hazel Reeve's love. He had no reason to doubt it—no good, substantial reason—but only his own impressions of the man and the negative things he had heard about him. Nor could Urbino accept Hazel's apparent belief that Gibbon had had no interest in her money, even though she had said that he always had plenty of money and even though three thousand pounds had been found on his body.

Precisely because such a large sum of money had been found on Gibbon, Urbino couldn't shake the conviction that the money had been ill-gained in some way. As he had said earlier to the Contessa, photographers were in a perfect position to blackmail someone. Whom might Gibbon have blackmailed? Xenia Campi had said that on the day of his death he had taken pictures of her until she had asked him to stop. But the list of possibilities certainly didn't end with Xenia Campi, who, in any case, would have been hard-pressed to come up with three thousand pounds or its equivalent in lire.

It was quite possible that Gibbon had been in the Calle Santa Scolastica to take incriminating photographs. He might very well have been blackmailing some of the men who frequented the area. Urbino wished he had access to Gibbon's photographs. They were in the hands of the police now. What chance did he have of convincing Gemelli to let him look through them?

As Urbino stepped off the boat, he remembered what the Contessa had asked him at Florian's—whether it was possible that Hazel had not loved Gibbon but hated him. Hadn't Urbino thought that there were interpretations of her emotional state other than grief? The Contessa, as she often was, might be right. He might not be seeing things clearly at all. Impartiality was something he strove for in his biographies. It was absolutely necessary. This didn't mean he didn't have his biases— as Gide had said, they were the very props of civilization— but he tried to be aware of them.

Urbino made an effort to empty his mind of all his confused—and confusing—thoughts as he walked slowly back to the Palazzo Uccello. When he turned down the Salizzada degli Specchieri, he thought about the vendors of mirrors who had given this alley, as well as another one near San Marco, its name. Mirrors were invented in Venice by the glassmakers of Murano, and ones of every shape and size, of every quality and design, could be found throughout the city. Many elderly men and women even had small mirrors, similar to the rear-view mirrors on cars, attached outside their windows so that they could see what was going on in the *calle* or *campo* below. Each of these little mirrors provided its owner with secret views of a city whose back canals, dead ends, covered passageways, concealed gardens, and tortuous, narrow alleys made Venice almost synonymous with secrecy itself.

A few moments later, as Urbino was walking past the baroque, theatrical facade of the Church of the Gesuiti with all its triumphant angels and gesticulating saints, something seemed to be suggesting itself to him. He didn't know what it was yet but he did know that he owed it to having set aside conscious thoughts about Gibbon's murder and musing, instead, about the city he had made his home.

Urbino started to walk faster, anxious now to return to the Palazzo Uccello.

23 WHEN he let himself in, Natalia was standing at the top of the stairs. Lines of concern marked her matronly face.

"Thank God you've come home, Signor Urbino."

"Is something the matter, Natalia?"

"Everything's fine, signor—I mean all your things are fine—but the police—"

She broke off and looked at him helplessly.

"What about the police, Natalia?"

"Commissario Gemelli called about three and again at four. I told him I didn't know where you were or when you would be back. He asked if a woman was here. I don't know what name he said but I told him I was the only woman here. Then about an hour ago two of his men came—"

She was all out of breath and sank down into the chair at the top of the stairs.

"What did they want?"

"They wanted to know if you were here. When I said you weren't, they wanted to come inside. I didn't know what to do but I said that you would be back soon and they should come back later. I hope I didn't do wrong, Signor Urbino. Maybe I should have let them in."

"You did fine, Natalia. This is surely no affair of yours. Don't worry."

He didn't even know what affair it might be of his but if Gemelli had called twice and sent some of his men over within a four-hour period, he was sure to find out soon.

As if on cue the phone rang, but it wasn't Gemelli. It was the Contessa.

"Urbino, what's going on? Commissario Gemelli was here at the Ca' da Capo just a few minutes ago looking for you. I told him you were probably at home—or on your way there. He went to Florian's first. Whatever is this all about?"

"I don't know. Natalia just told me that Gemelli called here several times and sent some of his men over. I'll give him a call as soon as I hang up."

Instead of calling the Questura right away, however, he fixed himself a whiskey and got ready to take a shower. He knew he should get in contact with Gemelli but he needed a few minutes to collect his thoughts. As he was stepping into the shower, the doorbell rang. By the time he had thrown on his robe again and gone out into the hall, Gemelli was hurrying up the staircase ahead of two of his men. His face was set in a determined expression.

Before he said anything he took in Urbino's black robe.

"I think you know why we're here, Macintyre."

"All I know is that you've called several times and sent your men here. The Contessa da Capo-Zendrini just told me that you went to see her."

"So you don't know why were here? Didn't your *domestica* tell you?"

"She said something about a woman but she didn't know who this woman was, she didn't remember the name. I have no idea."

This wasn't completely true but there was no sense in complicating things if he was wrong—or implicating himself if he wasn't. His heart was starting to race in fearful anticipation.

"Since you say you have no idea, I'll tell you," Gemelli said drily. "We're looking for Signorina Reeve."

"Hazel?"

Although this was the name he had expected, it still took him by surprise.

"I believe that's her Christian name, although she's not on a first-name basis with the Questura. This is an official visit, in case you didn't know."

He indicated his men, then gave another glance at Urbino's robe.

"I was going to call in a few minutes," Urbino said lamely. "I wanted to take a shower first to clear my mind."

He should have realized it was the wrong thing to say before he said it, but he felt confused and at a distinct disadvantage standing there half dressed in front of the uniformed Commissario and his men.

"Is she here?"

"Here? Of course not. I haven't seen her since about ten last night."

"It appears, Signor Macintyre, that you were the last person to see her."

For one heart-stopping moment Urbino thought Gemelli was going to add "alive." It showed how confused he was. Hadn't Gemelli just asked if Hazel was with him at the Palazzo Uccello?

"And it also appears that Signorina Hazel Reeve"—he emphasized her first name—"might not have spent the night at Porfirio Buffone's. In fact, he can't even say for sure if she came back after going out with you. We'd like to know how you and Signorina Reeve spent the evening—and perhaps the night."

Urbino asked Gemelli to wait a few minutes while he went to dress.

24 AFTER the Commissario had left, Urbino took his interrupted shower and called the Contessa. She picked up after only one ring.

"That was fast. You must still be home."

"Sitting here with my second whiskey."

"Whiskey! It must be serious. What did Gemelli want?"

"He wanted to know about Hazel Reeve. It seems she's disappeared."

The Contessa's immediate response was silence. Her considered one, after a few moments, was "I told you that woman meant trouble for you."

She hadn't said exactly this but he supposed she had implied it—and obviously she had been thinking it since he had first mentioned Hazel Reeve.

"She's the one who's in trouble, Barbara—one way or the other. I was the last person to see her as far as Gemelli knows. From the time I said good night to her in the Campo San Barnaba last night, she seems to have dropped from sight. Neither Porfirio nor his maid has seen her since yesterday evening when we left together for the Montin. Her bed doesn't seem to have been slept in."

In a rush, knowing that he had to tell her what he hadn't told her earlier at Florian's, he described the strain that had developed between Hazel and him near the end of the evening, how remote and preoccupied she had become, declining to have him walk her back to Porfirio's and striking out alone in the general direction of the Accademia Bridge and the Piazza San Marco.

"The Questura is checking the hospitals and the hotel registers," Urbino continued. "Gemelli has his hands full—what with Hazel's disappearance and Gibbon's murder. To make it worse, he said that London might be sending down two men to help with the investigation into Gibbon's death."

"That's unusual!"

"It is, especially since Gibbon doesn't seem to have any immediate family who might be putting on pressure. I suppose it could be Hazel's doing, although she didn't say anything about it. Her family has some prominence."

He quickly filled the Contessa in on Hazel's family background.

"It would be more than a little embarrassing," Urbino went on, "for these men to come down and learn not only that Gibbon is dead but that another British subject—the woman engaged to marry the murdered man—has disappeared and the police can find no trace of her."

"What do you think happened to her?"

"Maybe she got ill," he said without conviction. "She might have fallen. She could be in the hospital."

"In that case the Questura should know soon." She paused. "You don't think the obvious possibility is the answer, do you?"

Urbino knew this had to be faced. He had been avoiding thinking about it, so etched in his mind was the image of Hazel disappearing into the crowd.

"That whoever killed Gibbon has done something to her," he said.

Little relief came from saying it, from getting it out in the open. He took the Contessa's silence for an acknowledgment of the gravity—and the sad logic—of his fear, but when she spoke he realized he had been mistaken.

"That's not what I meant, Urbino." She said it gently. "You're not seeing things clearly. A man is murdered—a man who refused to sign a prenuptial agreement—and then the woman disappears only a few days later. You can be sure that Commissario Gemelli can see what this might mean."

She paused, giving him the opportunity to complete her thought. To do it, however, would have been to betray not only Hazel but his own strong conviction—or was it only his hope? He waited. The Contessa took in and expelled her breath before going on. When she spoke, she gently couched her suspicion in the conditional.

"She could have been involved in Gibbon's murder and she could have disappeared because of it."

The way she had tentatively expressed her suspicion provided him with an escape as well as suggested yet another possibility.

"She might know something about Gibbon's murder—she might even know who the murderer is. She could have gone away for her own safety."

His satisfaction at having routed the Contessa—having turned her suspicion around in this way—was soon dissipated when his friend added, rephrasing his own earlier fear, "Or whoever killed Gibbon might have decided it was best to make her less of a threat."

The Contessa's euphemism, though quietly spoken, screamed at Urbino across the line. The Contessa seemed right either way. Either Hazel Reeve had run off because of her direct involvement in Gibbon's murder or she had been "made less of a threat" by the real murderer.

25 AFTER his conversation with the Contessa, Urbino could think of nothing but Hazel. He couldn't ignore the fact that she had changed so abruptly during the short time he was away from the table. Had she spent those moments reflecting on some of the things he had said—or perhaps hadn't said? Had it been his poorly concealed disapproval of Val Gibbon that had made her want to punish him by terminating their evening?

Urbino pulled himself back from these speculations when

he realized that there was a high proportion of the egotistical in them. He was presuming that Hazel's disappearance had something to do with him, with his treatment of her. Surely he was assigning himself an importance that he certainly didn't have in her life.

Yet he couldn't help going back over their time at the Montin, trying to find some reason for her changed behavior. It might have nothing to do with her subsequent disappearance but it was something that needed an explanation.

Urbino decided to call Porfirio. Hazel could have come back. Porfirio answered.

"It's Urbino. Commissario Gemelli just left and told me that Hazel didn't come back there last night."

"So it would seem—unless she slept on the floor or made her bed perfectly. What happened between the two of you last night?"

"We had dinner and then she wanted to take a walk by herself before going back to your place."

"And you let her?"

"It wasn't a question of letting her. It was what she wanted to do and there was no reason for her not to."

"You don't think so? The man she loved is murdered and you think it's all right if she just goes off in a crowd?"

"I don't know what you're getting at, Porfirio. I didn't call to have an argument over this. I called to find out if you might have had word of her."

"I would have mentioned it right away. *Albertine Disparue,*" Porfirio insinuated, referring to Proust's novel in which the narrator's beloved, Albertine, disappears and later dies in a fall from a horse. "Or should I say *La Petite Hazel Disparue*? At least we know she has little chance of dying in a fall from a horse—not here in Venice, anyway, unless she climbed to the top of the Colleoni monument. I suggest that the next time you have a young woman in your charge you see that she doesn't elude you."

26 BERENICE Pillow and her stepson had already arrived. When Urbino walked into the Contessa's, *salotto*, the scene seemed to be set up for a repetition of his first meeting with Berenice Pillow two nights ago. The tall, angular American woman was wearing the same belted dress with thin violet and black vertical stripes and the same chains and pendants. Her hair was pulled back in her characteristic bun, except that renegade strands had slipped out and were brushing against the nape of her neck. It gave her a less severe look and for a moment Urbino could see in her the mischievous, romantic young girl of the Contessa's reminiscences.

Berenice Pillow was even standing looking up at the Veronese as she had the first time. Her stepson—this evening, however, dressed in black trousers and a black turtleneck—was once again sitting in the rococo chair next to the sofa of which the Contessa had taken her usual gracious possession.

Here, however, all similarities to that first meeting ended. Berenice Pillow wasn't actually looking at the Veronese but staring blankly at the allegory of love with its buxom Venus flanked by two handsome courtiers. The frown on her face tonight wasn't one of aesthetic disapproval but of worry. Tonio Vico looked uncomfortable and a little afraid.

Urbino's entrance into the *salotto* made an understandable change in the scene. As Berenice Pillow turned in his direction, she exchanged her frown for a smile of welcome in which there seemed to be relief. Tonio Vico stood up, as if to attention, looking less apprehensive now than a little defiant, although the element of unease was still there.

Only the Contessa remained where she was and how she was.

"We couldn't be happier that you've finally come, Urbino," she said. "Fix yourself a drink."

Urbino went over to the liquor cabinet and poured himself a glass of Corvo. He had already had more whiskey tonight than was good for him.

"We've all been waiting for you with more than our usual anticipation," the Contessa said. "Not that you're late, *caro*," she added. "In fact you're right on time"—she glanced at the Louis Quatorze clock on the mantel—"but it's just that Berenice and Tonio were even more punctual."

Urbino walked over to a chair, waiting for Mrs. Pillow to reclaim hers before sitting down. Only Vico remained standing. He seemed to want to pace the room but the Contessa's *salotto* wasn't designed for anything more energetic than spirited conversation. Vico compensated by negotiating the cluttered space between his chair and the liquor cabinet, where he poured himself another whiskey. Then he went over to stand beside his stepmother's chair. Mrs. Pillow reached up to pat his hand.

"Before you came, Berenice said she had something to tell us."

"We both have something to tell you," Berenice Pillow corrected, looking up at her stepson. Having said this, neither of them said a word. With a deep intake of breath, Mrs. Pillow went on to explain. "My stepson knew this man who was murdered a few days ago."

The Contessa's gray eyes widened in astonishment.

"Whatever do you mean, Berenice? Tonio knew Gibbon?"

As soon as Berenice Pillow had spoken, certain things fell into place for Urbino about last night at the Montin. How blind he had been! He now realized what had been suggesting itself to him earlier as he had walked back to the Palazzo Uccello by way of the Salizzada degli Specchieri. His first feeling was satisfaction and relief. His second was fear for Hazel.

"Through Hazel Reeve, wasn't it?" Urbino directed the question not to Mrs. Pillow but to Tonio Vico. The young man exchanged a quick nervous glance with his stepmother.

"You're right, Mr. Macintyre," Vico said. "I knew him through Hazel Reeve. But how do *you* know Hazel?"

Either Vico was an expert at dissimulation or the young man really didn't know.

"She's here in Venice. I've met her."

He didn't think it would be a good idea to mention Hazel Reeve's disappearance. He hoped that the Contessa would realize this as well and say nothing.

Astonishment raced across Mrs. Pillow's pale face at the mention of Hazel Reeve.

"She's in Venice? But why?" She looked at her stepson for an answer but the next moment provided one herself. "She came down from London after the murder."

"She's been here for a week," Urbino explained. "She was at the same restaurant you and your stepson were at last night with Barbara, Mrs. Pillow. Didn't you see her?"

"We most certainly didn't. We didn't have a clear view of the entrance."

"Would someone please have pity on me and tell me what you're all talking about?" the Contessa asked.

Urbino, verbalizing the connections his mind had been quickly making, told her that Tonio was the man Hazel had been seeing before she met Gibbon.

"Yes, I knew him through Hazel," Vico repeated. "Or it would be more exact to say that I knew *of* him. I never met him. But I didn't kill him!"

"Of course you didn't!" his stepmother said.

"But Berenice dear, why didn't you mention that Tonio knew Gibbon? Gibbon was killed more than two days ago. You were here when Sister Teresa came over to tell us."

"I know, Barbara, but you don't understand. I—"

"Let me explain, Mother." Vico had put his glass down and seemed more in control of himself now. "My mother wasn't aware that I knew Gibbon. I didn't even mention his name to her until this afternoon. I didn't want her to know."

"Why?" Urbino asked. "Because you were embarrassed to admit that Hazel Reeve was in love with someone else?"

He was deliberately trying to provoke Vico.

"It wasn't that way at all! Hazel and I would have worked things out. She was just a little confused. Gibbon was a Svengali. Hazel would have eventually realized what he was really like. There was no reason to say anything to my mother. It would only have upset her and—and she might have held it against Hazel. *I* didn't."

Vico picked up his glass and came close to draining it. Mrs. Pillow was shaking her head.

"You should have told me, Tony. I had the feeling there was something strange about Hazel ever since Christmas but I believed you when you said she had been working too hard, and needed time by herself."

"I'm sorry, Mother. All that was true—I just didn't tell you about Gibbon. I didn't know him—except what I gathered from Hazel, and that was enough! She told me all about him on Boxing Day."

"On Boxing Day!" Mrs. Pillow said contemptuously. "She might have told you earlier than that if she was involved with him."

Temper flared behind Mrs. Pillow's words and Urbino could understand why her stepson might have feared that she would hold things against Hazel for having hurt him. It was an understandable reaction for a mother—and that was what Mrs. Pillow had been to the motherless Tonio.

"Please, Mother," Vico said. "It doesn't do any good now. Gibbon's dead and I knew about him. I can't deny that."

He looked at Urbino. What Vico was really saying was that Gibbon had been murdered and he had an excellent motive. Not only that, but Vico was appealing to Urbino for help. That was why they had both come tonight to the Ca' da Capo-Zendrini.

As if to demonstrate the validity of what he had just been thinking, Mrs. Pillow said, "Mr. Macintyre, we don't know what to do. It's not as if Tony has anything to hide, but he hasn't gone to the police yet. He didn't even know about this man's murder until today."

"Today?" It was the Contessa. "But he was murdered on Wednesday night. Today's Saturday!"

"Tony usually doesn't read the papers. And all I had was *The International Herald Tribune*. They didn't cover the story, of course."

"But, Berenice dear, surely you must have mentioned the murder to him. You learned about it here."

"She *did* say something about the murder of some Englishman but she had no idea that it could be someone I knew. Someone else might have run to the papers but I didn't. If she had mentioned Gibbon's name or even that a photographer had been murdered, it would have been different. As it was, I only found out about it when I was looking through the paper for the television schedule."

"What should we do, Mr. Macintyre?" Berenice Pillow asked again, furrows of concern across her forehead.

"It's obvious, Mrs. Pillow. He should go to the Questura at once."

"Isn't that what I said, Tony? You see, Mr. Macintyre, when Tony told me this afternoon that he knew this Gibbon fellow I didn't see that he had any choice but to go to the police. If he doesn't, he might be in trouble."

"He certainly might," the Contessa said.

"But I'm afraid, Mother."

Berenice Pillow got up and put her arm around him. Tears welled in her eyes and as she spoke, her voice quavered.

"I know you are, Tony. But we don't have any choice. He knows he has to go, Mr. Macintyre, but he said he would feel better if someone other than ourselves and the police also knew about all this. We of course thought of you—and Barbara, too," she added with a weak smile at the Contessa.

"She's right. I know I have to go, Mr. Macintyre, but will you go with me? And do you think we could wait until tomorrow morning?"

The way Vico appealed to him made him seem like a little boy trying to postpone the inevitable deserved punishment.

"Tomorrow would be all right, I suppose, but as early as possible. I'll be at the Splendide-Suisse at eight."

"I want to come, too," Berenice Pillow said.

The gentle arm she put around her stepson and the look she gave him—and them all—were more convincing than a monologue would have been to express her belief in his innocence.

27 LIKE all the palazzi on the Grand Canal, the Contessa's turned its aristocratic back on the activity of the alleys, squares, and bridges. It was into this bustle that Urbino now plunged on his way back to the Palazzo Uccello. Several horns were blown in his face and he was dusted more than once with confetti on the busy *strada* that funneled the crowds between the train station and the Piazza San Marco.

It might be past ten o'clock but it was the Saturday night of *Carnevale* and people were still pouring in from the train station.

Fortunately, it didn't take Urbino long to leave this commotion behind as he walked away from the Grand Canal deeper into the Cannaregio. In Venice just one turning could make the difference between the thick of things and an almost funereal calm. Sometimes the division was as sharp and as sudden as that between life and death. One moment you were at the feast, the next moment beyond feasting, beyond caring, beyond feeling.

His thoughts were consumed with how Hazel's disappearance might fit into what he had learned tonight about Vico and Gibbon. Berenice Pillow had explained that there was no way for her or her stepson to have seen Hazel leave the Montin from where they were sitting, but what about when they had come in? Urbino had little doubt now that Hazel had noticed the two of them coming in with the Contessa when he had left the table. That explained the change in her behavior.

Gibbon's murder, followed only a few days later by Hazel's disappearance after she had been in the same restaurant with Vico, didn't look good for Mrs. Pillow's stepson. Urbino felt that he hadn't been told the truth tonight, not the whole truth. One thing that he was convinced of, however, was that Tonio Vico had kept Hazel's involvement with Gibbon a secret from his stepmother. Vico would never have told her. That Mrs. Pillow hadn't known of Gibbon's existence was one thing, but it was not as easy to believe that Vico had been unaware that Gibbon was in Venice. Yet, if Vico had had something to do with Gibbon's murder, would he have waited for a whole day to "discover" that Gibbon had been killed? Wouldn't he have taken advantage of yesterday's *Gazzettino* article to come forth right away and admit his acquaintance with the murdered man? What would a guilty man gain by delaying the revelation except the suspicion of intentional concealment? Had Vico actually not read *Il Gazzettino* until today?

The faces of guilt and innocence were unfortunately sometimes the same, except in one respect. One was actually a face, the other a mask indistinguishable from it.

When he got back to the Palazzo Uccello, he tried to give his attention to Proust. He started to read at random. He was familiar with the vast gallery of characters as well as with the story—the plot—if you could give these names to the ruminative narrative that re-created the loves and disillusionments of its main character, a thinly veiled version of Proust himself.

He hoped that Proust would be able to soothe him tonight. He also hoped that, as often happened when he put aside a problem, he would be visited with some sudden clarity, an insight that would have eluded him if he had sought it out. Urbino supposed that it wasn't much different from the unexpected power of involuntary memory that was at the heart of *Remembrance of Things Past*. First there was the intuition, followed by rational examination. It was what Urbino always hoped for in his biographies. It was also what he hoped for in this present business with Hazel Reeve and the murder of Gibbon.

Tonight no sudden clarity came, however, and he had to be content with the pleasures of the text alone, with characters changing into their exact opposites, with a social world in which the reality behind appearances and illusions was only gradually revealed. It wasn't long before his mind was filled with Proust's notions about passion transforming our normal character, about the difficulty of ever knowing another person, about the inseparable trinity of love, suffering, and jealousy. He couldn't get Hazel, Val Gibbon, and Tonio Vico out of his mind as he considered Proust's belief that jealousy can not only outlive love but frequently can't be cured even by the death of the beloved.

But perhaps the thing he thought about most, so much so that he put the book down in his lap, upsetting poor little Serena, who had climbed into it, was Proust's notion that another person is not like some garden with everything blooming for us to see beyond its railing but instead a shadow we can never penetrate—a shadow behind which the imagination can alternately see, with equal justification, both the fires of hatred and those of love. This wasn't particularly encouraging for someone in the business of getting at the truth about people, but Urbino took Proust's belief as a sensible admonition more than anything else, as a warning about presuming to know too much too soon. He saw no solution except in pursuing the truth as quietly and methodically as he knew how, all the while hoping for one of those fortuitous stumblings on the truth that Proust said gave some support to the theory of presentiments.

To clear his mind Urbino went for a walk. The weather was still cold and crisp, but no longer completely clear. Clouds moved quickly, pushed by winds from the Dolomites.

By avoiding the Piazza and the main squares and thorough-fares, he had the solitude he wanted for his reflections. He moved deeper into the Cannaregio, going along quays and up narrow alleys, past shuttered palazzi and bars and hostel-ries. He went past the dilapidated House of Tintoretto and the leprous statues of the Moors, one of whose noses had been refashioned out of metal, and then turned up toward the Madonna dell'Orto. When he stood on the bridge by the church and looked down at the black funeral motorboats moored against one of the buildings, the image of Hazel Reeve lying injured or dead somewhere in the city drifted into his mind like some dark fog.

When he went to the Madonna dell'Orto boat landing and looked out over the lagoon toward the cemetery island, the image was even stronger. Hazel's body might be in the mortu-ary on San Michele along with Gibbon's. If this were centuries ago and Florence instead of Venice, her body could now be under dissection at Maria Novella for a *presente cadavere* lesson to which the public was invited twice a year during *Carnevale*.

Urbino turned from the lagoon and made his way back to the Palazzo Uccello by the most direct route.

A figure was leaning against the building next to the Palazzo Uccello as he came over the bridge. The person was looking up the *calle* away from Urbino as if he wasn't familiar with the area or at ease in it either.

Until Urbino got closer, he didn't know if it was a man or a woman. Everything seemed meant to camouflage. Not just the long dark coat with the hood pulled up but the stance of the figure that betrayed nothing about sex or age.

As Urbino approached, the figure turned toward him but the facial features were in shadow beneath the hood, pulled forward as it was. Then the figure spoke, and with one word all ambiguity disappeared. Sex, age, and personal identity were clear.

"Urbino!"

Hazel Reeve came forward and touched his arm, She didn't throw back her hood but looked nervously up and down the *calle*.

"Can we go inside?"

Urbino unlocked the door and preceded her up the stairs to the little parlor.

28 "GIVE me a brandy," Hazel Reeve said, throwing back her hood and taking off her coat, "and I'll explain everything."

On the two previous times Hazel had confided in Urbino she had obviously kept things in reserve. Was he really going to hear the whole story now? He doubted it.

Hazel settled into the deep blue cushions of the chair, closing her eyes and putting an arm across her face. Urbino handed her the brandy.

"I'm sorry for whatever trouble I caused you, Urbino. It wasn't until this morning that I realized that dropping out of sight like that after dinner might put you in a bad position."

"I was worried about you."

She took her arm away and looked at him with a smile before taking a sip of her brandy.

" 'Worried about me.' That's nice but I don't think I deserve it. In fact, I know I don't. I went to Mestre."

Mestre! It was only a few minutes across the causeway from Venice.

"But I don't understand."

"How could you? I wandered around for a while after I left you. I went to the Piazza and had a drink at Florian's. It was a madhouse! Then I took the boat as far as the train station and got on the first train that was leaving. Of course it stopped in Mestre like all the trains from Venice. I got off and went across the street to a hotel."

"But why Mestre?"

"Because it wasn't Venice. I realized I had to get away, if only for as long as this."

"Because of Tonio Vico?"

If she was surprised she didn't show it. She nodded.

"So Tonio told you. I didn't think he saw me."

"He doesn't seem to have—or his mother. I spoke with them at the Contessa da Capo-Zendrini's tonight. She and Mrs. Pillow used to be in school together. Tonio Vico saw the piece in today's paper. He didn't know Gibbon was dead until today."

"Today's paper? What about yesterday's? But I'm the one who's been behindhand, aren't I? I should have told you last night, I know. When I mentioned another man before Val, there was no reason to tell you who he was. But last night when I saw him come in with his stepmother, I couldn't believe it. I knew the woman who was with them was your friend the Contessa. Porfirio showed me some pictures of her. When I saw Tonio, I got very frightened."

"For yourself?"

She laughed without much humor and drank some of her brandy. With her cheeks flushed and her short haircut disarrayed from her hood, she looked even more girlish.

"For *him*—for Tonio. If Tonio was here when Val was killed, it might mean—"

She floundered and looked at him helplessly.

"That he killed Val Gibbon?"

Although he had finished her statement for her out of sympathy, the sudden anger in her eyes showed that she had taken offense. It went as quickly as it came, however.

"What I meant is that the police would be in a good position to make his life uncomfortable. He would be their major suspect. It's just the kind of violence most Italians understand. A crime of passion involving a faithless woman."

She put down her glass and took out a handkerchief. Urbino thought she was about to cry but she only blew her nose. Her words reminded him that the Italians—and many others as well—would also be able to understand another crime of passion, one committed by a spurned woman.

"Tonio is going to the Questura tomorrow morning and tell Commissario Gemelli everything."

"Everything?"

There was a note of fear in her voice.

"Everything about his relationship with you and about having known who Gibbon was. He says he didn't kill Gibbon."

"Of course not!" She shook her head slowly. "Well, it's obvious that nothing's going to be a secret now. Tonio's going to be humiliated."

She put away her handkerchief and took another sip before going on.

"Commissario Gemelli must be furious. I might even have broken the law but I don't care. Last night I was so frightened and confused that I had to get away! I had to think, and I knew I couldn't do it staying with Porfirio. I'm moving out."

Where she might be moving to close to midnight in a city without a spare room was something she had probably not worked out yet. There was a determined look on her face, however, that seemed to say she wouldn't go back to Porfirio's even if it meant sleeping in a vaporetto or going back to Mestre.

"I can't trust anyone but you, Urbino." When she said this, it was as if Urbino could hear the Contessa whispering in his ear to be careful. "Let me tell you about Tonio. I met him two years ago at a lecture on Palladian architecture at the V and A. I hadn't had a relationship in—well, a long time—and we got along from the start. Tonio was studying architecture in London then and we started to see a lot of each other. Surely you can see even after only a short time that he's Italian in the best ways and none of the worst, yet he's very much American, thanks to his stepmother. I thought he understood me better than any other man ever had or could. He was intelligent, handsome, sensitive—everything that a girl could want."

She hadn't mentioned "rich" but she was rich enough herself.

"But you didn't love him," he said, risking her anger again.

"But I didn't realize it, not until Val came along. And when Val did, then I knew. I was in love with Val almost from the first. As I told you, he appeared like magic just when I needed someone to photograph my parents' things at the house in Knightsbridge. He was completely different from Tonio."

"In what way?"

"Oh, he was good-looking and intelligent, too, but he didn't take himself so seriously. Maybe that came of being more than ten years older."

Her comment surprised Urbino because one of the things that had struck him about Gibbon was just how self-important he could be. But that had been with him, another man. He might have been completely different with Hazel.

"But who knows why we fall in love with one person and not someone else? *Le coeur a ses raisons*. It's true. And we don't fall in love with the one we want to or even with the better person—frequently the opposite, in fact."

She seemed to consider this before going on.

"Tonio didn't understand any of this. How could he? I still don't understand it myself. When I told him about my feelings for Val—on Boxing Day, far from the best time, I know—he wouldn't believe it. He said that I would feel different after a while, that he knew I really loved him."

Tears came into her eyes.

"Sometimes since then I've thought that Tonio might have been right. He's such a good person. Val had a nasty side to him when it came to Tonio. He was envious of him—not so much because of me or because Tonio had so much money but because Tonio was privileged in a way he had never been. Val would follow him around sometimes and take his picture as if he were trying to learn some secret about him that would show up in the photograph. Exactly what he got out of doing that, I never could figure out."

"And what about Mrs. Pillow? How did she feel about you and Val—about the problems between you and Tonio?"

According to Tonio and Mrs. Pillow, Val Gibbon's name had never been mentioned between them.

"Tonio said he didn't tell her, and he didn't want me to say anything either—as if I would! He even suggested that I come over to dinner before they both left for Naples, but I couldn't have gone through with that. It would have been a farce. His stepmother would have seen through it. She's an intelligent woman."

"How did you get along with her?"

"Well enough. I don't think that she was that taken with me. There was some girl back in America, a niece of Mrs. Pillow's from her second marriage, not any relation to Tonio, of course. I'm sure Mrs. Pillow would probably have accepted me in the end. She loves Tonio as much as if he were her natural son and I suppose you can't blame her for wanting to protect him. Who knows? Maybe another woman could see that I didn't really love Tonio even if I couldn't see it myself. Maybe that was why she didn't completely approve of me."

"Did Tonio know that you would be here in Venice with Gibbon?"

She stiffened slightly in her chair.

"I wouldn't quite say that I was 'here in Venice with him.' Porfirio invited me to stay with him. I had already accepted before I knew that Val would be here too. He came for

Carnevale, and once he was here he was asked to take photographs of the church and the convent. But you know that."

Hazel looked down into the brandy glass cupped in her hands. She still hadn't answered his question of whether or not Tonio Vico had known she would be in Venice. Urbino asked her again.

"I didn't tell him." Then, perhaps realizing that this wasn't enough, she added, "He didn't know. I don't know how he could have known. The only people who knew were Porfirio, my editor, and Val, of course. Besides, Tonio has been down in Naples with his stepmother for the past few weeks—or so I thought."

In her wide green eyes he saw puzzlement, as if she were asking herself how Vico had come to be in Venice at the same time she was. She took out her handkerchief again and this time she was crying, deep sobs that wracked her small frame.

Urbino went over to her. He put his arm around her shoulders and let her cry.

"You'll stay here tonight, Hazel. You say you don't want to go back to Porfirio's and I don't think you have much chance of getting a room at this hour, not during *Carnevale.* After a good night's sleep, Natalia will fix you breakfast and we'll go to the Questura."

She dried her tears and looked up at him gratefully. He went to get her a glass of mineral water. As he was bringing it back, he realized something with a start.

He had also promised Tonio Vico just a few hours ago that he would go to the Questura in the morning with him. It was a strange dilemma to be in. He might even have seen some humor in it if it hadn't been a question of murder.

29   BUT next morning he soon realized that it made no difference what impossible promises he had made. When Natalia went to the guest bedroom to see about Hazel, she came back with a puzzled look on her face.

"There's no one there, Signor Urbino." Then she added, as if to assure him that he hadn't been mistaken but had indeed had an overnight guest, "But the bed was used."

She picked up the bag of espresso beans and started to measure them out, more absorbed in the task than was necessary.

"I think there's a note on the dresser. Do you want me to get it?"

"No, thank you, Natalia. I'll get it myself."

A page ripped from an appointment book was propped on the dresser against the mirror. In an obviously hurried hand was the message:

Urbino,
I'm going back to Porfirio's for a few hours. I'll go to the Questura on my own. It might be better that way. Don't worry.

Hazel

When the phone rang a few minutes later, he was still holding Hazel's note. It was the Contessa.

"Are you awake, *caro*? I'm afraid I have bad news. We've got another violent death to account for. Porfirio's dead. His body was found in San Gabriele this morning." The Contessa paused. "It seems he broke his neck in a fall from the fresco you and Josef are restoring."

Part Three

BUT
THE TRUTH
NOT TO
EVERYONE

1 URBINO called Porfirio's apartment a few minutes later. Carmela, the photographer's maid, answered, but before Urbino could ask the breathless, abstracted woman for Hazel, the phone was taken from her and a male voice came over the line.

"The residence of Porfirio Buffone. Who is this?"

Urbino recognized Commissario Gemelli's voice.

"Urbino Macintyre. Is that Commissario Gemelli?"

"Are you disappointed that I'm here before you, Macintyre? Maybe you're thinking you should have accompanied Signorina Reeve back here from your place. It seems that you've been lacking in gallantry with this particular young lady."

"She's there then? Is she all right?"

"Yes, she's here and I suppose she's all right. She hasn't flown away again, which is the important thing. She's apologetic about her little excursion to Mestre and seems reasonably upset over the death of her host. Not any tears but she has a very white face."

"She came here last night."

"And spent the night—yes, I know—and told you how she stayed in Mestre after leaving you in the Campo San Barnaba. She told me all about Antonio Vico, the son of a friend of the Contessa da Capo-Zendrini."

"A stepson. Vico was planning to come to see you this morning. He still is, I'm sure."

"Is he? And how do you know?"

"I was with him last night at the Ca' da Capo-Zendrini. He told us—that is, his stepmother, Mrs. Pillow, the Contessa, and myself—that he knew Gibbon. He asked me to go to the Questura with him this morning."

"I'm impressed, Macintyre. It appears that you are the confidant of two very important people in our investigation into Gibbon's murder. I'm sure you realize that this carries a responsibility. And now there's this business of Porfirio

Buffone's death. I don't dare ask you what your theories are about the deaths of two photographers who knew Signorina Reeve, but I would like to know about your movements during the past twelve hours—that is, when you weren't entertaining Signorina Reeve and getting Antonio Vico's confidences."

"My movements?"

"Exactly. I know you've become involved in an amateur way in restoration and have been helping the Polish man with his work at San Gabriele. But we needn't discuss this over the telephone, Macintyre. Come to the Questura in about two hours. Bring along Antonio Vico, too. We wouldn't want him staying in his room afraid to face the police without you by his side."

Urbino next called the Splendide-Suisse and asked to be connected with the Vico-Pillow suite.

"Oh, it's you, Mr. Macintyre," Mrs. Pillow said with faint surprise. "Tony was going to call you but he wanted to be sure you were awake."

Urbino looked at the clock on the table. It wasn't even seven-thirty.

"Tony's being very brave about going to the police. I'm glad that you'll be with him."

"I don't want either you or your stepson to think I can work any magic with the Questura, Mrs. Pillow. I'm not on the best footing with them myself. Commissario Gemelli and I have had a strained relationship during the past few years. I don't know what I can do for your stepson other than accompany him to San Lorenzo and be with him for as long as Gemelli thinks appropriate."

He didn't mention that Gemelli wanted to see him in his own right. In fact, he didn't see any point in mentioning the death of Porfirio at all.

"I have a feeling that you're being too modest, Mr. Macintyre, but in any case I'm happy he'll be going with you. Tony and I have talked it over and he thinks it would be better if he didn't have his mother along. Someone like yourself has the virtue of not being biased in his favor."

Urbino didn't get a chance to talk with Vico, but Mrs. Pillow assured him that her stepson would be waiting downstairs in the lounge at ten.

2 GEMELLI'S door opened. The Commissario ushered out a white-faced Vico.

"Signor Vico is free either to wait for you or to go wherever he wishes—as soon as he reads and signs the typed version of his statement, that is. It's being prepared."

"I think I'll go back to the hotel when I'm finished here, if you don't mind," Vico said to Urbino.

"Good idea. I'm sure your mother is concerned."

From his first moments alone with Gemelli in his office, Urbino sensed a somewhat different attitude in the Commissario from his usual one of cynical forbearance and irony. Instead of asking insinuating questions about his relationship to the restoration of the fresco and the last time he had been on the scaffold, he smiled at him over the desk and thanked him for encouraging Vico to talk with him.

"I'm not sure how much I had to do with that. He would have come on his own."

"But he wouldn't have been quite as much at ease. He had little enough to tell us about Gibbon though—except that he knew about him. The big question is why Signorina Reeve didn't mention Vico."

"She says she didn't know he was in Venice until a few nights ago."

"But she didn't even mention another man to us."

"She said that she had been seeing someone else when she met Gibbon. Even if she intended to conceal her relationship with Vico, it doesn't necessarily mean that she had any motive other than sparing them both some embarrassment."

"But she told you about another man, didn't she? She must realize that every piece of information, no matter how insignificant it might seem or how embarrassing it might be, can be of vital importance to the police. What else did she have to tell you?"

Gemelli's little smile warned Urbino that it was unreasonable to expect the Commissario to relinquish completely an attitude that was probably as ingrained personally as it was professionally.

As gulls screeched outside, Urbino told Gemelli how Hazel had been engaged to Vico before meeting Gibbon, how she hadn't known Vico was in town until she saw him at the Montin, how she had gone to Mestre to think things through.

"And then came back straight to you, not us," Gemelli added. "She's told us all of this—although I see no reason why either of us should believe that it's all she has to tell us. She might be parceling out information from embarrassment, as you seem to think, or for some other reason. We're finished with her for the time being but we've made it clear that we would prefer her to stay in Venice for a while longer. I hope we made it clearer this time than we did last. If you learn anything from her that seems important, I'm sure you'll let us know. That goes for Vico and your friend Lubonski, too. In the light of Porfirio Buffone's death, we'll be going to the hospital to ask Lubonski about the scaffold. He can have visitors now. It's a remote possibility, but Lubonski might be able to tell us something that could link the two deaths. Gibbon and Buffone were both photographers."

Gemelli stood up and went to the window that looked out over the Rio di San Lorenzo, where the police boats were moored. He drew aside the curtain.

"I'm asking for your cooperation, Macintyre, the kind of cooperation without which we couldn't get our work done. I'm not asking you to do anything more than that. If these men come down from Scotland Yard on Wednesday, I would appreciate it if you would first tell us whatever it is you might have to tell them. Today is Sunday. Even a dedicated chief of police doesn't work seven days a week. But it's *Carnevale*. We have a lot to take into consideration. It would be a coup if we could get this case wrapped up before they come down."

Urbino, surprised and gratified by Gemelli's appeal, decided to seize an opportunity unlikely to come again.

"I understand you, Commissario. I've never had any other intention but to help. But if you want me to be able to help you as much as I can, I should know a few things—more than you were able to tell me on Friday."

The Commissario turned away from the window, his dark, handsome face troubled. He looked down at Urbino.

"What kind of things?"

"The things you already know yourself."

Urbino knew he was putting the Commissario in a difficult, if not impossible, situation. It would be far from orthodox to share police information, and it might be embarrassing to have to admit how little information they actually had. Gemelli hadn't told Urbino much on Friday. He might think it best to keep Urbino uninformed, to let him assume that the Questura was waiting only for the one or two additional pieces of information that Urbino—or someone else—might provide, so that the Questura could tie up a neat package for the prosecutor.

Whatever train of thought Gemelli was going through, the immediate result was a sigh as he dropped the curtain and returned to his desk.

"*Allora,*" he said, uttering that indispensable word of Italian conversation. Urbino sensed that it could only be a prelude to the information he was seeking. He wasn't wrong.

"There have been other times when I've felt it was necessary to—to share information with someone outside the Questura, with someone other than a legitimate authority, I mean." He shrugged. "We do what we can the best way we can. You have your own American ideas about orderly procedure, but I assure you that the book is not something that can always be followed as if it were the Bible, neither here nor in America. My cousin who is an *avvocato* in New Jersey pretends to believe differently but it's just the same there."

Having delivered this defensive prologue, Gemelli began to tell Urbino what he knew up to this point, giving him no opening to ask questions.

"As you already know, Gibbon was found dead in the Calle Santa Scolastica at approximately eleven-thirty on Wednesday night. Ignazio Rigoletti, who lives in the Corte Santa Scolastica, was returning home. As he was about to enter the Calle Santa Scolastica a man dressed in dark clothes was coming out. A dark, good-looking man not yet thirty, he said. The man showed no surprise on seeing him. In fact, Rigoletti said the man acted as if he hadn't seen him at all. Just walked right past him without a look or a comment and went toward the Riva degli Schiavoni. Rigoletti continued to the courtyard and noticed a form lying in the *calle* near the water steps— in the area where men have their assignations," he added pointedly. "He went over and found Gibbon's body. Rigoletti started to go out into the Calle degli Albanesi for help when he saw a young man slipping into the Calle Santa Scolastica. This man had light hair and definitely wasn't the one he had seen a few minutes earlier, but Rigoletti seems to have a less clear idea of what he looked like. This young man—he was also about thirty—turned back into the Calle degli Albanesi and went toward the Riva degli Schiavoni as the other man had. Rigoletti then went to a restaurant and called the Questura. We've spoken with most of the residents of the area. No one saw or heard anything out of the ordinary that night."

Gemelli paused and tapped out a cigarette from the crumpled pack on his desk. He looked at Urbino as he lit it, shook out the match, and dropped it into his Murano ashtray.

"Rigor mortis hadn't set in and lividity was evident. Brilli determined that Gibbon couldn't have been dead for more than three hours, that is, no earlier than eight-thirty. Corroborating this and narrowing it down further, as you're well aware, is the fact that Gibbon was seen leaving the Casa Crispina about nine-fifteen. Allowing for at least half an hour for him to get to the Calle Santa Scolastica, we can say that he was murdered sometime between nine-forty-five and eleven-thirty. As I told you on Friday, he was attacked and died in the *calle*. We've had the film developed from the camera he had with him, and also the rolls in his pocket and those back at the Casa Crispina. He had had some film developed in a local shop but the shop didn't have any other rolls. We're checking other places. There's a lot of film of the fresco at San Gabriele and of some paintings at the convent, some shots of the crowd in the Piazza and individuals in costumes, but there doesn't seem to be anything of importance. We're going through all the photographs again, however." Gemelli smiled. "I assume you'd like to see them. Here they are. Perhaps you'll see something we haven't."

He handed Urbino a small cardboard box. Urbino opened it and took out the large pile of photographs. These weren't the ideal conditions for looking at them—not with Gemelli sitting there waiting for him to finish—but he tried to be as thorough as possible. As Gemelli had said, they were mainly of the San Gabriele fresco, the convent, and *Carnevale*. What struck Urbino was how few there actually were of *Carnevale,* however. He recognized Giovanni Firpo in his costume in several, but the pharmacist wasn't focused on but was part of the background. Xenia Campi had been caught in one of her diatribes in front of the Basilica in one photograph, and in another she was frowning furiously at the camera. There were some shots of canals, buildings, and bridges but none of any of the guests of the Casa Crispina except Xenia Campi. For a second time, as Gemelli barely concealed his impatience, Urbino looked at the ones Gibbon had taken of revelers, but except for Firpo and several people in costumes that looked familiar to him, Urbino recognized no one. More time spent looking at the photographs might reveal something, but Urbino had to admit to himself that he didn't find anything that might be of help—unless it was what Gibbon *hadn't* taken photographs of.

He put the photographs back in the box and handed it to Gemelli.

"There doesn't seem to be anything there," Urbino said.

Gemelli nodded in agreement.

"Rigoletti says the same thing. He didn't find anyone who remotely resembles the two men he saw in the Calle Santa Scolastica. I'm arranging for him to see Nicholas Spaak, Lubonski, and Vico as well as some other men known to frequent the area. He'll be coming by in a little while to go through the photographs again on the chance he might have missed something the first time. We'll also show him our artist's composite of the two men he saw that night. By the way, the composites will be in tomorrow's *Gazzettino*."

Gemelli seemed pleased to be able to say this. It probably gave him the feeling that everything he was imparting to Urbino wasn't privileged information.

"Gibbon died of a stab wound to the heart. A lucky strike—or maybe not so lucky, maybe the person knew exactly where to stab him. He must have died almost instantly. There was some roughening and bruising around the wound, which might indicate a weapon relatively blunt, like a pair of scissors or a knife that wasn't too sharp. It was a single blade. Whatever it was was at least five inches long, possibly longer. We can be sure only of the minimum length. The weapon hasn't been found."

Gemelli smoked his cigarette for a few moments and then lost interest in it, extinguishing it forcefully in the ashtray.

"I'm sure you know the reputation of the Calle Santa Scolastica. There are several other areas like it in the city, but because it's so close to the lagoon and the Piazza it's one of the most popular with homosexuals. Its proximity to the Bridge of Sighs must be an added attraction. We've had complaints from the people who live in the Corte Santa Scolastica, but short of posting one of our men there—and at other assignation points— what can we do? It's low priority. But this murder puts things in a completely different perspective. The residents want us to clean up the area, and so does the Danieli, which uses it for its trash. I can't blame them. They're all saying that it's a homosexual murder and they want us to police the area more rigorously, make arrests—which we've been doing. But no one who meets Rigoletti's descriptions has turned up."

"Do you think it was a homosexual murder?"

"Sexuality is a mystery, Macintyre. Who knows? This is Venice! You know its history of these things better than I do, I'm sure. It certainly doesn't have the best reputation, especially during these days of *Carnevale,* when it's impossible to distinguish the men from the women. Some of these people running around in costumes probably don't even know themselves who they are!"

"Is there any reason to consider it a homosexual murder other than the fact that the Calle Santa Scolastica is a cruising area?"

Urbino was thinking about the money found on Gibbon that the Contessa had learned about from Corrado Scarpa, information that hadn't been made public any more than most of what Gemelli was telling him now. The presence of the money on Gibbon's body might strengthen the theory of a homosexual murder or a murder of passion. Urbino wondered why Gemelli hadn't mentioned the money. Was it an oversight or something intentional? Withholding this piece of information—and possibly others that Urbino couldn't be aware of—might indicate that there was a limit to what Gemelli was willing to tell him.

"Yes, there is another reason. Partially dried semen was found on the side of Gibbon's trousers, semen that the lab people tell us was not his. That's the most significant thing our scene-of-crime people came up with. It doesn't appear that Gibbon had an orgasm anytime immediately before his death and there was no indication of anal intercourse."

"Couldn't Gibbon have met or lured or followed a man to the Calle Santa Scolastica," Urbino said, "and then been murdered?"

"It's not unlikely. Obviously we're not talking about a well-adjusted homosexual or heterosexual here. Murder of men or women following sex happens more often than you might think. Of course, Signorina Reeve was very upset when I mentioned the possibility that her fiancé might have been sexually involved with a man."

"But if the Calle Santa Scolastica is used for assignations between men, isn't it possible that the semen found on Gibbon's pants had been left by someone earlier? That he might have brushed up against the wall or got it on his pants when he fell to the pavement?"

"Matching semen was found on the wall near him but that doesn't prove or disprove anything, does it? We're not ruling anything out. Gibbon was attractive to women—and was attracted *to* them, it seems. But there's such a thing as bisexuality. I've come across it plenty of times here in Italy. In fact, some of the men we've pulled in recently from the Calle Santa Scolastica and some other areas are married. Yet we've found nothing to indicate that Gibbon was involved with men."

The Commissario had failed to mention another possibility—that Gibbon could have been attractive to men without himself being attracted to them.

3   WITHIN twenty minutes of his conversation with Gemelli, Urbino was in the Campo Zanipolo by the equestrian statue of the fifteenth-century military leader Colleoni that Porfirio had mentioned. The huge man and horse rose above him in all their virile nobility, perhaps after all these centuries finally reconciled to the trick played on them by the Republic. Colleoni had agreed to leave a large part of his fortune to Venice on the condition that a statue to him be put up in front of San Marco. The Republic, ever wily, accepted the bequest, and after Colleoni's death blithely erected the statue in front of the Scuola San Marco instead of the Basilica San Marco.

It was the Scuola of this trickery that Urbino was interested in at the moment.

Formerly one of the six great guilds of Venice dedicated to religious and humanitarian purposes, it was now the city's largest hospital. As he approached the Renaissance building, with its heavily decorated facade of carved cornices, ornate columns and capitals, graceful arches, windows and lunettes, Urbino could think only of the fear, death, and misery behind the deceptive front. Ambulance sirens screamed as he approached the main door flanked with trompe l'oeil sculptures and pedestals adorned, inappropriately now that the building was a hospital, with carefree, dancing children.

Lubonski's room was in the back wing in the former monastery. As he was walking along the corridor, checking the room numbers, Urbino was startled to see Giovanni Firpo walking toward him. He couldn't have been more surprised if Firpo had appeared in all his full *Carnevale* regalia instead of the clean white shirt and dark slacks he wore for his work as a pharmacist. Urbino felt grateful for seeing the man, so easy to condescend to and not take seriously, in this new light.

"Good morning, Signor Macintyre. Lubonski's room is the next one on the right. He's just had breakfast and is looking much better. I stop in from time to time if I happen to be on the floor. He hasn't been aware of very much since he was admitted."

Urbino wondered if Firpo knew about Porfirio's death. That was a good possibility, working in the hospital as he did, but the pharmacist gave no indication.

"The night nurse told me that he was asking for you. She promised she would call you first thing in the morning. I assume she had a chance."

Urbino let his presence in the hospital early this morning provide Firpo with an ambiguous answer. The pharmacist waited for a few seconds as if he expected Urbino to say something and then continued down the corridor to the elevator.

Lubonski didn't look any better than a week ago. His Tatar cheekbones accentuated his cadaverous face. Two bright spots of color on his cheeks did nothing to diminish the ghastly effect.

"Thank God you're here, Urbino. I was afraid that the nurse would forget to call you."

As with Firpo, Urbino thought it best to let Lubonski assume that he was there in response to the call. He needed to proceed carefully with him.

"How are you, Josef?"

The Pole waved a thin hand weakly.

"Better. Urbino, you must promise me again that you won't go anywhere near the restoration work. Not until I get back to work myself first."

Urbino didn't know what to say. Was this the time to tell him, right at the beginning of his visit?

"You haven't, have you?"

Fear livened the Pole's deathlike face.

"No, Josef, I haven't." Lubonski smiled grimly and rested his head back on the pillow. Then, this time with a slightly different emphasis, Urbino repeated, "No, Josef, *I* haven't, but someone else has."

The look that passed over Lubonski's face was difficult to decipher. Was it surprise? relief? fear? satisfaction? It seemed a combination of them all.

"Not—not the photographer?"

"Which photographer, Josef?"

Lubonski was clearly confused.

"The one staying at the Casa Crispina. Gibbon."

"No, it wasn't Gibbon but Gibbon is dead. He was stabbed to death the night they rushed you here."

"Stabbed! I don't understand."

It would be best now for Urbino to explain things as quickly as he could. He told Lubonski about Gibbon's murder in the Calle Santa Scolastica but said nothing about Hazel Reeve or Tonio Vico.

"So he's dead," Josef said.

"Yes, and the police are speaking with everyone at the Casa Crispina. I was just at the Questura. The Commissario will be coming by to talk with you in a little while."

Urbino wondered what Gemelli's reaction would be if he found out that he had spoken with Lubonski first.

A look of fear came back into the Pole's face.

"But I had nothing to do with Gibbon's murder. I don't know anything about it! But you said that someone went up on the scaffold."

"Porfirio Buffone. He's dead, Josef. He fell from the scaffolding. Paolo, the sexton, found his body this morning."

Lubonski stared unblinkingly at him for what seemed an impossibly long time.

"You booby-trapped the scaffold, didn't you, Josef? But why?"

A quizzical look came over the Pole's face,

"I mean that you did something to the scaffold. You fixed it so that it would collapse, didn't you? That's why you made me promise not to go anywhere near the fresco."

Looking down at the dark-green blanket, Lubonski nodded.

"I didn't want anything to happen to you, Urbino, please believe me. I called you to warn you after I—I booby-trapped the scaffold. I didn't want anything to happen to anyone."

"Except Val Gibbon?"

"Yes!" Urbino was startled by the force behind Lubonski's affirmative. "I wanted to hurt him, I wanted to scare him, but I didn't want him to die. I didn't want anyone to die."

"Josef, I think you should tell me about Val Gibbon. I know you didn't like him."

"I hated him!" Lubonski almost shouted. "He was a terrible man, the worst I've ever known. I can't say I'm sorry he's dead. Many people will be happy, I think. But I am sorry for the other photographer. Do the police know?"

"About Porfirio's death, yes. The Commissario said he wanted to ask me about the restoration work. The police will obviously want to know exactly how Porfirio fell to his death. Maybe they've figured it out already."

Lubonski averted his eyes.

"It was my fault, God forgive me. I will tell them the truth. I will tell them you had nothing to do with it."

"But why, Josef?"

"Why? Because he was making my life miserable. He didn't do it only for the money but because he enjoyed it. When people aren't happy, they want to make other people miserable too."

"Money? What money?"

"Two thousand pounds that I don't have—not anymore."

The amount found on Gibbon's body was more than this.

"Why did he want you to give him two thousand pounds?"

Lubonski looked at him with an appeal in his eyes. Having admitted to rigging the scaffold, what was there that he was still afraid of?

"It was what you call—what is the word?—when someone wants money from you or they will do something to you? *Chantage*," he said, using the French word.

"Blackmail? Did he have photographs that you didn't want him to have?"

"Nothing to do with photographs, no. Something else."

From the way Lubonski settled back against the pillows and looked straight ahead at the wall, Urbino knew that he was about to give him an explanation. He sat down in the chair at the foot of the bed and waited.

"Gibbon I met nine years ago in London, may the day be damned! It was two years after I got there. I went to England the summer before martial law started in Poland. I went to make money, mainly for my mother. She has only me and my younger brother but my brother and his family don't have anything. I didn't have a work permit but I found little jobs. Once I got a permit I had more work, mainly construction, and that's how I got involved with Gibbon." Lubonski frowned and shook his head weakly. "But that's not right. I knew him *before* then. I was studying English at a school in London. He was teaching there—not English but art or photography or something. He took an interest in me." He reached for a tissue from the box on the night table next to his bed, giving Urbino a quick glance.

"Did he have a job for you?"

Lubonski gave a feeble laugh.

"He was always looking for ways to make money himself. Not that I am too much different, but he had only himself and I had to worry about my mother back in Cracow and I wanted to get married. My girlfriend—an English girl, but we never got married—didn't like me to send so much money to my mother. We had fights."

Urbino listened patiently to his story, sensing it was being told not only to inform but also to provide an excuse or justification for what was to come. When Lubonski paused, Urbino reminded him that he hadn't said why Gibbon had taken an interest in him. The Pole looked down at his tissue.

"It wasn't because of anything I said or did," he said. "I never even noticed him until he came up to me after classes one night, asked me my name. He wanted to have a drink or a coffee. I could tell what he wanted."

Urbino thought that he did too but he waited for Lubonski to tell him.

"I was a good-looking man back then." He looked at Urbino almost belligerently. "I know it wasn't so long ago but you can change very fast. One day you're not much more than a boy, and then—then you're something else." He ran a hand through his thinning hair. "When I told him I wasn't interested in such things, he said he didn't know what I was talking about. But I knew I was right. I saw him talking to some of the young men in my English class. He became very friendly with one of them, an Asian. He didn't bother me again in that way but sometimes I saw him looking at me. He left the school a little while after that. His friend in my class said that he was teaching in a hospital. I don't understand how you can teach art in a hospital, but that's what he said he was doing."

"What way was it that he *did* bother you. You mentioned blackmail."

"Yes, *chantage*. A few weeks ago, here in Venice."

"You hadn't seen him in nine years and then he tried to blackmail you? But why?"

"I didn't say that I didn't see him after the school, did I? I saw him many times but not in the way that you think. It was business. Maybe not business but money was involved." Lubonski sighed. "I know that I have to tell you all this and that I will have to tell the police, too, but I want you to understand and to tell the Contessa that I am a good man, despite what I might have done. Will you tell her that?"

"She knows that already, Josef. She got you the work at San Gabriele because she knew you were a good man, that you had done good work for her friend in London before he died."

Lubonski's face clouded. He was looking weaker. Urbino wondered how much longer it would be reasonable to expect him to go on. Any minute now one of the nurses might come in to interrupt them.

"That's it," he said so quietly that Urbino almost couldn't hear him. "I didn't do a good job—at least not an honest job."

"Her friend was pleased."

"He never knew. Rich people—rich old people who have so much—sometimes they don't notice things. I don't think he ever did, thank God."

"Notice what, Josef?"

"That I stole some things from his house!" Lubonski was breathless after saying it and started to cough. "Little things," the Pole amended as if their size ameliorated his culpability. "Little things, but they were worth a lot of money. I wasn't sure, but Gibbon, he knew they were. He got money for them. I didn't know what to do with them after I took them and then I met Gibbon in Bloomsbury, being all smiling and considerate, maybe because he was with his aunt and he wanted to show her what a nice boy he was. I thought he could help me. When I told him about the little things a few days later, he came over to look at them and said he would be able to help me. He did. It was a big mistake."

For whom? Urbino asked himself as Lubonski paused. For them both? In what ways?

"What were these little things?"

"Gibbon knew what they were. He gave them names but I didn't know what the names meant."

"What did they look like?"

"One was ivory and the other one was jade," he said almost proudly. "The ivory one was shaped like a seahorse and the jade one was oval, like a very small bowl."

Urbino would need more details than these to know exactly what these *objets de vertu* were.

"You're sure the man never knew they were missing?"

It seemed improbable yet not impossible. How long would it take the Contessa to notice that one or two of her ceramic animals were missing or something from one of her other collections either at the Ca' da Capo-Zendrini or the villa in Asolo? The Contessa had never mentioned anything about a theft in her friend's townhouse. Surely he would have told her, especially if he had discovered the theft after the renovation work.

"Sure? No, I'm not sure, but he never said anything. I never heard anything. My supervisor never mentioned it, and the Contessa didn't either."

"So Gibbon sold the objects and gave you some of the money."

"Half of it—or I think it was half," he added ruefully. "But I was happy to get it. It was more than two thousand pounds. I sent most of it to my mother."

"Did you sell"—he thought it a better word than 'steal' if he wanted to keep Lubonski talking—"any other things?"

"That was all. Gibbon said I should try to take one or two more but I refused. I could never have done it again. It was an impulse. Anyway, the job there was soon over."

But obviously things hadn't been over with Gibbon.

"Gibbon wanted you to take more things and when you didn't he started to blackmail you."

Lubonski nodded his head sadly.

"*Chantage,* yes, but not at first. At first he tried to get me to take other things, but then here in Venice he started with *la chantage.* Imagine my surprise when I saw him at breakfast two weeks ago! I thought he had forgotten all about me, but he found out I was going to be with the sisters when I was doing the work. He wanted the money back."

"All of it?"

"Most of it. He said he needed it, and if I didn't give it to him he would tell the police in London."

"Tell the police? But Josef, he was involved too. If he told the police, he would implicate himself."

"That's what I told myself. That's what I said to him but he just laughed. He said I didn't know what I was talking about, that I had been the one to take the things, that I was a foreigner even after all these years, and that when they found out that I had—back in Poland—"

Lubonski broke off and looked at Urbino with imploring eyes.

"What about Poland?"

"I took many zlotys from the man I worked for. He never paid any of us enough and had so much."

"Were you arrested?"

"No, he didn't know for sure who it was. I don't think the man wanted the police to poke around in his business. Everything wasn't as it should be. I was lucky. I couldn't take a chance. If the English police learned about the money in Poland or if they sent me back there the way Gibbon said they would, I would be lost—and so would my poor mother. Even though things have changed in Poland, this man could have me arrested. He's a big man now."

Instead of asking any more direct questions, Urbino sat and waited for Lubonski to continue, which he did after taking a sip of water.

"I didn't know what to do when Gibbon asked me for more money. My mother has used up all the money and I must send her more. He said that I could always get some from the Contessa, that she seemed to like me and would continue to like me as long as she didn't find out what I had done to her friend. I was in a very bad position. But I only wanted to frighten him. Men like him, men who want to get money through *chantage,* they are cowards who only want to frighten someone else. So I thought I would frighten him instead."

"By fixing the scaffold so that it would fall down? I could have gone up there, Josef!"

"But I told you not to, and you promised. No one else went on the scaffold but you, me, and Gibbon. Paolo was afraid to climb the ladder."

It was a feeble attempt at justification. Anyone might have climbed the ladder out of curiosity despite the sign forbidding it. But Lubonski, ill and desperate, couldn't have been thinking clearly the night of Gibbon's murder when he had gone to San Gabriele. What he had done to the scaffold hadn't killed Gibbon, but it had killed Porfirio several days later—or had it?

Couldn't Porfirio's head have been crushed some other way? Porfirio might not have been up on the scaffold at all. Someone could have followed Lubonski to San Gabriele, understood that the trap being set up was meant for Gibbon, and taken advantage of it as a convenient cover-up for murder. Porfirio could have been killed to obscure the real motive for Gibbon's murder, perhaps to implicate Lubonski.

But it was unlikely that anyone would believe that the ill Lubonski had gone all the way to the Calle Santa Scolastica to kill Gibbon. As the Contessa had said in reference to Stella Maris Spaak, the other semi-invalid of the Casa Crispina, it was "impossible," wasn't it?

4 GIOVANNI Firpo was waiting for Urbino by the elevators when he came out of Lubonski's room. There was a strained look on the little man's face that hadn't been there earlier.

"Could I talk with you for a few minutes, Signor Macintyre?"

He led Urbino to the end of the hall to a room with a few chairs, a sagging sofa, and a table littered with magazines. No one was in it. He closed the door behind them.

"I just heard that Porfirio is dead. I think there's something you should know. It's about Xenia Campi. When you asked me about her yesterday, I didn't think this was important. You wanted to know if I had seen her the night of the English photographer's murder. As I told you, I didn't, but I saw her yesterday in the Piazza with Porfirio. Just the two of them. They were in the corner by the bank. I couldn't help overhearing as I was going by. They didn't notice me. She was threatening him."

"What did she say?"

"She said he would have a fall and that she would be there to see it!"

5 FROM the café across from the hospital, Urbino first called Mother Mariangela and tried to allay her fears about how the death of Porfirio might affect the convent and the Casa Crispina. He didn't think it wise to tell her about Lubonski's role in Porfirio's death. Before hanging up, Mother Mariangela said that Mrs. Spaak would like to see him.

Next Urbino called the Contessa.

"I have a lot to tell you, Barbara, but I don't have the time now. I'd like some information from you though. Tell me about Xenia Campi."

"Because of her dislike for Porfirio? But Porfirio was killed accidentally, wasn't he? Or have you come across something else?"

"Later, Barbara. Just tell me about Xenia Campi now."

The Contessa sighed with impatience.

"All right but I'll expect a full accounting later. Xenia Campi and Ignazio Rigoletti were married for about twenty years before they divorced. She was a seamstress. They had only one child, a son. He was killed in a car crash on the autostrada on his way to Milan. There was fog, and a bus bringing tourists to *Carnevale* hit him. He was burned to death. The girl he was with was thrown from the car and survived. It was about ten years ago. There were some terrible pictures of it in the paper. You might have seen them."

Urbino hadn't, but he had known about the crash. Were the particulars of her son's death the reason why Xenia Campi seemed to see fiery auras around people and why she was so passionately against *Carnevale*? How had she reacted to the graphic photographs of the crash? And how did she feel about the girl who had survived, whoever she might be?

"At about the same time, Porfirio was trying to get them and another family out of his building," the Contessa went on. "They didn't have the money or the energy to fight him and moved out six months later. They found a room in the Castello but their son's death tore them apart. Eventually they got a divorce. She went back to her maiden name but insisted on the 'Signora.' That's when she started to say she had visions, could see the future, although always a bad one. You must have noticed her around the Piazza then."

"I saw her for the first time at a Biennale. She was handing out flyers by the boat landing."

"As I've said before, she has some sense. Much of what she says about Venice and the Biennale is true, as far as I'm concerned. If she were less extreme, people would pay more attention to her."

"How does she support herself?"

"The sisters take hardly anything. Rigoletti gives her a bit of money now and then."

"Did Porfirio feel any guilt over what he had done?"

"Not that he ever showed. He was happy to have his thoroughly modern apartment and his photography."

Urbino thought the Contessa was about to give him more details about Porfirio, but after a moment's pause, she asked, "Have you seen Miss Reeve yet today or is that one of the things you're concealing from me?"

"I haven't seen her. I assume she's at Porfirio's."

"Are you still not suspicious, *caro,* that the young lady has been so eager to tell you things about her private life?"

"I don't think 'eager' is the word to describe what she is, Barbara."

"I've made you cross but it's only for your own good. You need a woman's point of view, and as a woman—as a woman who is also your dear friend—I tell you that you might be putting yourself in a position to be deceived. It could ruin any chance you have for getting to the bottom of this business. I'm curious about something, *caro*. Does your Miss Reeve expect reciprocity?"

She drew out the syllables of the last word almost comically.

"What do you mean?"

"Does she want to know about you, too? Have you told her things about yourself?"

"Very little. She did ask me some things about my parents and about my life in New Orleans before I came here."

"And it was like pulling teeth for her, wasn't it, the poor dear? I know just what she must have gone through! It was years before I got your whole story, and I'm still not sure I know all the important parts! I'd be absolutely furious if I found out that she knew even one tenth of the little I've been blessed with. Oh, she's a crafty one, your Miss Reeve—and also Gibbon's Miss Reeve and Tonio's Miss Reeve! Maybe even Porfirio's Miss Reeve! Very crafty! And only another woman can see the extent of it!"

6   LITTLE Stella Maris Spaak was sitting in the room's only chair, dressed in a dark-blue pants suit. Fluffy childlike pink slippers, similar to the ones her daughter wore, were on her feet. She didn't look as well as she had a few days ago. Her face was flushed and her breathing was a little labored. Urbino detected an occasional wheeze that sounded like the cooing of a dove. Her machine squatted on the floor next to the bed and her medications were scattered over the night table.

He sat self-consciously on the edge of the bed that was covered with magazines, clippings anchored by scissors, and a paperback biography of a movie queen of the thirties and forties.

Mrs. Spaak didn't spend any time on small talk.

"It's about Nicky. No, he isn't here at the Casa Crispina now. He and Dora went shopping and are eating out at a restaurant. I wouldn't have had a chance to talk with you like this if he were here. You're a son, of course, Mr. Macintyre. You know how sons want to protect their mothers from the time they're little boys. And mothers want to do the same for their children, of course. It's even more natural. But once I'm gone there's not going to be anybody who will look after them the way I do. Not even if they marry. Dora came close to marrying two years ago but the young man—he was a doctor at the hospital—broke off their engagement. As for Nicky, he could marry if he wanted to. But even if they have a husband and a wife, they still won't have a mother."

She shook her head slowly.

"A mother always worries about her children, Mr. Macintyre, is always looking for ways to help them through life. I feel Nicky needs me now, needs me to take you aside like this and talk to you. It's not going behind his back," she was quick to assure him, "even if I wouldn't be able to talk to you like this if he were here. I know my son well, maybe more than most mothers know their sons. Ever since he was a little boy he's told me almost everything that has happened to him. When he was away at college, he called me at least once a week and wrote me every single day. Do you know what that means, Mr. Macintyre? Every single day! He wanted to include me in his life. I know that he couldn't tell me everything, of course. He needed to keep things to himself—for his sake and for my own sake, he thought. But compared to your average son, you could say he told me just about everything."

Mrs. Spaak paused. Urbino didn't know what to say or even if he should say anything.

"He still feels it's necessary to keep things from me, and it's only the way it should be. He's a young man now." Urbino was happy to see that Stella Maris Spaak at least made this concession. "But if he's trying to protect me and doing some possible harm to himself, then, in that case, I can't allow it, can I, Mr. Macintyre?"

"I wouldn't think so, Mrs. Spaak."

"There you are. It's for his own good that I tell you. But you needn't tell him that I told you anything."

The concealment, deception, and even self-deception woven through the fabric of what Stella Maris Spaak was telling him

struck Urbino as touching, pathetic, and typical of the majority
of love relationships, whether or not loves of passion. Where
was the love that existed without them?

Urbino believed he knew at least part of what Mrs. Spaak
wanted to tell him about her son. It might be kind if he indicated he already knew, but he didn't want to reveal anything
that would be better kept from her. He smiled to himself.
The trouble with concealment and deception was that they
reproduced themselves. The instinct to protect other people
with benevolent deception was a strong one, especially when
you knew that the person preferred it that way and would most
likely reciprocate.

So sure was he of what Mrs. Spaak had on her mind, however, that he decided to say something.

"It's about your son's walks after you're in bed, isn't it?"

She sat back in her chair, showing the soles of her slippers
more fully.

"How do you know?"

"Your son told me when I spoke with him last week. He
didn't want you to know that he leaves you alone at night."

"Leaves me alone! Now isn't that just like a son! That's
what I was talking about. I know he goes out late at night,
and not because Dora told me either, because she didn't. I
figured it out on my own." She nodded her head proudly at
powers of divination that might rival those of Xenia Campi.
"It doesn't bother me at all, but it bothers him to think I might
know about it. Dora is always here to look after me. She's the
nurse and not Nicky!" she added with a little laugh. "I'm so
happy he told you about his walks, Mr. Macintyre. It makes
it easier for me and it shows that my Nicky understands that
it might put him in a bad position not to tell certain things.
You're a sophisticated man, Mr. Macintyre. I saw that right
away. You speak Italian so well, you live here in such a
famous and beautiful city. Someone told me that you live in
a palace. Is that true?"

"It's called a palace, Mrs. Spaak, but it's probably no bigger
than your house back in Pittsburgh."

She first looked disappointed, then skeptical, but she didn't
pursue the point.

"A man like you, Mr. Macintyre, wouldn't judge my Nicky.
You have a good heart. You can't hide a good heart, not from
a mother, even if it isn't your own mother! You should be able

to find some way to have Nicky confide his secrets in you. I can tell he trusts you, that he likes you."

Urbino doubted this. His impression of Nicholas Spaak was that the American considered him a nosy intruder, someone not to be trusted with a lie, let alone the truth.

"I'm not formally educated myself but I read a lot. Nicky has always bought me books, and sometimes I'll even read his, the ones he might not think are proper for a mother. I know what the world is like even if I've spent most of my life in Pennsylvania. I love my son and I love him no matter what. Some of us are born one way and others a different way. People should stop blaming the mothers. Not that my Nicky has ever blamed me for anything. Even if I had something to do with—with making him that way, there's still nothing to be blamed for. After all, there's Michelangelo, Tennessee Williams, that Russian composer with the long name. I understand my Nicky and I'm proud of him. He's mine forever. That's the way mothers feel about their children."

She coughed and turned her face aside as she took out a handkerchief and expectorated into it.

"Maybe if Nicky were to tell you about himself," she continued, turning back to Urbino, "and it could be handled so that it didn't seem as if I knew. The problem, Mr. Macintyre, is that I'm worried about the rumors I've been hearing here at the Casa Crispina. The Campi woman has been spreading them. She says that everyone knows that Mr. Gibbon was murdered in a place that—that men like to go to and that the police know just the kind of person they're looking for. I could tell it upset my Nicky. So you see, Mr. Macintyre, if he isn't honest with someone about certain things it might look very bad for him. The police would think the worst!"

Mrs. Spaak left little for Urbino to say. He told her that he would see her son as soon as possible.

"And not here at the Casa Crispina if you wouldn't mind, Mr. Macintyre. Somewhere else, maybe your palace. That would be nice. Tonight would be fine, I'm sure."

"Why don't you tell your son to meet me at Harry's Bar tonight at seven, My place is a little difficult to find."

Mrs. Spaak seemed disappointed.

"I suppose that's all right, But don't breathe a word of our little talk. The important thing is to get him to tell you the truth. It has to come from him."

Urbino was relieved to be able to leave Mrs. Spaak with the feeling that, despite her apparent need for concealment and deception, she still had some belief in the truth.

7 AS Urbino was leaving the Casa Crispina, the elderly nun who was reading *Oggi* at the reception desk said that the Contessa da Capo-Zendrini had called and wanted him to call back. He could use the phone at the desk.

"I would like to see you here at the Ca' da Capo about five," the Contessa said.

There was a restrained excitement in her voice. What could possibly have come up in the hour and a half since they had last spoken? He had some more people he wanted to see this afternoon. It would be difficult to see them all and be at the Ca' da Capo-Zendrini at five.

"I'll try, Barbara."

"Don't sound so eager, *caro*! I hope it's not a duty you're performing. Don't think that we Venetian widows are wandering around from room to room in our palazzi rearranging the bibelots and turning the pages of *Casa Vogue* waiting for our entourages of lean, young—or should I say leanish and youngish—American men to show up. I want to see you not for my own misunderstood self but for your own dear sake. This is a completely altruistic appeal. Come at five. I have a surprise for you."

"A surprise?"

There was no further clarification. The Contessa had already hung up. He handed the receiver back to the sister, who was looking up at him curiously after this almost entirely one-sided conversation.

8 IGNAZIO Rigoletti was still at home after the midday meal. He was a dark muscular man in his late forties with an intense, hawklike face. Urbino and Rigoletti were sitting in the dark, underfurnished living room above the Corte Santa Scolastica. Rigoletti had been napping and his face was still rumpled from sleep. He yawned several times as he sprawled on the sofa under a collection of photographs of his days as a rowing champion. Rather than having a cup of coffee, which might have helped make him more alert, however, he was sharing a bottle of red wine with Urbino—and doing most of the talking and drinking himself.

"This area has changed during the last three years since I moved in. We didn't have all this business of *finocchi* coming in to have their bit of dirty fun. I lost my son almost ten years ago. He was a fine specimen of a man, nothing like the ones who come into the Calle Santa Scolastica. I used to think that they were foreigners, tourists—Xenia, my ex-wife, said they were—but I hate to admit we have more than enough of these so-called men living right here in Venice. Things have changed so much I wouldn't be surprised if six of them joined together and rowed a *caorlina* for the Regatta. Why not? They let women row in the *mascarete*!"

He shook his head in disapproval and took a sip of his wine. Urbino's glance went automatically to the photographs above Rigoletti, where he could make out much younger versions of the man, smiling confidently and proudly. A carefree, smiling Xenia Campi had her arm around a boy of about thirteen, both of them standing next to Rigoletti as he held a trophy in his hands. Another showed Xenia Campi on the Lido with her son and a petite dark-haired girl. One photograph seemed to be of the golden Bucintoro, the ceremonial barge that had carried the body of Pope Pius X in his crystal coffin down the Grand Canal. Urbino asked Rigoletti if it was.

"It certainly is. I helped row it."

Rigoletti's eyes seemed to be looking at something beyond the room. He raised his glass in an ostensible salute to this past honor. Urbino did the same and took a sip of the wine. He realized that it was a mistake, however, to encourage Rigoletti to talk about his rowing days. He might not get the information he wanted until it was too late for him to be at the Contessa's at five. There was no question in his mind that Rigoletti would have willingly delayed returning to his job as a delivery bargeman for the sake of reminiscence.

Urbino put the conversation back on the track by mentioning that Commissario Gemelli had told him that Rigoletti had seen two men in the Calle Santa Scolastica the night of the English photographer's murder.

"Two *finocchi,* of that I'm sure," Rigoletti said scornfully. "I didn't recognize either of them from the *calle* or the neighborhood. One of them was coming out when I was turning in. We practically bumped into each other but he was as cool as you could imagine. Just kept right on smiling! Hardly a flicker of surprise or worry on his pretty face. Someone like that could probably have just come from stabbing a man to death and act and look as if he were on his way to Mass! I tell you, Signor Macintyre, appearances are deceiving, though *he* looked enough like what he was to leave no doubt in my mind. He probably spends hours in front of the mirror to get himself to look so good." He grinned. "Well, he wasn't looking so good this morning at the Questura."

"You saw him at the Questura?"

"I went there to look at the drawings the artist made from my descriptions, and there in the flesh was the dark-haired guy I saw coming out of the Calle Santa Scolastica."

It must have been after Urbino had finished talking with Gemelli and was on his way to the Casa Crispina.

"Didn't look at all as cool and collected as he did the night I saw him. They brought him into another room. An Italian, he was. I guess the police have a list of these people. I hope they do. In a little while I'll be looking at some more police photographs from Rome and then I'm going to the Casa Crispina with the Commissario." He sighed. "Maybe I'll be lucky and Xenia won't be there. She'll sure as hell start in on me about something."

"What about the light-haired man you saw coming into the Calle Santa Scolastica after you found the body?"

Rigoletti shook his head.

"I haven't seen anyone who looks like him. They had me go through the photographs in their books, also loose ones like snapshots."

"Did you see anyone else suspicious the night of the murder?"

"Anybody wearing a costume or a mask looks damn suspicious to me. I saw plenty of them. There was a whole bunch coming up from the Riva degli Schiavoni, laughing and passing a big bottle of wine back and forth. I went to the restaurant in the Calle degli Albanesi to call the police, the place where the young kids hang out. You should see the kids in there! Some of them have their heads shaved. Now why would a guy want to go and do that? And the girls! They might not have been wearing costumes but they weren't wearing normal clothes either. My son never hung around places like that. Neither did his girlfriend, although I hear she's changed since those days."

"Why didn't you call the police from here?"

Rigoletti's face betrayed a certain tension as he looked quickly at the telephone on a stand next to Urbino's chair.

"It was quicker to go to the restaurant."

Urbino got up to look more closely at the photographs of Rigoletti's rowing days. Only when he was about to leave did he mention Porfirio.

"Good riddance! He came to the end he deserved, too, just like that scum down in the Calle Santa Scolastica! Broke his neck, didn't he? Well, he broke what was left of Xenia's heart when he forced us out of our home. Made me look like less of a man, too, when we had to live in one ground-floor room in the Castello. Maybe there's some justice in life if we wait long enough. I just hope Buffone suffered before he died, the way my Marco did."

9 NEXT Urbino went to the restaurant in the Calle degli Albanesi that Rigoletti had made his call from. It was little more than a small snack bar with booths and a counter in the back. A television beamed down from a corner above the counter. It was crowded with youths, most of them not in costume. Loud music competed with the video music program on the television. Smoke was thick in the air.

A young woman was painting a boy's face as his friends watched and laughed. She looked vaguely familiar and for a moment he thought she might be the girl in the Piazza who had pointed him out to Leo and the other boys, the girl Xenia Campi was trying to interest Giuseppe in. But she gave him only a quick glance and turned quickly back to her work. He must be mistaken.

Urbino went up to the counter and asked the waitress, her black hair cut at oblique angles, if she had been working the night the English photographer was murdered.

She shook her head.

"Do you know anyone who was here that night?"

"Lupo," she shrilled out above the noise. "This man wants to talk with you."

A tall, thin young man with closely cropped hair dyed blond came from the back. It looked as if he had black eyeliner on. "What do you want? Are you with the police?"

"No."

"You're not Italian, are you?" he said, picking up on Urbino's slight accent.

"No, but I live here in Venice,"

"So what do you want with me?"

"The girl tells me you were working here the night they found the man in the Calle Santa Scolastica."

Instead of answering, Lupo stared back at him.

"I was wondering if you noticed anything unusual that night."

"What's it to you if I did? I've already talked to the police. It was very busy here that night. It's *Carnevale*. I didn't know anything was wrong until that man who lives in the Corte Santa Scolastica came in to call the police. He has a problem, that one."

"What do you mean?"

"Always complaining about the music, about the kids who hang out here, about how we're weird and not normal. He should talk! He's an old relic. We like to have our fun with him."

He returned to his friends. On the way out Urbino looked for the young woman painting faces. She had left. As he was going down the Calle degli Albanesi toward the Riva degli Schiavoni, he heard footsteps behind him.

"Excuse me, signore, you were asking Lupo about the night they found the man in the Calle Santa Scolastica?"

Urbino turned to see an emaciated boy about eighteen.

"Do you know something?"

"I might," he said, looking nervously behind him and running his tongue over his lower lip.

Urbino knew what he was dealing with and held out a ten-thousand-lira note. The boy frowned and Urbino took out another. He grabbed them and stuffed them into his filthy jeans.

"So?" Urbino prompted.

"I was in the place that night. A man with short light hair came in about ten o'clock. He was by himself. He had a drink but he stayed by the door, looking out, as if he was looking for someone or expecting someone to come along. He didn't pay much attention to anybody in here. He was young, younger than you, but not young like the kids who hang around the restaurant. He stayed for about ten minutes. I went out a little while after he did. I saw him going down toward the Calle Santa Scolastica. And there was another thing."

He paused and licked his lower lip again. Urbino gave him another ten thousand lire.

"He was like you," the boy said with an air of triumph.

"Like me? What do you mean?"

"He was an American. He spoke Italian with an American accent. His Italian wasn't good, not like yours, but he was an American just like you."

He went back up the *calle* to the restaurant.

10 A few minutes later, in front of Harry's Bar, Urbino was confronted with the sight of Xenia Campi thrusting flyers into the hands of the people pouring off the vaporetti.

"Turn around, go back to where you came from!" she shouted in Italian. "Venice isn't your playground. I'm speaking to you Italians as well as to you foreigners. Venice won't take it anymore. Venice *can't* take it anymore. You're all murderers! Cities and civilizations can die just like people."

She pushed a flyer at Urbino before she recognized him.

"Oh, it's you, Signor Macintyre. Are you going or coming?"

"Going."

"Good for you! Go back to the Palazzo Uccello and stay there until Wednesday!" She gave him a sharp look, pausing in her distribution of the flyers. "You were at the scene of the crime."

Xenia Campi said it without qualification or tentativeness. She looked away from him to thrust flyers into the hands of a group of people who didn't even glance at them but crumpled them up and dropped them to the pavement. Did Xenia Campi realize that she was contributing to the very problem she was decrying?

"How is Ignazio? I know you saw him! To think that he was the one who found the photographer's body! Now he has something else to talk about besides his old rowing days!"

Urbino detected a slight wistfulness underneath her criticism of her husband. He thought of the picture of the three of them—her, Ignazio, and their dead son, Marco.

"You know the boy Giuseppe staying at the Casa Crispina?"

A wary but somewhat sad look came into her eyes. She nodded.

"From Naples."

"Did you ever see him or the two other boys talking with Gibbon?"

"He's a good boy! He's being led astray. If he was talking with the photographer it was only hello and good-bye. He keeps to himself. The other two are looking for trouble. I wouldn't be surprised if they thought the photographer had a lot of money and followed him to the Calle Santa Scolastica that night. The Neapolitans always carry knives! But not Giuseppe. He's different."

"There's a young woman who paints faces in the Piazza. Do you know her?"

"There are a lot of girls who do that."

"When I saw her she had her face painted red. She has short dark hair."

Xenia Campi narrowed her eyes but didn't say anything.

"Someone said that she had been seen with Gibbon."

No one had told him this, of course, but he wanted more information about the girl from Xenia Campi and he wanted to get it without mentioning Giuseppe again.

"That's impossible!" she said. "I know who you mean. She's a good girl. She would never have had anything to do with a man like that."

"Are you sure she isn't someone you might have seen with Gibbon yourself in the Piazza? You told me that he was always being friendly to young women."

"I meant only Signorina Spaak!"

She thrust a flyer at a couple who had just left a motorboat.

"Do you think that Porfirio's death has something to do with Gibbon's murder?" Urbino asked, taking a different tack.

When she answered, she did it through the mask of Xenia Campi, clairvoyante and seer.

"I saw flames around Gibbon, an aura that promised no good. And around Porfirio Buffone the flames were even brighter, like the flames of the inferno! He was fated for a fall. He was trying to climb too high. I told him in the Piazza but he just laughed like the fool he was! A fall, I told him! The wheel would turn as it does for us all!"

Was it Urbino's imagination or was there something peeping out from behind the crazed glitter of Xenia Campi's eyes? He had often wondered how intentionally histrionic and controlled the woman was when she let herself go this way. He had never considered it a reason to take her less seriously, however. In fact, it seemed all the more reason to pay close attention, for it suggested a cool, calm, almost chilling lucidity behind what might be the camouflage of her rantings and ravings.

She had just given him, without being asked, a good explanation for what Firpo had overheard in the Piazza. Urbino was inclined to believe her, but he couldn't be 100 percent sure.

She was now vilifying photographers.

"They're all ghouls," she said, "ghouls feasting on other people's flesh and blood!"

Handing Urbino a flyer, Xenia Campi turned away to address a newly disembarked group. As Urbino walked out to the landing platform to wait for the boat, he looked at the flyer. It was the same one Xenia Campi had been handing out in the Piazza the afternoon of Gibbon's murder. He read the first few lines and then threw it in the overflowing metal basket on the wake-washed, rocking *pontile*.

11 THE Contessa had an enigmatic smile when Urbino went into the *salotto*. If it didn't say as much—or was it as little?—as the smile da Vinci had painted on the lips of his Gioconda, it was nonetheless just as intriguing. The almost imperceptible curve on one side seemed to tease him with a knowledge that was hers alone.

The Contessa, however, wasn't frozen in time in a marble chair among rocks and a winding river but was a woman of flesh and blood whose main reason for having a secret was being able to impart it to the privileged in her own good time. Urbino knew he would just have to wait and let his friend indulge the pleasure of keeping her secret until she was ready to give herself the equally, if not even more, intense pleasure of revealing it.

"*Caro,* you came, and it's not even five yet," she said with a languid glance at the ormulu clock on the mantel. She leaned back against the Tunisian cushions she had brought back from her autumn cruise of the Mediterranean with Oriana and Filippo Borelli.

"I doubt if you want tea any more this afternoon than you

usually do." She looked down at the table in front of the sofa. Usually during their tête-à-têtes there was only the one china cup for herself. Today there was her cup—filled with tea—and an empty, waiting one. "Fix yourself an *aperitivo*. I think Mauro put in a new bottle of Campari yesterday."

Urbino went over to the bar and fixed himself not a Campari soda but a Cynar. It was his way of letting the Contessa know that she wasn't as much in control as she liked to think she was. She wrinkled her nose when she saw the brown liquid in his glass.

"I don't know how you can drink something made out of *artichokes*! Alvise used to say it was swill fit only for pigs."

For answer he sipped the Cynar and sat in his accustomed Louis Quinze chair with its view not only of the Contessa but also of the Veronese behind her, the one that had disturbed her friend Berenice Pillow so much.

"Well, aren't you going to *say* anything?"

"Like what, Barbara?"

"Such coyness, *caro,* would be no crime, if we had but world enough and time," she said, twisting the poet's words. "But instead we have poor Porfirio dead." This was said as if the departed photographer were lying in state right there in the *salotto*.

"I wasn't aware you had such feelings for Porfirio Buffone," he said disingenuously.

"Urbino! How can you! I didn't care for the man but I certainly didn't wish him dead."

"I've finally succeeded in provoking a straightforward response!"

"I'm the most straightforward person I know," she said with a devious inflection, the smile back in place. "You're playing with me, *caro,*" she informed him in a bold attempt at projection. "Don't I look famished for information? You promised you would tell me everything."

He began with his and Tonio's visit to the Questura. This time he held back nothing that Hazel had confided in him last night about her relationship with Vico and Gibbon and then went on to tell the Contessa about Lubonski, Firpo, Mrs. Spaak, Rigoletti, the two young men from the restaurant, and Xenia Campi. Throughout his long explanation the Contessa looked less like a woman whose appetite was being appeased than someone thinking about a meal she was planning.

But when he finished, her comments indicated that she had been paying attention after all. Understandably, it was Lubonski's admission that she first focused on.

"I feel responsible! I got him the commission. To think that he took those things from Sir Rupert's. I've misplaced my trust abominably!"

"Josef isn't a bad person, Barbara. He was concerned that you not think he was."

"Does that make him better? There was enough talk when we didn't get an Italian for the restoration work, and now with a Venetian dead, probably because of Lubonski, it's going to be that much worse." She settled back and sighed. "Oh, well, I'll go to see him tomorrow. Would you come? You don't think the police will arrest him and take him out of the hospital, do you?"

"He isn't well enough yet to be moved even to another medical facility. Gemelli will probably post a policeman outside his room."

"His poor mother. They're so devoted to each other. You don't think she'll have to give back the money, do you? That would be terrible!"

The Contessa was probably considering how she might be of help to Mrs. Lubonski back in Cracow.

"It's logical, isn't it," she said after a few moments, "that if Gibbon was trying to blackmail Josef, he was doing the same to others? Maybe he was doing it through•photographs, even though you say there isn't anything incriminating in the ones you've seen."

"But I could easily have been missing something. The only thing that struck me was how few photographs of *Carnevale* there actually were. I wonder if there are any other rolls of film around somewhere. Gemelli is checking some of the shops but a professional photographer like Gibbon wouldn't be likely to send most of his film out to be developed. He'd do it himself when he got back—unless he needed the photographs right away."

"What do you think of Gemelli's idea that Gibbon was murdered by a frequenter of the Calle Santa Scolastica?"

"In a fit of passion someone might have done it—or after the passion."

"Does that mean he was that way himself?"

"Who knows?" Gemelli's comment on the mystery of sexuality came into Urbino's mind. "I didn't care for him although I didn't know him that well. If I had, I might have a different opinion of him, as you pointed out. Maybe he had to pretend to be something he wasn't and that was what made him as irritating as he could be."

"But he was engaged. He flirted with women. Women were attracted to him."

She delivered these declarations as if they were indisputable proof of the dead man's heterosexuality.

"It's also possible," Urbino said, "that he just happened to be in the Calle Santa Scolastica without knowing what it was like, was approached, and was a bit too contemptuous in his refusal."

"Then there's Xenia Campi and Rigoletti. I understand now why you wanted to know more about her, but she couldn't have had anything to do with Porfirio's death, could she?"

Urbino told her what he had been considering earlier—that Josef's booby trap might have provided someone with a convenient cover-up for murder.

"Rigoletti and Xenia Campi—together or separately—might have killed Porfirio out of revenge for what he did in turning them out of their apartment right after their son's death. Plenty of murderers have claimed to 'discover' the body as Rigoletti did. And even though I feel Xenia Campi was telling me the truth this afternoon about what Firpo overheard, I still have my doubts about her. Telling the truth about that and not lying about other things aren't the same thing at all. Of course, if we knew why Porfirio was in San Gabriele to begin with, we would have a better chance of figuring out if his death and Gibbon's are related in some way other than through Josef. Perhaps Hazel Reeve knows why Porfirio was in the church."

"Hazel Reeve?"

Urbino couldn't tell if it was satisfaction or surprise that he detected in her tone.

"She's a more logical connection between Gibbon and Porfirio than either Xenia Campi or Rigoletti."

Did the Contessa realize how difficult it was for him to admit this?

"Do you have any theories?" the Contessa asked.

Urbino shook his head.

"I don't believe you. You always have theories, and you

almost always hug them too close for too long. Well, I can have theories of my own! I can have secrets of my own!"

After this little outburst, the enigmatic smile was back in place.

"When I spoke with you from the Casa Crispina, you said that you had a surprise for me."

"Did I say that? Maybe I was mistaken—or maybe you don't deserve to have the pleasure of a surprise."

"Surprises aren't always pleasurable, Barbara."

"Aren't you the sly one! You might be right in this case. But pleased or not, don't disappoint me by not being suitably amazed."

"So what is it?"

She looked at the mantel clock again.

"It shouldn't be long. Keep your mind on other things," she said, as if he didn't have more than enough to occupy him. "It might be a good idea to talk about Hazel Reeve even though you don't seem to want to. Actually, that's the very reason why you should." She hesitated as if considering what she should say next. "So what do you think of her?"

The question was, he felt, intentionally ambiguous and meant to lead him astray. The Contessa took a sip of her tea and looked at him from across her cup and saucer, her eyes shining with what he found to be an inappropriate merriment.

He got up and poured himself another portion of Cynar. He didn't return to his seat but walked to the corner table with its collection of Byzantine and Russian icons and reliquaries of Saint Catherine of Siena and Saint Nicholas of Bari. He picked up the wooden cross with a bone shard of Saint Nicholas encased under a delicate bubble of glass.

"It was a lot easier knowing what you believed a thousand years ago," he said. "Haven't you ever wondered what it would have been like to have lived back then? Things were much simpler."

"And also a lot more unbecoming, especially for us women. Are you going philosophical on me or just being evasive? If you don't want to answer my question about Miss Hazel Reeve, just say so."

When Urbino put the reliquary down and turned to face her, her enigmatic smile was more irksome than it had been before.

"Evasive, Barbara? Is it evasive not to answer a question

when you're not sure of the answer? And, I might also add, when you know what answer is expected?"

"And what kind of answer is that, *caro*?"

"That Hazel Reeve is Lucrezia Borgia!"

He tried to carry it off as a joke but it somehow rang hollow. The Contessa was amused.

"You're such a boy, Urbino—such an innocent, sweet little mischievous boy!"

What she said was unexpected enough but her clear, honest laughter made it even more so. Before she could add anything to it, there was a knock on the door. Lucia, the Contessa's maid, entered tentatively. She went over to the sofa and handed the Contessa a folded slip of paper. The Contessa thanked her and opened it.

She frowned, folded it again, and slipped it into her pocket.

"Bad news, Barbara?"

"Not bad news, but disappointing." The frown gradually disappeared. "Disappointing, I should add, mainly for you. *I* can deal with it."

"Does this have something to do with your secret?"

"It has everything to do with my secret, *caro*, but if I tell you anything more than that it won't be a secret any longer, will it? Stay and have dinner. I promise that your curiosity—I can see it shining in your eyes!—will be sated before the end of the evening."

"I'm sorry, Barbara, but I'm meeting Nicholas Spaak at Harry's at seven. I told you about my conversation with his mother. She thought it would be a good idea for us to meet at the Palazzo Uccello but I suggested Harry's instead. Neutral ground, so to speak."

"To discourage any amorous notions in Mr. Spaak? You don't think his sweet mother could have had such things in mind when she suggested the privacy of your quarters, do you? You're a good catch, you know! Why Harry's, though? You know what it's like at this time of the year! But since you're going there, you must promise me two things."

"What?"

"That you will absolutely *not* order a Bellini and that you will do everything you can to be back here by nine—even if Mr. Spaak is pouring out his heart to you!"

12 AN hour later at Harry's, Urbino kept his first promise to the Contessa by ordering a glass of wine. And it seemed he would easily be able to keep his second one as well for Nicholas Spaak didn't seem inclined to speak much at all, let alone pour out his heart to him.

Harry's was impossibly crowded with masqueraders, people in formal dress, and bewildered tourists in anoraks and jeans relegated to remote tables in the smoke-filled downstairs room. Urbino and Spaak were standing at the bar by the entrance. Every seat at the bar and at the tables was taken. Perhaps he should have followed Stella Maris Spaak's suggestion and asked Spaak to meet him at the Palazzo Uccello. Harry's wasn't particularly conducive to the kind of conversation he hoped they would have.

Spaak had downed his martini in the first few minutes and was already half through his second. He seemed paler than he had several nights ago, his blue eyes duller.

"My mother put you up to this, didn't she?"

"I was at the Casa Crispina today to see Mother Mariangela. It was my idea that we meet here at Harry's."

Spaak gave him a knowing smile.

"Have it your own way. Don't forget that she's my mother. I know her."

Then why try to protect her so much? thought Urbino. Nicholas Spaak and his mother seemed to understand each other very well, yet neither bothered—or risked—telling the other the extent of their understanding.

"So why did you want to see me?"

There was a false bravado in Spaak's challenge. He pushed a lock of blond hair from his eyes.

"Very well, then," Urbino said. "But let's be honest with each other. I don't think you would have even shown up here this evening if you didn't want to talk with me. You realize that you're putting yourself in a vulnerable position the longer you say nothing."

"Say nothing about what?"

"About being in the Calle Santa Scolastica the night Val Gibbon was murdered."

Urbino hadn't been absolutely sure that Nicholas Spaak had been there, but his reaction now removed any doubts. An incredulous look came over Spaak's face. Something seemed to collapse in his shoulders. He ran his hand through his blond hair. Urbino could tell that he wasn't even going to make the feeblest attempt at a denial.

"How did you know?"

The best—and perhaps kindest—way to answer this was to tell him that he had been seen in the Calle Santa Scolastica. When he did, Spaak almost shouted, "But that man couldn't have known it was me! I've never seen him before and I haven't seen him since. I haven't even been anywhere near that place since the murder."

"You might very well be seeing Rigoletti at the Casa Crispina later. He's going there with the police."

Spaak started slightly.

"If you get back after they've been there, it would be wise of you to go to the Questura first thing tomorrow. You were at the scene of a crime and you haven't told the police yet. Why don't you tell me what happened?"

"What is this, a dry run? Maybe you'll compare notes and see if I tell the same story to you both."

"Do you have any reason not to tell the truth?"

Spaak finished his martini and ordered another.

"I might have a lot of reasons for not wanting to say I was there on that night—or on any other night—but they don't have anything to do with having murdered Gibbon. I've already told you that I didn't like him," he added, as if this previous openness would compensate for whatever he had also held back. "I didn't like him but I didn't kill him. I'm not the killing kind, Mr. Macintyre."

"You were in the Calle Santa Scolastica that night. Maybe you saw the person who did kill Gibbon."

"Let's get out of here. I'd prefer to talk somewhere else."

But once they were outside they had to decide where to go. Certainly not up the Calle Vallaressa toward the Piazza San Marco with its crowds nor along the Molo toward the Piazzetta, the Ducal Palace, and the Calle Santa Scolastica. It was Urbino's town, and if he had made a mistake in having them meet in Harry's, then he might be able to rectify it.

"Let's take the local boat up the Grand Canal," he said. "With luck it won't be too crowded."

But it was. Maskers were on their way to parties or dinner, residents were returning home, and weary tourists were taking the slower and cheaper vaporetto back to the train station. Urbino and Spaak made their way through the noisy enclosed area to the stern. Here, fortunately, there was only a young man in a tall Pulchinello hat embracing a girl with a white-painted face and chartreuse wig. They were oblivious to anything or anyone but themselves. Urbino and Spaak sat down across from them.

The wind that had been blowing earlier had died and the air had turned warmer. Fog was starting to roll in across the water. The boat pulled out of the San Marco landing for the short passage to the Salute.

Spaak was huddled into his coat, his scarf tightly wound around his neck, his hands thrust into his pockets. He made no effort to pick up where they had left off inside Harry's. There was a somewhat wary look in his eye now as he glanced out at the Custom House.

Perhaps Urbino could help things along by falling into the role of a guide.

"That palazzo there," he said, drawing Spaak's attention to a small Gothic building with lacy balconies and ogive windows, "is sometimes called the House of Desdemona, although I doubt if it had anything to do with her."

When Spaak gave no reaction except a desultory glance at the building, Urbino said, "Desdemona was Othello's wife."

Spaak's humorless smile made his face seem skeletal.

"Have you forgotten that I'm an English teacher, Mr. Macintyre? I know the play and some of the criticism on it. Do you remember what Coleridge said about Iago? That he had a 'motiveless malignity,' that he was like a devil, a fiend?"

Urbino nodded as they pulled into the Salute landing.

"Do you think a person can be evil just for the sake of being evil?" Spaak asked.

The boat bumped against the landing.

"It's possible, but it would be an example of pathology, don't you think?"

"Pathology or, if you believe Coleridge, theology. Devils, Satan, and all that."

The vaporetto was soon moving again slowly up the Grand Canal to its next stop on the other side. The low line of lights in the far distance that was the Lido was barely visible because of the fog.

Urbino gave a quick glance at Spaak, who was staring at a row of palazzi. He sensed that Spaak was working up to something and that he should keep quiet. They were approaching the next landing when Spaak said, "One of my professors in graduate school said that Iago might have been homosexual, that he was jealous—envious—of Desdemona and that was why he did what he did." He turned to Urbino with an earnest look. "What do you think of that?"

"There are more plausible reasons to explain Iago's behavior than that." Spaak looked at him expectantly. He wanted more than this. "Besides," Urbino added, "Shakespeare was a genius, wasn't he? Your professor seems to want to make him into a bigot."

This light note seemed to be the right one.

"Aren't you forgetting Shylock and *The Merchant of Venice?*" Spaak said with a smile. "Maybe Shakespeare saved his genius for his other plays and put all his bigotry into the ones set in Venice. Venice!" He shook his head slowly as the vaporetto left the landing and continued its zigzag course up the Grand Canal. "I think you know why I was in the Calle Santa Scolastica. And I think you also know why I'm not particularly fond of my old professor's interpretation of Iago."

"How did you find out about the Calle Santa Scolastica?"

"The way I've found out about many other things in my life! It was an accident. Not quite an accident, perhaps. Let's just say that I was led there."

"You followed someone?"

"I like the way I put it better. Oh, I know you can lead a horse to the river and all that. I was led but I wanted to drink. No one had to force me. I knew what I was doing."

"Are you talking about the night Gibbon was murdered?"

"I was there before that night. I told you last week at the Casa Crispina that I usually go for long walks after I see my mother to bed. I wasn't telling you the truth, though, when I said that I didn't know where I ended up the night Gibbon was murdered. I went to San Marco the way I usually do. That night I didn't find anyone along by the water and I thought I would go to that alley."

"You stopped in the little restaurant in the Calle degli Albanesi where the young kids hang out, didn't you?"

"I'm impressed. Yes, I did. I wanted a coffee. After I had it, I went to the alley that leads to the canal, the place where they found Gibbon."

"I know you got only as far as the first part of the *calle*. That's where you saw Ignazio Rigoletti and became frightened and turned around."

"You don't know as much as you think you do. You're talking about the second time I was there that night. Yes, I went there twice."

This was completely unexpected.

"The first time was about ten-thirty. I had been walking by the water for about twenty minutes and then I decided to go to the alley. As I was turning into it, I got a quick glimpse of someone standing to my right in the passageway behind the hotel. He was much shorter than me, with one of those cheap yellow masks, the kind I bought for my mother. He was just standing there, waiting in the shadows. It was strange. He seemed to step forward and then stop, and I thought maybe he had seen me before in the area. He seemed a little familiar— I can't put my finger on exactly why, since I couldn't see his face. I kept walking into the Calle Santa Scolastica."

Spaak stopped and looked at the young couple who now seemed to be paying more attention to their surroundings. But a few moments later they got up and left. The vaporetto was approaching the Accademia stop.

"When I got into the courtyard," Spaak continued, "I saw another man by the canal. He was very attractive—handsome, I'd say. He had a strong face with full lips. I wanted to go up to him but something made me stop. Maybe it was the look on his face, so self-assured, so impassive. I thought of the short man I had just seen. I felt as if it was a trap so I turned around and went out. The other man was still standing there. I went down by the water."

"Did you recognize either of the two men?"

"No," he said hesitantly, "but I had a feeling that I had met one—or both of them—before, maybe when I had been in the alley. But neither was Gibbon. That's why I saw no point in telling the police. If I had, it couldn't have been any help to them, and I would have had to admit everything."

"You went back to the Calle Santa Scolastica again later, though."

"About half an hour later. I knew it would be best if I didn't. The same two might be there and this time they might mug me or do something worse. But somehow I felt compelled to go back." He looked down at his hands. "I feel that way a lot when I—I'm walking around. I stopped for coffee in that place where all the kids were hanging out and then went down toward the alley again. I didn't see either of them this time. I turned into the alley and then I saw that man—what did you say his name was? Rigoletti—coming toward me. I got frightened and ran away toward the lagoon. I could tell right away he wasn't there for the same reason I was. I was frightened but not because of Gibbon, believe me! I never even saw him. My God, I didn't even know he was there! Dead, I mean. But hc wasn't lying there at the end of the alley the first time I came. When I saw that man coming toward me, all I could think of was that he was the police. It would kill my mother if I were arrested for something like that. It would kill her if she even knew about the way I am."

"If she loves you, as she obviously does, I'm sure it wouldn't make any difference."

Spaak gave a hollow laugh as the vaporetto moved away from the landing where a crowd waited for the other boats. The boy in the Pulchinello hat and his girlfriend in the wig were being greeted enthusiastically by their friends, who were partying in the little square in front of the art gallery.

"Aren't you the optimist!" Spaak said. "Well, it might be true, but I wouldn't want to find out. It might be too hard on her."

Where did protecting his mother end and protecting himself begin? Were they really distinguishable to him?

"And Dora? Does she know?"

"I've never told her, if that's what you mean, but I think she's known since I was in college. My sister is very loyal. *She* wouldn't say anything to Mother."

"Would your sister do anything for you?"

Spaak frowned.

"What the hell is that supposed to mean?"

"You just said she's very loyal. Your mother said the same thing the other night."

"Well, she is! And I've always looked out for her, too. Stop beating around the bush. Are you going to say anything to my mother?"

"It's not my business to tell her; I leave that to you. But you must go to the police. What you saw in the Calle Santa Scolastica could be very important. At any rate, you could be arrested for withholding information." He let this impress itself on Spaak. "Did you see anyone in the area of the Calle Santa Scolastica that night other than Ignazio Rigoletti and these two men?"

"Not until I got out by the lagoon."

"Rigoletti has identified one of the men. You're the other one. When you go to the police, tell them about the short man in the mask. The man you saw at the end of the *calle* might be the one Rigoletti has already identified."

"Has he been arrested?"

"I don't know but I doubt it. Just because someone was in the Calle Santa Scolastica around the time Gibbon was murdered doesn't make him the murderer, and it's certainly not enough to have the Questura arrest whoever it is." Urbino paused before going on. "I'm sure you realize that the police will want to know if you were physically attracted to Gibbon. If you and he might have—"

"I couldn't stand the man!" Spaak almost shouted. He shook his head. "I guess I look guilty either way, don't I? Whether I say I liked him or if I say I didn't!"

"Do you think Gibbon could have gone to the Calle Santa Scolastica for the same reason you did?"

Spaak's mouth twitched with amusement. " 'Could have'? Who knows? That's why he might have been so snide with me. Too bad he isn't here for you to ask him if he was physically attracted to me, instead of the other way around!"

This marked the end of their conversation. They sat side by side in the stern of the vaporetto, looking at the Grand Canal and the palazzi lining its banks. They could see the decorative Murano chandeliers in the parlors and could hear the sound of laughter and music drifting over the canal from open windows. The Sant'Angelo and San Silvestro stops came and went and they still were silent.

As the boat was approaching the Rialto landing, Spaak stood up.

"I know the way to the Casa Crispina from here. Don't

mention anything to my mother. If she has to know, I should tell her. I hope you can see that."

Urbino did. He also saw that the circle of benevolent deception between Spaak and his mother was likely to continue.

"And the police?" he asked as Spaak opened the door into the cabin.

"I'll tell them everything tomorrow. Tonight I just want to take a long walk."

He closed the door behind him and went down the aisle to the exit.

13 FOR the remaining trip only occasionally did Urbino give his attention to the passing, familiar scene along the Grand Canal. At first he thought about his conversation with Nicholas Spaak. Was his story of his two trips to the Calle Santa Scolastica to be believed? Had what he had seen there—someone in a plastic mask standing outside the *calle* and someone else unmasked at the end of it by the canal—played a role in the death of Val Gibbon? Did Spaak know something more about Val Gibbon's sexuality than he was willing to say? And did he really not realize that his mother knew about his own homosexuality? Or did he know, yet not want to acknowledge that she actually did, even to himself? And what about his sister? How much did she know about her brother?

There seemed to be no limit to people's capacity, not to say their need, for self-deception. We wear masks as much for ourselves as we do for others, Urbino thought. Masks covered faces, and these days there were any number of examples of them. But the face could be the ultimate mask, one thrust not only at strangers and loved ones, friends and enemies, but also at oneself.

Much of his work as a biographer was to penetrate masks—in some cases to peel successive ones away—and to seek out the concealed selves behind them, yet all too often there was little that could be found. Proust, sounding a warning, had said that no one could truly say he knew another person. Urbino had little doubt of this. He was being particularly sensitive to it as he worked on his book on Proust in Venice, and now he reminded himself of it in reference to the deaths of Gibbon and Porfirio.

Because of the turn Urbino's mind had taken as he sat in the stern of the vaporetto after Spaak had left, everything around him seemed to feed his thoughts—the water reflecting darkened impressionistic images of the reality above them, the veil of fog wreathing in, the palazzi stretching and curving like some long, deceptive escarpment or series of embellished masks on either side of the Grand Canal. Sitting there in the stern, Urbino for a few confused moments felt that he himself wasn't moving but that an elaborate screen was being unwound on either side of him, giving the illusion of motion and of depth.

Inevitably, this sense of disorientation led back to his thoughts about the murder in the Calle Santa Scolastica, thus completing the circle.

What was true and unfeigned about the things he had been told so far? Even in the best, most usual of circumstances, when little except social discomfort was at stake, people pretended, exaggerated, indulged in mental reservations or outright lies. It wasn't immoral except by the strictest of standards, and it certainly wasn't villainous. But murder was an entirely different matter. Loss of face and loss of reputation were the least things for the murderer to fear.

As the vaporetto pulled alongside the San Marcuola landing, Urbino felt oppressed as if by a frieze of masks showering down upon him their lies and deceptions. Among these lies and deceptions were the ones biding the truth of a brutal murder. These had to be recognized and exposed, but as for the others, he would leave them where he found them.

14 THE surprise the Contessa had been teasing him with earlier with her insinuations and enigmatic smile was immediately evident when Urbino walked into her *salotto* shortly after nine.

It was on the sofa next to her. His face must have shown a great deal of what he was feeling because the Contessa, barely able to keep the laughter from her voice, said,

"No, you're not seeing things, *caro!*"

"Hello, Urbino," Hazel Reeve said. She was wearing a forest-green dress of simple lines that brought out the color of her eyes. "I'm sorry I wasn't here earlier when you stopped by but I—I had to leave in a rush."

"Don't go into that right now, Hazel dear," the Contessa said, reaching out to pat the young woman's hand in a proprietary way. While she was doing it, however, she wasn't looking at Hazel but at Urbino with just the faintest suggestion of her Gioconda smile from several hours ago.

"I'm also sorry that I left your place the way I did this morning. And I wish I could have spoken with you later from Porfirio's but Commissario Gemelli wouldn't let me."

She gave him a brave smile. It was as if she needed to apologize all at once for whatever she might have done.

"I've been busy for most of the day myself," he said. "I should have given you another call. I'm sure Porfirio's death has hit you hard, coming as it does right after Val's."

He fixed himself a bourbon, something that the Contessa kept especially for him. She looked at the glass.

"You've given up Cynar, I see. Be careful, *caro*. You know how too much bourbon gives you a restless night. When you're finished with that bottle, I'm not so sure I'm going to be nice enough—or inconsiderate enough—to get you another."

Urbino sat down and took a sip of what might be one of his last bourbon and waters at the Contessa's. Hazel took a sip of her own indistinguishable but tall drink and said, "I came here about two this afternoon, Urbino."

"You came here?"

"Yes, *caro,* she came here. Don't act so incredulous. The Ca' da Capo isn't a St. Anne's Home for Young Girls, I know, and our own sweet Hazel here isn't in any way the wayward kind, are you, dear?"—once again she reached over to pat the girl's hand—"but here she is and here she can stay for as long as she cares to."

This was said with a slightly uptilted chin as if she expected Urbino to demand at once that Hazel Reeve be returned to her original quarters.

"The Contessa—Barbara"—Hazel corrected herself—"came over to Porfirio's this afternoon and insisted that I return here with her. She helped me pack my things, not that there were all that many, and we were here before I knew it."

The Contessa glanced at her sharply, perhaps at the possibly implied criticism she might have detected in Hazel's "before I knew it." When the Contessa spoke, however, it was without a trace of anything except a sincere desire to leave nothing in question.

"I certainly couldn't leave her at Porfirio's, poor girl! And a room in a hotel just would not do, even if we could have found one. As far as the Palazzo Uccello is concerned, *caro,* we couldn't have Hazel staying there unchaperoned. I know that Natalia and her husband are living in the *attico* but that's not enough to keep all the tongues in this city from wagging." She took a sip from her glass of Corvo before adding, "One night couldn't do much damage but, beyond that, we have to be concerned with appearances, especially since Hazel knew a man who has been murdered." She looked away from Urbino and said to Hazel, "Urbino is considered something of an interloper, I'm afraid, Hazel dear. People are only too eager to talk in the most unkind ways. *Dio mio!* Even after more than thirty years here, I have to watch out for myself. Tongues are like knives here, believe me!"

It was to Hazel's credit that she gave no indication that she might have found the Contessa's last image disturbing.

Urbino sipped his bourbon and water and mulled over the Contessa's volte-face. Only a very short time before she had been brimming with disapproval of her young compatriot. Now she was benevolent and protective, traits much more natural to her. But what bad brought about the change?

"She's all alone here in our serene city, Urbino dear," the Contessa said, eerily answering his unspoken question, "although it isn't particularly serene at the moment, is it? And she has no father, no mother." This must have started an unwelcome train of thought for she quickly added, "And I thought it only right that I offer her some sisterly shelter and comfort. We are both English after all. She's suffered enough."

For the first time since coming into the *salotto* he noticed the dark shadows under Hazel's eyes. On top of Gibbon's murder and her fear that Tonio Vico might have been involved—a fear that had caused her to flee to Mestre—there had come Porfirio's own death. The poor girl was understandably at loose ends, and it had been a commendable act of charity for the Contessa to invite her to stay at the Ca' da Capo-Zendrini—even if he didn't fully understand the reasons for his friend's abrupt change of mind.

"I hope it doesn't compromise you, Barbara. I certainly seem to be in the thick of things," Hazel said with an embarrassed smile. "I knew Val, and he's dead, and I was staying with Porfirio and now he's dead, too. I know that they died in different ways, that there's no connection between their deaths," she was quick to add, "but it doesn't make me feel any less—less peculiar. Commissario Gemelli didn't make me feel any better this morning, especially not when I told him about the key."

"The key? What key?" the Contessa asked.

Hazel flushed.

"Things have gone so fast today, Barbara, that I haven't had a chance to mention it before now."

The Contessa put down her wineglass and waited for Hazel to go on.

"You see, there was a key to the church. Val gave me one. He had it made from the one he had. We would meet in the church late at night, just to be alone together, just to talk and walk around. It was like being in another world. He gave me the key because he didn't want to have anyone interrupting us. On evenings when we didn't have dinner together he would go in and lock the door behind him, then wait for me. I would let myself in with my key. Porfirio took it. That's how he got into San Gabriele the night he—he died."

"Didn't you take the key with you to Mestre?" Urbino asked her.

"I left very quickly without going back to Porfirio's. I intended to come back. I *did* come back. But why would I want to take the key anyway?"

"How did Porfirio know about it?"

"One night he saw me going into San Gabriele. He was walking across the square. It was obvious I had a key."

"So he took it and went into the church—but why?"

"I haven't the slightest idea. Maybe he wanted to see the restoration work for himself."

"But he could have come in to look at it anytime."

"He might have wanted to look at it when no one else was there," interjected the Contessa. "With Gibbon dead and Lubonski in the hospital, he could be sure no one would interrupt him."

"Porfirio *was* upset that Val was taking the photographs of the restoration instead of him," Hazel said tentatively, picking up her tall glass. "Do you think he might have wanted to take his own photographs now that Val was dead?"

"Paolo told Sister Teresa that Porfirio had one of his cameras with him," the Contessa said.

This didn't mean very much, although Urbino would have liked to know what the film in Porfirio's camera showed when it was developed.

"When do you think Porfirio took your key?" he asked Hazel.

"Does it really matter that much? I don't really know. I kept it on the dresser in my room. I didn't put it on my key ring because I knew I would have to give it back to Val soon. It wasn't there this morning, but I'm sure it was there the last time I bothered to look a few days ago. Porfirio could have taken it just about anytime after Val died—or before—and either used it or had a copy made."

"I doubt he had a copy made since the key wasn't there this morning. The key he used to get in must be yours. It must have been found on his body."

"And now there's this trouble for Tonio," she said, shaking her head and looking at the Contessa. "Can I tell him now?" she asked hesitantly.

"Whatever do you mean, Hazel dear? You can tell him whatever you want, whenever you want. Urbino, would you mind getting me another glass of wine? And perhaps Hazel would like to have her drink freshened."

The girl shook her head. Urbino got up and poured out another Corvo for the Contessa and put another ice cube and dollop of bourbon into his own glass.

"What is this about Tonio Vico?" he asked as he gave the Contessa her glass and returned to his seat. "I went to the Questura with him this morning. Everything seemed fine, although he was nervous, of course." But before he finished speaking he thought he knew what Hazel had meant. "Rigoletti said he identified someone at the Questura. Was it Tonio?"

"After you left," the Contessa said.

There were a few moments of silence.

"It can't be true!" Hazel said. "I know it's not true! Tonio could never have done anything to Val."

It wasn't the time to remind her that she had fled—albeit only across the bridge to Mestre—when the sight of her former fiancé at the Montin had led her to suspect that he had had something to do with Gibbon's murder.

"I told you that last night," she said to Urbino. "Tonio swears he's never been anywhere near the area."

"You've spoken with him?" Urbino asked.

"She's seen him. She went to the Splendide-Suisse this afternoon."

"That's why I couldn't see you then, Urbino." This explained the note the Contessa had received when he had come earlier, the note that had quickly banished her enigmatic smile. "He found out that I was here from his stepmother—Barbara told her—and he phoned me. I went to see him as quickly as I could. He was very upset."

"He's not arrested then."

"Of course he's not arrested, Urbino," the Contessa said. "How could he be? Just on Rigoletti's identification? Just because he might have been in the Calle Santa Scolastica that night? It doesn't mean he killed Gibbon."

"But he wasn't there that night—or any night!" Hazel leaned forward, gripping her glass tightly. "I know he wasn't! This man is mistaken."

"Or he's lying," the Contessa said. "He might have his own reasons for lying. And it was night. How could Rigoletti be sure of who he saw?"

"Mrs. Pillow swears he wasn't out that night. They were in the whole evening!" Hazel said in a choked voice.

"If Berenice says so, it must be true," the Contessa affirmed. "She wouldn't lie about a thing like this."

"Not even when it came to her stepson?" Urbino said. He had no doubt that Mrs. Pillow or almost any mother trying to protect her son would lie. He was sure Mrs. Spaak was capable of it. It made Mrs. Pillow no better or worse than anyone else, and it certainly didn't make her a villain. Some might even say that it made her something very much different.

Hazel looked at him coolly.

"Believe me, Urbino, she wasn't lying. I've known her for several years and she was telling the truth. She's seldom passionate about anything, but when she is, you know it's because she believes in what she's saying or doing. I wish I had reason to doubt that."

The Contessa nodded in agreement with Hazel's assessment of her old friend.

"Was she unpleasant to you this afternoon, Hazel?" the Contessa asked.

"Not at all. She was actually quite nice. She knew I was there only to try to help Tonio."

"But what can you possibly do for him, Hazel dear? You mentioned before Urbino came that you hadn't seen him before tonight. It would be fine if you could provide him with an alibi, yet—"

"He doesn't need an alibi! He didn't do anything, I tell you!"

She put her glass down on the table and buried her face in her hands. The Contessa slid over to her and put a consoling arm around her shoulder.

"I'm sorry, Hazel. I didn't mean to upset you but you have to be open-eyed. Tonio is in love with you and it's quite obvious you still have feelings for him"—her gray eyes slid quickly in Urbino's direction—"but you can't tear yourself apart like this. It's not going to do either of you any good. Urbino will help Tonio, won't you, *caro*? He's already been helping him. He went to the Questura with him this morning, didn't he?"

Hazel lifted her hands from her face to look at Urbino. Tears glistened on her cheeks.

"You can help?"

Her words were less questioning than imploring.

"Of course I'll do whatever I can," Urbino said, keeping his promise vague.

Before coming to the Contessa's tonight, he had believed that Vico hadn't been in the Calle Santa Scolastica the night Gibbon was murdered, but now that Rigoletti appeared to have identified him, he wasn't so sure. He supposed it was more than possible that Berenice Pillow, to protect her stepson, had lied and said that he was in the suite all that night. Yet he hadn't detected anything in Mrs. Pillow's words, tone, or manner that might have indicated she was wrongly if understandably giving a mother's protection. If anything, what had come through clearly was her own certitude about what she was saying.

Nonetheless, Urbino wanted to be careful of what he promised Hazel. He didn't want to mislead her. To do that would have seemed too much like getting caught up himself in the web of lies and deceptions that was seriously impeding his progress toward a solution.

"I'll speak with Commissario Gemelli. I'll see Tonio tomorrow," he said, still keeping his promises within reasonable bounds.

The Contessa, who had taken her arm away from Hazel's shoulder, looked at him expressionlessly. Hazel's response was more easy to gauge. She was now smiling. She took out a lace handkerchief and wiped her tears.

"You won't have to wait until then, Urbino," she said. "Tonio and Mrs. Pillow are coming over in a little while. Oh, I hope you don't mind my inviting them, Barbara. I knew Urbino was going to be here and I wanted to be able to explain poor Tonio's situation before they came." She looked at her thin gold watch. "They should be arriving in about five or ten minutes. You really don't mind, do you?"

The Contessa had slipped during the past several moments into her inscrutable mode. What she was thinking or how she was feeling were mysteries that her fine smooth manner did nothing to reveal. And when she spoke, her words gave nothing away except their surface meaning.

"Berenice is one of my oldest friends, Hazel. She and Tonio are welcome here whenever they wish to come."

This was what she said. What she meant, however, could have been something else entirely. The extent to which she was in control was clear when she looked at Urbino with no expression on her face at all.

"Excuse me for a moment," she said, starting to get up from the sofa. "I would like to tell Lucia and Mauro that we'll be expecting Berenice and Tonio in a few minutes."

"I've already mentioned it to Lucia, Barbara," Hazel said, putting her handkerchief back in the pocket of her dress.

"How kind of you, Hazel."

The Contessa settled back against the Tunisian cushions, still managing the feat of an expressionless face. Urbino couldn't help noticing, however, that this time she didn't look in his direction.

There was one topic that Urbino wanted to bring up with Hazel but he wasn't sure this was the best time or place. It had to do with Gibbon's presence in the Calle Santa Scolastica. If they were alone, it would be easier. Now with her staying at the Ca' da Capo-Zendrini, he wondered how often he would be able to see her without the Contessa around. Could the Contessa's consideration in taking Hazel away from Porfirio's have been complicated by an additional motive? He remembered the enigmatic smile on her lips. Had it been pure anticipatory amusement or the smile of someone who had made a countermove soon to be revealed? Knowing the Contessa for as long and as well as he did, he had to admit that it was probably a little of both.

The silence that had come over the three of them made it seem as if they had nothing to say to each other until the arrival of Berenice Pillow and Tonio Vico. Urbino decided to risk asking his question.

"Do you have any idea why Gibbon happened to be in the Calle Santa Scolastica the night he was murdered?"

"I didn't know he was going there. I didn't know he ever went there."

It wasn't really an answer to the question he had asked, but before he could ask it again, without seeming rude or importunate, Hazel said,

"I know what you're getting at. Commissario Gemelli, of course, has asked me the same thing in about five different ways, but I told him that I have no idea what Val was doing there that night. Commissario Gemelli made it clear what kind of reputation that area has, but my answer was the same after he told me as it was before. I thought Val might have been there to take pictures until I saw that there were none of that area among Val's photographs—and not anything that might help us find Val's murderer either, from what I could see."

"I'm surprised at you, Urbino," the Contessa said. "Poor Hazel here was engaged to Val Gibbon. Whatever are you implying by such a question?"

"Oh, it doesn't matter, Barbara, really it doesn't. We all live in the modern world." Hazel smiled weakly. "Although maybe I'm mistaken about Venice. It's not quite right to call it part of the modern world, is it?"

"And why not, my dear, if it's filled with at least some enlightened people who think in modern ways?"

The Contessa had abandoned her inscrutability. Now she was all passionate defense of her adopted city and, it would seem, her own enlightened self.

"Commissario Gemelli isn't one of them, though," Hazel said. "He's more than a little benighted. 'Are you sure your fiancé didn't like men, Signorina Reeve? Are you sure he wasn't having an assignation in the Calle Santa Scolastica? Have you any reason to believe that he might have been homosexual? Have you noticed anything unusual along these lines during the time you've known him?'"

The Contessa seemed uncomfortable as Hazel made her recitation.

"If he could have proof of any of that, he would probably be happy to write off Val's murder as a meeting between an all-too-willing victim and a pathetic murderer of whom you couldn't expect much less," Hazel continued. She shook her head in exasperation. "I told him I had no reason to think any of those things, and he just smiled at me. Then I told him that it wouldn't have made any difference to me anyway. That took the smile off his face! And I meant it, too! I judged and loved Val by the way he treated me, what he was like with me. I believe he was faithful. I wanted him to be, and I certainly don't like the idea of his sneaking around in dark alleys looking—looking for someone, something. Val was a very attractive man. He was an artist. I know what the world is like. I know—"

She didn't finish her sentence but burst into tears again. This time they flowed more copiously. Before she reapplied the hastily drawn handkerchief to her eyes and before the Contessa once again reached over to comfort her, for one brief, somewhat unsettling moment she looked at Urbino through her tears. It didn't strike him as a look soliciting sympathy but one assessing his reaction.

The door to the Contessa's *salotto* opened. Mauro announced the arrival of Berenice Pillow and Tonio Vico. The two of them started to enter the room but stopped abruptly when they saw Hazel weeping in the arms of the Contessa as Urbino looked on.

15 WHAT happened in the first few moments of the arrival of Mrs. Pillow and Vico determined the direction of the rest of the evening.

Tonio hurried over to Hazel and took her hand. The Contessa gave her seat to the young man and went up to her friend Berenice, guiding her to one of two chairs near her collection of eighteenth-century ceramic animals. After Urbino had fixed the drinks—a Corvo for Berenice Pillow, a Courvoisier for Vico, and another bourbon and water for himself—he went back to his own chair, feeling very much alone and very much the spectator.

This feeling of exclusion, however, lasted only as long as it took Berenice Pillow to exchange greetings with the Contessa and turn to him.

"We've come here tonight because of you, Mr. Macintyre. I don't mean it in a rude sense, Barbara dear, but Tony and I are very frightened by this latest development. Who wouldn't be? Can you believe that someone would say that they saw him in that terrible place the night Mr. Gibbon was murdered?"

"What happened, Tonio?" Urbino asked the young man who now had both his hands around one of Hazel's.

"After you went in to talk with Commissario Gemelli, I went to another part of the Questura to wait for my statement to be typed up. It took forever and then I read it more than once. I kept thinking that what I had said had become all scrambled up and meant something completely different. When I finally finished and was walking along the *fondamenta* past the pharmacy, a man—I later found out it was this Ignazio Rigoletti—was walking in the opposite direction, toward the Questura. He stared at me in the strangest way. When I passed him, he stopped and turned around, then started to shout after me. I stopped too. Before I knew it I was back in the Questura. Unfortunately you had already left."

"How long did they keep you?"

"For another hour. This Rigoletti swore up and down that he recognized me from the Calle Santa Scolastica, that he wasn't mistaken. I told them it was impossible, that I never left the hotel that night. I wish to God there was some way we could prove that we were in that night, but the simple fact is we can't, and I won't pretend anything else. I took a shower about ten o'clock and my mother was already in her room on the other side of the foyer. She knows I didn't go anywhere. If I had, she would have heard me. She's a very light sleeper."

"I wasn't even asleep yet," Mrs. Pillow said. "I have my little rituals before bedtime."

"I told the Commissario to ask if anyone saw me leaving the hotel that night, that no one possibly could have because I didn't! He said he had already spoken with the hotel personnel on duty that night and with some of the guests. He didn't say what they told him, but he did say that it was *Carnevale* and everything was in a state of confusion, that unfortunately the Splendide-Suisse wasn't set up in such a way that anyone could be sure if someone came in or out. He's right, of course, if you know the hotel. There are two entrances, but is that my fault? Does that make me guilty?" Vico sighed. "Fortunately it was my word against Rigoletti's, and I was eventually told I could leave. But I could tell that the Commissario didn't believe a word I was saying. As it was, he hadn't believed me when I told him that I didn't even know that Gibbon had been in Venice—let alone that he had been murdered—until I read it in the paper yesterday."

Berenice Pillow's face was mottled with anger.

"I wanted to go right to the Questura and tell the Commissario what I thought of his tactics. Tony didn't tell you some of the terrible things he accused him of."

It seemed a somewhat inappropriate comment. What after all could be more terrible than the suspicion of having murdered someone? But Urbino could understand why Commissario Gemelli's insinuating questions about the Calle Santa Scolastica could rile Berenice Pillow and throw things somewhat out of perspective. The poor woman was visibly agitated. He sensed something in her that he both admired and feared: a righteous anger. Her son—it made no difference that technically he was her stepson—had been accused of terrible things, things that he couldn't possibly have done from her point of view, and she was seething.

"There is no way anyone is going to say that Tony was in the *calle* that night. He was in the hotel with me."

"We were," Vico said. "You have to believe us."

"This man is mistaken, and no wonder that he is," Berenice Pillow said. "Look at the chaos out there! How does this man know what he saw? There are many handsome young men in this city. It could have been any one of them—someone who resembled Tony superficially. In the dark, who would know for sure? I wouldn't be surprised if other people say they saw Tony—but no matter how many might say it, it's not true! He never went out that night—and he certainly had nothing to do with the death of Mr. Gibbon!" Her voice was taut with anger. "Anybody wanting to do something wicked and evil would probably wear a mask anyway, wouldn't they?"

"Poor Tonio," Hazel said. She reached out and touched the side of his face with her free hand.

Mrs. Pillow looked at her with a tight-lipped smile.

"I didn't have a chance to thank you, Hazel, for coming to our suite as quickly as you did this afternoon after Tony spoke with you. I'm afraid I was in such a sorry state that I might have ended up being rude."

"Not at all."

Mrs. Pillow got up and went over to the sofa, slipping in on the other side of Hazel. There was a strain on her face as she placed her hand on Hazel's, the hand that her stepson had just been holding. Vico looked on, taking a sip of his cognac.

"I'm also afraid I've been guilty of not taking your own feelings into consideration. I know we've had our differences, and I hope you can understand how upset I was when I found out yesterday that you had broken—that you and Tony had decided to break off your engagement. Tony can certainly keep a dark secret but I could tell that something was troubling him. I want you to know, Hazel, that I couldn't be more upset by all this for your sake. Whatever differences you and Tony have— that's your business. I only wish you well."

"I should certainly hope so, Berenice dear," the Contessa said with a laugh. "The good sisters at St. Brigid's raised us for that and more!"

Mrs. Pillow smiled, patted the sleeve of Hazel's dress, and returned to her chair. Vico looked after her with a pleased smile on his dark, handsome face.

"So what do you think you can do for my Tony, Mr. Macintyre? We'd like to leave as soon as we can, by Ash Wednesday at the latest. Tony has to return to a project in London and I must be back in New York. I know Ash Wednesday is only two days from now and things move slowly here in Italy, but do you think Tony will be free to leave by then? If he isn't, I'll stay in Venice for as long as necessary."

"And you'll stay right here," the Contessa offered.

"We wouldn't impose on you, Barbara dear," Mrs. Pillow said, glancing at Hazel. "But if we can't leave by the end of *Carnevale,* perhaps you could help us find another hotel."

"You should be at the Danieli or the Gritti if you can't be here. Don't worry about it. That will be my welcome little task. But I doubt if it will be necessary. We can all count on Urbino to do his best, can't we, *caro?*"

Urbino nodded, not at all sure of what he was committing himself to.

16 LATE though it was, Urbino went to the Splendide-Suisse after leaving the Contessa's. Mrs. Pillow and her stepson were obviously going to be at the Ca' da Capo-Zendrini for at least another half hour and he thought it was best to take advantage of their being away from the hotel.

After getting off the vaporetto at the fog-shrouded Rialto, he hurried as quickly as he could through the clogged *calli.* He became trapped among a boisterous group of men in fur skins and women in black shawls singing an almost incomprehensible song about a wild man who loved an elfin spirit. When one of the men, wearing a chaplet of twisted leaves on his head, shoved an open bottle of red wine at him, it fell to the stones and shattered. This only added to the group's excitement. Up ahead a man in a domino and white mask was preparing to jump from the parapet of a bridge into a tarpaulin-covered boat. Urbino didn't wait to see what happened but heard a splash and loud laughter a few moments later.

There was a merciful break in the crowd and Urbino quickened his pace. The paving stones were treacherously slick from the fog and he almost slipped and fell down the stairs of the bridge nearest the hotel.

A canal ran along one side of the two buildings that housed the Splendide-Suisse. The reception area was in the first building off the *calle* that led to the Piazza. Urbino went up to the desk and waited while a French couple in matching feathered masks were given directions to the Danieli. When they left, the clerk was at first reluctant to give Urbino any information, but when Urbino showed that he was willing to persuade him as he had the boy in the Calle degli Albanesi earlier in the day, the clerk was more cooperative. He told him that he had been on duty the night in question and had given the key about eight-thirty to Signora Pillow and Signor Vico and that he hadn't seen either of them leave the hotel that night.

"I've told the same thing to the police, signore, and so have my colleagues."

Urbino went out through the connecting alley into the other part of the hotel, where the lounge, rooms, restaurant, and bar were located. The lounge was filled with guests in costume, the air stridently alive with their voices. Occasionally words and phrases in English, Italian, French, German, and Spanish were distinguishable, but most of the time all he could hear was the confusing but universal language of excitement and expectation. It might be past eleven o'clock on Sunday night but the night was still young for *Carnevale*. Many people wandered in and out. There was no need for them to go across the alley, past the reception desk, and out the other doors.

Urbino spoke to several other employees who had been working the night of Gibbon's murder and got the same information as he had from the desk clerk. It was obvious that the only alibi Vico had was the one provided by his stepmother.

Given all the chaos of the lounge during *Carnevale* and the ease with which someone might bypass the reception desk, the fact that no one had seen him leaving or returning around the crucial time meant little.

As Urbino plunged back into the mad Carnival crowd, retracing his steps, he reminded himself of something that Hazel had said at the Montin—that it was usually the guilty who had alibis. He went over all the alibis he had been given during the past several days.

Lubonski had perhaps the best of all. He had been lying very ill at the Casa Crispina, soon to be rushed to the hospital. Yet he had already been out once that night. Poor little Stella Maris Spaak had her asthmatic condition, her breathing machine being set up near her bed in case she needed it. Xenia Campi claimed to have spent the evening on the chair in the reception area in full view of the front door of the Casa Crispina and of Sister Agata—that is, when the old nun hadn't been snoring—but Giuseppe had seemed to imply that he might have seen her around the Piazza. Giuseppe, along with the other two boys from Naples, had been in the Piazza, and Nicholas Spaak had been cruising the area. Dora said she had been in the Casa Crispina for the whole evening after dinner and, according to Mrs. Spaak, had checked in on her mother twice during the evening.

And what about Hazel Reeve, now the pampered guest of the Contessa? Where had this young woman with the green eyes and the perfect Italian gone on her walk during the time her fiancé was being stabbed in the Calle Santa Scolastica?

Urbino was so lost in thought that it took him a few moments to realize someone had grasped his shoulder and was speaking to him. He looked up into the face of a brown bear with sad eyes. Around his neck was a heavy metal collar with half a dozen links of a chain attached to it.

"Hide me, signore, hide me! I've broken away from my post in the Campo Santo Stefano but the dogs are still after me. They want to bite and scratch me to death! Look!"

Holding up a mangled paw glistening with wet, he touched Urbino's cheek with it, leaving something sticky behind.

"Help me or I'm finished!"

As Urbino took out his handkerchief to wipe his cheek, the bear plunged madly along the *calle* toward a couple in scowling leather masks and repeated his plea.

Urbino stopped in front of a brightly lit shop to look at his handkerchief. It was smeared with what looked like blood.

As he continued to the Rialto, all he could think of was the look Hazel Reeve had given him at the Contessa's when she had burst into tears for the second time.

17 WHEN the phone rang only five minutes after he got back to the Palazzo Uccello, Urbino knew who it was even before he picked it up. If he hadn't, he might have been somewhat mystified by the voice that came through the receiver. It was the Contessa, but the Contessa speaking in unusually hoarse, low tones as if she had strained her voice or were afraid of being overheard. Having left her only an hour and a half before in what seemed to be full possession of her well-modulated voice, he could only assume that his friend was taking precautions.

"Where are you speaking from, Barbara?"

"From my bedroom. Where else would I be at this hour? And where have *you* been?"

He told her about his quick trip to the Splendide-Suisse and his walk back home and also filled her in on his conversation with Nicholas Spaak earlier in the evening, which they hadn't had a chance to discuss. But it was Tonio Vico she wanted to talk about.

"No one saw Tonio come out because he didn't come out. It's as simple as that," she said in almost a whisper.

"I admire the trust you put in the word of an old friend."

"It has nothing to do with Berenice at all! The Berenice I remember was completely capable of lying for someone she cared about. She did it for me a few times in the days of St. Brigid's, and I'm sure I did the same for her, though I'm also sure we both ran to confession as soon as we could." The Contessa sighed, perhaps in recollection of those simpler days of simpler faults. "No, *caro,* if I believe that handsome young man it has nothing to do with Berenice. It has everything to do with his eyes and his mouth. He was telling the truth."

He could barely hear her.

"Barbara, why are you whispering?"

"I am not whispering, Urbino." She said this no louder than anything she had already said. "Why do you say I'm whispering?"

"Because you are. It wouldn't have to do with Hazel Reeve, would it?"

"With her? Whyever should it?"

"Because she's staying with you, Barbara, and perhaps you don't want her to hear you."

Could the Contessa be having second thoughts about her act of charity?

"However could she hear me?" She was almost shouting now. When she went on, he was happy to hear that she was now using her normal voice. "Oh, I suppose I am being silly, *caro*. That girl makes me feel not quite comfortable. I can't shake it from my mind that she knew Gibbon, and he's dead, and she was staying with Porfirio, and now he's dead, too. I'm not superstitious but—"

"But you think you might be the next one to go? You are being superstitious, Barbara. You might say with much more sense that I could be the next one to go, or Josef."

"What do you mean?"

"Gibbon and Porfirio were both associated with the fresco, weren't they? So are Josef and I."

"But the fresco is only a thing!"

She said the last word disdainfully.

"I stand corrected. I forgot that 'things' never bring about misfortune. Never has money or jewels or a painting by a Great Master or an incriminating letter brought death and discomfort."

"Shame on you, Urbino, you're making fun of me—and you're saying nonsensical things." She paused. He could almost hear her thinking. "But you don't really think the fresco has something to do with all this, do you?"

"I would be surprised if it did."

"More or less surprised than if Hazel Reeve has something to do with it?" Once again she was almost whispering. When he didn't respond immediately, she added, "I mean something more to do with all this than just being an attractive, intelligent young woman who was engaged to a murdered man and was staying in the home of another man who's just met a violent death."

"And now she's staying with you, Barbara."

"That's right, *caro,* and don't forget it!"

With this parting warning the Contessa hung up.

18 URBINO read Proust for a while and then went to bed. He fell asleep right away but was visited by disturbing dreams.

A scowling Xenia Campi lamented the destruction of Venice, handing out her ubiquitous flyers on which there was nothing but a bloody hand print, while Giovanni Firpo, dressed in his full *Carnevale* regalia, laughed and mimicked all her movements, except that he was handing out not flyers but photographs of himself.

Hazel Reeve stalked the rooms of the Ca' da Capo and approached the Contessa's bedroom. When Hazel opened the door, however, it wasn't the Contessa lying in bed but a man. His face was in *profil perdu.* The profile remained lost until he turned in his sleep, revealing Val Gibbon, his eyes closed, his face masklike but smiling. Suddenly, however, it was no longer Hazel approaching the bed but Nicholas Spaak, and the man in the bed wasn't Gibbon but Tonio Vico, also smiling and with his eyes closed. When Vico started to get up from the bed, Urbino woke up.

He looked at the clock. It was three-thirty. He wouldn't be able to get back to sleep easily and was in no mood for lying in bed. Not until he started to put on his clothes, however, did he realize he was going for a walk.

After leaving the Palazzo Uccello, Urbino turned in the direction of San Marco. The *calli* were almost completely deserted. He walked quickly and was soon in the Piazza. All the festival lights were off, and workers were clearing away the debris. A few drunken revelers were sleeping under the arcades until the *carabinieri* came along again.

Urbino went past the Basilica and into the Piazzetta where

Saint Theodore and the lion of Saint Mark on their columns looked off into the darkness. To the far right all the kiosks were shuttered. Fog was thick here by the water. He could see only the dark outlines of the moored gondolas, but could hear them creaking and hear the water slapping against their sides and against the wooden piers and the stones of the embankment.

He turned left toward the Riva degli Schiavoni. He now realized where he was going, where he had been going ever since leaving the Palazzo Uccello.

The Ducal Palace, phosphorescent in the fog, was more like a ghost of a building than the real thing, its heavy upper stories looming eerily above the ground as if supported by nothing but the air and fog beneath. Urbino went over the bridge, not bothering to look this time at the Bridge of Sighs. He went under the arcades and through the narrow gap between the old prison and the wing of the Danieli Hotel into the Calle degli Albanesi.

It was completely deserted. He went into the service alley on the right where Spaak had caught a brief glimpse of someone in a cheap plastic mask. Urbino could see how someone standing in the shadows of this area could be fairly well concealed and yet have a good view of the entrance of the Calle Santa Scolastica across the way.

Urbino stepped into the first section of the Calle Santa Scolastica. Near this spot Spaak had been frightened by Rigoletti hurrying out to phone the police. Farther along, the apartment windows of the courtyard were all dark except for one. It was Rigoletti's window.

Beyond the *corte* the alley continued at an oblique angle. It was this angle that prevented anyone on the far side of the courtyard from seeing what might be going on by the water steps. The Ducal Palace gleamed wetly across the canal.

Why Urbino had felt compelled to revisit the spot at this time in the early morning he didn't know, but he stood there for more than ten minutes, thinking.

He suddenly remembered something that Mrs. Spaak had said. It hadn't impressed itself on him at the time but now, standing on the spot where Gibbon had been murdered and with the fog drifting around him, it came close to chilling him.

"He's mine forever," Stella Maris Spaak had said about her son.

Was this a supreme confidence in her son's devotion—or something else entirely? Could it be a comfort to this widow that her son was gay, and that by being gay he was, in a very real sense, "hers forever"?

There was, of course, another way that someone could be yours forever—in death. Hadn't one of Browning's characters strangled his beloved with her own hair after she had said she wanted to give herself to him forever? That the name of the strangled woman had been Porphyria—the female version of Porfirio—seemed one of those peculiar coincidences meant to confuse and even mock with a meaning that wasn't there. It was like a mask you were meant to take for flesh and blood.

Urbino no longer wanted to be there at the end of the Calle Santa Scolastica where Gibbon had been found stabbed to death with all that money on him. He looked at his watch. It was almost five o'clock. He would get no more sleep, but it didn't matter. He had a lot to consider. His dreams and this visit to the Calle Santa Scolastica had left him with the feeling that he might be close to an understanding of what had happened on the night Gibbon had seen the face of his murderer.

Part Four

———————————

BALLO
IN
MASCHERA

1 THE next morning's *Gazzettino* brought a surprise. There on the front page was Tonio Vico's face.

It stared up at Urbino as he took his *caffelatte* and croissant at the refectory table in the library. Although the black hair was closer to the head than Vico wore his, it was the same strong aquiline nose, sensuous mouth, and large eyes. Fortunately, Vico's name wasn't mentioned in the accompanying piece, but Rigoletti's was. The article was brief, mentioning only that Ignazio Rigoletti of the Corte Santa Scolastica had given the Questura's artist a detailed description of two men he had seen in the Calle Santa Scolastica shortly after the British photographer was murdered. The police were conducting a search for the men who met the description and would appreciate any information.

Next to the drawing that resembled Vico was another one of the light-haired young man Rigoletti had seen. It was less distinct and didn't bring Nicholas Spaak immediately to mind.

The Questura was playing it careful—and crafty. They didn't have anywhere near enough evidence to arrest Tonio Vico and they couldn't very well mention his name or provide a photograph. Instead, they had released the artist's composite of the man Rigoletti claimed to have seen and identified yesterday as Vico.

There were several aspects of all this that Urbino was turning over in his mind. Was Rigoletti telling the truth about the dark man in the Calle Santa Scolastica? Could he possibly be mistaken in some way? Did Vico only resemble the man or had he actually been in the *calle* immediately before Rigoletti discovered the body? Could Xenia Campi's ex-husband have an ulterior motive in identifying Vico as the man? And how did what Spaak had seen fit into the picture?

The Contessa believed Vico hadn't been in the Calle Santa Scolastica. So did Hazel Reeve. Mrs. Pillow, however, in a different position. For her it wasn't a matter of should be one of knowledge.

He would have to talk with her again, but not with her stepson there. Fortunately, once again it was Mrs. Pillow who answered the phone when he called the Vico-Pillow suite at the Splendide-Suisse.

"Mrs. Pillow, this is Urbino Macintyre. I was wondering if we might meet for a little while sometime today."

He hoped she would understand that he meant without Tonio.

"Of course, Mr. Macintyre. I've been left completely on my own. Tony is giving Hazel a tour of the Palladian churches. He wanted to rent a car and go along the Brenta Canal but he wasn't sure if he would be allowed."

Had Mrs. Pillow and her stepson seen the picture in the paper?

Urbino suggested that they meet at a wine bar not far from the Teatro Goldoni and told her how to reach it from the hotel.

After saying good-bye to Mrs. Pillow, Urbino went to the Casa Crispina. It was only nine o'clock but the *calli* were filled with maskers making their way from the train station and the hotels along the Lista di Spagna. The day was crisp and clear after last night's fog. If the weather held through Tuesday, it was going to be a record crowd for the final days of *Carnevale*.

In the Campo San Gabriele a group of schoolchildren were having a *regata di carriole*, racing their wooden wheelbarrows across the uneven stones between the church steps and the covered well head in the center of the square. A muzzled terrier chased them.

The same elderly sister from yesterday was at the reception desk again. This time she was reading a copy of *Gente* with a photograph of Lady Diana on the cover. As Urbino waited for Dora Spaak to join him in the lounge, Sister Teresa came walking from the direction of the chapel.

"I'll be visiting Signor Lubonski at the hospital this morning," she said. "I called to see how he was doing. He's better, but there's a policeman outside his room. Do you know why that is?"

"It has something to do with Porfirio's accident in San Gabriele, I believe," he answered vaguely.

Sister Teresa was about to say or ask something else but they were joined by Dora Spaak, whose round face wore a worried look. She asked Sister Teresa if she had seen her brother, Nicholas.

"Not since yesterday morning. Is something the matter, Signorina Spaak?"

"It's Mother. She's having even more trouble breathing. It seems to be the beginning of one of her bad attacks." She finally acknowledged Urbino when she looked at him and said, "She's affected by the change in the weather."

"Would you mind if I stopped by to see her for a moment?" Sister Teresa asked.

Before the girl could open her round mouth to say anything, Sister Teresa was already hurrying toward the staircase.

"Don't frighten her, please," Dora Spaak called out after them as if the woman had some malevolent intent in going to her mother's room. Her voice held an unmistakable note of tender worry.

"You wanted to see me, Mr. Macintyre?" She looked up at Urbino with a troubled but guarded look in her dark-brown eyes. "It's not the best time."

"I'm sorry, Miss Spaak. This shouldn't take more than a few minutes. Would you like to sit down?"

She shook her head more vigorously than was necessary, her hair giving off a somewhat rancid, unwashed odor.

"If it's only going to take a few minutes, it's just as well I stand. What is it? You want to know something more about Val Gibbon."

She said it almost defiantly.

"Yes. Would you mind once more going over your meeting with him the night he was murdered?"

"Why? To see if I tell it the same way again? I'll never forget that night, or anything about it." A momentary look of fear crossed her face. "As I told you, I wasn't feeling well and was having some tea in the dining room when Val came by."

Once again, just as she had before, Dora Spaak went through the whole encounter—how Gibbon was obviously on his way out, carrying his camera case and wearing a scarf, how he had offered to stay in that evening to keep her company, how he had mentioned lines from Dante that still seemed to puzzle her. Urbino asked her for more details about the few minutes they had spent together in the guests' dining room but either Dora Spaak didn't remember anything more than she had told him already or chose not to share anything more with him.

"Did Gibbon have anything else with him?"

"Anything else?"

"Anything besides his camera?"

"I—I didn't see anything else."

"He didn't have a mask, for example? He was going to the Piazza, you said."

"I said I thought he was going to the Piazza. And he wasn't wearing a mask!"

Dora laughed.

"He might not have been wearing a mask, Miss Spaak, but maybe one was around his neck or in his pocket."

"I doubt if photographers wear masks when they're taking pictures." She stared at him for a few moments as if considering something, then said, "I suppose he *could* have had one in his pocket or his camera case."

She said it as if to appease him.

"Was your mother well when you looked in on her that night?"

"As well as a person with a chronic asthmatic condition could be."

"Was she asleep?"

"Yes, she was asleep, Mr. Macintyre."

"Are you sure?"

"I'm a nurse, Mr. Macintyre. I can tell when a person is asleep, I assure you. My mother was."

"And the other time you looked in on her that night—was she asleep then too?"

Dora Spaak seemed flustered, her eyes wide.

"I don't know what you're getting at, Mr. Macintyre, but my mother is a semi-invalid. She was in her bed and asleep on both occasions. She wasn't out and about, if that's what you're thinking."

"And your brother?"

"Are you trying to make trouble for my brother, Mr. Macintyre? He was in all night—just as he told you."

Urbino stared at her silently. If she was aware of her brother's walks, as Nicholas said she was, then she was deliberately lying—unless she actually believed her brother had been in that night. He might have told her that he was.

Was Dora speaking out of knowledge, ignorance, or the attempt to deceive him? Could Nicholas actually *have* been in that night after only a short walk? If he had, then why had he told such an elaborate story about the Calle Santa Scolastica, the kind of story that could only make him a stronger suspect?

Dora, obviously uncomfortable under Urbino's silent scrutiny, was about to turn away when her attention was caught by the folded copy of *Il Gazzettino* that Urbino was holding under his arm. She went white.

"That picture, Mr. Macintyre." She pointed down at the newspaper—at the police artist's drawing of the dark-haired man Rigoletti had seen. Urbino unfolded the paper. Both pictures were now visible. Dora Spaak looked at the picture of the light-haired man but her gaze went immediately back to the other picture. She was about to say something, then stopped. She seemed undecided if she should go on.

"What about the picture, Miss Spaak?"

"I—I've seen that man." There was a hesitancy in the way she said it. "Yes, I've seen him." She took a few moments to collect her thoughts before going on quickly. "I saw a man who—who looked just like him talking to Val a few days before he was murdered." She took the paper from Urbino and studied the picture. "Yes!" she said with more force. "It's the same man. I'm sure of it. I thought it was suspicious at the time but I'd forgotten all about it until this very minute."

"Where did you see him?"

"Out in the square a day or two before Val's murder. I'm not sure exactly when. I was going for a walk. Val was talking with this man"—she indicated the picture of the man who resembled Vico—"and he seemed angry with him."

"Did you hear anything they were saying?"

"No, I just kept walking. I was too far away."

Urbino thanked her and told her that he hoped her mother's condition would improve. As he watched her hurrying up the staircase, he wondered why he found it so hard to believe anything she had to tell him. Was it that she herself wasn't sure of the truth of what she was saying or was it that she was making much of it up as she went along? In either case, he had a hunch that Dora could end up shedding more light on what had happened in the Calle Santa Scolastica than she already had—or than she ever would want to.

2 AFTER leaving the Casa Crispina Urbino called the Questura from a public phone in a bar in the Calle dell'Arcanzolo. When the receptionist put him through right away, he took it as a further indication of Commissario Gemelli's spirit of cooperation.

He wondered if Nicholas Spaak had made his promised visit. Perhaps Dora couldn't find her brother because he was at the Questura or on his way there.

Urbino mentioned the pictures in that morning's *Il Gazzettino*.

"Remarkable likeness of your friend Vico, wouldn't you say? Could hardly have been more like him if it had been a photograph taken by Gibbon or Buffone."

"I'm sure you would have liked to give *Il Gazzettino* a photograph if you could have."

"In time, in time—before the end of *Carnevale* most likely. But even the Italian police have to do things in the proper, orderly way. And don't forget Lubonski. He's a strong suspect in Gibbon's death even if he was rushed to the hospital in the middle of the night." Gemelli paused. "I don't think I have to tell you what I learned from your friend Lubonski, do I? I know you learned the same things during your visit to him but saw no reason to inform us."

"Have you had any response to the pictures yet?"

"Not to the one of the blond man but the phone has been ringing off the hook about the other one. Quite a few people have said they saw the handsome Signor Vico the night of the murder. And Ignazio Rigoletti has called us two or three times. He seems to think he keeps seeing Vico parading around. Says he made an obscene gesture at him when Rigoletti's boat was coming into San Marco—then he ran off in the crowd. He wants to know why we haven't arrested the insolent young man yet. I think he's trying to get us to pull him in as a public nuisance. It might not be a bad idea."

When Gemelli said nothing about Spaak, Urbino assumed

he hadn't been to the Questura yet. He realized he was once again withholding information. But what held him back was not that he wanted to keep the information for himself but that he wanted the Commissario to get the story first from Spaak. He had told Mrs. Spaak that he would try to help her son. This might be the best—and only—thing he could do for him.

"Anyway," the Commissario was saying, "aside from Rigoletti, Vico was seen by at least half a dozen people that night, and he was just where you would expect him to have been—along the Molo, in the Piazza San Marco—someone even saw him in the Mercerie not far from the Splendide-Suisse. He seems to have been having quite a good time. If he has nothing to hide, then why doesn't he just admit that he was out? His stepmother is obviously providing him with an alibi. In the stories I read when I was a kid the stepmother used to throw her stepchildren to the wolves! I wonder if Vico knows how lucky he is to have the one he does?"

3   THE Commissario's question sounded in Urbino's ears as he listened to Mrs. Pillow in the crowded wine bar.

Did Tonio Vico know how lucky he was? Urbino didn't doubt that Vico loved his stepmother. But was he aware of the depth of her own feeling? If he could have heard how passionately she was defending him now, he would have considered himself very lucky indeed.

"Tony was in the whole night, Mr. Macintyre. Neither of us is a gadabout. I know people have traveled hundreds, thousands of miles to be here during *Carnevale,* but we've been content to stay in most nights, reading or watching television. When we've gone out to eat, we've usually made it a point to go in the opposite direction from the Piazza. We've found some quiet little restaurants that I'm sure you know all about."

She cast her eye quickly over the noisy, smoke-filled room. Many people were in costume but only a few wore masks since they made eating and drinking almost impossible. Those who were indulging in the wines and little snacks of the *enoteca* with masks on were wearing either half masks or three-quarter ones designed so that the mouth, although concealed by a long beaklike protrusion, was free to take drink and nourishment.

"Tonio prefers to be away from the madding crowd," Mrs. Pillow went on, looking away from the exuberant diners and drinkers, "and so do I. He's a quiet boy. Sometimes I think he would have made a wonderful priest or monk although I would have been devastated to lose him that way."

Urbino didn't see any point in disagreeing, in telling her that having a son in the religious life was sometimes the very way of never losing him—at least not to another woman. He couldn't help but be reminded of Stella Maris Spaak's comment. But although Mrs. Pillow, according to Hazel and Mrs. Pillow's own admission, didn't care for Hazel, Urbino didn't think she was the kind of mother to stand in the way of her son's true happiness.

"Maybe I should have gone with Tony and Hazel." She gave a laugh that had less humor in it than self-deprecation. "Not as a chaperone. I mean for my sake. San Giorgio Maggiore and the Giudecca might be only a few minutes away but they're worlds apart from this madness."

Once again she took in the noise and confusion of the wine bar and the festive crowd outside. A couple with their faces painted half white and half black and wearing red fright wigs had their faces pressed against one of the windows and were grimacing. Mrs. Pillow turned away with a moue of distaste. Urbino wondered why she had put herself in the middle of *Carnevale* when she seemed to dislike it so much, although it was completely possible that her patience with it had been worn thin because of the serious problem her stepson now had.

"Yes," she went on, "all the cleanness and logic—the sanity, you could say—of the Palladian churches would have been restorative today. But Tony and Hazel need it more than I do, although the young can bounce back so much more easily."

A look of tired sadness passed over her sharp features. It was hard to believe that she was the Contessa's contemporary, or even only a year older. Her skin had a grayish pallor that she made no attempt to conceal with cosmetics, and the lines

in her face didn't give it character so much as a worn, weary
look. Her graying red hair, however, looked as if it would
be thick, rich, even lustrous when it was unbound. If the
immediate impression of Mrs. Pillow was one of fatigue and
austerity, a considered one couldn't fail to register the slightly
mischievous young girl looking out from her blue eyes. When
searching for the long-ago girl from St. Brigid's in the mature
Mrs. Pillow, it must be these eyes that the Contessa focused
on. These eyes were turned now on Urbino.

"Tony didn't see the paper this morning, Mr. Macintyre."

"I assume you did."

"Yes, after you called but not before Tony went to
Barbara's. It was a shock to see Tony's face—or almost
Tony's face—looking out at me. Surely it's some grotesque
mistake!"

"You'll have to prepare yourself for more and he's going
to find out soon enough. He probably knows by now."

"What do you mean that I should prepare myself for more?"

"I wouldn't be surprised if other people say they saw someone who looked like the picture."

He didn't mention this had already happened. If possible,
he wanted to be the one to tell Tonio Vico.

She nodded her head slowly.

"I had thought of it myself but I was too afraid to admit it.
It could make Tony look very bad."

Urbino asked her if Tonio had ever been to San Gabriele.

"San Gabriele? Where's that?"

"In a quiet part of the Cannaregio quarter. Not too far from
the Ghetto."

"Don't try to trick me, Mr. Macintyre. It's where the Casa
Crispina is, isn't it? Where Mr. Gibbon was staying? What
good would it be for me to say that Tony hadn't been there?
The truth is that there's no way for me to know, is there, the
way there is about that night at the hotel? But ask him yourself.
He'll tell you the truth."

She looked for her purse.

"Do you think we could leave? It's getting a little close
in here."

She got up and waited for him outside. She seemed even
taller as she drew up against the window, disdaining any close
contact with the crowd that surged past her and fixing her gaze
on the upper story of the building opposite.

4 ON the way back to her hotel, Mrs. Pillow commented occasionally on the passing scene, asking Urbino to identify a particular costume or to give her the name of a building, but she was obviously preoccupied with her thoughts.

She didn't show much real interest until three figures appeared suddenly around the corner ten meters ahead. They wore black tunics of oilcloth, wide-brimmed black hats covering their ears and hair, large black-framed glasses, black gloves, and golden masks with a long pointed beak over the nose and the mouth. These masks made them look almost ducklike, but the effect was far from comical. The slow, silent way they moved through the crowd added to their ominous quality. Each was carrying a wooden stick. One of them raised his and touched Mrs. Pillow gently on the shoulder. She shrank back. The figures passed by and silently turned a corner.

"Who are they?" she asked in an unsteady voice.

"Plague doctors. It's used as a costume now but it was how doctors caring for plague victims dressed hundreds of years ago. They put a piece of cloth soaked with some kind of medicine in the cone of the nose. Its fumes were supposed to protect them from the plague. Every opening of the body was protected."

"And the stick?"

"They used them to examine the victim's sores at a safe distance."

Mrs. Pillow shivered.

"Some doctors today don't act much different," she said. "I've seen a lot of illness in those I love, Mr. Macintyre."

Her face was touched with genuine sorrow. He wondered if she herself could be ill. It might explain why she looked so much older than the Contessa. He felt a surge of sympathy for her.

After they parted at the Splendide-Suisse with a few words about the Contessa's *ballo in maschera* tomorrow evening, Urbino started off for the Piazza.

The faint glimmers of something were starting to form in his mind. Sometimes his own research and his understanding of his biographical subjects proceeded from hunches and intuitions that led him in the right direction. When he was wrong in these cases, all he had wasted was time and energy, and he could make up for his unprofitable detour. In the case of murder, however, it was much different. He didn't have much time to indulge himself. Ash Wednesday was only the day after tomorrow.

The narrow alleys were clogged with revelers. Urbino pitied the relatively few people who were trying to make their way from the Piazza against the surge of people. There were full minutes when Urbino moved barely a foot as he waited for the bottleneck ahead to clear up. The individual costumes and masks were almost indistinguishable, so packed together was everyone. Only occasionally could he concentrate on a detail—an astronaut's helmet, an odalisque's veils and scarfs, an astrologer's cone-hat with crescents.

As he was held up for several minutes in front of a souvenir shop where two men—one dressed as Fu Manchu, the other as an American Indian—stood arguing, he went over everything that Dora Spaak had told him about meeting Gibbon in the dining room the night of his death, about her visits to see how her mother was doing, about her assurance that Nicholas had been in all night, about her response to the artist's drawing in the newspaper. He thought of Berenice Pillow's impassioned denial that her stepson had been out on the fateful night and reviewed what Rigoletti had said about the men he had seen, especially the one he had identified yesterday as Vico. Urbino kept coming back to what Dora Spaak actually knew and might not be telling him.

Urbino would also have to ask Nicholas Spaak and Tonio Vico some more questions. He checked his watch. Hazel and Vico wouldn't be back for a while yet, but lunch must have just finished at the Casa Crispina. He might be able to catch Spaak there if he had returned.

Urbino slowly made his way across the swarming Piazza to Florian's. The family of white-costumed acrobats was in front of the Campanile forming a human pyramid. The one balancing at the top was pelted with an egg by a rabbit-eared *mattaccino*, as Urbino had been a few days ago.

A line of people, most of them in elegant costumes, were

waiting in the foyer for a table. Urbino went up the stairs to the telephone and called the Casa Crispina. The sister who answered said that Spaak was in and she would see if he was free. His mother was very ill.

Urbino waited for what seemed a long time. Finally, Nicholas Spaak's voice, sounding strained, came over the line.

"It's Urbino Macintyre. I'm sorry to disturb you at a time like this. I hope your mother isn't too ill."

"Dora says she'll have to be put in the hospital but Mother's afraid of going to a foreign one, and she seems even more afraid of being brought there in a boat. What do you want? I don't have time to tell you what happened with the police but as you can see I wasn't arrested."

"I just want to know one thing about your trip to the Questura. Did Commissario Gemelli ask you to look at any pictures?"

"Why do you ask me questions that you know the answer to? Yes, I did look at a drawing—one of the ones that's in the paper today. The one that's supposed to be me is ridiculous. It could be almost anyone as far as I can see."

"And the other one?"

In a weary voice, Spaak said, "Yes, it was the tall man I saw in that alley. Now you all can see that I'm telling the truth. Good-bye, Mr. Macintyre."

5   HALF an hour later Urbino was glad to see that Giovanni Firpo was on duty at the hospital pharmacy.

Firpo had a worried, puzzled look on his face that didn't clear up when Urbino mentioned the afternoon when he had seen Firpo in the Piazza San Marco taunting Xenia Campi— the last afternoon Gibbon was alive.

Firpo had just time to give him the address of the person who had, unknowingly, contributed to Xenia Campi's anger that afternoon when a doctor required Firpo's attention.

Urbino walked from the hospital toward the Calle Santa Scolastica. The shops were starting to open again after the midday break. People were waiting to get in and creating even more confusion in the narrow passageways. In the middle of a bridge a group was gathered around a Cleopatra with a boa constrictor around her shoulders—or rather *his* shoulders, because beneath the kohl-rimmed eyes and other heavy makeup, it was obviously a man. A Pharaoh standing next to her was playing a reed flute. As she gently cradled the head of the snake, Cleopatra recited in Italian-accented English:

> *"Dost thou not see my baby at my breast,*
> *That sucks the nurse asleep?"*

As Urbino left the scene behind, he heard a man make a lewd comment. The crowd laughed loudly, drowning out the sound of the flute.

The mask shop Urbino was looking for was already open. The proprietor, Matteo, a genial, broad-faced man in his mid-thirties, was explaining commedia dell'arte masks to two young women. He smiled in greeting.

The relatively recent revival of *Carnevale* in Venice had brought with it a renewed interest in masks and the art of mask making, and every quarter of the city had its mask shops and artisans.

Matteo had pulled out a large well-worn book from under his counter to illustrate his little lecture.

"Arlecchino—perhaps you know him as Harlequin—is the servant of the miser Pantalone," Matteo said. "Arlecchino loves love and loves his polenta. You see his costume is made of red, orange, and green patches that remind us of his poverty. This is his mask." He held up a small dark-brown mask with a misshapen nose jutting out above a bushy moustache. "Columbine, the woman he pursues, who doesn't have sense enough to resist him, usually doesn't wear a mask, but you see from this picture how lavishly she is dressed in her bright-colored skirts. Sometimes she wears an apron, too, since she's a servant like Arlecchino. And then, completing the eternal triangle, is sad-faced Pierrot with his black skullcap and floppy white suit. He seldom wears a mask either, but why does he need one, ladies? His face is itself a mask."

He pointed to the face of Pierrot in the book. "It is painted white, sometimes with one tear to show his sorrow at losing his beloved Columbine to the more crafty and sensual Arlecchino. Let me show you one of my Pierrot masks." He went to the wall and took down a simple white-faced mask with a large black tear on its cheek.

"You will see many people in the *Carnevale* crowd dressed like Harlequin, Columbine, and Pierrot, sometimes in groups of three, sometimes just two of them, sometimes one alone. But there are also the Harlequins, Columbines, and Pierrots who wear no costume, ladies, for remember that the commedia dell'arte characters are ones we see around us every day. I myself am the brokenhearted Pierrot who sees all you lovely ladies come into my life only to leave a few minutes later."

The two young women giggled, thanked him, and said they might come back to buy a mask before they left Venice. Matteo went out into the *calle* to direct them to the Piazza San Marco although his parting words—"Just follow the crowd"—were the best directions he could give them.

"How can I help you, signor?"

When Urbino mentioned Giovanni Firpo and one of the masks he had worn that afternoon last week in the Piazza, Matteo nodded. "Yes, I make all of Vanni's masks for him. He's even more of a perfectionist than I am! Of course I remember that particular one. I had a lot of fun doing it." He laughed as he remembered. "A man who spoke Italian with an English accent—or maybe it was an American accent—asked me to make one of them for him, too. Maybe Vanni Firpo recommended me, but this man wanted it in a hurry and I couldn't do it. I suggested he see Pierina. She just got started as a mask maker and is looking for business. She has a very good eye and steady hand."

"Where can I find her?"

"She doesn't have her own shop yet. She shares a space near Santa Maria Formosa with a cousin in the secondhand-clothing business, but until the end of *Carnevale* she has a booth in the Campo San Maurizio. She's there almost all the time when she isn't strolling around the Piazza, trying to do business there."

Urbino thanked him and set off for the Campo San Maurizio. It was slow going as he moved against the current of the crowd,

but he soon entered the maze of back alleys where there were
only a few masqueraders and local residents going about their
business. As he neared the Campo San Maurizio, however, he
was once again in the thick of things.

The square not far from the Accademia Bridge had rows
of canopied booths selling masks, hats, and costumes as well
as books, calendars, and posters of the Venetian Carnival. A
couple dressed as Beauty and the Beast were performing a pan-
tomime in one of the aisles. Làughing tourists were trying on
bizarre and fanciful cloaks, robes, pants, dresses, and headgear;
others were carefully considering between two or three masks
as if the one they chose would make the difference between a
completely successful *Carnevale* experience or a fiasco. Three
Gypsy children ran up and down the aisles, distracting the
proprietors and their clients.

Urbino had to ask at several booths before someone pointed
out Pierina's booth.

It wasn't until he was only a few feet away that he recognized Pierina. She was the young woman who had been
painting faces in the Piazza on the day he had spoken with
the boys from Naples. He was also fairly certain that it was
the same girl who had been in the restaurant in the Calle
degli Albanesi when he had spoken with Lupo. Without her
face paint, he saw that she was a little older than he had first
thought, perhaps twenty-five or twenty-six. She was small and
birdlike, with short dark hair feathering around her face and
dark expressive eyes. Her face was very pale and she looked
like a porcelain doll—a slightly damaged doll, however, for a
small scar marred her right cheek.

She was just finishing a sale of one of the many masks
that glared, grimaced, and laughed from the counter and the
support beams.

Pierina's eyes widened when she saw him.

He didn't indicate that he recognized her. Before he asked
her any questions, he examined some of the masks and bought
a black velvet oval *moretta*. He would give it to the Contessa.

While Pierina was wrapping it in pages from *Il Gazzettino,*
she looked at Urbino warily. He said that Matteo near the
Campo San Filippo e Giacomo had told him where he could
find her. He asked her about the man Matteo had mentioned.

She busied herself with a piece of cellophane tape before
answering.

"I remember him. He came to the shop I share with my cousin. He paid me a lot but it wasn't easy. You have to go from something flat to something three-dimensional. I saw many flaws in it myself but he was pleased."

She handed him the package. He had the impression she wanted to end their conversation. She looked over his shoulder at the shoppers milling around.

"Was he American or English?" Urbino persisted.

"He wasn't French or German. I could tell that. As for the other man, he was very handsome, but I don't know what nationality he was, of course."

"Have you seen either of them since two weeks ago?"

She tried to look at him steadily as she answered but the eye over the scar twitched slightly.

"No."

"Are you sure?"

She nodded her head but Urbino wasn't convinced.

"You know Xenia Campi, don't you?"

"Most people know her. She's a real character."

"But you know her better than most. You've known her for ten years. You were close to her dead son."

"Did she tell you that?"

"No. Giuseppe, the boy from Naples, did."

She made an annoyed face.

"Yes, I know her. And I knew Marco." A sad look came over her face. "I was almost killed in that accident, too."

"Does Xenia Campi bother you?"

"Bother me! She watches me all the time! You would think I had been married to Marco. I was only a kid at the time. She thinks she has to watch out for me. I've got a mother of my own!"

"Did she bother you about Signor Gibbon, the English photographer who was murdered in the Calle Santa Scolastica?"

Pierina paled and her scar stood out more.

"I don't know what you're talking about, Signor Macintyre! Yes, I know who you are! Xenia Campi pointed you out to me in the Piazza. You like to poke your nose into everything. She said I would have trouble because of you."

"Trouble from her if you spoke with me?"

"Excuse me, Signor Macintyre, I have work to do."

She started to straighten some of her masks but he had one more question.

"Do you have any inexpensive plastic masks, a yellow one, perhaps?"

She seemed surprised, looking at him with disbelief.

"Only what you see. I make and sell only quality masks. Good day."

The next moment she was shouting angrily at the three Gypsy children who had come up to the booth and were eying a row of small porcelain masks. Urbino left.

6   BY the time Urbino was approaching the Palazzo Uccello a chill wind was blowing through the dark alleys. He could sense an abrupt change coming in the weather. The last day of *Carnevale* might see not only confetti and streamers flying through the air but snowflakes as well. He hoped so. Cloaks of snow covering the domes, bridges, and gondolas of the city would only add to the festive air. Venice would seem even more enchanted. He wished he were in a better position to be able to enjoy this year's celebration.

His walk back to the Palazzo Uccello was at many times like moving against an incoming tide. Crowds flooded the main *calli,* shouts poured out of cafés, and dancers eddied madly within the larger human maelstroms of the squares as music played loudly over speakers.

So difficult was it to make his way that once again he left the main route. He was happy to reach his neighborhood where the noise and activity were replaced by an almost funereal stillness. Occasionally the quiet was broken by the waxing and waning of voices and other sounds, sometimes loud and other times muted, which seemed to come from everywhere and nowhere. Where only a few moments before he had encountered crowds of merrymakers, he now met only an occasional neighbor with whom he exchanged a quick greeting.

Was it his imagination or did everyone he met now seem just a little eager to get to their destination? Fortunately, he didn't have far to go.

He had only to turn the corner at the end of the *calle*, go over the bridge, and apply the key to the lock. He quickened his steps.

As he walked up the steps of the humpbacked bridge next to the Palazzo Uccello, he looked up at the lights Natalia had put on. They gave him a warm, secure feeling. He paused in the middle of the bridge to look down at the narrow melancholy canal. He never tired of peering into it from here or from the windows of the palazzo.

Sometimes on overcast days or evenings like these, with the building reflected in its murky waters, he was reminded of how Poe's House of Usher had been mirrored in the tarn that ultimately claimed it. As on these other occasions, he now found himself searching the walls of the Palazzo Uccello for some barely perceptible crack that might eventually bring the building to the same fate. It was clearly an irrational fear, considering all the work that had gone into the building's restoration ten years ago when he had inherited it through his mother.

The thought of a drink and Serena's greeting after not having seen him all day pulled him out of his reverie. He went down the steps and bent to fit his key in the lock.

"Everything is going to come crashing down around you, Signor Macintyre."

The voice—a woman's—seemed disembodied, as if it had been whispered urgently in his ear and yet projected from an impossibly long distance. The effect was all the more eerie because, only a moment ago, the *calle* that stretched from the bridge past the Palazzo Uccello and beyond had seemed deserted. Surely his mind was playing malicious tricks on him. These words, spoken in Italian, were too close to the unreasonable fear that had just visited him on the bridge to be anything but a figment of his imagination.

He was wrong, however.

A tall figure dressed in a dark knee-length cloak stepped slowly from the shadows of the building next to the Palazzo Uccello. He didn't recognize the figure, although the resonance of the voice in his mind sounded familiar. A quick laugh preceded another step forward into a dim pool of lamplight.

It was Xenia Campi, her face looking like stone.

"You're in danger, Signor Macintyre. I've brought you a warning of danger," she intoned. "A red aura bleeds around your head. And tell your friend the Contessa to stay in her palazzo until it's all over."

"Until what's all over?"

It was more a startled, automatic response than a question. In any case Xenia Campi didn't answer but instead smiled without mirth or apparent meaning. It was an indication of Urbino's confusion and uneasiness that, as he watched her go over the bridge and turn the corner, he could think of nothing more to say to her.

7   "WHATEVER did the poor deluded woman mean, Urbino?" the Contessa said over the phone ten minutes later. "Stay here in the Ca' da Capo until *what's* over?"

"I asked her the same question. She only smiled and went away. I assume she meant *Carnevale*."

"*Carnevale*! I'd be most content to stay here until Ash Wednesday, but it just isn't possible. I have my obligations, you know," she said as if a long list of social, personal, and charitable missions kept her in perpetual and exhausted motion. "And unfortunately—because of your own insistence—tomorrow the Ca' da Capo will be in the mad middle of *Carnevale* itself. Like Mephistopheles in that play I'll be able to say, 'This is hell nor am I out of it'! But, seriously, Urbino, do you think there was anything behind Xenia Campi's warnings?"

"It isn't the first time that she's been apocalyptic."

His response expressed more confidence than he actually felt.

"That may be true but it's the first time she's been *personally* apocalyptic. I would prefer it if she would keep me out of her computations or her prognostications or whatever you want to call them. Either that or be more specific. Have you ever noticed how these people manage to be specific enough to frighten you but vague enough to wriggle out of it in the end? I wouldn't give another thought to what that silly woman said. She could have been born with *two* cauls for all I care!"

Urbino asked her if she had seen the police artist's sketch that looked like Tonio Vico.

"How could I miss it? Even if I had, Berenice called me up right after she saw it herself. It certainly looks like Tonio although he's much more handsome."

He told her that many people had seen Vico in and around the Piazza San Marco the night of Gibbon's murder, that Dora Spaak had said she had seen him talking with Gibbon in the Campo San Gabriele, that her brother—who looked very little like the other sketch—had identified him as the man he had seen in the Calle Santa Scolastica.

"Are you saying that Tonio is the murderer? You might as well say that poor Berenice did the deed! Stabbed Gibbon in the heart because he had taken away her stepson's fiancée!"

"So that her stepson could marry a girl she didn't even like?"

"You're right. If she were the murdering kind, she would have done in your dear little Hazel, I'm sure!"

"She didn't even know that they had broken off the engagement."

"Poor Berenice. Tonio had nothing to do with Gibbon's death! I don't think you believe that, do you? You seem so determined to ignore the obvious!"

"And what is that, Barbara?"

"That your cherished Miss Hazel Reeve is up to her shelllike little ears in intrigue! And to think that because of you I'm harboring her here in the Ca' da Capo!"

"Because of me . . . ?" he began but wasn't allowed to finish. The Contessa hung up.

Irritated though he was by her accusation that he was protecting Hazel Reeve, the precipitate end to their conversation had solved—for a time—the dilemma of whether or not to tell her what he had learned from Firpo and Pierina.

8 SERENA'S cries and ankle rubbing reminded Urbino that in his eagerness to talk with the Contessa, he had forgotten to feed Serena and that he, too, was hungry. After giving her something to eat, he rummaged through the kitchen and fixed himself a plate of prosciutto, Gorgonzola, and an apple. He brought it to the library where he poured himself a glass of Corvo, leaving the bottle near for replenishment. He also put his Proust within easy reach but knew that he wouldn't be able to concentrate on it tonight until he had thought some things through.

The first thing he turned his mind to was Xenia Campi. What was she in a position to know? She was staying at the Casa Crispina and therefore had an insider's perspective on the other guests. Because of her self-proclaimed clairvoyant abilities, most people considered her a *pazza*—a crackpot—and a meddler, someone to be avoided and not to be taken seriously. Dora Spaak and Giuseppe were frightened by her. Most of the time she was very much in evidence in the Piazza San Marco, predicting the doom she saw for the city and handing out her leaflets. Surely she recognized the same people day in and day out, evening after evening, their faces when it wasn't *Carnevale* and probably even their masks now that it was. Her best camouflage might very well be her notorious publicity. The quickest way to put yourself in a vulnerable position when you had something to hide was to underestimate the intelligence of someone ideally placed to observe you. Xenia Campi was easily underestimated, was quickly dismissed. Didn't the Contessa do it? Hadn't he himself done it from time to time?

Xenia Campi had gone out of her way to come to the Palazzo Uccello to warn him and, through him, the Contessa. Was her warning based on something she had actually seen or heard or was it the product of the fevered workings of her imagination? Could she have been thinking less of their safety than of giving herself—or someone close to her—a clear field during the final frenzies of *Carnevale*?

Xenia Campi had been sitting in the chair in the vestibule the night Gibbon had been murdered. Had she told him everything she had seen? Sister Agata had been asleep for a while. What might have happened during that period that Sister Agata wasn't aware of? Had Xenia Campi herself been sitting there for that entire time? Had she actually stayed in her room after Gibbon had left the Casa Crispina?

Urbino tried to fit Xenia Campi into what he had learned from Firpo and Pierina. Might she not know something she hadn't told him about the night of Gibbon's murder? If she did, she could be putting herself in a dangerous position by going around giving people warnings. Perhaps it was she who should remain close to home "until it was all over."

He next went over what Lubonski had told him the other day about Val Gibbon, about the man's maneuverings and deceptions, and kept coming back to one thing that the Pole had tossed off in passing. If he could get more details from Lubonski, it might be all he needed.

Serena jumped into his lap and started to make herself comfortable, as if she were sure of having a long, undisturbed nap. He helped her settle herself, stroking her soft, glistening coat. Her purr of contentment soothed him and he ate some of the prosciutto and cheese, followed by the Corvo. Although Serena had just eaten, she showed an interest in the Gorgonzola, one of her peculiarities being a taste for cheese, the more pungent the better.

Urbino was restless and he shifted his position in the chair several times. Each time he did, however, Serena accommodated herself to it, always managing to find a comfortable way to nestle again. When his changes and movements eventually became too much for her, she would always jump down and seek her comfort elsewhere. But her patience sometimes amazed him, even if at other times her lack of it made him realize that she was, after all, only a cat.

As he looked down at Serena, who at the moment was the perfect embodiment of her name, he wondered at the patience of people, at their ability to adapt themselves to things much more shattering for them than any shift of his position could ever be for Serena.

He took a sip of his Corvo and considered the adjustments Berenice Pillow had to make. She hadn't cared for Hazel to begin with. Yet she hadn't had the brief and bitter comfort of knowing that the girl had fallen in love with Gibbon— brief because death had now ended it and bitter because any sorrow of Tonio's was surely her own. She was a true mother in this respect. But although Tonio had concealed from her that Hazel had broken off their engagement, he wasn't doing the same now with what seemed to be their reconciliation. Berenice Pillow had her own adjustments to make and to judge from her behavior at the *enoteca* that afternoon she was doing a fairly good job of it.

The Italians called it making a *bella figura*—cutting a good figure, putting a fine face on things, even sometimes pretending to feel other than you did. It was something that Urbino admired in Berenice Pillow and in the Contessa, who was a mistress of its more benevolent forms. It was almost equal parts the art of deception and the deceptiveness of art. Without it the precarious structure of social life couldn't be maintained, but with too much we all wandered confused, trying to fathom the true thoughts and feelings even of those we loved and who loved us. Our intelligence and our awareness were our Ariadne's thread through this labyrinth, but even these could take us only so far to the open air.

As Urbino stroked Serena's coat and she rearranged herself with a murmur, he hoped that the Ariadne's thread that he had begun to spin out of the facts he already knew and the assumptions he couldn't help making—the kind of assumptions that had proved him right so often in his biographies—would be strong enough to get him out of the labyrinth.

And he hoped that no one else would be seriously hurt before he did. He was worried mainly about Tonio Vico, yet there was also room—and doubt enough in his mind—for him to worry about what harm Vico might do to someone. But who might that someone be?

9 NEXT morning, on the last day of *Carnevale*, Urbino called Gemelli and told him what he had learned from Pierina.

"All of this simply raises more questions," Gemelli said. "It complicates things, as you well know. The men from London are arriving tomorrow. Maybe they don't want to be corrupted by our Latin excesses and are waiting until all the celebrations are over. But unless we make some sense of all this, we stand a chance of being put in our place."

Urbino allowed himself to assume that he was included in the Commissario's "we." It was unlikely he was going to receive any more recognition than this.

"Alibis provided by mothers—even stepmothers, as in this case—are even more suspect than those provided by wives," Gemelli went on. "Signora Pillow can lie until she's blue in the face, and Pierina from the Campo San Maurizio can come in here and swear to her statement, but the prosecutor would just shake his head and frown. Annoying him is the last thing anyone wants to do, believe me. This is far from the most straightforward murder case I've ever dealt with and what you're telling me now makes it seem as devious as— as I don't know what!" he finished lamely for lack of an appropriate example. "*Carnevale* be damned! None of this business will get into *Il Gazzettino,* Macintyre. I'll see to that. It would be a big mistake if it did, so don't mention it to anyone. And although we'll put a police guard on Vico, I don't want him to know that we are. That way you and I will both be satisfied. You can assume that my men are protecting him and I'll be glad to have them watching him in case anything else develops. A nice, neat package and an economical use of the taxpayers' money. You *do* pay taxes here in Italy, don't you, Macintyre?"

Pleased that his conversation with Gemelli had gone so well, Urbino next called the Contessa. She was on her way out but she said she would be coming back in a few hours.

"If you think everything has already been taken care of for the masked ball tonight, you're sadly mistaken. I have plenty to do and I'm not sure I'm going to forgive you even if it all turns out to be a smashing success!"

"You said you wanted to go to the hospital to see Josef today, didn't you?" Urbino reminded the Contessa. "We can go in late afternoon and be back and forth in less than an hour. In addition to Josef, I'd like to see Mrs. Spaak. Sister Teresa called a little while ago and said that she was rushed to the hospital late yesterday afternoon and would like to see me."

Urbino arranged to be at the Ca' da Capo-Zendrini at five. This should give them enough time, since the ball didn't start until nine.

10   A dark gray sky with a flat, stony look was pressing down on the city like a slate roof when Urbino, in his cape and a heavy scarf, went for a walk half an hour later in the bone-numbing cold.

Ever since he had been a boy in New Orleans, deprived of a bicycle by his overcautious father, he had been a walker. The habit had carried over into his adult years and now he couldn't feel comfortable in any city that wasn't walkable. Fortunately, Venice was eminently so, and on those rare occasions when it wasn't, it more than made up for it by being floatable. The Contessa chided him about his love of walking, avoiding the activity herself whenever possible, but she understood that it could cure him, clear his head, put things in perspective.

This morning it might help him see something other than an impossible chaos in the details of Val Gibbon's life and death and in the lives of the other people Urbino had become familiar with.

At first Urbino sought out the quieter areas of the Cannaregio and in fifteen minutes, after crossing over a wooden bridge and going under an archway, he was in the isolated Campo Ghetto Nuovo.

The square, surrounded by tall narrow tenement buildings, had its usual weekday activity far removed from the frenzies of Carnival. The only people in masks were three young children chasing each other back and forth from a bare tree to one of the covered stone wellheads. They wore yellow plastic masks beneath their woolen hats, the kind of mask Nicholas Spaak had seen on the face of the person standing suspiciously across from the entrance of the Calle Santa Scolastica. Two women, their shopping baskets on the ground, looked with amusement at the children and chatted, occasionally casting apprehensive glances at the lowering sky.

Urbino didn't stop but continued to walk briskly out of the square and over the bridge past the synagogues and the shops of metalworkers and carpenters.

Urbino's mind was filled with thoughts and speculations about Val Gibbon and his murder. Something was glimmering there in the darkness of his meditations, of this he was sure—something thin, silver, hopefully more strong than it looked. Last night he had called it his Ariadne's thread and this late morning he still felt the aptness of the image.

He reviewed most of what he believed was important. His review didn't begin with Sister Teresa's summoning him from the Ca' da Capo-Zendrini the evening after Gibbon's murder but with the days immediately before.

The reach of his review also extended back into the pasts of the people he had spoken with or been told about, pasts either reluctantly or eagerly confided in him. It wasn't just Gibbon's life he tried to understand but the lives of all the others it had touched—the Casa Crispina guests, Rigoletti and Firpo, Tonio Vico and his stepmother, and, of course, Hazel Reeve. His mind was a kaleidoscope of masks and faces, and he wasn't at all sure that he was yet able to distinguish between them.

He bought a pastry, eating it as he entered the dark alley that led to the *sottoportego* running beneath several buildings. Beyond, framed at the end of the passageway, he saw the water traffic of the Cannaregio Canal and people hurrying along the quay.

He was soon walking against a steady flow of people hurrying to the Piazza from the train station. Most of these were day tourists who would return on one of the last trains after getting their taste of *Carnevale*. They tended to be among the most boisterous of the revelers but seldom wore elaborate costumes, only paper or plastic masks. Many of them used noisemakers and threw handfuls of confetti. A shower of the brightly colored pieces of paper fell soddenly over Urbino as he entered the Campo San Geremia.

Looking across the square to the church where the preserved body of Santa Lucia, patron saint of the eyes and sight, reposed in her crystal coffin, Urbino said a quick prayer for the kind of vision that would allow him to see the one true but camouflaged thing in all the confusing falseness. If it were given him, he promised Santa Lucia that he would add his own testimonial to all the discarded eyeglasses, ex-votos depicting eyes, photographs of the cured, and doctors' certificates of restored vision that the faithful left in homage to the little saint.

After threading his way through the jammed Lista di Spagna with its trinket shops, restaurants, and hotels, he was happy to reach the Ponte Scalzi that lifted its stone arch far above the busy waters of the Grand Canal. He stopped in the center, surveying the people streaming down the steps of the train station and piling into the waiting water-buses or hurrying on foot toward the Piazza. The sound of shouts and laughter competed with that of all the water traffic.

The noise and the crowds abated as he went through narrow alleys to a *campo* he treasured for its unpretentious yet secret air. Though relatively unknown to tourists, this unadorned square, set in a nest of confusing alleys not far from the Rialto and the train station, was typical of a city that flaunted its openness to the eye and the elements while also turning almost incestuously in on itself.

He stopped for an *ombra* of red wine and called the hospital. Stella Maris Spaak had been moved from intensive care and could have visitors for short periods of time.

After leaving the bar he paused to lean against the parapet of a narrow bridge. It was the infamous Ponte delle Tette— the Bridge of Teats—where in the sixteenth century courtesans were permitted by law to expose their breasts to entice reluctant youths into heterosexuality. Some of the prostitutes, however, had more success by simply dressing as boys in doublet and hose.

Urbino pulled his scarf up further against the cold wind gusting along the canal. Soapsuds were slowly drifting along on the surface of the water and a small plastic bag of refuse nudged the water steps where a group of cats were huddled.

From a window above the canal a woman in a knit cap shook out a dusty mop.

Into this less than romantic scene a black gondola with two reclining figures drifted into sight from beneath the bridge. On such a cold day it was unusual for anyone to venture on a gondola ride. These two people must be both hardy and incurably romantic to do it, and their preference for these secret waters could be said to bespeak a fine discrimination. Gondola traffic was usually concentrated on the Grand Canal between San Marco and the Rialto Bridge and in the network of canals in the San Marco quarter.

The two figures were so bundled in their scarves and in the blankets provided by the gondolier that they wouldn't have been out of place in a sleigh in nineteenth-century St. Petersburg. This association amused him and he imagined them as some latter-day Kitty and Levin out for a ride and was about to leave them to their relative privacy when one of the two figures turned around to look up at the bridge. Despite the swaddling of the scarves around the face he could tell that it was a woman, and that the woman was indisputably Hazel Reeve, but she didn't seem to recognize him, perhaps because of his own scarf pulled up above his chin. Whether she recognized him or not, he didn't know; she definitely didn't acknowledge him but turned back to her companion. Urbino's first thought was that her companion must certainly be Tonio Vico but his second was the admission that he couldn't even be sure whether it was a man or a woman.

He watched the gondola make its slow way down the canal and then, preceded by the warning cry of the gondolier, turn down into another waterway that would eventually bring it out into the Grand Canal.

11 "DON'T be upset with me, *caro*," the Contessa said when Urbino came into her *salotto* at a quarter to five. "I've already seen Josef. Berenice, Oriana, and I were over on Murano and when we were coming back across the lagoon I asked Milo to take us to the hospital. We were practically there as it was. I thought it would be better to do it then because the Lord only knew what I would be faced with when I came back here. And I was right!" she said triumphantly. "Mauro said that Alvise's sister Siviglia called from Vicenza and will be here at seven, instead of eight-thirty as she had said she would be. She'll be all ready to go and I'll look like a frump!"

"You should be all the more thankful then that it's a masquerade, Barbara. You can hide behind one of the masks you haven't decided on yet. I bought you a new *moretta* yesterday."

He gave her the packet that she had been glancing at since he had arrived.

"Thank you for your generosity, but I have no intention of hiding behind anything!"

"And if you do end up looking like a frump, Barbara— which I doubt could ever happen—I'm sure everyone will assume it's the costume of a frump."

She stared at him, trying to figure out if he had paid her a compliment or not.

"But about Josef, Barbara," he went on, "how did it go?"

"Not too well at first, I'm afraid, but that was my fault. Oriana left us to see her friend who lives by the Querini-Stampalia. Berenice came with me. All I told her was that Josef was restoring the fresco at San Gabriele. I didn't tell her anything else, don't worry. Josef seemed pleased enough to see me when I stepped through the door, although he was obviously uneasy, but when he saw Berenice come in, trying to beam good cheer despite her troubles, poor dear, he realized we weren't going to be alone. I had thought he might prefer it that way since we wouldn't be able to get into anything that might upset him. But he was upset already so I asked Berenice to wait for me outside."

"Did you talk about Sir Rupert?"

"Not directly. Josef didn't seem up to it, and I wasn't either. I told him that you had mentioned your conversation with him and left it at that. I said that all I wanted to hear was that he was all better and that when he got out of hospital he was to come here with me for as long as he wanted or needed. He seemed happy to hear that."

"I'm not sure how free Josef is going to be once he does get well."

"I didn't notice any policeman standing at attention outside his door, thank God. They can't be too concerned about him if he's left alone from time to time like that—though what a bedridden man who still looks half dead is supposed to do, I'd like to know!"

"Maybe it's better that you went without me, Barbara. This way Josef gets two visits instead of one."

"He's had plenty of visitors already today. When Berenice and I were leaving, Sister Teresa was going in to see him with the young woman I saw at Florian's with Gibbon."

"Dora Spaak."

"Right. I invited her to come tonight. I told her she could come with Sister Teresa and not to worry if she didn't have any costume or formal clothes. I was afraid she might be offended at the invitation since her mother was in hospital but her face lit up."

"I should be on my way, Barbara," Urbino said, getting up. "Do you think Milo could take me to the hospital?"

"Of course, *caro*." She smiled, picking up one of the Tunisian cushions and cradling it against her chest. "He won't be going the most direct way, though. I hope you don't mind. He'll be going the whole length of the Canalazzo. I promised Hazel that Milo would take her to Harry's. You don't mind being with her as far as there, do you?"

Something akin to the enigmatic smile she had worn several days ago was on her lips, and once again it had to do with Hazel Reeve. Exactly what she was thinking or feeling behind that smile was impossible to fathom. He hoped his own face was as much a mask as hers.

12 FOR the first five minutes of his trip down the Grand Canal in the Contessa's motorboat with Hazel Reeve, Urbino couldn't help thinking how much less romantic it was than riding in a gondola on a back canal. Did Hazel, looking out at the palazzi and water traffic, think the same thing? If she did, she gave no indication.

"This is absolutely marvelous, isn't it! Barbara is so lucky. Oh, don't tell her I said 'lucky,' will you?" She reached out to touch his arm gently. "She has the taste and the imagination to do wonderful things with the money she has. I don't suppose that's luck, is it? Enough people have the money—maybe *that's* where the luck comes in—but they don't have the taste and the imagination."

She shook her head slowly as if she were contemplating her own sad position. Surely she didn't place herself in the latter category.

"What about the ones with the taste and the imagination but without the money?" Urbino said. "Would you say they're *un*-lucky?"

"Oh, Urbino, I'm enjoying myself too much to get involved in a serious discussion. All this is such a fantasy!" She indicated the golden lights, the glimpses of ceiling frescoes, chandeliers and warm interiors, the water taxis with their costumed groups pulling up in front of the water entrances of the palazzi, the decorated facades of the buildings, the festive groups crowded on the boat landings, the dark lustrous waters and the other craft gliding soundlessly by. "Why break the spell?"

Her rhetorical question described just what Urbino hoped to be able to do before they reached Harry's—break the spell of this trip down the Grand Canal and get Hazel Reeve to tell him a few things.

Hazel kept asking him to name the various palazzi, churches, and buildings doubled in the dark waters of the Grand Canal. She wasn't content with mere names but also wanted histories, lineages, operatic tales of love, passion, and death. He was happy that his own knowledge and the rich human history of the Grand Canal made it possible to give her what she wanted.

Her hunger, however, made him a little uneasy. Was there something else behind it? Could she be keeping him occupied so that they wouldn't have to talk seriously, as Berenice Pillow had seemed to be doing for part of their walk back from the wine bar yesterday? Did she hope that her enthusiasms and his encouraged accounts would keep them away from other topics until she was safely deposited at Harry's?

He intended to try to find out.

His first opportunity, and perhaps his best, came when they were passing the Ca'Rezzonico where Browning had died more than a hundred years ago.

"You might know that Browning died here." He indicated the magnificent facade of the palazzo. "I've often thought that Venice was an appropriate place for him to die. After all, he was a poet of masks wasn't he? He's always wearing one in his poems. He's Porphyria's lover, he's the brother in the Spanish cloister, he's the Duke of Ferrara and Fra Lippo Lippi and Abt Vogler and Andrea del Sarto and all the Italians in *The Ring and the Book*—even the Pope himself! I don't feel as if I know Browning but I love him."

Hazel looked at him with her widely spaced eyes that glimmered from the lights outside the Contessa's boat. Urbino started to recite a stanza from one of Browning's poems about Venice:

> *"Past we glide, and past, and past!*
> *Why's the Pucci Palace flaring*
> *Like a beacon in the blast?*
> *Guests by hundreds not one caring*
> *If the dear host's neck were wried:*
> *Past we glide!"*

"That's from 'In a Gondola,' " Hazel said, and started to recite some lines from the poem herself.

> *"Dip your arm o'er the boat side, elbow deep,*
> *As I do, thus: were death so unlike sleep,*
> *Caught this way?"*

Neither of them said anything as they passed under the Accademia Bridge. As its shadows flickered over her face, Hazel pulled her coat more tightly around her. The scarf she had muffled her face with earlier in the gondola was loose now around her neck.

"But we can't dip our arms in the water in this boat, can we, Urbino?" she said. "Things have changed since the days of Browning and Elizabeth Barrett."

"And don't forget that the gondolas had a *felze* then, a little black cabin with louvered windows where the passengers could shelter from bad weather and be private."

She didn't say anything. Was she thinking that he had finally broken the spell? She was staring at the Gothic Palazzo

Barbaro. Perhaps he could still provoke her into a revelation.

"Browning stayed there. So did Sargent and James. In fact, James had one of his characters, an American heiress, die there after she found out that the man she loved had betrayed her."

The Contessa's boat passed the Palazzo Barbaro and several other palazzi before Hazel said, "Women seldom die for such things except in books, Urbino, and when they do they don't just 'turn their face to the wall' and expire the way she did. And neither do they will all their money to the man who deceived them."

It was obvious she knew James's story well.

"The days of fine renunciatory gestures like that have gone forever," Urbino said, thinking of how she had refused to put aside her promise to her father about the prenuptial agreement.

"If they ever existed. And if they did, I'm not sure they should have," she surprised him by saying, given what she had told him about her own scruples.

"That palazzo there," he said, indicating the low white building to their right, "is the Peggy Guggenheim museum. The 'Unfinished Palazzo' as it's called. If it had been finished it would be the largest palazzo on the Grand Canal."

She stared at the building with its horse and rider by Marino Marini facing the Grand Canal through the water gate.

"To think of all the modern art behind those walls," Hazel said, "It strikes me as being out of place in the city of Carpaccio and Titian, Veronese and Tintoretto. Venice doesn't belong to the modern world, even if we are going down the Grand Canal in a motorboat."

"Peggy Guggenheim was the last to have her own private gondola."

"Did it have a *felze* that she could hide inside?" She smiled. "Are we playing games with each other with all this talk about gondolas, Urbino? That *was* you on the bridge today, wasn't it? You probably wondered why I didn't say hello but at first I wasn't quite sure if it was you. I *am* a bit nearsighted." She avoided his eyes for a few moments and stared at the landing stage of Santa Maria del Giglio where a crowd of people waited for the boat. She turned back to him. "When I realized that it was you, I didn't say hello because I was a little embarrassed. To tell you the truth I wasn't absolutely sure you knew it was me either. *You* didn't indicate that you had."

"You were rather muffled up."

"Could you see who I was with?"

"As I said, I could barely recognize you."

She looked at him assessingly. He could sense her suspicion and nervousness.

"It was Xenia Campi, you know." She laughed. It sounded genuine. "Yes, Xenia Campi. I'm embarrassed to admit it." There was an awkward smile on her face. "That's another reason why I didn't say hello."

"I didn't know that you knew her."

"I met her when I went to the Casa Crispina a second time. I wanted to see Val's room but the police still had it sealed. I spent a few minutes outside and Xenia Campi came down the hall. We started to talk and—and I'm afraid I encouraged her. I suppose I'm in a rather vulnerable state. I thought I was handling things so well but now I'm not so sure. It hasn't even been a week since Val was murdered. Xenia Campi spoke to me in such a gentle way. She said that she knew what it was like to lose someone you loved and that she could help me—help us all—find out what happened to Val. She said something about auras and fire. I wasn't listening too closely but when she said that everyone was concerned about where Val was killed but no one seemed to be paying any attention to how he had got there, it made a lot of sense, at least at the time."

Urbino silently agreed with her. All that he knew about Gibbon's last day was that he had spent much of it in the Piazza, came back to the Casa Crispina for dinner, seen Dora in the dining room, and then left.

"She said she could find out but I would have to help her. We went outside and she stood there in a trance for a few minutes and then went to the water steps on the other side of the Casa Crispina. 'A water trail,' she said. 'We have to follow his water trail.' I know it's silly, but I believed she knew what she was talking about, so I told her that we'd go in a motorboat. She didn't want a motorboat. She said it would disperse the influence and that motorboats were also bad for the city. So that's why you saw us in the gondola. We followed what she said was the water trail. It seemed we were going up and down every back canal. Right after I saw you on the bridge, she said she had lost the trail. She blamed it on the suds she saw floating on the water. She insisted on getting out immediately and I went back to the Molo feeling very foolish."

"Xenia Campi can be convincing in her own way," Urbino said, thinking about her visit last night to the Palazzo Uccello. "I don't believe any of her business about auras and flames and whatever else she sees, but there's a definite passion—confused and misdirected though it might be—in what she says."

Hazel smiled wryly.

"Isn't that often the case with passions?"

They were approaching San Marco. There was still something Urbino needed to know. Their time alone together was so short now that he knew he had to risk being abrupt but abruptness might end up serving his purposes. He might get a more direct answer or be better able to gauge her response if it was evasive.

"Forgive me for asking this, Hazel, but do you have any reason to believe that Val Gibbon betrayed you?"

Her response wasn't one of the ones he had expected. She laughed.

" 'Betrayed'! What a perfectly Victorian word, Urbino. It almost has furbelows on it. You have to admit it sounds strange when you use it for someone not in a novel. The word's on your mind because of that Henry James novel, isn't it?"

He reminded her that during dinner at the Montin she had mentioned something about a woman Gibbon had been involved with.

"Could he have continued the relationship?"

"Is there a difference between continuing a relationship and trying to end one gracefully?"

"Is that what he was trying to do?"

"I don't have the slightest idea. Of course there were other women. Val was charming and handsome. I'm not saying that he had relationships with them while we were together, but don't forget that neither of us expected to fall in love. I was involved with Tonio and I believe Val was involved with someone, too. We never talked about it, but once when we were at his flat the phone rang and I could tell there was a woman on the other end. I didn't hear what he was saying but I could tell that he was talking to a woman."

"It couldn't have been another man?"

Milo was carefully maneuvering the boat between the pilings of the quay. The Molo and the Piazzetta blazed and clamored in front of them.

Hazel didn't answer but got up. Not wanting to leave her this way Urbino told Milo that he would get off here and walk the rest of the way to the hospital. Milo could bring the boat to the Rio dei Mendicanti and wait for him there.

Hazel and Urbino joined the crowd on the Molo and began to walk to Harry's in silence. The kiosks flanking the gardens were crowded with customers buying trinkets and postcards. An old man with a bored expression was demonstrating neon yo-yos by one of the stone benches that gave a view of the lagoon and the island of San Giorgio Maggiore floating in the distance. A few feet away a younger man, who looked like his son, was fashioning pink, yellow, and green neon bracelets and necklaces. The pavement between the kiosks and the marble wall by the water was dense with people, moving in both directions and jockeying for a good position from which to see the water processions that would be starting in about an hour. Out in the lagoon by San Giorgio was a barge from which multicolored lasers crisscrossed the sky.

Groups leaving the vaporetti pushed Urbino and Hazel against the buildings after they went down a bridge. He put his hand under her elbow to steady her. They stopped in front of Harry's in the Calle Vallaressa, drawing as close to the door as they could as the people flowed around them on their way to the Piazza.

"Thank you, Urbino, thank you for everything," she said as they had to make way for a Doge who was emerging from Harry's.

There was something valedictory about her thank-you. She was thanking him in a way that seemed also to be saying good-bye, not just for the evening but for a longer time. Yet he must have been mistaken, for the next moment she said, "Come in and have a drink with Tonio and me."

Before he could protest, she opened the door. He had no choice but to follow her in and immediately wished he hadn't.

One reason was the sheer noise of the place; another was the thickness of the smoke that set his eyes watering. But it was the look Tonio Vico, standing with a drink at the far edge of the crowded bar, gave him from his dark eyes that had Urbino wishing he weren't there.

13 THE three of them were outside now, having decided against staying in Harry's, and were moving slowly toward the Piazza San Marco. It had started to snow, a wet snow that stung the face.

As they made their way down the narrow Calle Vallaressa with its fashionable shops, four-star hotels, and expensive restaurants, it was impossible for the three of them to keep together and soon Urbino found himself ahead of Hazel and Vico. How far ahead he was he couldn't tell because whenever he looked behind all he saw were shouting, unfamiliar faces and impassive masks. He didn't know if he should stop and wait. When he reached the glass shop at the intersection, he stepped into the entrance. They would be lost to him forever if he joined the crush coming from three directions and inching toward the Piazza.

In a few minutes the couple appeared, arm in arm, apparently unconcerned about the crowd or the stinging snow that was coming down faster and harder now. When they saw him, they ducked into the shelter of the shop opening.

"I'm going to avoid the Piazza and go to the hospital."

"But you can't, Urbino! It's the last night of *Carnevale*! I know you'll be celebrating later with us at Barbara's but can't you come into the Piazza for at least a few minutes?"

She tugged at his sleeve as she plunged into the crowd with Vico, looking back at him. He followed.

The Piazza was seething. What Napoleon had called the finest drawing room in Europe was like a masked ball in Bedlam.

People crowded under the long, golden corridors of the arcades, sat and sprawled on the steps, and danced and swarmed in the Piazza. Bright lamps tossed on their wires, and the huge chandelier in the middle blazed and swayed perilously in the gusts of snow-laden wind. The windows above the arcades had lights, and rows of illuminated white masks marched on poles above the crowd. Blue and green lights played over the domes of the Basilica, and the gold of the facade mosaics glowed so brightly, even through the driving snow, that it looked as if the building was on fire. Cameras flashed everywhere and even the music pouring out of the loudspeakers and being played by the orchestras at Quadri's and Florian's couldn't drown out the roar of the crowd. A line of masqueraders crossed the stage, posing and bowing. Urbino recognized many of the more elaborate costumes he had seen during the last week. Now, at Carnival's end, after wandering through the stage set of the city, the maskers were on an actual stage.

There was too much to see and hear to be able to do either without becoming confused and disoriented. One moment everything was an indistinguishable swirl of colors and material. The next moment you became entranced by one grotesque or comical detail—a man with two heads, a spray of feathers instead of a face, a grimacing figure apparently walking backward, a replica of the Campanile teetering between two gravestones with flashing lights, a tall, thin man with a dripping piece of meat impaled on a huge pitchfork.

Walking in stately procession near the stage was a mock cortege, complete with a shining black coffin and six pall-bearers draped completely in dominoes, their faces covered in black masks. The coffin was followed by a group of laughing mourners dressed as Harlequin, Columbine, Pierrot, and other commedia dell'arte figures who were dancing and pelting the coffin and onlookers with flowers. Every few steps Harlequin stopped to make an obscene gesture with his *batocchio,* a stick used for stirring the character's favored dish of polenta.

In the midst of all this chaos were silent, costumed figures, either alone or in clusters. They had an eerie stillness as they stood immobile against a column or in a doorway waiting to be photographed. One of them was Giovanni Firpo in his blue and green robe, high headdress with silver baubles, Oriental turquoise and silver mask, and large black feathered fan inset with tiny mirrors.

Most of the time Urbino was tossed by endless and unpredictable waves that seemed sometimes mainly colors, at other times shouts and laughs, at still others a dominant scent.

The three of them, buffeted by the crowd, walked under the arcade toward Florian's. Urbino was several feet behind the couple. Maybe Florian's could be their safe haven, and he could part from them there. Hazel turned, however, and beckoned Urbino to follow as she and Vico went down the steps into the Piazza and almost disappeared in the swirl of bodies lanced by snow.

He entered the thick of it himself. It was a deluge that put him in mind of the storming of the Bastille except that the object here was a different, more frightening kind of liberation. Pleasure was the object, in the pursuit of which there seemed to be no rules or thought of bridling the self but only a frenzy of letting it go. These were all thoroughly modern men and women, most of whom during the rest of the year kept to the straight and narrow. During *Carnevale*, however, they were allowed to be something else, and they were allowed to do it all together. It was intoxicating and seductive.

Pushing through the crowd Urbino thought he had lost Hazel and Tonio until he saw the young man's profile standing out against a cream-colored feathered headdress loaded down with wet snow. He caught up with them. Still arm in arm, they had stopped and were looking at the people dancing and posing and pushing at each other in the middle of the Piazza and on the ramp, the inclement weather only seeming to add to their spirits. A long sinuous line of maskers linked arm in arm rushed up one incline, scattering people as they ran and slid across the platform and down the other incline. The whip of revelers got longer and longer as others joined. Urbino thought he caught a glimpse of the small, birdlike face of Pierina in the crowd on the platform, a light-colored mask pushed to the top of her head.

"Isn't this thrilling!" Hazel said. "I wish we had our masks with us." She waved a program she had picked up near the tourist office. "There's going to be a laser and Bengal lights show in half an hour and then some fireworks!"

Excited as a child, she gave Vico a kiss on the nose. He didn't seem anywhere near as excited as she was.

"Oh, I wish we could stay here all evening! Don't tell Barbara I said that, Urbino. Of course we'll be there for her ball but all this is so overwhelming!"

As the evening progressed the throng would get thicker and more frenzied, the air more charged with abandon. Even if the snowstorm got worse, it would probably only animate the crowd even more. Yet at midnight the madness would come to an end, ushering in a period of silence, ashes, and repentance— or, its contemporary equivalent, recuperation.

Hazel brushed snow from the front of her coat.

"Why don't we have the drinks we didn't have at Harry's?" she asked Urbino. "We could go to Florian's."

"I have to get to the hospital. I'll cut across the Piazza. I'll see you later at Barbara's—unless you feel you can't pull yourselves away from all of this."

"Oh, we'll be there, won't we, Tonio?"

Urbino was about to leave them when he was elbowed violently by someone passing him from behind. A figure dressed in a dark jacket and slacks and wearing a knit cap and yellow plastic mask streaked past. Urbino thought he was hurrying to join the end of the long line of men and women now snaking back in the opposite direction. Instead he went straight for Tonio Vico, knocking aside Hazel, who almost fell to the pavement. His hands closed tightly around Vico's throat, and Vico put his hands up to rip away the throttling grasp. Hazel screamed.

The person in the mask shouted a muffled curse in Italian but Urbino couldn't tell if it was a man's voice or a woman's. He hurried forward to come to Vico's aid but once again he was elbowed aside, this time by a man with a swarthy face. Hazel was still screaming as the other man went up to Vico and his attacker and withdrew something from inside his coat. It was a truncheon. He raised it and clubbed Vico's attacker on the back of the head. Vico was free, and his attacker fell to the snowy pavement. The mask had fallen off. It was Ignazio Rigoletti, a crazed, derisive look on his hawklike face.

14 EVERYONE else in the *salone da ballo* of the Ca' da Capo-Zendrini probably thought that the Contessa's main emotions this evening were relief and excitement—relieved, as they all were, that Ignazio Rigoletti had been caught before he could do any real harm to Tonio Vico or anyone else and excited that her *ballo in maschera* was going so well.

Urbino, however, could detect the apprehension in his friend's face. Even if Rigoletti was now in police custody and her ball was going smoothly, there was still an hour and a half until midnight and something could still go wrong. It would all be on Urbino's head if it did since he had, as she kept reminding him, "instigated" the whole thing. The Contessa had gone to a great deal of trouble and expense to ensure that nothing could be laid at her door.

Conviviality had been building during the last hour and, in the true spirit of *Carnevale*, the Contessa's diverse friends and acquaintances—old aristocrats and shopkeepers, dress designers and clerics, artisans and councilmen, journalists and businessmen—mingled freely and without any apparent reservation. A small orchestra was playing tasteful music— "no Piazza San Marco show tunes or popular songs," she had made clear to the conductor—on a platform by the wall with the sixteenth-century tapestry of Susanna and the Elders. Soon a tenor, soprano, and baritone would sing some arias and duets from *Un Ballo in Maschera*. When the orchestra wasn't playing, music from the opera came over the speakers.

A buffet table offered its savories in front of the closed doors of the loggia overlooking the Grand Canal where a flesh-cutting snow, more ice now than anything else, was still falling. At strategic points in the large room were baskets of fresh flowers, large pots of scented herbs, and bronze chafing dishes burning incense. The Contessa had decided against any streamers, but Urbino suspected that many of the guests had brought them, along with confetti, to toss at the appropriate time.

Urbino, conforming to the theme of the ball, was dressed as Renato, the Creole secretary to Riccardo the Governor. His blue coat with scarlet sash tied in a knot on the left was the costume of the conspirators who planned the assassination of the Governor. There were other conspirators at the ball, most of them wearing large plumed hats and fancy masks. Urbino wore a matte-black half mask that the Contessa had given him. Alvise had worn it to a memorable *ballo in maschera* the first year of their marriage.

The Contessa, at the moment consoling and congratulating Berenice Pillow for what must have been the fifth time that evening, was dressed as the veiled Amelia in a simple Fortuny silk gown that had belonged to Alvise's mother—soft blue with a mother-of-pearl sheen. Her blue veil, pulled away from her face, was of delicate Burano lace, supposedly of the same design as the one that Philip II ordered for his bride, Mary Stuart.

Only about a third of the guests were in elaborate costume, the predominant one being the eighteenth-century disguise of the domino with wig, black tricorn hat, black cape, and stern *bautta* mask. Most of the guests wore black tuxedos and evening gowns topped with feathered or jeweled masks. The only exception to these two categories was Sister Teresa, who wore a simple gray suit in lieu of her religious habit, which would have looked too much like a costume. In fact, several people had come dressed as nuns and cardinals.

Dora Spaak, with whom Urbino was talking now, was wearing an oversized Laura Ashley party dress in a summery floral pattern. Urbino didn't know if it was meant to be a costume or not.

"I stopped in to see your mother earlier this evening."

"How kind of you. I was with her for most of the day."

"She was doing fine," he said. So fine, he didn't add, that she had once again urged him to help her son but to do it so that Nicky wouldn't realize that she knew anything he didn't want her to know. Urbino had assured her he would do his best, but that he doubted her son needed his help, mentioning Rigoletti's arrest an hour before in the Piazza. As he had hoped, this had satisfied her and she hadn't asked any more questions that he wouldn't have wanted to answer, although he had asked some questions of his own.

"She said that she hoped you would have a good time this evening and not to worry about her. Your brother will look in on her. You see, she knows that your brother sometimes goes for walks here and that you cover for him, so to speak. The night of Gibbon's murder, for instance. She told me again that you stopped in her room twice, shortly after your brother put her to bed and several hours later. She wasn't sure of the time but she said she thinks it was about midnight. She remembers the church bells. She wasn't asleep either time, it seems. So you see, she's aware of your concern for her, Miss Spaak, and she wants you to have a good time tonight."

It seemed as if a great many things were going through Dora Spaak's head but none of them were verbalized. She was as pale as a corpse.

When Urbino asked her to dance, she shook her head. "I'd rather not, if you don't mind. I'm feeling a little warm. It must be all this excitement. It's like a fairy tale—a masked ball at the palace of a countess!"

He went to get them something to drink. As he was moving through the crowd it seemed as if the main topic of conversation wasn't the costume ball or *Carnevale* but Ignazio Rigoletti. By the time he reached the bar and was working his way back to Dora Spaak, he had heard several convincing theories as to why Rigoletti had murdered Gibbon and then tried to kill the "handsome young man" whose likeness had been in the newspaper. Though ingenious, however, none of them was correct or could ever hope to be, and Urbino, with his own knowledge, felt like a real conspirator among them instead of only someone dressed as one.

When he got back to where he had left Dora Spaak, she was gone. The Contessa was standing where she had been.

"Don't look so disappointed, *caro*. I asked Filippo to ask Miss Spaak to dance and told him that no one would mind if he monopolized her for a while. I didn't add that the last person who would object was Oriana since it would give her a chance for a tête-à-tête with her latest admirer."

She took the mineral water he had brought for Dora.

"I was sure Miss Spaak was the type to drink only champagne and to be thrilled to have a headache and soda water the morning after."

"Everything is going well, Barbara," Urbino said, telling himself that he wasn't being hypocritical, that things *had* been going well so far. "Aren't you glad you allowed yourself to be persuaded?"

"If I am, I'll never admit it. And don't forget that the evening is far from over yet."

She gave him a slightly questioning look, the kind of look a sophisticated child might give to a magician she suspected of having something up his sleeve that had been secretly put there hours before. The Contessa would forgive him almost anything except an intentional unkindness to her, and of this he knew he was—and hoped he would always be—innocent.

They surveyed the guests mingling and dancing. As Urbino had noticed before, there were several veiled ladies, but none veiled and gowned as strikingly as the Contessa. There were numerous fortune-tellers, the character of Ulrica being the most colorful one in the opera. Vico, who had arrived only a short time ago from the Questura, was wearing a red half mask and a well-cut black suit with a black cloak. The cloak, made of a heavy material, was obviously meant for outerwear and was probably a part of Vico's regular wardrobe. Inside the Contessa's *salone*, however, it made the handsome young man sweat as he danced with Hazel in her geometric-print silk dress and half mask with red and white lozenges.

"I was afraid," the Contessa said as she deposited her half-finished mineral water on a passing waiter's tray, "that the attack on Tonio and Rigoletti's arrest might be sobering for everyone here tonight but it seems to have had the opposite effect. It's our *coup de théâtre*! It's more of a theme than Verdi! And I have you to thank for that."

The Contessa's praise made him uncomfortable.

"I had little enough to do with it. It all happened so fast. Fortunately, Gemelli's man hadn't lost Vico in the crowd or else your lovely ball would have been completely ruined."

" 'Completely'?" Her brow furrowed as she tried to understand what he might mean. "I'm sure you have a lot of explaining to do, the kind that makes me feel like a *cretina*, but it will have to wait until tomorrow. Ash Wednesday is the time for reflection and remembrance of things past, for plans for a better future. I don't insist that you explain anything now, *caro*. How did you find Josef?"

She seemed eager to change the subject.

"He was looking very well, much better than when I saw him last. I think your visit did him good."

"I'm glad to hear that. I was afraid it might have been somewhat of a setback at first."

"We talked about that. He explained what the problem was. He was glad to be able to see you alone. His mind is more at ease now."

Once again she gave him her questioning look but he stared back at her, with, he hoped, as little expression as possible.

"I also spoke with Dora Spaak's mother. She was worried about her son but I tried to put her mind at rest."

"Doesn't poor little Dora get worried about? I'm happy she came tonight. How much of *Carnevale* can she have seen? Although I saw her last week in the Piazza with Gibbon, she probably has been keeping close to the Casa Crispina."

"Not quite. Mrs. Spaak says that she thinks she has slipped out one or two nights to see what was going on."

" 'Slipped out'? At her age she shouldn't have to 'slip out.' "

"Mrs. Spaak would agree with you. She found it rather amusing when Dora came in the night Gibbon was murdered and borrowed the mask her son had bought for her a few days before."

"But I thought she said she had stayed in that night—that she wasn't feeling well?"

Urbino nodded but didn't go into more detail. The Contessa stared at him quizzically and turned away to look out on the dance floor, at the president of the district assembly dancing with the young wife of a senator, at Oriana Borelli in the arms of her latest admirer, at the architect Rebecca Mondador with a journalist from *Il Gazzettino,* at Filippo Borelli with Dora Spaak, and at many other couples Urbino himself couldn't recognize because of their costumes.

Urbino wished there had been some way he could have convinced Commissario Gemelli to provide a police officer for the ball. But Gemelli would have said, with good reason, that Vico didn't need any more protection or observation, did he? And before his trip to the hospital to see Lubonski and Stella Maris Spaak, Urbino hadn't been in much of a position to give Gemelli the kind of reason that would have inclined—or compelled—the Commissario to comply. Gemelli was confident that Rigoletti would now tell the truth about what had happened in the Calle Santa Scolastica.

"It's time for our little concert," the Contessa said as the orchestra finished their number. "Excuse me."

She went on the platform and introduced the tenor, soprano, and baritone from Milan.

"They will be singing three arias and a duet from *Un Ballo in Maschera.* The first is Signor Massimo Carlini as Renato singing 'Alla vita.' "

Urbino was less than impressed with Carlini but Annamaria Terisio, who sang "Morrò," moved him. For several minutes he forgot everything and was caught up in the soprano's rendition of Amelia's impassioned gallows request to her husband not to kill her until she can see her only son once again. Amelia, along with Bellini's Norma and Puccini's Suor Angelica and Madame Butterfly, was one of the memorable mothers of opera. As she sang, Urbino saw that Filippo Borelli was translating for Dora Spaak:

> *"I shall die—but one last wish,*
> *By God, at least grant me.*
> *My only son let me*

> *Hold close to my heart. . . .*
> *Do not reject the pleas*
> *Of a mother's heart.*
> *I shall die—but this body*
> *May be consoled by his kisses,*
> *For the end is in sight*
> *Of my fleeting hours. . . .*
> *His hand he will extend*
> *To close the eyes of his mother*
> *Whom he will never see again"*

Extended cries of "Brava!" sounded after her performance. The duet that followed between Terisio and the tenor, Michele Altieri, in the role of Riccardo, though good, was under the shadow of her aria. It wasn't until Riccardo's "Ma se m'è forza," with its expression of foreboding and fated desire, with its advice to Amelia to imprison her memories in the secret depths of her heart, that the guests were captivated again.

The three then sang "Tu qui" and when they had finished there were rousing cheers. The Contessa went up on the platform. A waiter brought bouquets of flowers that the Contessa presented to the singers. If the Contessa's ball had ended now, there would have been good reason to consider it a thorough success, but there was still an hour until midnight.

No sooner had the Contessa and the singers left the platform than Tonio Vico stepped up on it. He had discarded his cloak. His hair was damp with perspiration and a purplish bruise marked his neck. In his flawless Italian, he addressed the guests, many of whom had already started to move toward the buffet table and were engaged in conversation. As he spoke, Urbino saw that once again Filippo Borelli was translating for Dora Spaak.

"Ladies and gentlemen, after such a wonderful performance I cannot hope to give you anything except what makes my own heart happy. Most of you hardly even know me but you know that some sorrow and difficulty came to an end for me this evening in the Piazza San Marco. Carnival isn't over yet but I can't wear my mask any longer." He pulled his red half mask from his face and threw it into the air. "I must express the truth of my heart as our wonderful soprano, Signora Terisio, did a few minutes ago. Ladies and gentlemen, I am proud to announce my engagement to Signorina Hazel Reeve!"

To initially weak, but gradually growing applause Hazel joined Tonio Vico, her mask with its red and white lozenges now around her slender neck. She looked embarrassed, even a little frightened, and for one brief moment her eyes locked with Urbino's.

The Contessa, who had joined an astonished-looking Dora Spaak, Filippo Borelli, and Berenice Pillow in the corner by the icons and triptych, had a fixed smile on her face. Here was some entertainment she hadn't planned herself and she must be wondering if it was going to be a good addition to the evening. She was a woman who found it difficult to trust in the unforeseen or unprovided-for, no matter how many times they had brought her pleasure. For her they were almost synonymous with the chaotic.

The Contessa had a bottle of champagne brought to the engaged couple and told her guests to join her in a toast.

"Please, Mother, would you come up here with Hazel and me?" Tonio said enthusiastically.

Berenice Pillow smiled and walked slowly to the stage. Her stepson took her hand and helped her up. She kissed him, then Hazel, and was given a glass of champagne. The orchestra, at Vico's request, started to play "Nel Blu Dipinto di Blu," but not before the conductor had looked at the Contessa for her approval. It seemed her costume ball was going to have some popular songs after all. The guests, clearly enjoying the music, started to dance.

Tonio Vico seemed somewhat at a loss as to what he should do next—dance with Hazel or with his stepmother, whom he had called to join them. Urbino was going to the stage to ask Mrs. Pillow to dance when shouts came from the grand staircase at the entrance of the *salone da ballo*.

Xenia Campi, melted snow glistening on her knit cap and dark cloak, was arguing with Mauro at the head of the staircase. When he put his hand on her shoulder, she shook if off violently. The orchestra continued to play but gradually most of the couples stopped dancing. Those who didn't slowed down their movements and tried to see what was going on. The Contessa hurried over to Xenia Campi and Mauro, saying something to the woman and taking her hand. Mauro started to help Xenia Campi off with her cloak but the woman moved away from the staircase and into the *salone* itself. The first place she looked was at the stage where Hazel Reeve, Vico, and Berenice Pillow were standing in front of the orchestra, now silent. Hazel's eyes were large with nervousness but her future mother-in-law had a tentative smile on her face as if she expected to witness another installment of the evening's entertainment. Vico had his arm protectively around Hazel's shoulder.

Urbino went across the room to Xenia Campi.

"Signora Campi, what a pleasure that you've joined us. Can I get something for you? Perhaps you would like to go into one of the reception rooms for a few minutes."

Urbino knew he would have the Contessa's eternal gratitude if he could maneuver the woman out of the *salone*. But Xenia Campi would have none of it. She shook her head and stepped forward a few more feet.

"Maybe she's upset about Rigoletti," the Contessa said to him in English.

At the sound of her former husband's name Xenia Campi turned to glare at the Contessa.

"The password is Death!" she shouted.

The Contessa was visibly taken aback at Xenia Campi's words. Some of the guests started to laugh uneasily and Urbino heard one of the Contessa's Dorsoduro artist friends explaining to a young American girl who worked at the Guggenheim that these were words from the opera.

"It's the password of the conspirators at the masked ball." The artist thought that Xenia Campi was playing a role. "She's Ulrica, the soothsayer, you see. Delightful! Barbara has such an imagination."

Did Xenia Campi know the opera or know that it was the theme of the Contessa's own *ballo in maschera*? Or were her words merely coincidentally appropriate? Perhaps because he had as recently as yesterday been thinking of "The Fall of the House of Usher" right before being accosted by Xenia Campi, Poe's "The Masque of the Red Death" now came into his mind. Prince Prospero, to escape the plague ravaging his country, throws a voluptuous masked ball only to discover that the uninvited guest, dressed in a winding sheet and with a masklike death's-head, is the Red Death itself. Prince Prospero and all his guests die.

As Urbino looked into Xenia Campi's glittering eyes, he involuntarily shivered.

"Conspirators all of you!" she shouted, still keeping Urbino guessing as to whether or not she was familiar with the opera. Her gaze swept contemptuously over him, the Contessa, Sister Teresa, Dora Spaak, and some of the guests. She raised her hand. "You all dance and sing while Venice is being destroyed! You're just as bad as the ones out in the Piazza, screaming in the snow. You're all guilty. All of you. Blood is on your hands and on your feet, too!"

She found this immensely funny and started to laugh wildly. By now it was evident that there was no point in trying to pacify her. She had to be removed from the ballroom. Urbino nodded to Mauro and took one of Xenia Campi's arms. She pulled away and moved deeper into the crowd of guests, scattering them and making a path for herself. Before Urbino and Mauro were able to grab her she had focused her attention once again on Hazel, Vico, and Mrs. Pillow, who were still on the stage.

"You've got blood on your hands!" she said, gesticulating wildly at the stage. "May God forgive you!"

Hazel Reeve fainted into Vico's arms while his stepmother stood there, the smile frozen on her face.

15 XENIA Campi had been brought to one of the reception rooms off the *salone* and was being calmed by Sister Teresa, who assured everyone there was no need to call the police. Hazel Reeve was in another reception room with Vico, Berenice Pillow, the Contessa, Dora Spaak, and Urbino. Samuele Picardo, a physician from Padua who was one of the Contessa's guests, had revived the girl with Dora Spaak's help and had pronounced her out of any danger. After giving instructions to Dora Spaak, he had gone to see to Xenia Campi.

Hazel was reclining on a high-backed tapestried sofa with a damp cloth over her eyes. The least of the Contessa's worries seemed to be that the old fabric might be stained. She was by the door, having said for the second time that she should return to the *salone* to retrieve what she could of her evening. The prospect mustn't have been pleasing for she didn't look as if she was going anytime soon. She kept staring at Urbino, as if to say, "I told you so, and it's all your fault!"

Vico was standing next to the sofa and Berenice Pillow was in a deep armchair by a carved walnut table displaying a collection of jasper cups. The soft look on her face was evident in the light of the Oriental bronze lamp hanging from the ceiling above her. She kept looking from Vico to Hazel.

Dora Spaak stood by the door, staring at Vico.

"Are you all right, Hazel darling?" Vico chafed the girl's hand. She reached up to remove the piece of cloth but Vico told her to leave it. "Just rest. You've been through so much. We won't wait to get married. We'll get married as soon as we can, right here in Venice. Wouldn't that be nice?"

Hazel shook her head so violently that the cloth almost fell off.

"No, never here. Never!"

"Of course not, Hazel. What was I thinking? But why don't we marry here in Italy, down in Naples? How long would we have to wait until we are able to marry, Mother?"

Berenice Pillow didn't say anything for a few moments.

"I don't know, Tony," she finally said in a quiet voice. "I married your father a long time ago. I've forgotten. I'm sure Barbara knows."

She looked over at the Contessa.

"I'm afraid I don't know for sure either, Berenice dear, but I don't think you have to wait a long time, not if you have all your documents. It used to be harder to get married here, and in those days you couldn't even get divorced."

The Contessa seemed to ponder this as if she wanted to draw a conclusion from it all but just shrugged her shoulders. She looked weary.

"And, Mother, I'd like you to help Hazel with all the plans. She has no mother. She'd appreciate it, wouldn't you, Hazel?"

The reclining girl gave no indication. She seemed to be waiting for Vico to go on—or waiting for Mrs. Pillow's response.

Berenice Pillow was breathing heavily. She saw Urbino looking at her and stared back at him almost defiantly. When she turned her eyes away to look at the jasper cups, he was sure that the defiance was still there. She picked up one of the cups and ran a finger over its lip.

Dora Spaak was still staring at Tonio Vico. Urbino remembered how Xenia Campi had said that the ghost of death—of murder—could be seen in this young woman's eyes.

"You recognize him, Miss Spaak, don't you?" Urbino said.

Dora Spaak's eyes flew from Tonio Vico to Urbino.

"He—he's the man in the newspaper you had."

"But you saw him somewhere else, didn't you?"

Dora was speechless. Everyone stared at her—everyone except Hazel, who was still lying on the sofa with the cloth over her eyes. She seemed to be holding her breath as she waited for Dora Spaak to answer.

"You did tell me yesterday morning that you saw Mr. Vico in the Campo San Gabriele talking to Val Gibbon, didn't you?"

Vico jumped to his feet.

"What's this? Talking to Gibbon? Where's the Campo San Gabriele?"

"It's where the Casa Crispina is," his stepmother said quietly, "the pensione where Mr. Gibbon was staying. Mr. Macintyre asked me if you had been there but I told him I wouldn't know."

"I certainly wasn't! I never saw Gibbon here in Venice. I didn't even know he was here until he was dead."

Hazel put her hand up to the cloth as if she was going to remove it but didn't.

"Well, Miss Spaak," Urbino said, "he is the same man, isn't he? The one you saw arguing with Val Gibbon."

For a moment Urbino thought that Dora Spaak was going to brazen it out. She opened her round little mouth to say something but nothing came out. She made her way to the nearest chair and sat down in it slowly. Fear gripped her face as she looked at Urbino.

"I—I must have been mistaken," she said in a quiet voice. "It must have been someone else."

"You seemed so sure yesterday morning, Miss Spaak. But of course you were upset over your mother being taken ill. So you never saw Mr. Vico in the Campo San Gabriele talking to Val Gibbon?"

She shook her head.

"What about in the Calle Santa Scolastica? Could it have been there that you saw someone who looked very much like Mr. Vico?"

She put her face in her hands and started to cry.

"Oh, poor Nicky, what's going to happen to him? I wanted to be so careful! I knew I had to watch everything I said! Poor, poor Nicky!"

"Don't worry about your brother, Miss Spaak."

"What is going on, Urbino?" the Contessa said.

"I'm trying to settle some very important points, Barbara. You see, Miss Spaak didn't stay in the night of the murder, did you, Miss Spaak? You thought your mother was asleep when you came in and borrowed her scissors and her mask to follow Gibbon, but she was awake—and she was awake when you brought them back about midnight. She was only pretending to be asleep, as she frequently does, so that you wouldn't worry about her. You followed Gibbon to the Calle Santa Scolastica. Tell us about the mask, Miss Spaak—the portrait mask that looked like Tonio."

"A mask that looked like me? What are you talking about?"

"Miss Spaak knows. She saw Gibbon put it on at some point and go into the Calle Santa Scolastica. And then she saw her brother go in—and come hurrying out after only a short time, looking very nervous. But he didn't know it was you there, did he, Miss Spaak? You were wearing the yellow mask. You went back to the Casa Crispina and returned the scissors and the mask to your mother's room—and ever since you found out that Val Gibbon was murdered you've been trying to protect your brother."

Dora Spaak nodded.

"Are you saying that Miss Spaak killed Gibbon? Or her brother?" the Contessa asked. "I thought that Rigoletti—"

"Forget about Rigoletti, Barbara. He had nothing to do with Gibbon's death."

"Oh, poor Nicky!" Dora Spaak wailed.

"I told you not to worry about your brother, Miss Spaak. He hasn't done anything wrong. It would have been better if you hadn't lied to protect him. But now is your chance to help. Before you left the area of the Calle Santa Scolastica, did you see anyone else there that you recognized—or perhaps no one you recognized at the time but whom you do now?"

"I didn't go into that alley. I was so surprised when I saw Nicky there. I figured what he was up to. I know my brother very well although we never talk about a lot of things. I knew what he was looking for, but when he went into that alley after

Val did and then rushed out, I was so shocked that I went right back to the Casa Crispina."

"You're sure you didn't see anyone else?"

"I saw many people once I got out by the water but I didn't recognize anyone. I was in a state!"

"Of course you were, Miss Spaak. You were in such a state that you could have passed by any number of people you might otherwise be able to recognize now."

"I suppose so."

Hazel sat up quickly, the damp cloth falling from her eyes onto the sofa. The Contessa didn't seem to notice—or if she noticed, not to care. She was staring at Urbino.

"Because there is someone here who was also there that night, one of the few other people who know about the mask that looked like Tonio Vico."

Urbino turned toward the handsome young man who was standing ramrod straight a few feet from the sofa, looking back and forth from Urbino to Dora Spaak.

"Tonio, do you still say you were in the hotel during the time Gibbon was murdered?" Urbino asked.

"Of course I do! I was in all night! Tell them, Mother!"

"I already have, Tony." She looked levelly at Urbino. "I assure you my son was in that evening, Mr. Macintyre."

She put down the jasper cup that she had been holding in her hand during the last few minutes.

"But you don't know for sure if he was, do you, Mrs. Pillow? You couldn't swear to it?"

"Are you accusing my mother of lying?"

Urbino ignored Tonio and continued to look at Mrs. Pillow. From the tail of his eye he saw the Contessa moving slowly away from the door.

"Why don't you admit that when you said Tonio was in the hotel during the time of Gibbon's murder you couldn't swear to it?" Urbino pursued.

"But I *was* in that night! Mother, tell them I was in!"

"She's already said it several times, Tonio, but it doesn't mean that she knows you were in that night. Tell him, Mrs. Pillow, tell him and Hazel and all of us that you don't know, you couldn't possibly know whether Tonio was in during the crucial time."

"Of course he was in!" Mrs. Pillow said. "Why are you trying to make it seem as if Tony has something to hide? If you think my son had anything to do with—with Mr. Gibbon's death, you are wrong, Mr. Macintyre."

"Urbino, what is going on?" the Contessa said again, more nervously this time.

"I'm sorry, Barbara. Why don't you sit down. Your guests can wait a little longer," he added as if this was still her main concern.

Almost sheepishly, the Contessa complied, going to an armchair on the other side of the table with the jasper cups.

"He *was* in that night, Barbara," Berenice Pillow said, looking at her old friend.

The Contessa reached out and took her hand.

"Of course he was, Berenice. I don't know what's got into Urbino. Is this some kind of Carnival prank?"

"My son was where he said he was, Mr. Macintyre."

"Why don't you tell us about the mask, Mrs. Pillow? The mask that looked like Tonio."

If Mrs. Pillow had any doubts before that he knew what she had hoped no one else knew but herself, she couldn't delude herself any longer. Where her face had looked only unnaturally soft earlier, now it seemed to have collapsed. She pulled her hand from the Contessa's and stood up. She looked regal standing there next to the walnut table with its collection of jasper cups. Her eyes blazed under the bronze lamp.

"You're very astute, Mr. Macintyre. You're right. I don't know if Tony was in the hotel that night."

"But Mother!"

"It's all right, Tony. There's nothing for you to worry about. I just hope you won't hate me when you learn the truth. I never wanted to do anything to hurt you or—or Val. Don't ever think that! All I ask is that you be gentle in your heart with me, Tony darling. If I can count on that, I don't care about anything else."

She was speaking only to her stepson now as if no one else was in the room.

"You see, Tony, Val Gibbon and I—" She stopped and took a deep breath and said with quiet emphasis, "What I did I did because I loved him—I still love him—and because I love you. But nothing is your fault, Tony, nothing!"

Hazel got unsteadily to her feet.

"Loved him? Loved Val? What are you talking about!"

"Yes, Hazel, I loved him! Is that so hard to believe? And I'll tell you something else," she said moving closer to Hazel, who took a step back. "Val felt something for me, too! When you all look at me—even you, Barbara, who should know better—you see only a woman who isn't young any longer, who isn't attractive. What does she have to do with love? What could that kind of love have to do with her? I'm just a silly old fool to you, aren't I? But I see something different! I see what I used to be, and not that long ago, the woman Val could have loved, the one I still like to believe he once felt something for. I felt everything you feel, Hazel dear, and maybe a lot more. But now I finally have to say good-bye to all that. I said good-bye to it in that alley."

Stunned, Hazel sat down on the sofa and put her hands to her face. Once again Tonio seemed caught, as he had been on the stage earlier, between his fiancée and his stepmother. He stood rooted to the carpet. The Contessa was staring straight ahead, blank, amazed, and shaken. Dora Spaak had settled back in her chair and looked exhausted and still a little fearful.

"It was because he loved me that you killed him," Hazel shouted. "You didn't want anyone else to have him. You're hateful! Thank God you're not Tonio's real mother!"

"Hazel! That's enough!" Tonio said.

"Was it because of the money Gibbon wanted, Mrs. Pillow," Urbino asked, making an assumption that could prove wrong despite how strongly he felt about it, "or because he was planning to marry Hazel?"

Berenice Pillow appeared to ponder the question. They all waited expectantly but no one, it seemed, more than her stepson, who was still standing between her and Hazel.

"He humiliated me," Berenice Pillow said with quiet emphasis. "After everything we were to each other, he had to humiliate me. He couldn't let me go in dignity. And he threatened to humiliate me in your eyes, Tony. I would have continued to give him just about anything, as long as he treated me with some tenderness and consideration—or as long as I believed he did. No, Mr. Macintyre, it wasn't the money and it wasn't you either, Hazel. I felt as if I were losing everything that meant something to me—my son, Val, and my dignity. I snapped. I loved him but at that moment I was filled with hatred. No, I wasn't thinking about the money. If I had been, I might have taken it back. And I wasn't thinking of you, Hazel. If I was thinking at all, I was thinking of myself and of you, Tony. You can't imagine what it was like to do what I did when he was wearing that mask!"

"You're an evil, selfish woman!" Hazel screamed, her face livid with anger.

Tonio Vico, poised between Hazel and his stepmother, made his decision.

"Mother," he said, going over to Mrs. Pillow and taking her in his arms. "You didn't know what you were doing. You did it for me."

His two contradictory explanations seemed to echo through the heavy air of the room. Outside in the *salone* the orchestra was playing "Funiculì-Funiculà." In the Contessa's absence her *ballo in maschera* seemed to have taken an even more festive turn, which was only fitting since, as the ebony clock on the mantel indicated, it was almost midnight.

Epilogue

ASHES

"*T*HE question I keep asking myself, Urbino, until my head is spinning, is whether you're to be thanked or not."

In the middle of the Contessa's forehead was a black, ashy smudge that she wore like a badge of honor. In her deep purple dress of simple lines, she looked reserved, almost chastened, her honey-brown hair pulled back from her face and fastened with a black comb that had belonged to her mother and that matched the onyx beads around her throat.

It was early afternoon of Ash Wednesday, the day after her *ballo in maschera*—her "notorious" *ballo in maschera* as she lost no time in calling it as soon as she had seen Urbino.

Urbino and the Contessa were sitting in her *salotto*. She would have preferred the Oriental salon at Florian's now that the crowds had left the Piazza, but the café was always closed after Carnival for several days of what the exhausted management referred to as "recuperation."

"I lose my dear friend Berenice for a long time," the Contessa went on with intentional vagueness, "and just when she's found again she's swept away from me like this—and all because of you!" She looked at his forehead pointedly for what must have been the fifth time since he had arrived ten minutes ago from the Questura. "And you're not even the slightest bit penitential, are you!"

"Barbara, I'm sorry that it had to happen the way it did."

"I'm all in a muddle. It makes everything so much easier when good people are killed and terrible ones do the killing! That's the way it should be! Poor, poor Berenice! I'll tell you one thing, *caro*. I'm going to help her as much as I can. I know she has to be punished but I intend to see that it's as painless as possible."

Exactly how she was going to accomplish this she didn't explain but Urbino was sure that she had already considered various possibilities.

"When I said last night that you could make me feel like a

cretina today," she went on, "all I thought you had to explain was about Rigoletti! Now there's Berenice!"

"Don't forget Dora Spaak."

"I've managed to piece together some of her sad little story. Correct me if I'm wrong." Her gray eyes narrowed. "She went to the Piazza after borrowing her mother's mask and scissors. I assume the scissors were for protection. But what did she hope to do?"

"Follow Gibbon and then reveal herself. She slipped out the front door past the sleeping Sister Agata while Xenia Campi was having her anisette and after Xenia saw her coming out of her mother's room. Dora thought she would have a drink with Gibbon afterward and they would laugh about it. What happened was different, of course. She found him in the Piazza taking pictures and then followed him to the Calle degli Albanesi where he put on the portrait mask. When he slipped into the Calle Santa Scolastica, she went into the service alley for the Danieli across the way, waiting for him to come out. Her brother came along but didn't recognize her, and then he went into the Calle Santa Scolastica. She was surprised, of course, but she knew Nicholas was gay and that he might wander around in places like this. What was shocking to her was that Gibbon was in the *calle,* too. When her brother came hurrying out, apprehensive when he saw Gibbon in the portrait mask waiting for him—although he didn't know who it was—she got frightened. She waited a few minutes longer but when Gibbon didn't come out she realized she should leave herself, that it was a silly game she was playing."

"Did she think that her brother had killed Gibbon?"

"Not then, but she did when she heard that Gibbon had been murdered. She couldn't imagine what the scene of only a few moments between them in the alley could have been like, but she was determined to protect her brother. That's why she didn't want to admit knowing anything about a mask, but she saw a chance to put me off the track when she saw the artist's drawing in *Il Gazzettino*. If she could make me—and perhaps through me, the police—believe that Gibbon had been arguing with the man pictured in the paper, then this man became an even stronger suspect, and her brother less of one. She wasn't thinking completely clearly, of course, or else she would have wondered what had happened to the portrait mask."

"What did happen to it?"

"Berenice took it from Gibbon's face. She couldn't leave it. The finger—or the face—would have pointed right to her stepson. Taking the mask was the first thing she did that was completely intentional. Murdering Gibbon wasn't, and that will be in her favor. She stuffed the mask into the pocket of her coat but didn't realize it was gone until she was out in the Calle degli Albanesi. She heard someone walking toward her from the direction of the restaurant where the kids hang out, so she hurried to the Riva degli Schiavoni and from there back to the hotel. Needless to say, the realization that the portrait mask was out there somewhere made her very nervous. She expected people to say they had seen her stepson in different places that night. In fact, she said more or less the same thing to us, if you remember, when she and Tonio came over the night Hazel was here. She must have prayed that the mask wouldn't surface— and it didn't until the early hours of this morning."

"Where?"

"In a trash bin on the Riva degli Schiavoni. Whoever found it after it fell out of Mrs. Pillow's pocket seems to have made good use of it for *Carnevale*. Maybe it was the person Mrs. Pillow heard walking toward her. I have no way to prove it, but I think the person who found the mask was someone associated with the restaurant in the Calle degli Albanesi, possibly Lupo, who not only dislikes Rigoletti but might be a frequenter of the Calle Santa Scolastica himself. Lupo— or someone else—could have been on his way there, found the mask somewhere along the first stretch of the Calle Santa Scolastica or in the courtyard, and taken it. For some reason, he didn't notice Gibbon's body. He might have just taken the mask, thought no one of interest was in the area, and left."

"So this person probably wore the mask until Monday when the artist's sketch was in the paper."

"Possibly even after Monday, since it wasn't found until early this morning. You'd be surprised how infrequently some people read the paper."

"But Rigoletti says he saw Vico—or the person wearing the mask—several times, that once or twice the person seemed to mock him."

"That's why I tend to think it could have been Lupo or someone else who also knew Rigoletti and disliked his busy-body ways enough to have some fun with him. I mentioned it to Gemelli this morning and he's checking it out."

"Perhaps it's because of Berenice and memories of St. Brigid's and all," the Contessa said, "but this afternoon I feel very much in the position of a catechumen being instructed in the faith. I suppose the analogy isn't a bad one, given my ignorance and your greater knowledge of the mysteries—the secular ones, that is—and it does rather suit the religious spirit of the day." She gave another brief glance at his unmarked forehead. "I'm not quite up to hearing about Berenice yet, though. What about Rigoletti? He had nothing to do with Gibbon's murder, did he?"

"Not at all, but everyone seemed to be willing to believe he did after he attacked Tonio in the Piazza—even the Questura. 'How crafty,' I heard someone say last night. 'The man who finds the body is the murderer. Ingenious!' "

"I thought it wasn't so much craft as derangement. Rigoletti might not have taken an extreme turn like Xenia Campi but their son's death has affected him too."

"Of course it has. His rancor toward *Carnevale*, Porfirio, and the men who visit the Calle Santa Scolastica was in large part fueled by the loss of his son. He believed Marco would have grown up to be a 'real man,' not someone like Firpo, and especially not the kind who meet in the Calle Santa Scolastica. He attacked Vico out of a combination of righteousness and personal affront. He told the police that he was furious they let Vico go after his identification, and when he saw him in the Piazza, he lost control of himself."

"But why was he wearing a mask if he hates *Carnevale*?"

"The same reason why many other people wear them—he didn't want to be recognized by Vico. He felt that he was being taunted by him and he didn't want to give him any warning. The last night of *Carnevale* was the perfect time for his revenge. He wanted to pounce on Vico unawares."

The Contessa shook her head and took a sip of her tea. This afternoon Urbino was joining her in her preferred drink. It was a little gesture he was making to try to soothe his friend whom he realized he had upset and, to a certain extent, also deceived.

"How did you know that a mask of Vico was involved?"

"For one thing I didn't believe that Tonio had been out that night. And even though Mrs. Pillow couldn't know for sure that he hadn't left the room, she believed it so strongly that

I did too. She had been the one to kill Gibbon and she was determined no one would suspect her stepson."

He paused to take a sip of his tea.

"There was another thing. Rigoletti said that the man he first met coming out of the *calle*—the one he later identified as Tonio—showed no reaction on his face at all. And Spaak said that the man at the end of the *calle*—Gibbon in the mask—looked particularly aloof and unruffled. Then, when Gemelli told me that people claimed to have seen Tonio in and around the Piazza that night, it seemed even more unlikely that it could have been Tonio. He just doesn't seem the type. Of course, that's a rather inane thing to say considering how well everyone seems to have been able to conceal things, but for some reason I just didn't believe that Vico was out that night. The only explanations then became either malicious misidentifications or sightings of someone who resembled him or of someone wearing a mask that looked like him. I doubt if a portrait mask would even have occurred to me if Firpo hadn't had one made of Xenia Campi and I hadn't seen it the afternoon before Gibbon was murdered. Through Firpo I was led to a mask maker, a young woman named Picrina who had a booth at the mask fair in the Campo San Maurizio."

He explained how Pierina had been Marco Rigoletti's girlfriend—the girl who had been thrown from the car on the autostrada.

"Xenia Campi won't let her go, keeps looking after her, warning her. She probably saw Gibbon flirting with her in the Piazza but didn't want to draw my attention to her. Pierina said that Gibbon—although she didn't know who he was at the time—came to her with a photograph of a handsome young man and had her make a portrait mask."

"You didn't tell me that!" the Contessa said accusingly.

"I found out only late Monday, and I didn't want you to act any differently around Mrs. Pillow or Tonio, perhaps even say something, But the main reason was that I knew it would occur to you, as it did to me, that there was a possibility that Gibbon hadn't been the intended victim but that Tonio was if Gibbon was wearing the mask when he was attacked."

"But why did he want to have a mask of Tonio?"

"Gibbon had a playful, malicious streak. He knew he would be meeting Berenice Pillow and he knew how she felt about her stepson. It was just to have some fun. He probably thought he would have even more fun with it with Hazel but he never got the chance."

"I can't understand why Berenice ever got involved with Gibbon."

"Oh, yes, you can, Barbara! He was a good-looking man and from what she told the police and me today he was very flattering to her, very attentive."

"But she's so much older than he was! The difference between them must—" She stopped. "It's a little unusual, I mean."

"Perhaps, but certainly understandable. She met him when he was working as an art therapist at the London hospital where her second husband, Malcolm Pillow, died. about eight years ago. She could have looked much back then—those eight years cover a crucial period in son's life." He pulled himself back from going into any more details on this aspect. "Of course, she had the great equalizer that made whatever age she was—or however she looked— unimportant. Money. Gibbon was desperate for it, something he managed to conceal from Hazel. He saw his chance with your old friend and he took it. He seems to have got quite a bit out of Berenice Pillow—money, I mean."

"Let's draw the veil, *caro*, on whatever else he might have got out of her."

"And she out of him?"

"Urbino!"

He didn't say anything. He wanted what he had been saying to make its impression on his friend. There was a lot here for her to absorb. After taking a sip of her tea and looking very thoughtful, she said, "So let me see, then. Berenice and Gibbon were having a relationship of some kind and then her stepson's fiancée ends up with him? But Urbino, this sounds like some Oscar Wilde comedy or Restoration drama or bedroom farce or whatever!"

"But it's not so strange when you realize how it all came about and once you know what kind of person Gibbon was. Tonio and Hazel met very innocently at the Victoria and Albert, started seeing each other, and planned to marry. She claims she was particularly vulnerable at the time, her mother having just committed suicide. Mrs. Pillow didn't care for Hazel that much but perhaps she wouldn't have cared for anyone her stepson wanted to marry—not at first anyway.

There was, though, the American niece she favored. But Mrs. Pillow was being reasonable about it. Both Hazel and Tonio knew she had reservations about Hazel but wasn't making any real problems for them."

"All the while, though, she was carrying on some kind of relationship with a man almost as young as her stepson."

"There were thirteen years between Gibbon and Tonio. She met Gibbon before Tonio went to the university. When Mrs. Pillow heard that Hazel was looking for someone to photo-her parents' art collection, she thought of Gibbon, but ldn't tip her hand too much, so she mentioned Hazel to r big mistake—and he showed up. Hazel told me that med strange how Gibbon just suddenly appeared. Gibbon soon saw what kind of circumstances Hazel came from, saw she was attracted to him, and made his move. The fact that she was engaged to marry Tonio just added extra spice to it. He had been having his relationship with Mrs. Pillow for more than five years at this point and I'm sure that he had to hear a great deal about how wonderful her stepson was. He must have resented Tonio for a lot of things—his money and background, and probably, in some twisted way, Berenice's devotion to him. Mrs. Pillow sent Gibbon into a perfect situation and he took full advantage of it."

"But how was everything kept a secret?"

"Hazel never knew about Gibbon's relationship with Mrs. Pillow. Neither of them wanted it to come out. Tonio didn't know anything about it either. He didn't know Gibbon at all except as a man he had met once or twice at the hospital when his stepfather was dying. And Tonio didn't know about Gibbon and Hazel—not at first, anyway."

"It *is* like a Restoration comedy—or I should say a tragedy! What about Berenice? Didn't she know about Hazel and Gibbon? Did Tonio really keep the breakup of his engagement a secret from his mother?"

"Yes. He hoped everything could be patched up between him and Hazel and his mother need never know."

The Contessa shook her head.

"So many lies and deceptions. It makes my head spin."

"Mrs. Pillow didn't know about it until the night she killed Gibbon. He told her there in the Calle Santa Scolastica, where he had asked her to meet him. The remote location must have played to his strange sense of fun. He might have known its reputation and might even have had an adventure or two there, if we can believe what Josef said about him. When she saw him in the mask, she was shocked for a few moments. She thought it was Tonio, but when Gibbon laughed she knew it was he. Gibbon told her about Hazel, threw it in her face. He said he planned to marry Hazel but that he wanted money from her anyway. Obviously he needed money to keep up his pretense with Hazel of not being concerned about hers. Berenice Pillow was aware of the promise Hazel had made to her father. I wonder if Hazel would eventually have broken it?"

He considered this for a moment before returning to what had happened between Gibbon and Mrs. Pillow in the Calle Santa Scolastica.

"At first Berenice refused to give Gibbon the money. She always gave him cash, of course, and always, it seems, in unusual places that he suggested. She used to think it was exciting and romantic."

"Poor Berenice. And then she just snapped when Gibbon made fun of her and said he would tell Tonio all about them."

"He called her a ridiculous old woman. He said that the only way he could take an attractive picture of her was to cover the lens in gauze. She hardly remembers reaching for the letter opener in her lap desk. She brought the lap desk instead of her purse because it was hefty enough to use as a weapon if she was approached by someone. After the murder she planned to lose it. When she saw me at the *traghetto,* she decided that would be a good time for the accident."

"Why not just say it had been stolen?"

"It might have seemed more suspicious than something as public as what happened."

"To think we're talking about little Berenice Reilly from St. Brigid's!"

"Very much the same, it would seem, from some of the stories you've told about her."

"Poor Berenice! Why couldn't Gibbon have let her have some illusion that he cared for her just a little? I know there were so many lies and deceptions involved—not only with Berenice, Tonio, Hazel, and Gibbon, but the Spaaks as well— but one more deception, especially one like that, would have been kind. And it could have saved his life. How terrible it must have been for Berenice to stab him when he looked like Tonio!"

"It's very much on her mind. She says that's all she can remember of those few seconds. Tonio's face."

The Contessa looked puzzled.

"But how did you ever figure out that Berenice and Gibbon were involved with each other?"

"Let me explain something else first. Hazel said that Gibbon was involved with someone when they met and that he was trying to break it off. What he was doing was keeping Mrs. Pillow in the picture and continuing to get money from her. Then Josef told me he met Gibbon with his aunt in Bloomsbury but Hazel said that Gibbon's last living relative died when he was about eighteen. That's where you come in."

"Me?"

"You brought Berenice to the hospital to see Josef and he recognized her as the 'aunt.' He told me last night after Vico was attacked." Urbino got up. "I think I'd like something a little more bracing than tea, if you don't mind."

"Good idea," the Contessa surprised him by saying. "I'll join you. There have been few occasions when I've felt so compelled to have a drink at this time of the day."

Urbino poured out two glasses of Corvo and handed one to the Contessa. When he returned to his chair, he finished explaining about Berenice Pillow.

"You know, Barbara, in the excitement and confusion of the murder and all, we forgot about something."

"What?"

"Why Berenice Pillow was so anxious to see you."

The Contessa nodded.

"She was going to mention something about Gibbon. I don't think she knew exactly how much or how little she was going to tell you, but when she knew she would be in Venice to see Gibbon—he had arranged the place of their meeting as he usually did—and that you were here too, she thought she would talk to you about him. She had kept it a secret for so long from even her closest friends. You were going to be the one she finally confided in. All those years since St. Brigid's she's remembered you."

"But why didn't she confide in me? She had plenty of opportunity. And if she had done it right away, she might not have ended up killing Gibbon."

"Remember how you were waiting for her at Florian's last week and she didn't come? I don't mean when I was with you, but the first time you arranged to meet each other."

"How could I forget?"

"Gibbon and Dora Spaak came up to your table and you spoke with them for a while. She saw you through the window from outside. There you were talking with the very person she wanted to tell you about. She lost her courage. She thought that you couldn't be as objective as she had thought you might be. And then there was the business over *Casa Vogue*."

"What about it?"

"When she saw that you knew Gibbon, she thought that he might have taken the pictures for *Casa Vogue*. She had read most of the article but not the first page where the photographer's credit was given. That's why she wanted to see the whole article."

The Contessa stood up.

"Would you mind if we took a little walk? I don't mean outside, but only out to the loggia. Let me get a shawl."

While she was gone, Urbino went to the bar and took the Corvo and two clean glasses. When the Contessa returned with a large wool challis scarf, they walked toward the *salone*.

"I was just thinking of a few things," the Contessa said. "Why was Porfirio in San Gabriele? Why did he go up on the scaffold?"

"We'll never know for sure. Maybe he wanted a closer look at the restoration. He told Josef he didn't think he was doing a good job. Or maybe he wanted to take photographs of the fresco himself now that Gibbon was dead. If Porfirio had lived, he might have approached you about finishing up Gibbon's work in San Gabriele."

The Contessa shook her head.

"He had too much pride for that. If he didn't get the commission to start with, he wouldn't have wanted it after Gibbon had been murdered. You're lucky he finished taking the photographs for your Proust book."

They were passing by the private chapel where the Contessa had received her ashes that morning. One of the priests from the Madonna dell'Orto came over several times a month to say Mass. It was one of the Contessa's sorrows that she had never had any children who would have been baptized at the ornate marble font.

The altar was bare of flowers and the statues of the Blessed Virgin, Saint Teresa, and Saint Nicholas of Bari were shrouded in purple material that matched the color of the Contessa's dress. She kept to many of the old traditions, among them this veiling of the statues in penitential purple for the forty days of Lent. It created a solemn effect that brought Urbino back to the days of his youth when all the churches used to do it.

As they entered the *salone*, the Contessa started to sing softly a patch of Amelia's "Morrò" aria that had been such a success last night. The words about the acceptance of the inevitability of death and the consolation of a son's kisses touched her face with melancholy.

"You know, Urbino, I can't help thinking how much of a role mothers and sons played in all of this sadness. There's Berenice's love for Tonio. She was more of a mother to him than many natural mothers are. And there's Xenia Campi, who lost her son in the accident."

Urbino nodded.

"And don't forget Stella Maris Spaak and Nicholas," he added. "Or Josef and his mother back in Cracow."

What exactly it might mean, however, he didn't know, except that without the tender bonds between these particular mothers and sons—without the delicate system of their interdependence—there might have been less sorrow, but also, certainly, less happiness.

The Contessa regarded the scene of last night's ball. Workmen had removed the stage and the buffet table. They were now in the process of putting back the Aubussons and the furniture that had been brought to the storeroom.

"Did it all have to come out at my ball?" the Contessa asked. "You might have arranged things differently."

"I didn't arrange things at all, Barbara. I certainly didn't set up Xenia Campi to come in with her accusation, spouting that the password was death as if she were intentionally playing the role of Ulrica!"

"I'm not so sure of that. I had an uneasy feeling you had something up your sleeve."

"As far as Dora Spaak is concerned, it was your fault that her story came out in the little parlor and that she was there to hear Mrs. Pillow's revelations."

"My fault?"

"Do you forget that you snatched her away from me and gave her to Filippo? If I could have spoken with her privately, things might have been different."

"Well, thank God it didn't happen in front of everyone! I keep hoping that most of them didn't even know what happened in the reception room."

"I'm sure they didn't—and they still might not."

"Not until they read the paper—and *my* friends, I assure you, read the paper!"

She greeted the workmen and asked one of them to open the doors to the loggia. When he did, they stepped outside. Yesterday's storm had blown out to sea and had left only a small deposit of icy snow that had soon melted with the coming of the new day. The sky was a clear blue, the air fresh and bracing. The Contessa gathered her scarf more tightly around her throat.

"I don't know what's going to happen to Josef," she said, "but he can stay with me for as long as he wants."

"I wouldn't be surprised if the prosecutor overlooks his role in Porfirio's death." He paused. "How is Hazel?"

"Oh, didn't you know, *caro*? She's left already."

"Left?"

"Not Venice, but the Ca' da Capo. She's staying at the Danieli for a few more days before going up to London."

"What about Tonio?"

"I doubt he has anything on his mind now but his mother—and that's the way it should be. I don't think your Miss Reeve conducted herself very well last night in the reception room, even if she was under a strain. Perhaps Tonio saw something in her that he didn't find attractive. And there's another thing. I don't think that Miss Reeve is ready to doff the role of lover for the equally difficult and perhaps less gratifying one of beloved."

She looked sideways at him quickly.

"Do you remember how I said at the Regatta in September that you might be on the verge of a mistake? You were feeling so ridiculously guilty and saying that you wanted to 'do' something, as if you had been the prince of indolence! Well, you *have* ended up doing something, you see, something that neither of us could ever have imagined at the time. I don't think I would have even remembered Berenice's name then. And as for your mistake, well . . ."

" 'Well' what, Barbara?"

"You were in danger, but you never quite went over the verge, did you? I commend you for that."

They looked down at the Grand Canal. Everything seemed calm and arrested: the vaporetto nursing against the landing across from them, the mirror of the water, the almost motionless figures in the opposite *campo*, a woman drawing aside the drape of a palazzo window. Midnight had released the city from the thrall of *Carnevale* and restored it to its former serenity.

"Thank God it's all over," the Contessa said. "Next year I intend to be far away."

"It's a long time between now and then. Whether you realize it or not, your *ballo in maschera* was a success. You might have started a new tradition here at the Ca' da Capo."

"I doubt it." She sighed and shook her head, looking across at the palazzi on the other side. "I can't help thinking of poor Berenice. What's to become of her? She won't recover from this, not with her spirit intact. She's parted from something forever." There was a gentle sadness in her voice. "Poor fiery little Berenice Reilly of St. Brigid's. Oh, *caro*, it was all such a long, long time ago."

He put his arm around her waist.

"But you're here now, Barbara." He looked at her. "Did little Barbara Spencer at St. Brigid's ever think she would be standing on her own balcony above the Grand Canal?"

"If she did, she certainly never thought it would be with you, *caro*."

She rested her head against his shoulder.

"I've had enough of remembrance of things past," she said. "And you're too young to indulge in such things. Save Proust for your old age. That's what I'm doing."

But then, as they stared down at the Grand Canal sweeping like a flood between the double row of palazzi, she started to reminisce about her days at St. Brigid's, and Urbino poured them each a glass of wine to warm them.

ELLIOTT ROOSEVELT'S DELIGHTFUL MYSTERY SERIES